FINDING THE VOID

Michael Quinn Sullivan

"Come, my friends, 'Tis not too late to seek a newer world."

– ALFRED, LORD TENNYSON

PROLOGUE

For untold millennia it had rested in the twilight of a distant star, bathed in the soft radiation of interstellar space. Meant to greet the deep of space, the object instead suffered the indignity of strikes from the dust, ice balls, and small rocks that more naturally occupied this region at the edge of the solar system.

It rests just inside the far edge of the jumble known as the Kuiper Belt, but not yet approaching the hazy line of the Oort cloud. Its ancient exterior originally glistened brilliantly, but now floated as a silent monument in opposition to the notion that the vacuum of space is clean. It was now covered in a film of dust, obscuring the surface and all but eliminating the reflection of any light.

It was gripped by gravity the Sun, though so distant it was distinguishable only by being the brightest star in the heavens. The illumination was barely measurable.

Once, very recently – *compared to its ancient origins* – it had come close – *compared to the scale of the cosmos* – to being approached by an artificial object. But that object had sped on toward infinity. The sensors, pointed in the wrong direction since passing the orbit of the last of the major planetary bodies in the system, never detected the object's presence.

Decades later another object, with more powerful sensors and a more robust design, happened to pass close enough that had its masters been paying attention, they might have noticed it.

But they were not. And they had not.

The tantalizing hints of data collected by that visit sat

unexamined. To those in charge, it was worthless noise. It was not what they were looking for when the data came in, so they did not see it. There were just too many objects to study, which was not even the worry of that particular voyage at that particular time.

The internal heat and the object's gravitational divot could possibly have sparked interest, even alarm... had they been detected. It wasn't entirely the fault of those who had sent that most recent probe. So much dust had gathered on and around the object, insulating its heat and hiding it from most of the electromagnetic spectrum, it was rendered all but it invisible.

And the full appreciation of gravity was, at best, in an inconveniently stunted infancy.

Even if the object's presence had somehow been noticed, the biases of those observers would have most likely misinterpreted what they were seeing.

PART I

Innovation

CHAPTER 1

Near Seminole, Texas, USA

"This is pointless. I really have better ways to spend my time," said an exasperated Miles Oliver, senior science correspondent for the Associated Press. He had recently completed three months on the decrepit International Space Station thanks, in part, to the sponsorship of the corporation whose event Oliver did not want to cover–but was nonetheless driving to at this moment.

The sponsorship had not come with any expectation of future coverage; it was yet another public relations stunt by a globe-spanning company that could do such things in its corporate sleep. Miles Oliver knew that intellectually. The sponsorship had been an advertising decision. And he knew he had been assigned to this event because, allegedly, Quantum Advantage's CEO Ian MacGregor would be announcing a technological advancement of "unprecedented" proportions with deep implications for space travel. *Right.*

"You just hate MacGregor."

Miles opened his mouth to protest the assertion of his cameraman. It was a bald-faced, mean-spirited, pernicious... truth. The reporter took a deep breath and fumbled with the rearview mirror of the rented Ford before responding.

"Josh, I don't hate him," Miles Oliver said, knowing his words convinced no one, least of all himself. "I just really doubt anything worthwhile is going to be unveiled today. Out here. MacGregor was a one-trick pony, and he's fading from the spotlight."

"Out here" was west and north of Midland, Texas, near

Seminole, and not yet to New Mexico, and south of Lubbock. If there was an uglier place on planet Earth, Miles Oliver was certain he had not seen it. In his career he had seen every continent, so he felt justified in his opinion. The steppes of Kazakhstan from which the Russians launched their space vehicles was virtually a paradise compared to this place. That MacGregor called this area home might have had more than a little to do with Oliver's assessment, a fact the cameraman decided not to voice.

"It was, what, 20 years ago? Get over it." Josh Padden had pieced together the story in his years with Miles Oliver. The veteran newsman had been assigned to cover the second New Horizons mission. As the data came in from the fly-by of the Kuiper Belt's dwarf planet Quaoar, he'd nearly missed being present – thanks to a younger Ian MacGregor.

Apparently Miles Oliver had tried to bully who he thought was a young intern out of his desk so the journalist could pre-file a story. That "intern" was Ian MacGregor, Ph.D., who was responsible for interpreting a section of the probe's data stream. The young MacGregor was indignant, called for security, and said he felt physically intimidated. A furious Miles Oliver was in the process of being escorted from the building before cooler heads prevailed.

It was true that Ian MacGregor had drifted from the center of both scientific and commercial attention in recent years. The computer company he founded continued to redefine computational science, and in doing so opened new frontiers in basic science. But these days, rather than Ian MacGregor, it was the young researchers who announced their findings and ran the various sections of the privately held Quantum Advantage. It was a commonly whispered slur that most of what "QA" did now was iterative, not breakthrough.

No one would say that aloud because no one could say the company was on the decline. In any given quarter, QA could misplace more cash than the Gross Domestic Product of several small countries. Its annual revenues rivaled several large countries.

"Besides," Josh Padden continued, "his company let you go into space. He obviously doesn't hold a grudge."

"Why should he? He wasn't almost kicked out of JPL..." Miles stopped himself. Ahead was the turn off, marked only by a low-slung, 3D-printed building. It was the only interruption in what had been miles of triple-layered fences.

A uniformed guard stepped out as Miles Oliver turned the car into the driveway. After producing the requested IDs and invitations, the guard told the journalists to pull around back and leave the car. A shuttle would take them the rest of the way.

"How far is it from here?"

"Just a couple miles is all," came the reply of a man, whose tone of voice indicated he had said it several dozen times already.

Oliver's rental joined thirty or more already parked behind the building. He and Padden gathered their equipment and walked inside to wait. Among the half-dozen people in the lounge, he recognized the chairman of the U.S. House Committee on Science, Space and Technology. They chatted for a few minutes before being interrupted by the head of Ford Motors. Everyone, it seemed, had a theory about what Ian MacGregor was – or was not – going to announce.

It wasn't long before a corporate shuttle emblazoned with the QA logo arrived to take the assembled crowd on the final leg of their trip.

"I'm surprised they wouldn't let you fly out here, congressman," Oliver remarked as they boarded the bus. "Surely MacGregor has a landing strip?"

"Strict no-fly-zone here," the politician said. "No exceptions." He caught the reporter's eye. "And, no, I have no idea why, either. He pulled strings way over my head to get that designation."

Miles Oliver committed that little nugget of information to memory. Nice bit of color, if it checks out. He looked out the window.

Up ahead appeared a large building, with an architectural style that evoked memories of science fiction movies from the mid-1960s. To Miles Oliver's eyes, the building appeared – from this vantage point, anyway – to be roughly octagonal, made of metal and glass. It seemed wildly out of place in the Texas desert. It should have been printed adobe, like the guard house. It didn't seem to even sit right on the ground.

Of course, the reporter wasn't sure where such a building would sit right. Maybe it would look right *only* in one of those sci-fi movies.

The bus deposited its passengers outside a large set of open doors. As the last person in their party entered, Oliver noticed the outer doors begin to close.

One side of the hallway was lined with pictures of aviation and space history, from sepia-toned photographs of hot air balloons to the latest imagery from a robotic Europa lander. The other wall had publicity photos of Quantum Advantage and its various employees. Curiously absent were any photos of the company founder, a point Padden whispered to the newsman.

Miles Oliver ignored him. "I think we've been conned. This is going to be Ian MacGregor's Segway moment, I can feel it."

Padden arched his eyebrow in a question.

"The Segway, you know? Maybe it's was a little before your time. It was a two-wheeled scooter held upright by a gyroscope and hyped by its maker and early investors as a revolutionary change to city life. One guy claimed it would change the way cities were designed. Instead, it was a dud product used for mall cops." He shook his head. "You see them sometimes for tourist groups?"

Josh Padden feigned recognition as a set of large doors closed behind him.

With the clap of the doors, Miles Oliver felt a slight jump

in the pit of his stomach. Something wasn't right.

"Ladies and gentlemen, please make your way to the auditorium," came a faintly mechanical voice. "Follow the lighted markers to the auditorium, if you please, so that the program can begin promptly at 2 p.m."

The auditorium was, roughly, on the other side of the building. Chairs were arranged on steps, facing a window wall, and a small podium. There were already several dozen people in attendance, including competing journalists, Miles noted. There were politicians, a few business and industry types, and an assortment of academics.

There. Standing by the window. That was Ian MacGregor.

Miles Oliver, of course, recognized the 44-year-old from an endless parade of news magazines and television interviews, though he had not actually laid eyes on him personally since that night two decades earlier.

The woman with MacGregor had to be his wife, Jessica. Standing a little ways from them were three children who Miles assumed were theirs. Girl, boy, girl. Still young enough that their height order matched their age order.

The MacGregors had gone to great lengths to keep their children out of the public eye. Obviously, that was not an easy task considering their father was one of the wealthiest men in the world. Curiously absent, the reporter noted, was Ian's on-again, off-again business partner – his sister. Miles knew he would have to ask about that. In his mind, it demonstrated she had the sense to stay away...

Curtains began to close, darkening the room, as a video screen lowered from the ceiling. It was emblazoned with an animated QA logo.

CHAPTER 2

Paris, France

Charlie was going to scream if she had to listen to this debate much longer. She had heard it all before; it wasn't even a debate. It was just her older brothers goading their father into – loudly – defending his latest theories. Those theories, of course, were generally either ignored or treated with gentle amusement by the rest of the academic world. She looked at her mother, Adele Durand, pleading with her eyes to make it stop.

Charlie wouldn't be able to hear the television if they continued.

"Charles," Adele said to her husband, her French accent purposefully stronger than it had been when Charlotte – Adele refused to call her "Charlie" – was a girl growing up in England. "Can you and the boys lower your voices, just a bit?"

Charles Smith-Davies didn't respond... or miss a beat in his argument. "Even years ago, the Abri du Maras textiles were acknowledged to be highly sophisticated and were conclusively of Neanderthal design!"

"So father," said Henry, the oldest son, with a smile, "you are basing your argument that the Neanderthals were technologically advanced because they made string? That's a far cry from being an analogue to modern society. Were they dashing about on motorcycles?"

"That's not what I said," the older man replied, "I said they were more advanced than they are given credit for having been! That's all! And, to be clear, my theory has never been about the Neanderthals at all – and you know it."

Switching sides without notice came Gabriel, who – like his sister, Charlotte – was visiting Paris from the United States. "Given the age of the Earth, why couldn't it have been possible for a civilization to have–"

"–Oh, please, Gabriel! No, no, no," began Henry, a professor in Department of Earth Sciences at Université Paris Sciences et Lettres. In a few minutes, following the longstanding script, they would switch sides and drive their father, mother, and sister to the point of insanity – though for decidedly different reasons. This is how life went in the family of Charles Smith-Davis, Adele Durand, and their three highly intelligent children.

"–to have risen and fallen?" Gabriel smiled with a wink at his brother. "You're going to tell me about your precious rocks now aren't you?"

"Boys!" Adele said more sternly, getting the attention of all three men. "You will be silent. Or, you may go outside. But Charlotte and I wish to watch this, as she so kindly asked over dinner."

"Yes, ma'am," a chagrined Gabriel spoke for the trio. "I really should tackle the mid-terms I brought to grade. I suspect that won't be too disruptive?"

Truth be told, Adele was as interested in what Ian MacGregor would be announcing as her daughter. Still a lecturer for Université PSL's graduate engineering program, it was Adele who had introduced Charlotte to the MacGregor family. That had resulted in a "gap year" during which Charlotte worked as the MacGregor's *au pair*.

Charles *harrumphed* as he grabbed the ever-present pen and notebook by his chair, so that he could jot down a rejoinder to whichever of the boys it was who had raised whatever it was they had said. It would be brilliant, he knew, if he could remember what that thought was...

Smith-Davies came from an extravagantly wealthy English family that had never managed to get itself titled by the crown. It seemed at the various important points in history, the family patriarchs always happened to have taken the correct – if politically disadvantageous – position on important matters of state. One ancestor had vocally supported the American cause of independence. That particular stain had lasted into the late 19th century, just in time for another family member to suggest the continued presence of royal colonies amounted to little more than enslavement of those peoples. Those were just two high points.

But they had, to put it modestly, *enough*. In real terms, the family could buy and sell the entire monarchy a time or two over without it so much as denting the Smith-Davies petty cash fund.

And then there was the matter of the endowment which Charles oversaw. The fund provided research grants across a variety of disciplines each year. It was in the awarding of one of those grants two decades earlier that had brought Adele Durand and Charles Smith-Davies into contact with the MacGregor family. Not Ian himself, but his younger sister Teresa, who had been doing truly groundbreaking linguistics research.

The sheer amount of money awarded by the Smith-Davies Fund for Excellence in Research allowed Charles – a retired professor of anthropology – to hold his rather eccentric theories without being too loudly mocked... if not taken entirely seriously, either.

"Well, I think the boys should be more open-minded," Charles said to his wife. She replied only with a smile, which had made him melt since they first met a half-century earlier. "I'm sorry, Charlie," he added to his daughter. She could have been a clone of her mother.

When Charles and Adele became "empty nesters" after their second son Gabriel left home for university, they were not exactly expecting to start baby-proofing their homes. But from her first scream at the world until this most recent exasperated moment, Charles could think of no more perfect third child than his beautifully intelligent Charlie.

She was so perfect, he had insisted, she could only be named after him. "What is your friend Mr. MacGregor going to be announcing," he inquired.

"Father, you know full well I'm bound by more non-disclosure agreements than most lawyers can count. But... I'm pretty sure QA has been underselling it."

CHAPTER 3

As a boy, Ian MacGregor could not sleep at night. His earliest memories were of telling his parents, and an endless line of doctors, that he just wanted to see the stars. At various points he was diagnosed with every sleep disorder and psychological condition for which his family could afford the treatment.

His mind raced faster the more he learned. And he retained it all.

His story never changed: he wanted to see the stars. That he was intelligent was never questioned; tests placed his IQ at impossibly high levels. At the age of four, he was found to have not only a photographic memory but one which entered his long-term memory. The psychologist doing the test told his parents that seeing someone with a true photographic memory, like Ian's, was the researcher's equivalent of seeing a white buffalo driven from a watering hole by a bevy of black swans.

It wasn't until his father took employment in far west Texas, near the famed McDonald Observatory outside Fort Davis, that young Ian discovered astronomy could be pursued in daylight hours. He was soon a fixture at the observatory.

At age 9, Ian pushed four years of high school into a summer. At 14 he had a masters degree, and at 18 he was the youngest doctoral staff member at the Jet Propulsion Laboratory. By the time he could buy a beer, he held three doctorates and had graced the covers of both scientific journals and popular magazines.

Along the way Ian MacGregor's fascination with stars

had evolved into a fascination with gravity and the fabric of space itself. He mostly kept his heretical views to himself while finishing his first doctoral dissertation, but it was his opinion that Einstein's universal speed limit could be broken as freely as any imposed on the straight, flat highways of west Texas.

That speed was limited to 299,792,458 meters per second offended Ian intellectually and personally. If the speed limit was 'c,' he would grumble after a few beers, it was only because scientists and engineers were too lazy or stupid to comprehend anything faster.

Ian MacGregor was neither lazy nor stupid. He was, however, arrogant. Very arrogant. Frustrating. Demanding. At least, in his early adulthood. Marriage, and then three children, would eventually change that.

But at 25 years old, two years before marriage and several before the first child, Ian MacGregor was at the height of his demanding, frustrating, genius-level arrogance. He decided that the public study of outer space no longer interested him because the "close-minded fools in the field make it impossible to explore new ideas." That quote came from an essay he penned for the *New York Post*. He burned every bridge, and set the ashes on fire.

By then, he had shifted his mind to something infinitely smaller: quantum computing.

It wasn't a new field for him, per se. Just a new area of professional devotion. He had published several articles on quantum theory in his teens, and remained fascinated with the promise of quantum computing.

It was a promise he turned into a reality because it served his original fascination with the stars.

With Quantum Advantage, Ian, his sister Teresa, and their best friend Chris Stoddard successfully took quantum computing to the consumer market. A series of innovative devices and services made QA what the *Wall Street Journal* called "the most essential enterprise in the world." Within a decade its annual revenues dwarfed every rival. The company was kept purposefully private, allowing it to experiment and innovate without the pressures of appeasing quarterly targets or capitulating its efficiency to activist investors. And when significant resources were devoted to Ian MacGregor's quixotic intellectual indulgences, it was no one's business.

He had stopped needing to prove he was right to anyone; he just wanted to prove it to himself.

Despite Ian MacGregor's brusque personality, the company's staff was fiercely loyal – a point of pride internally, even if viewed from the outside as somewhat cultish. But it was what they were loyal to that had the outside world confused.

In one of his rare interviews, Chris Stoddard scoffed at claims the company was a cult of personality built around his friend.

"No one here likes Ian, except maybe me. Everyone loves Teresa, but that's because she's actually pleasant and has mostly stepped away from the business. Everyone else is here because they want to change the world. We let people do that. This is why me and Ian almost never talk to the media, or stand on stage hawking the company's products. Most of them we didn't create, so why should we take the credit? We've created an environment where people can innovate, and we fiercely guard that environment. That's it. And, we pay really, really, really well."

CHAPTER 4

Near Seminole, Texas, USA

"Thank you all for making the trip out here," Ian MacGregor began. He wasn't using notes, to the chagrin of his wife and public relations team. Jessica and the kids were now seated on the first row, furthest from him and closest to the drawn curtains. It was the view the kids had wanted. He smiled at them.

"I know getting out here wasn't easy," he said. "I grew up not terribly far away, but that's ancient history and not why we're here. We're here because this remote area has allowed us to test a technology that will revolutionize the world like nothing since the wheel." He paused. "And I mean, nothing."

Ian caught the eye of Sam Jenkins, whose new line of personal quantum computers was challenging QA's dominance in the consumer market field essentially created by Ian MacGregor. Reportedly fierce competitors, they in actuality met every few months for chess and margaritas. The world would be shocked when it learned Ian and Jessica were silent financial investors in Jenkins' work.

Josh Padden nudged Miles Oliver. "Where do you think this is going?"

"No idea," Miles whispered back. "My gut's telling me this is going to be the end of Ian MacGregor. This kind of build up makes me think he's lost it. Segway, calling."

MacGregor spoke of QA's breakthroughs in quantum computing, which had been called "impossible," without sounding like he was bragging. The success of the company did the bragging.

"Some of you know that Albert Einstein was referring to quantum communications as 'spukhafte Fernwirkung' or basically, spooky action at a distance. To say he was skeptical about quantum entanglement and its implications would be an understatement," said Ian. "While I suspect the news in coming days of our latest development in quantum work will be overshadowed by the reason I brought you here, the team at QA has developed a fully operational, repeater-less, communications system that will make conversations with explorers on Mars instantaneous. No more light-minute lags in communication."

There was a smattering of applause, eclipsed by more than a few suspicious scowls. Ian marched passed it, and began touching on his frustrations with the accepted views on physics and space travel. Even still, many in the audience heard a subtle note of humility in MacGregor's voice that they had never heard before.

"It's not that Einstein was wrong, that Von Braun was wrong, that anyone before us was necessarily wrong. It's just that they didn't have the data necessary to understand the universe as we can today. They weren't as right as they could have been."

Oliver smirked at his cameraman. "Here comes his crazy." Others in the crowd no doubt were thinking the same thing. There was a distinct murmur building.

"Thanks to quantum computing, we've been able to dig more deeply into data, and tease out the secrets of the universe, in ways our forebears could only imagine." MacGregor sensed the audience was turning against him. His PR team had warned him this would happen, but he couldn't resist the big reveal.

"It comes down to gravity. It is a force we live with every day, a force we have spent untold fortunes overcoming, or cheating. But it is a fact of life which we still, today, know so little about." He paused. "Well, publicly. We," he stressed it, and pointed at a group sitting in the front row, "have learned a great deal about it. We have found that it is a force that can be manipulated, created, and defeated."

Several loud protests rose.

"Please, please, my friends. Let me show you. We have developed technology that harnesses the power of gravity, it creates gravity, it offsets gravity. Well..." he turned slightly and smiled at his wife, "Let me just show you, Curtains, please!"

Oliver felt smug in knowing that everyone in the room now considered Ian MacGregor a rich fool. They'd never forgive him for wasting their time. Whatever silly, impractical contraption was floating outside those windows would...

Everyone gasped as the windows revealed *SPACE*.

Where had been the expanse of desert, now there was the curve of the Earth, the fragile band of atmosphere, and the deep black ink of... space.

"Welcome to low-Earth orbit," Ian MacGregor said, smiling. "Brought here quickly and effortlessly by our new gravity drive system that – I think some of you might even still believe – is impossible."

"There's no way," said a professor of engineering from the second row. "There is no way. This can't be possible. It's a trick." But even as he said it, the professor's conviction fell away. He knew, instinctively, that what he saw was real.

"If you believe it's a trick, then by all means head to the door — the airlock — and take a look around," MacGregor said with smile. He glanced over at his wife, who was shaking her head, telling him to keep the sarcasm in check. "But let me propose a better way." He motioned to the staff on the wing of the large room.

"The gravity drive engaged at the moment the airlock doors closed. Some of you might have felt a slight jump in your stomach. I never have, but my kids all three claim they know exactly when the grav-drive takes over."

Lucy, the youngest girl, shouted, "We do!" Miles thought of his own lurching stomach from a few moments ago. *Surely not...*

Ian smiled at her and then continued. "We launched as soon as the curtains closed. The effect is mitigated by gravity plating in the floors, which have kept us at a comfortable one-G while eliminating the effects of inertia. As you can imagine, we've travelled very fast to this orbit. With a conventional rocket, we would have been plastered to the floors."

He paused, remembering what he'd been wanting to point out. "The team here is setting up an area that will reverse the gravity plating effects and give you the opportunity experience weightlessness in a way not even astronauts in free fall have experienced."

With stanchions in place, two of the staff members jumped into the air, and hung there. They began doing a series of rolls familiar to anyone who had watched videos of space station crew members over the years.

"This is ridiculous!" Miles Oliver had finally found his voice. He was certain it was all an elaborate hoax. He stood and walked down the two steps from his chair and marched to the cordoned off area. "You, Ian MacGregor, are a fraud."

With that, Miles stepped across the boundary into a... weightlessness. He had felt it before. He had lived with free fall for three months. He gasped. "It's real."

"Of course it's real, Miles," said Ian, smiling. "And, please, everyone is welcome to give it a try. And press your noses up to the windows. You'll have some truly extraordinary views coming up."

A petite blonde employee of QA took the microphone to announce that, in fifteen minutes, MacGregor and his engineers would be answering questions on the theoretical and practical aspects of the program.

Meanwhile, Ian dropped in the chair beside his wife. "How was it?"

"You did just fine, Ian," she squeezed his hand while watching their son, Peter, jump into the zero-gravity area. "You started to be a little hard on Professor Hindmann, but you recovered nicely."

As Ian began to respond, a small German woman appeared and grabbed him by the arm. "Does this mean you've solved renormalization?"

To steady himself, Ian looked at his wife. It wasn't too long ago that he would have berated the woman for interrupting a conversation. Instead, he smiled with a practiced – if forced – graciousness. He stood and walked her toward the podium, where he had left a massive binder of notes.

CHAPTER 5

Kansas City, Kansas, USA

Maxwell Prasadh was not having a good day, because everything was going fine. Perfectly, in fact. But he couldn't get his colleagues to take their eyes off the news long enough to care.

He wanted to shout, "We're doctors, not astronauts!" But the ghost of his father restrained him. Propriety would not let him raise his voice at his colleagues. As a well-educated man of Indian heritage, he must be more reserved.

He could hear his maternal grandfather saying *Well to hell with that crap, boy.* Being the son of an Oxford-educated Indian and a white girl from rural Louisiana meant he had to suffer internal arguments between the particular views of his own heritage more than most anyone else.

"Excuse me," he said to his assistant, "but could I have you double-check these results?"

The young man looked up with something akin to horror. "I am so sorry Dr. Prasadh. I'll get right to it."

"Not a problem," Maxwell said to the graduate student who was barely five years his junior.

It was a problem, of course.

There was a narrow amount of time to study each sample before it degraded, and the samples really did not care much about billionaires and their toys.

"Forgive me, everyone, but unless we want to be unemployed after this grant expires due to a lack of publishable results, I would appreciate you diverting your attention away from outer space and back on the tissue samples." That got their attention.

To the layman, Maxwell Prasadh's research was focused on hibernation. In fact, he was looking more broadly at the many ways in each various species could slip into a form of self-imposed stasis. Hibernation was the most gross, and perhaps least informative, of their study.

Yet it was included because, as his department head said, pictures of cute sleeping bears would help popularize the research in pop-science magazines. Maxwell Prasadh couldn't name a pop-science magazine, and was relatively certain he would burn to the ground the forests which produced the pulp to make the paper used in publication of any such magazine were he to know them.

He took a deep breath. "Publish or perish" wasn't just a cute phrase in academia used to justify work of dubious value – though it was that also. The people granting dollars for high-level research expected results, or they wouldn't pour their cash onto the Bunsen burners of the world's universities.

In this case, the grant was from a private science foundation, through the National Endowment of Science, to the University of Kansas' School of Medicine, and finally his own department. No one said it, but it was believed to be a pharmaceutical company looking for a new take on the century-old "medically induced coma" brought on with barbiturates.

"Uh, Dr. Prasadh, you really need to see this."

He turned to an assistant who had, dutifully, turned his head back to the computer display and microscope.

With a glance, he knew the young man was right. This was it.

CHAPTER 6

Near Yalinga, in the contested territory of Central Africa

She was the wealthiest missionary in the world. Or that's how *Forbes* had described her, anyway. In fact, Teresa M. Schultz was not a missionary; she was a translator. Her husband, Hank, was the missionary.

"There is great joy in reading words that were written thousands and thousands of years ago, in understanding the thoughts, dreams, fears and hopes etched into stone, carved into wood, or inked into hide or paper," she had told *National Geographic* when they profiled her a decade earlier.

More than simply being a talented translator who brought dead languages to life, she was a linguist who created written languages where none had previously existed.

Their profile centered on her successful efforts to decode the mesa-American Isthmian script. She demurred in accepting credit, deflecting to the work of epigraphers John Justeson and Terrence Kaufman, as well as their critics Stephen Houston and Michael Coe. It wasn't false humility. In point of fact, she had read every word written by each man, and she knew beyond a shadow of a doubt that were it not for their work she would have gotten nowhere.

But Teresa was not known popularly for her work in breathing linguist life into dead languages, nor for supporting her husband's work by creating new written languages in which scripture could be translated.

"Hey, sis – sorry to call so late. You up?"

Teresa looked over her reading glasses, reminding herself for the thousandth time that she needed to change the settings so her brother couldn't just beep in when her computer was on.

"Quite the show today," she told Ian. "From what I hear, half the world went on alert because they thought a new missile was being launched."

She was proud of her brother, barely two years her senior. He was less of a mess than he had been in the past, a feat accomplished by her former college roommate and now sister-in-law.

Ian offered an exaggerated grimaced. "I probably should have filed a flight plan…"

"But you didn't want to spoil the fun," she said with an arched eyebrow. "So sorry we couldn't be there, Ian, but –"

"Stop apologizing, will you? Hank's like, what, the first American honored by their Congress? That's pretty awesome."

It wasn't a "congress" that had honored her husband; it was a tribal confederation. While they resented his zealous evangelism, they appreciated the education and medical services provided by his team.

Teresa knew that Ian similarly resented Hank's zealous evangelism, but he appreciated the intensity of the preacher's beliefs. Perhaps, she often thought, the thing the two men shared most in common was an unwavering view that they were right. It wasn't so much that either man had a "faith" defined as believing in something they could not see, but that they both operated from the absolute conviction that they were simply working from facts that were as obvious as the rising of the sun.

"When did you return to Earth?" she asked, noting that the image behind him was his home office and not a view from low Earth orbit. "And, for the record, I think it's very cool I get to ask my brother, 'when did you return to Earth?' That becomes even more cool of a question, the longer I think about it." They both laughed. "Cool" had never been a word used to describe Ian.

"About two hours ago. Pretty sure some of the guests

are still playing on the grav-plates–" he looked off camera at someone speaking to him "– I'm on with Teresa, can I call him back?" Long pause. "Yes, I will." He smiled. "I promise." His attention returned to his sister. "I've got some congratulatory phone calls I need to return, apparently."

"You should get to those," she said, marveling yet again at how much more sociable her brother had become even in the last few years. Before Jessica entered his life, Teresa served not only as the lead architect of their company's quantum computing programming language, but as her brother's life coach. She was still occasionally called on to help interpret the world of human interactions for him.

"No, wait," he said. "Don't hang up. I need your help with something."

"Okay..."

"This new project is going to be bigger than anything I've done before, than anyone's done. I don't trust anyone else to do it. I know you said probably no, but I want you to reconsider that because you wouldn't even have to start until next year, and Chris says he thinks the structure would take about a year to create and he and the rest of his team could take it over which gets right where we'd need to be on the construction deadline that I'm really convinced we could–"

"Wait."

He paused. "I jumbled my words, didn't I?" He made a show of clamping his mouth.

"It's not that. You've tried to sell me on this for, what – three years?"

"What is it, then?" He asked, fearing she was going to reject him.

She smiled. "I'll do it."

"You'll do it?"

"Yes, Hank has pled your case for the last six months."

"He has?"

"Yes. I'll do it."

"Tell Hank he can be the first missionary on Mars, or

whatever planet he chooses!"

"I'm sure that will please him."

"This is great! It'll be like old times, but even better." He beamed liked a child. "This is great. Okay, so I need to jump off now. Bye."

The computer screen switched to blue as he disconnected the call.

Teresa smiled, re-adjusted her reading glasses, and went back to the notes she was studying. She would have the structure of his new programming language ready earlier than he needed it.

"I better get a trip around the moon for this," she said to herself.

CHAPTER 7

Near Seminole, Texas, USA

On the other side of Earth, Ian turned from his computer, pleased that Teresa had agreed to help.

Laying on his desk was the massive scroll of blueprints for the support complex Ian intended to build over the next two years. It would be critical to the construction of his orbital station. While many other private companies had launched rockets, placed satellites in orbit, and even ferried humans to the various space stations, QA was now the first entity – governmental or private – to take a hundred people into orbit at once.

In five years, he'd have a space station that would be home to five hundred times that number. And then he would be part of the way to solving the puzzle that consumed him for the better part of two decades.

Ian tapped two keys and the room lights dimmed, calling up a holographic projection of the proposed QA station. Five years. Before he could get lost in his thoughts, he reminded himself of the calls he needed to make.

Those had to be done. But maybe tomorrow. He could have this station built in five years.

Several hours later his wife appeared in the doorway to his study. The holographic display was on, but the security settings meant viewing it required special glasses or contact lenses. Otherwise, the room was merely awash in a sea of pinprick lights bouncing off every surface.

Jessica didn't need the lenses to know what Ian was doing. He was standing in the room, leaning forward, with his hands manipulating data points invisible to her. He was lost in the details of the farthest reaches of the solar system.

"Honey," she said softly as she tapped the door frame.

He turned around the wrong way, before calling out the command for the projection to end. "How long have you been talking to me?"

"Just now," she said. "You wanted me to remind you that you need to go to bed at a reasonable hour tonight."

"Why did I do that?"

She laughed, not sure if he was kidding. That made her laugh even more. "Site visit? For the... I don't know, the interior wall manufacturing?" She waved her hands. "You said it was a big deal."

He tried to pretend that he remembered and had been kidding with her, but gave up. "Thanks. Everyone in bed?"

She nodded and Ian called out for the projection to resume, without security. The room became cluttered with holographic projections representing distant objects. But not the station. He was drawn back to this every night.

"This looks different," she said, surprising even herself that she noticed.

"It is. I finally had time to import the E.U.'s deep-space observatory data. Took about a week to process."

Jessica stepped further into the room. She joked with friends that she couldn't find the Moon without help, which was only a slight exaggeration. But this section of space she knew almost as well as her husband, because it was important to him.

There.

The displays wanted to show... something. Even she could see that. And maybe that was the problem.

"Ian, I know I always ask this, but is it possible that you so badly want to see something there that you're biasing the results?"

He shook his head, like he always did. "There is something. I've tried to program out the possibility of something there, and yet–" he bit his lip "–the data keeps showing this... unnatural void."

"An unnatural void in the void of space? Be careful or you might yet be a poet."

Ian waved his hand like a conductor bringing the orchestra to its finale. The holographic display ended and he made a show of dancing across the floor in his bare feet. "I think my desk has a better chance of being a poet first," he said as he grabbed her hand and they left the study.

"In less than a decade I'll be looking at that void with my own eyes."

It would be much longer.

+++

Two decades and several regional wars would pass before the orbital infrastructure finally took form.

Australia's government weaponized QA's gravity drive before the first ship went past the orbit of the moon. The immovable Chinese government was toppled, twice. The Union of South America was formed and dissolved. The civil war in Central Africa continued apace.

Through it all, that void mocked Ian MacGregor.

CHAPTER 8

High Earth Orbit; 42,192 KM above sea level

Chris Stoddard never liked being the bearer of uncertain news. Yes, he came with a plan, well, an idea, anyway... Someone else's idea... But, still...

He checked the running timer on his tablet. It had been twenty-one years, three months, and fourteen days since the world learned about the secret gravimetric experiments QA had been conducting in rural West Texas.

As QA's Employee Number Three, he on numerous occasions had been the one to deliver Ian MacGregor with news things were really bad. More often, thankfully, he was the one to deliver good news about really great things.

But sometimes Chris had to deliver ambiguous information, partial data, uncertain news. The worst possible news was easier to deliver than an ambiguous set of facts. Ian was wired to find solutions; he considered ambiguity a mortal enemy and would spend hours debating facts that could not be known.

That was the worst kind of news, Chris reflected, as he prepared for the morning's briefing with his friend and business partner of forty-some years.

Chris Stoddard knew he could have easily cashed out a decade (or many decades) ago and spent his days sipping drinks on a private island. The thought occurred to him a time or two... Or thirty.

Every time he thought about retiring, he'd dismissed the notion. Like Employee Number One himself, Ian MacGregor, and Employee Number Two, Teresa MacGregor Schultz, Chris

Stoddard simply enjoyed what he did. He took vacations and spent large portions of the fortune he had amassed at QA, but he found fulfillment in his work.

True, Teresa had now twice left the daily work of the company they had founded. Both times it had been to devote herself to her religious and linguistic interests, but she was never really gone.

Chris knew he couldn't leave. It wasn't that Chris feared leaving the business in Ian's hands. He wasn't a bad man, a horrible boss, or an inept businessman; he was none of those things.

Nor did he believe there was no one more competent to take his place; he could name a dozen replacements from within the company off the top of his head.

Chris was certain the several hundred department heads and senior managers could competently and smoothly run the collection of companies and enterprises QA controlled. In fact, the businesses ran very well – and sometimes ran better without either he or Ian's intervention, especially these days.

What kept him from leaving was something akin to parental pride. Despite the waxing and waning public focus on Ian, QA in practice and operation bore more the markings of Chris Stoddard than either Ian MacGregor or his sister Teresa. This was not a matter of hubris; Ian himself had said it regularly and publicly through the years.

While Ian provided the vision for QA, it was Chris who gave it structure and muscle. Where Ian would be distracted for days or weeks or months on a singular problem – or, conversely, chase hundreds of ideas down rabbit trails in a single afternoon – it was Chris Stoddard who steadily got things done. He created the practical systems that implemented Ian's vision. He took the ideas and made them real.

Teresa, though, was the heart of the business. She demanded that the company, its products and portfolios, produce a tangible good – and a "profit" simply was not enough. She expected QA to be a force for improvement in whatever parts of the world or the systems of man it touched. She didn't care if a thing could be done, she wanted everyone to be on board with why it would be done by them.

Neither of her two departures from the company had left them heartless – she remained a majority shareholder in the company. If anything, her most recent departure from the daily grind of the company actually increased her impact. She no longer worried, even a little, about the thousands of details that went into running one of the largest business enterprises in the history of the planet.

Every conversation about a new or expanded project was met with her simple questions, "Who does this serve? Who does this benefit?" If you weren't ready to be confronted with that question, then you shouldn't propose your project anywhere near her... and hope she never found out.

Chris thought of that as he waited for the elevator to Ian's suite. It was remarkable that not once, ever, had he heard her ask *those questions* about *this* project. She had never asked about building a space station, or fleet or ships. Not once.

He had only recently learned why.

The elevator door opened into the suite Ian had reserved for himself. It was perched on the lead side of the station, or Station, as it was called. That was Ian's most demanding decree. He had insisted that it not carry a name. Not his, not the company's. He didn't want to call it anything other than Station; not now, not ever. This was not the destination, but a transfer point.

There was no small irony to that. Ian maintained an office and home Earth-side, but rarely visited them these days. Chris knew Jessica MacGregor was down there now on the North American continent, dotting on her first grandchild. She would be back in a few days.

The suite Ian had chosen for himself had the worst possible views, aesthetically speaking. The peculiarities of the Station's orbit meant Earth was almost never visible from here, though the moon would often come into partial view.

If this were a hotel, it would be among the cheapest rooms based on view. In fact, when the Station's hotel finally began accepting guests in three months, the cheapest rooms would, indeed, have very similar views – though not as bad and advertised as "moon side."

Though, frankly, none of the rooms' views were quite this bad.

Ian had picked this spot because it afforded him the best view of the construction platform on which a fleet of vessels would be built. These were the very first vessels designed and built in space for the singular purpose of space exploration.

"So, you're here to tell me about delays." Ian stated without looking up from his tablet. "And, before you make jokes, I do occasionally pay attention to news sources not named Chris Stoddard and read reports from our department heads."

"Probably a month, but we're not entirely sure. Next Thursday is the deadline for our round of material orders, of course." The only thing worse than delivering uncertain news, Chris realized, was when Ian beat him to the punchline. "The war in South America slowed production more than anticipated, again. And if you aren't going to get all your news and data through me, how am I supposed to manipulate it for my own purposes?"

"You'll get by," Ian said as he set the tablet down and smiled at Chris. "Can't we just end that war? That should be easy, shouldn't it? They've blamed us for both their wars, so we should just be able to say, 'Enough,' right?"

Chris nodded his head and sank into a chair across the room from the table were Ian worked.

"Seems like it, doesn't it? After all, the Brazilians seem to have very little fight left in them and the Chinese, in a bit of sickening historic irony, seem to be running low on manpower."

"That many 'seems' so close together doesn't exactly

inspire confidence, data-man."

"Would you like for me to deliver the full briefing I had planned, or do you want to criticize my word choices? And I thought we long ago agreed I wasn't here to give you confidence, but facts?"

Both men laughed, as Ian slid a cup of coffee to Chris. "Don't worry, it's decaf. I'm not getting another irate phone call from Mrs. Stoddard." He looked up in mock horror. "And, hold on. I thought you were here to pamper my fragile ego? What do we pay you for otherwise?"

As Chris rolled his eyes, Ian continued: "I've been looking at the expedition designs by Mr. Roberts. I like the plans, and I see he is keeping himself in as the first test pilot. You think that's wise?"

They were now, officially, off of Stoddard's agenda before they could even really get on it. It was going to be that kind of Ian MacGregor morning. Chris knew his own briefing would have to wait, so he set his tablet on the table and settled in for whatever Ian needed to discuss.

"I was impressed," said Chris. "He's more than qualified, he designed the ships, and he could probably build everything but the engine from scratch without a set of blueprints. I think he's the right man. He knows how the ship is supposed to react."

Ian stood and stretched. "My thoughts, too." The years were catching up to him. Standing too long made his knee hurt, sitting too long made his back hurt. His doctors said he really needed to replace the knee, but he was putting it off.

No time for self-pity. Too much still to do.

"Peter will be upset that he doesn't get to fly the first bird," Ian said wistfully of his son. In the blink of an eye, the boy had become a man. But unlike every little boy since the dawn of the space age, Peter hadn't been forced to give up what was once a childish fantasy of exploring the stars.

"He'll get his turn soon enough," said Chris. "The test flight is being configured as a two-man crew, but I suspect

Roberts would be happy to include—"

"No, no," Ian interrupted. "That's not what I meant. The crew design for the test flight calls for a life-support specialist, not another pilot or drive engineer. I'm not going to compromise the plan to advance my son's professional interests. Hell, Peter would punch me in the face if he thought I'd ever consider that. He understands the importance of getting all this right."

Ian turned to gaze out over the construction field where flashes of light indicated a welding team was at work. "And, besides, if he works hard, he'll be in line to take the first of those big birds on the real mission."

Chris Stoddard looked at his business partner and friend for a long moment. "Does he really understand the importance of this to you? Does he really not know what you're looking for—"

"No. He doesn't. No one should. I don't want anyone biased on this." Ian walked around the table and then perched himself on it across from Chris. "And that includes you, my old friend."

"Watch who you're calling old, or Peter will have to get in line to punch you in the face," said Chris, hoping the joke would cover his frustration at having only recently been let in on Ian's obsessive secret.

On reflection, Chris knew he was mostly frustrated with himself. How could this have been what had driven Ian MacGregor all these decades, and Chris never once even have had an inkling? He could, now that he knew, understand why Ian had kept it to himself. Yes, they were friends. Close friends, even. But they had always respected each other's privacy, their need for space. In this case, apparently, literally.

So, no, Chris' frustration was not that Ian had not told him. It was that he himself had not been able to reverse-engineer everything they had done to arrive at the motivation. *But then, let's face it,* Chris told himself, *only a mad man would have been able to assume...*

To stop himself from finishing the thought, Chris leaned across the table intending to pick up his own tablet. In doing so, he brushed past a bound stack of papers.

"Some light reading?" he asked Ian, picking up what was stamped "DRAFT" in red ink.

"Met this guy at a speech and he asked me to review the math of his thesis," explained Ian.

Chris read the title page, doing a passable impersonation of a movie trailer, "Temporal Distortions As A Necessary Component of Einstein-Rosen Bridge Phenomenon: Or, That Wormhole Doesn't Lead to When You Think, by W.J. Williams."

He flipped through the pages. "I thought the official line was that the gravity steam our drives create isn't a wormhole."

"It's most definitely not," said Ian. "But the math suggests that might not always be the case."

Chris could hear the tone of Ian's voice, and he didn't have the time to follow his friend down this theoretical path. So he brought the conversation back where he had started.

"So, let me tell you how your daughter thinks the war can be ended and our schedule maintained." Without looking up he could almost feel the surprised smile spread across Ian MacGregor's face. "Didn't see that comin', did you boss?"

Shaking his head with a smile, Ian asked, "Could she have it done before next Thursday?"

CHAPTER 9

Construction Bay, Station, HEO

Jason Roberts secured his phone in the front pocket of his blue utility suit. A month-delay at this point meant a three month delay for the first test flight. There was no getting around it. Stoddard seemed to think this would be the final delay.

Were it not Chris Stoddard himself who said it, Jason would have written off the prediction as the irrational optimism of a madman. In the face of everything that had been transpiring on the world below for the last two decades, such a commitment was silly. Though, admittedly, not much more so than the thought of floating in a massive zero-grav assembly area to inspect progress on engines that would be the first real step in making humanity an interstellar species. So maybe this latest war would, indeed, come to an end without obliterating mankind.

Dare to dream big, Jason, he said to himself.

The original grav-drive and related technologies pioneered by MacGregor and Stoddard were good mostly for maneuvering around the gravity well of a planet. In fact, those engines worked – by design – almost entirely by manipulating that irresistible tug of a gravity well. Essentially, the first-generation drives worked by using gravity against itself.

The second generation of drive-systems were far more complex by several orders of magnitude. The third generation would be even more so.

"A caveman driving a Porsche" is how Ian MacGregor described moving from these second-generation engines to the theoretical third-generation of grav-drive technology. Of course, that's not exactly how it worked. Using a focused point of gravity to create a straight-line slipstream in which a ship was inserted meant vast spaces could be covered in something like the blink of an eye, yet it was a wholly inefficient means of making complicated maneuvers to enter orbit. For that, the first-gen drives – or even old-fashioned rocket propulsion – would always be necessary.

Note, do not say that around Stoddard or MacGregor. They imagine a rocket-free world. Whatever. Jason knew how to turn a wrench; they could do the futuristic scheming.

Somehow the caveman allusion resonated with the construction crews. Hence, the first two ships of the line were nicknamed *Australopithecus* and *Denisovan* by the nerd-dominated shipyard teams. Jason Roberts, who had taken the most minimal biology classes possible way too many decades earlier, had to look up the references. He hoped fervently those would not become the actual names.

And for the life of him, he did not understand why the construction guys didn't call them Barney and Fred. Those names, he could have appreciated. But when he'd suggested it, the kids – his teams – looked at him like *he* was a dinosaur. *There's just no respect for the classics.*

Jason caught his own reflection in a polished panel. They might not be wrong about his age. The heavy bags under his eyes were a reminder he needed to actually get rest, not just sleep, but rest. This (last?) delay would at least guarantee him some extra sleep which might accidentally provide some rest.

But not today. After this tour of the *Denisovan* – XCE-G2-2, he corrected himself – he would need to review the crewing options for the first test-flight.

A voice from across the bay shouted out: "Mr. Roberts, have a minute?"

Jason turned from his checklist and peered halfway across nearly two acres of assembly space. Standing at the gravity boundary was the voice of his most eager drive engineer, Peter MacGregor. As Jason Roberts pushed toward him, the younger man took several steps backward before making a running leap into the zero-grav zone.

"Peter, I just got off the phone with your old man," Roberts said as they met halfway. "What's going on with you?"

"I've got the perfect life-tech for your test run," he began. "She was a Royal Navy pilot, highly professional, and she might be second only to you in understanding how every system works on these things."

Roberts blinked twice. "I thought you were going to lobby me for the second-seat?"

"Look, I really want to be riding shotgun when you initiate the drive, but that isn't going to happen," Peter began. "Now, I'm fine with everyone thinking I want the gig, but I figure if I'm being reasonable about this you'll feel morally compelled to guarantee me a spot on the second set of test flights." He waited a beat. "Seriously, I've memorized your test protocols; you'll need me."

Without taking a breath, it seemed to Roberts, the young MacGregor launched into the rather impressive resume of the woman overseeing the gravity-support design team. Roberts, of course, knew her – though not well. If Peter was this excited...

On most days, Roberts forgot the young man was the son of the company's owner. But at times like this, when Peter got an idea from which he would not be dislodged, Jason Roberts saw instead the man who lured him from NASA more than two decades earlier.

+++

"So you're saying that in five years, you'll have a space station up and running with five thousand people on it?" Jason Robert smiled at the multi-billionaire across the table. This was a month after the infamous launch from *middle-of-nowhere* Texas. Jason had had a particularly profound – and worrisome – view of the launch, as it had occurred while he was coming up on the end of his tour commanding ISS-II.

The ISS-II had been crossing over the northeastern tip of Colorado, on a flight path that would have them very quickly passing over Kansas, Oklahoma, and a small tip of Jason's home state of Arkansas, before then passing over into Louisianna. At a carefully timed moment, he was going to wave his home state's flag at the window while one of his colleagues took a photo. The plan had been to present that flag to the governor in Little Rock.

This was the last opportunity to do so before his scheduled departure from the station.

But then, just before saying "Wooo Pig Sooie," every alarm system in the ISS went off, with hurried communications from mission control in Houston and their counterparts in Europe. A fast-moving unidentified flying object was leaving a no-fly zone in west Texas headed for space. *For them?*

The lone Russian crew member looked at the American, European, and Japanese citizens with whom he had been living for four months. He had his hand covering a small ear bud.

"My people say it's a missile. They want me to move into the escape craft."

The British astronaut was speed-reading a text message on her tablet. "This missile is huge..."

"Houston," Jason Roberts said as calmly as he could, "we are getting mixed reports of a huge missile launch from Texas. Can you confirm?"

It wasn't a missile. It had been Ian MacGregor and several dozen dazed and confused VIPs.

"You owe me and my governor a photo op in space holding an Arkansas flag," said Jason, sipping his latte. "You scared the hell out of me."

"I'll fly your governor up with you, if that's what it takes," Ian responded. "I'll take Mrs. Smith's third grade class from Little Rock Elementary School, if that's what it takes. But everyone tells me if I want someone overseeing the construction and flight-testing of our second-generation ships, it has to be you."

"Sold. I'm sure Mrs. Smith will enjoy that." He set the coffee cup down.

They were sitting at a chain coffee shop just off Interstate 45 in Webster, Texas, a few miles from NASA's offices.

"What I think you need to understand about me, Mr. MacGregor, is that I do not like surprises. I spend my time planning away surprises. What my experience in the military and in the space program tells me is that surprises kill people. If I were to leave the Air Force, and leave NASA, to come work for you, these little stunts of yours must come to an abrupt end. You might think its fun to surprise the world with your little toys, but people's lives were literally at stake. Including mine and my crew. You want me to work for you? Then you better be prepared to work for me."

Ian MacGregor took a relaxed sip of his own drink. "Sold."

CHAPTER 10

Construction Bay, Station, HEO

Everything every produced by QA had specific development names, and the two ships – *Australopithecus* and *Denisovan* – were no exception. They were Experimental Craft Engine Generation-2, one and two. Or, XCE-G2-1 and XCE-G2-2.

They could comfortably carry a crew of 150, depending on the mission parameters. The ships themselves were feats of engineering, but they were – ultimately – bubbles of air. Humanity had been building variations on the theme for a long time. What made these ships truly special were the engines themselves. These two ships, once flight-testing of the engines was complete, would be part of a fleet of generic vessels fulfilling a variety of mission profiles. On one mission, a ship could be operated by as few as a dozen people carrying cargo. With a reconfiguration, the same vessel could carry more than two hundred souls in a pinch – though they would be crammed in like a budget airline.

The engines were designed to travel within the solar system. They could go beyond it, but not too far. They just were not that powerful.

Jason Roberts still had a hard time with the physics, but he had resigned himself to not *needing* to understand it all. He simply had to be able to make sure the engines and ships attached to them were safe. Well, as safe as hurtling through gravity-induced distortions in the fabric of space could be.

He knew these engines would be obsolete in another twenty or thirty years. His boss, Chris Stoddard, made a good show of being ready to hang it all up and retire, but Jason had seen the schematics for the third generation of gravity drive engines. There was no way Stoddard was going to let someone else build those.

The galaxy was going to be getting smaller for humanity when those engines came online. But not yet, not with *this* generation of engines.

Neither XCE-G2-1 nor XCE-G2-2 would be cruising to Alpha Centauri or any other star system. The engines needed an hour to reset between initializations, and would operate better with a longer reset. So with a little trouble and time, one could get safely outside the solar system's heliopause – but, functionally, that was the limit until the third generation came online.

These engines, though, operating at maximum efficiency, could take a ship approximately two astronomical units at a time, or 300 million kilometers – twice the distance from the Earth to the Sun – in under twenty minutes. Light took 16 minutes to cover that distance, so Ian MacGregor's frustration with Einstein's speed limit had not yet been rectified.

The theoretical problem, however, was the yet-to-get-off-the-drawing-board third-generation engines. Those bad boys would be able to get to Alpha Centauri, and they would most definitely be breaking Einstein's speed limit. Again, after innumerable briefings, Roberts decided he didn't need to understand the physics.

In the face of the engines now traveling just under the speed of light, and despite their long-standing assertion such a thing wasn't possible, when confronted with engine designs that would allow a ship to functionally exceed "c", the physicists on Planet Earth had agreed that, yes, it all worked out. From Jason's perspective, every single physicist uniformly agreed it was, now, apparently, possible for these engines to create a space-bubble and achieve *apparent* speeds without... This is where Jason Roberts usually excused himself to get coffee. These were *grown men* talking about *space bubbles*. For heaven's sake... *Whatever*. That was their job.

He chose not to debate the physics. That was most definitely *not* his job. He wasn't even sure he could debate the physics. What he knew, was that the engines worked. His job was to make sure the engines and the vessels to which those engines were affixed operated efficiently and safely.

Neither ship would be tested until both ships were ready; this had been a point on which Jason would not budge. He wanted the ship *not* being tested to be configured precisely as its mate, so system problems could be addressed in real time. After all, 300 million kilometers from home was a long way away to work a problem.

The first test would be to the L2 point beyond the Earth-moon system. While the test did not need the gravitational steadiness of a Lagrange point, it served as a convenient marker – and one to which a theoretical rescue mission of the test pilots could be achieved using the first-generation craft that were now buzzing regularly between Earth, Station, and moon.

Jason decided a valid rescue option would be nice, since he would be onboard for that first test.

The engines themselves had already been tested. The latest model had a perfect record. Strapping craft around those engines, filled with fragile human cargo... that point was rapidly arriving.

+++

The month moved quickly, and sleep remained elusive for Jason Roberts. But, honestly, he'd never felt more alive.

All in all, his work overseeing the development of these ships should be at the top of his professional achievements at this point. But, he decided, it was not.

That honor, he decided, would be in preventing the ships from retaining their caveman nicknames.

It seemed Ian MacGregor thought the names were funny, and rather enjoyed the thought of making two-bit journalists spell *Australopithecus* and *Denisovan* or, worse, pronounce them on the air.

Fortunately, good sense prevailed and they were, instead, named the *Shackleton* and the *Henson*, two men who happened to be in the pantheon of personal heroes of Ian MacGregor and Chris Stoddard.

That was a bonus; Jason had been willing to see them named after the lead singers of 1980s hair metal bands.

Because these first two vessels were named after famous explorers, the entire series of ships – at least four more were contemplated for construction – would be named similarly and collectively referred to as the explorer-class.

By way of random draw, it was the *Henson* (XCE-G2-2), that Roberts took out for the first flight. The vessel was officially crewed by himself and the life-support engineer, Adriana O'Neil.

Unofficially and unrecorded, Ian MacGregor and Chris Stoddard sat quietly behind them on the bridge.

It was, after all, their ship. No amount of coaxing was going to change their minds about tagging along.

The *Henson* moved slowly out of the docking bay where it and its twin called home. With a slight smirk and loud enough to be heard by his bosses, Roberts said, "Maneuvering rockets at seventy-five percent starboard." The only response was Stoddard's snort of amusement.

Before the grav-drives could be enabled, the *Henson* had to be outside the effective field of Station's own gravity systems. In what felt all the world to Jason Roberts like a Ghostbusters reference, the physics required that the competing gravity drive waves not cross each other. The result of such a thing, Ian MacGregor had said years ago, would be "horrendously deadly for everyone."

Avoiding "horrendously deadly," was at the top of Jason Roberts' list of best practices on most days. As a test pilot and astronaut, his entire professional life had been devoted to putting as much distance as reasonably possible between his people and "horrendously deadly." Everything was about minimizing any risk that could reasonably be minimized. Hence: avoid "horrendously deadly."

Five minutes after leaving dock, the *Henson* was in place, relatively speaking.

"Station, this is *Henson* preparing for initiation of the gravity drive," said Roberts. "Matthew Henson once said, 'It'll work, if God, wind, leads, ice, snow, and all the hells of this damned frozen land are willing.' *Henson* out, but we'll be right back."

"Nice words," came Stoddard from the back of the room. As the engine light switched from standby to ready, Jason Roberts glanced back at the two men. A smiling Ian MacGregor caught the glance, and nodded. "Punch the button and let's go."

And punch the button Jason Roberts did, though it felt like nothing happened. There was no jolt, no bump. No push of inertia. Nothing. That was, actually, a good thing. The safety systems were specifically designed to resist inertia. If they had felt something, it would just as likely have been their bodies turned to liquid by the almost unimaginable speeds they were traveling.

Someone inside the vessel would have no idea they were moving unless they were looking at the secondary monitors on the display wall, showing a rapidly vanishing Earth.

"Mr. Roberts," said Adriana, with only the slightest hint of concern in her voice. *Peter had been right; she is a professional.* "We've gone way past the L2 point."

"Have we now?" Jason responded with a smile. "I probably should have mentioned that Mr. MacGregor and I decided we'd take it just past the orbit of Mars before turning back."`

The life-support tech laughed. "Well, it is his boat." O'Neil began running – more leisurely than she had planned, since she had more time – a carefully prepared battery of tests.

For as unremarkable as the engagement of the grav-drive felt, their arrival at Mars' orbit was even less so. They were not actually at Mars; the red planet was inconveniently a quarter of the way around the Sun. Instead, they were staring at the empty space which, in a few months time, Mars would occupy.

Of course, they were not really staring at the empty space. They were, in fact, staring at the images of empty space from the hull-mounted cameras. There were only a couple small windows scattered around the ship where they were absolutely necessary because – ninety-nine percent of the time – there was literally nothing to look at. More importantly, even the most advanced transparent metals created unnecessary stress points for the ship, and therefore dangers for the crew. Instead, a generous number of faux windows were almost everywhere, rendering the exterior as if they were actual viewing ports.

"This might be the most beautiful and expensive expanse of nothing I have ever seen," said Ian to no one in particular. He looked knowingly at Chris and added, "But the next one will be even better."

The vagaries of slipstream travel and quantum mechanics prevented communications in transit. So, not surprisingly, the communications system had been practically screaming with frantic messages the moment the engines cut off on their outbound leg. Station-side crews and even Earth-based personnel were losing their collective minds at why the *Henson* had over-shot its mark. What should have been seconds had instead been agonizing minutes.

"Station, this is *Henson*. Once onboard we'd made the decision that this would make for a more optimum test. I'm pleased to report, we were right. All systems have operated nominally. We'll be heading back to the barn as soon as we finish transmitting the outbound data."

Less than an hour later, the *Henson* – having gone further, and faster, than any manned craft in human history

– slid carefully into its docking bay at Station. Jason Roberts and Adriana O'Neil disembarked to loud cheers from the construction team, a collection of dignitaries, and friends on hand for the test. Amidst all the celebrations, no one noticed Chris Stoddard and Ian MacGregor leave from a secondary hatch and mingle in with the crowd of well-wishers.

Almost no one; Peter MacGregor could only shake his head in amusement when he greeted his father with a hug.

INTERLUDE 1

Space is big.

The span of space is almost impossible to fully comprehend. If the solar system were the size of a football field, the Sun would be the size of a dime. Pluto would be approximately eighty yards away; the Earth would be the size of a grain of sand.

Using this scale, and placing the solar system in Miami, the nearest star – Proxima Centauri, which is more than four light-years away – would be a thousand miles away, just outside Columbus, Ohio.

Yet for all that distance, near misses still occur.

In 2013, it was discovered that a small star – named Scholz's for its discoverer, Ralf-Dieter Scholz – and its brown dwarf companion had passed through the solar system's Oort cloud some 70,000 years earlier. Their passage disturbed the detritus remaining from the early solar system that was far enough from the Sun and former planets to not be pulled in, but close enough to remain under the Sun's gravitational influence.

That jostling rearranged the dust, pebbles, boulders, and even planetoids that comprise the Oort cloud. Some of those objects eventually became comets and astroids that would eventually enter the inner solar system – though because of the immense distances and their relatively slow speed, it would not be until long after Scholz passed through the celestial neighborhood.

Other objects, however, merely moved within their established orbits, breaking out of the ecliptic plane of the system and moving in irregular directions even while still gripped by the distant star.

To the denizens of Earth, clubbing each other with sticks and rocks, the concept of distant rocks nudging each others' orbits was beyond meaningless. But as man took small steps, and then giant leaps, from the blue planet of humanity's origin, the theories of celestial mechanics would eventually present very real challenges.

Some more immediate than others.

PART II

Discovery

CHAPTER 11

The Shackleton, *Kuiper Belt*

These alarms should not be sounding.

Peter MacGregor's first thought was not, "Oh, no!" or "I wonder what the alarms mean?" or "This is serious!" No. His first thought was, "These alarms should not be sounding." And that alone worried him more than what any of the automated alarms – save perhaps the alarm indicating a hull breach – could have communicated on their own.

Even a hull breach, among an astronaut's worst nightmares, could – theoretically – be repaired depending on the size and placement. But this alarm, quite literally, should not be sounding. There were, literally, only a few places in all of space where this alarm should sound. The closest was some forty-nine astronomical units away, at Station. Others would be wherever the *Shackleton*'s sister ships were to be found – none were anywhere nearby.

The alarm was to sound when the grav-drive system initiated and dedicated the presence of an artificial gravity source – or, rather, the attendant waves – within its established course. An entirely different alarm sounded if someone were foolish enough to set a course through the interaction area of a natural gravity well.

Frankly, he would have been less surprised by that second alarm. They were constantly discovering Pluto-rivaling hunks of rock and ice out here. That alarm had become almost-common.

That it was *this* alarm sounding raised the horrifying possibility that the intricate systems which existed to protect life on this vessel were flawed and failing. In that case, it meant the systems and the automated alarms could not be trusted.

And *that* thought is what had Peter MacGregor very worried, with panic a not-too-distant feeling. He pushed that down. Neither he nor his crew could afford the ship's captain to be panicked.

The *Shackleton* was now more than five years old. After a series of tests, it had spent thirty-six months, alongside its twin, *Henson*, ferrying people and cargo between Station and the Mars orbital platform. In the meantime, three more second-generation ships had come into service specifically for that task and so *Shackleton* and *Henson* were given new assignments.

Actually, they were released to perform their intended first major assignments. Going back and forth to Mars were, frankly, little more than extended shack-down cruises.

Space is big.

That is another way of saying it is incredibly easy to get lost. From the surface of Mars, the Earth appears to be just another twinkling light in the sky – just as Mars does from Earth to the casual observer.

From anywhere in the solar system, even past Neptune and well into the Kuiper Belt, the sun is the brightest object in the sky. But trying to get home requires a little more precision than "head for the Sun and brake when you see the blue marble."

Making the system easier to navigate was the primary mission of the *Henson* and the *Shackleton*. They were responsible for placing small satellites in a system-wide analogy to the Earth's Global Positioning System. The first set of hops had been to place beacons in orbits around each of the planets and each of their moons.

By happenstance, Peter MacGregor and the *Shackleton* had drawn Jupiter and its many moons. He wasn't sure he had ever been so happy to leave a place.

Now, they were distributing the outer-system beacons.

All of the beacon satellites operated on the same quantum-based technologies that allowed real-time communications that would otherwise be unwieldy with frequencies limited by the speed of light. By triangulating the various beacon signals, future grav-drive ships could more easily and safely navigate around – and through – the solar system.

But not if the ship alarms went off for no reason.

When the alarms sounded, Peter had been brushing his teeth and preparing to hit the rack. Yes, they were about to make a jump into the gravity stream that propelled the ship at sci-fi like speeds two astronomical units at a time. But, frankly, he'd pulled a couple double shifts so his second-in-command could rest up after what everyone agreed not to call food poisoning and instead refer to as a food disagreement. Being nearly 50 AUs from home, *no one* wanted to think about food poisoning. *Not again.*

With his second in command – Linda Bletchley – back on her feet, Peter was ready for bed. She could oversee things. After all, their only real job was, basically, to tell the helmsman "press the glowing green button on your screen," which the helmsman knew to do since that was his job. Being in command of a spaceship and 136 highly intelligent and talented men and women was usually an exercise in being superfluous.

Except when alarms were going off that should not be.

And so that is when Peter dropped his toothbrush and sprinted down the hall – grateful he was still wearing his utility overalls and not his pajamas. No one wanted to see their 40-year-old captain running through the ship in his pajamas. No one.

Thanks to science fiction movies, generations of people have been trained to place the command center – the bridge – of a spaceship at the front of the vessel, or on the top of it, presumably so that at any point the erstwhile captain could whip out his sextant and find land or fight off seven-eyed aliens. Or, as with the old American space shuttles, perhaps pilot the craft to a landing strip.

The *Henson*, the *Shackleton*, and their sister ships, as well as the contemplated third-generation of craft, did not land on landing strips. They did not really have windows, except at airlocks. And even then, day-in and day-out, the windows on the airlock doors were themselves hidden behind heavy doors. Every room had a splendid view of the outside of the craft... by way of ridiculously high-definition video feeds. Every vantage point from the outside of the craft was accessible by video feed.

And so the command center of the *Shackleton* and the other vessels in the explorer-class was placed where it was the most easily accessible and structurally efficient.

Ironically, it also happened to be near the "front" and "top" of the vessel – if such designations can truly have any meaning in space.

"As soon as the grav-drive activated, the warning sounds alarmed," said Linda Bletchley, as Peter dashed barefoot into the room. "I've already ordered a full system check. These alarms shouldn't be sounding out here."

"I had the same thought. Kyle, what else is breaking?" Peter looked at the engineering section's representative in the command center. Kyle Moons' boss was the chief engineer, who was no doubt barking orders four floors down at this very moment.

"Sorry, Peter, but nothing is broken. The boss-man says the same thing from downstairs."

Going around the room, every section gave the same report. There was no reason for the alarms to have sounded.

"But we did all hear those alarms, right?" asked Peter with a nervous chuckle. Hopefully they weren't all getting space happy. "If our systems check out then that means something out here has a gravity signature our computer systems have mistaken for artificial. That's at least more interesting than the dingy red color of the sixteenth moon of Jupiter. I guess today is the day we get to do some real-life space exploring."

CHAPTER 12

Station, HEO

"Did my brother really use the phrase 'real-life space exploring'?" asked an incredulous Lucy MacGregor Hyde. She smiled and looked over at Chris Stoddard, who just happened to be in the mission control center when *Shackleton* was making the abortive jump to the next set of coordinates for a beacon drop.

"Yes, he did," Chris answered. "It is a testimony to Peter and his crew. They have been at this tedious task for months yet seem excited about taking up this challenge, like they are fresh out of the dock."

"Why were you up here, again? I mean, it's great that you are, Uncle Chris, but you're peeking in on the Missions Control center when you could be doing... well, whatever you retired people do?"

"I guess I missed the memo where I was retired," he said, smiling at his goddaughter and successor. It was true that Stoddard kept a light load of special projects he oversaw for the company – none of which were the various space-based missions operated out of this massive, controlled-access room on Station. And it was equally true that he spent a significantly larger amount of time perfecting his fly-fishing techniques. "Since I was on Station for the day, I just figured I'd pop in and – bam! – lots of excitement in here. Figured I stick around, and maybe you'd show up since you never call."

Lucy knew she was going to lose this round. Like she lost all the others.

Unlike her older siblings, she had a deep and abiding

interest in the business of the QA business. She was a technophile only because it was technology company. She was a space aficionado because it was now the default space company for the planet. But it was the business of it all, the interactions between the people and the products of the company with the public they attempted to serve, that excited her.

"Alright, my wise mentor, what should my reaction be to a flurry of panicked messages I got from missions control followed by my brother sounding like he and his crew are suddenly space-faring versions of Lewis and Clark?"

"I'd say exactly what it is: incredulousness, mixed with concern and pride. Basically, the emotions I felt at least once every day working around your dad."

"Why did you let me take this job?" Before he could say anything, she added, "Did he ask you to babysit me?"

"No, he did not. Seriously, you are better at this than I ever could have been, at your age or any other. I just happened to be in the neighborhood." He glanced at his watch. "Hey, I need to run, but if anything interesting occurs, maybe you'd let me hang out in the back of the room? And, also, you should give your dad a shout." Stoddard turned and headed for the door before Lucy could respond.

And then the technician monitoring the *Shackleton* called for her. "Mrs. Hyde, *Shackleton* Actual is requesting to speak with you."

Lucy looked at the door through which Stoddard had just exited, wondering what the old man knew. He had definitely been there at her father's request.

"I'll take it in the conference room... uh, room three," she said, looking at one of the small rooms set up specifically for private conversations. Lucy entered, letting the door close, and pressed her authentication badge to a panel next to the large monitor. The QA logo was replaced with the logo of the *Shackleton*, and then her brother appeared.

"So, have you broken our ship?" she asked, hoping it

sounded funny. She wasn't feeling funny. She was feeling incredulous and concerned. Pride wasn't yet anywhere on her emotional map.

"I'm sure the records office can tell you how many times I've been on a ship that activated the drive and slipped into the stream, but this is the first time I have ever experienced anything like this."

"So what are you doing about it?"

"Engineering, computer sciences, life sciences, our helm and navigation teams, all report there is nothing wrong with the ship or its sensors. We've done every test imaginable, and they've even created a few new ones. So we're going to plot for a slightly different set of coordinates, power up the drive, and see what we get."

Lucy put her finger to her chin. "When you say 'slightly different,' what do you mean?"

"Basically, we're going to aim a little shorter and little over our original target."

"And you felt the need to tell me...?"

"Because I'm thinking no matter what we find, you are going to need to put your Dad-sized brain on this."

"Thanks... I think. While I have you, Uncle Chris was here when all the alarms started ringing here. He said he thought I should give Dad a call. That strike you as strange?"

"Does he usually hang out in the Space Operations Center?" Peter used the proper name for what everyone colloquially called 'Missions Control.'

"Not that I've seen, and I think I would feel really bad checking the logs."

"Strange. Well, I know Dad always likes a call from his star pupil."

It was an old joke the older siblings shared at Lucy's expense. Some people teased that one child was the emotional favorite of a particular parent; sometimes it might even be true. In the nerdy world of the MacGregor siblings, it came down to GPAs and SATs. Numerically, she was, indeed, their father's star pupil. Even if not by that much.

"Well, have fun exploring outer space. I need to make sure you and your crew get paid." They both waved as Peter cut the connection.

Lucy looked at her schedule. Her afternoon was already shot, so maybe a call to her dad would make... No, it wouldn't. He and mom were visiting Samantha in France, so it would be – she glanced at her watch – midnight there. She decided she'd call at a more reasonable hour for them.

+++

When Lucy was three, she could do long-division. But besides that and a fondness for hearing her mother read Shakespeare, Lucy was a normal child. Or rather, as normal as a child could be when growing up in the home of billionaire.

But that wasn't fair.

Her parents never acted like what Lucy would later find to be the common traits of unfathomably wealthy parents. They ate meals together, did chores, had fights, played games, got in trouble. They did, she had to admit, take very nice vacations.

Two different times, when their mom – Jessica – knew she was going to be immersed in a work project for an extended time, the family hired an *au pair*. The first one was Charlotte Smith-Davies. She came to live with the MacGregor's when Lucy was four and half. That was a pivotal year.

Looking back, Lucy vividly remembered telling the very old, very mature Charlotte – who was, in fact, only 19 and taking a year off from her studies – that "Charlie" was a "boy's name" and that as such she could probably never be friends with her. That lasted an afternoon.

For the next 11 months, everyone knew where to find Lucy – she would be within inches of Charlie. She was infatuated with Charlie's accent and clothing. Everything that a four-year-old could possibly be impressed by in an adult,

Lucy was impressed by in Charlie.

That was the year when the family had moved to Seminole, close to the grav-drive test facility. The move – no one knew at the time, of course – had been precipitated by the development of those amazing grav-plates.

On occasion, Ian would take the three children to the test facility. They were told not to tell anyone what they saw or did there, and the children obeyed.

Except for the star pupil. It had been a Saturday afternoon shortly before Charlie left to return to college. The children had gone to "daddy's work."

"Did you have fun, Muffin?" Charlie asked Lucy.

"Yeah, we just stayed in the flying room. They wouldn't let us go in the ship this time."

"Ohhh," was all Charlie said. This was a common fantasy for the young girl. She would tell Charlie all about playing "flying tag" with her siblings. Lucy said she really wished that, before Charlie left, she could come play flying tag, too.

"Why don't we just play that here?" Charlie had asked, playfully tapping Lucy's shoulder as if starting the game..

"Well, because we don't have right kind of floor here, of course!"

Lucy dashed to the kitchen where her mother was dishing up small bowls of ice cream for the kids. Charlie hadn't realized it, but Ian had been standing in the door frame.

"She has such an imagination, Mr. MacGregor," Charlie had said.

The man stared at her for a moment, smiled, and said, "Yes, she does. But let me take this opportunity to remind you, before you head off, about the non-disclosure agreements. Even little things, like my daughter's, uh, stories, are covered. Okay?"

Charlotte Smith-Davies was momentarily taken aback, but quickly assented. "Absolutely, Mr. MacGregor. This has truly been the most wonderful year. You, Jessica, and the kids have all been amazing."

"Thank you for your understanding," he had said, and followed Lucy to the kitchen. "Are y'all leaving any ice cream in there for me and Charlie?"

+++

Lucy MacGregor Hyde again passed her authentication badge over the reader. The communication system activated.

"Call *Henson* Actual," she said. Several moments passed before the QA logo was replaced, this time by the *Henson*'s own mission logo, and then a young man's face appeared. The shock at to whom he was speaking flashed heavily across his face.

"Uh, Mrs. Hyde, I'm very sorry," he stammered, "but Captain Smith-Davies is about halfway through her sleep period. The signal wasn't marked urgent or I would've just patched it through directly and I didn't realize..."

"No, that's quite alright, I should have checked the duty roster before calling. Let me ask you this, has the *Henson* been operating alright?" The young man looked like he was about to faint, so she added, "No, I'm sorry, that didn't come out alright. I was just checking in to make sure everything was good there. Captain Smith-Davies and I have been friends a long time, and I was just checking in on her, to see how things were going."

He didn't look much relieved, but the young communications officer appeared to be steeling up his composure.

"Yes, ma'am. Everything is five-by-five, unless you count the chef wiping everyone out at our poker tournament on Saturday."

"Sounds like Karl. Alright, I'll send the captain a message, but if you cross paths, let her know I called. And what was your name?"

"Jeff Prasadh, ma'am. I'm a junior comms tech."

"Thanks, Jeff, for your time. Nice to chat with you."

"Likewise," he said as she cut off the call.

She called the Martian insertion team leader, who

oversaw the three ships doing the Earth-Mars runs. They had had no problems.

This left a mystery that Lucy was in no position to unravel. She did not like mysteries.

CHAPTER 13

The Shackleton, *Kuiper Belt*

Charlotte Smith-Davies awoke two minutes before her alarm. She rose, a little stiff from the workout before bed, but it was the "I'm glad I finally got a workout" stiffness that she told herself was a good thing and not another sign of being well past 50.

In the dim light of the quarters, as she slipped into her utility overalls – the closest thing QA had to a "uniform" – she could see her reflection in the mirror. Her disheveled red hair would need to be tamed before she could get coffee. That was a disappointment.

She silenced the alarm before it would go off and awaken her husband. Thomas Newcome was a good sport about many things, but interfering with his sleep was not one of them. He was the only non-crew member on the *Henson*. That she was allowed to bring her husband, when no one else could bring theirs, had been a minor source of contention leading up to the voyage.

Yet that had been her requirement for taking the job. She still smiled at the memory of being invited to Chris Stoddard's office, where she was asked to consider running the *Henson*'s half of the solar system navigation project. After graduating college she – like every other young engineer on the planet – had applied for a job with QA's nascent space program. Unlike every other engineer on the planet, she had Jessica and Ian MacGregor's private number.

For twenty years she had worked in various positions on the second and even third generation engine design teams.

At the time of the meeting with Stoddard, she was heading up a team of almost 200 engineers tackling the new docking structures for non-QA ships at Station. Captaining a spaceship had never been in her plans.

Saying *yes* took a while. Stoddard praised her performance, noted the various evaluations she had received. But in the end, it came down to one thing: Ian MacGregor trusted her, and had specifically requested that she consider the job.

She and her husband had a teenage son, but he attended the boarding school near Oxford where Thomas had gone... as had every other male in the Newcome family since almost back to the Middle Ages. Thomas was from one of the families in that special club which her father – still – refused to accept had been denied to his own family. The Royal Peerage.

And despite the hereditary titles, the Newcomes all actually had to work for a living, and not entirely for reasons of personal fulfillment. Thomas' line of work just happened to be as an astronomer for the Royal Astronomical Society, specializing in exoplanet research. That Charlie came from money, and had money, did not lessen Thomas' *need* to work. Not surprisingly, the RAS had been pleased to let one of their own go on the trip.

Therefore, he was the one person on the ship who was doing true, actual, science for the sake of science as his one and only thing to do. For everyone else, the mission was the mission.

Like the *Shackleton*, the *Henson* was placing quantum beacons around the outer edge of the solar system. These beacons would provide highly accurate navigation tools for the expanding fleet of QA ships – and anyone else's ships – buzzing about the system. For the traditionally powered ships, the navigation beacons were a navigational bonus. For the grav-drive QA ships, the information generated by the beacons approached the realm of necessity.

On occasion, when the specifics of the mission came

up, Thomas would bring out his dead-on impersonation of the actor Harrison Ford, playing Han Solo. "Traveling through hyperspace ain't like dusting crops, boy! Without precise calculations we could fly right through a star or bounce too close to a supernova and that'd end your trip real quick, wouldn't it?"

It almost always got a chuckle. Charlotte grinned when she remembered Chris Stoddard genuinely having no idea what Thomas was referring to the first time he quoted the old movie line. She briefly wondered if, in his quasi-retirement, maybe the old guy was catching up on the popular culture of the last century.

Her tablet showed a number of unread messages about routine ship business. That was common for any day ending in "y" out here. There would be status reports, department head logs, and a variety of inquiries from the Space Operations Center.

She glanced at the list, and was pleasantly surprised to see her old charge – and now her boss – checking in. That one would be read first, though it would be read after a cup of coffee.

Walking to the galley, Charlotte wondered if Lucy was finally going to clear her little side-trip. The *Henson* was ahead of schedule, and Charlotte wanted to do something special for Thomas... and the world.

After their next jump, the ship would be positioned such that with a few – numerous, actually – extra jumps they would be flying alongside Voyager 2. There were, of course, some very valid scientific reasons to go. While the ship still sent a faint signal to Earth, no one knew precisely what kind of shape the probe itself was in. It was last seen by human eyes in the mid-1970s before being strapped on a Titan IIIE rocket and blasted on the so-called Grand Tour of the solar system. Seeing what effects flying through space at more than 38,000 miles per hour had on the probe would offer a fascinating look at how to improve the design of future spacecraft

And it would just be really cool.

In all capital letters, the subject line from "Hyde, L." screamed "EYES ONLY."

"Dear Charlie," the encrypted text message from Lucy began, "I haven't forgotten about your request. The committee finally gave its blessing, so you are free to go check it out."

Charlotte almost squealed – which would not have been a good look for the captain in the ship's galley. She wasn't sure why this was encrypted. "Their only requirement – which you know but I promised I would reiterate – is that this is a look-not-touch operation. The nice folks at NASA want their antique to keep right on flying. Before you start making these jumps, I do need to check in with you about a hiccup on the *Shackleton*. Nothing major, and maybe by the time you see this, more information will be in your message queue. But it is potentially something I need you to be aware of and watching out for." That is why it was encrypted, Charlotte thought just before reading, "As you can imagine, this is potentially sensitive, hence the encryption. P.S. Tell comms tech Prasadh he did a great job. Pretty sure I terrified him."

The captain of the *Henson* wasn't sure what that last line meant, but assumed if she needed to actually know she would be told. Despite the casual tone of the message, an encrypted reference to a problem on the *Shackleton* was more than a little troubling. Another message, unencrypted, from Lucy indicated a series of times she would be available for a conversation. Charlotte picked one, but noted there were no other messages pertaining to either her own vessel or its sister.

She reasoned that was good news, because it seemed bad news was the fastest moving object in the universe.

CHAPTER 14

The Shackleton, *Kuiper Belt*

"This is either going to be good news, or bad news," Peter said to the ship's helmsman as the young man finished manually programming the jump details into the navigation computers.

The entire mission had been meticulously plotted long ago by Peter's father when he dreamt up the quantum positioning beacons. Each one was to be set in a specific location relative to the Sun, Earth, and Station. So this little *alarms-going-off-you-have-never-heard-before is-our-ship-losing-its-mind* experience meant the navigation team had to actually plot courses by hand.

Yes, they had done it several times before in real life, departing from Dear Old Dad's program charts. They had made two unscheduled return trips to Station, but once those were done – the first time was to replace a batch of spoilt food, and the second to get a crewman home for a family medical emergency – they had returned to the pre-plotted schedule.

This was different because they were plotting to somewhere new – even if just by a few kilometers.

"It's ready to go, bossman."

Peter clicked the microphone to address the entire crew – most of who seemed to be either on the bridge, or crowded around the doors leading in.

"For the three of you not on the bridge and at your duty stations, let me remind you that we are activating the drive protocols but we are not actually going to initiate a jump. Whether the alarm sounds or not, we are going to power down the engine, plot a second set of coordinates, and repeat. We'll do it a third time, and then, after that, the senior staff and I will confer on our next step with input from our friends at missions control. So this was just a long way of saying, because I love the sound of my voice almost as much as you guys do, don't expect much."

Linda Bletchley smiled at his informality, toggled the intercom at her own station and added, "Prepare for drive initialization." Peter chuckled, "I knew I forgot to say something."

The drive initiated, but the alarm was silent for the first test. An hour later, the second initiation produced no alarm. On the third test, the alarm sounded. That one had been plotted to be less than a hundred meters from the original coordinates. The ship wasn't at fault; there was absolutely something out there causing the alarms in this very localized region of space.

The third test had a weaker "feedback" strength, indicating it was further from the anonymous gravity source than their original attempt. Theoretically, jumping to the first or second set of alternative coordinates would be perfectly safe.

Theoretically, this sound should not be happening since by definition artificial gravity didn't happen naturally. The consensus of the senior staff was that they use the first set of test coordinates and jump there.

"I know we covered this hours ago, but neither visual nor radio telescope data shows anything there, right?" Linda asked the assembled staff.

The lead navigator, Fritz Stuenkel, scoured again the available data – information loaded before the mission at Station, and all the observational they had collected along the way. "This is about as unremarkable an area of space as you get. We cannot see or detect anything sitting there, but obviously there is."

Peter nodded. "Thank you all for your input. I'm going to

notify missions control and see if they want to countermand this. Otherwise, I'd like for you to go ahead and get things set to jump to the first test. Linda, will you stick around?"

Everyone filed out, and then he initiated a call to Station. He was patched immediately into a conference room on Station's executive level. Around that table were support personnel whose jobs mirrored his own team. They had been receiving real-time updates as the tests proceeded, and no doubt just concluded a similar conversation. Whether or not they agreed on the best approach would be shortly revealed.

Lucy was in the room, but – as was her custom – not at the head of the table. "Everyone here liked the way your team designed the tests. Probing the surrounding space was a good call."

"Thank you," he said. "That would be Mr. Stuenkel's doing. I'll pass along your compliments."

"Before we go further," Lucy said, "I need to warn you that your crew might be starting to realize they aren't getting messages from home. As soon as all this started, I locked the doors on the *Shackleton* mission. We didn't want to risk anything getting out until we knew what we were confronting."

"Glad you did, ma'am," came Linda, "but there shouldn't have been anything inbound through Station. I gave that same order here."

Once again, Peter was glad Bletchley was his right hand.

"That's great, thanks Linda. So our top-line decision here at Station was not to be the armchair quarterback. You two and your crew are in the thick of it, so we want to hear your decision about how to proceed. We do have a recommendation, if you want to hear it."

Peter nodded and thanked Lucy, on behalf of his crew, for that trust. "We do want to hear your recommendation. What the team here decided was to jump into the first set of test coordinates." He could tell from the nods around the Station table that was their recommendation, as well. "Our intention is to leave the communications system active when we make the jump. I know that's a little wonky, what with the travel blackout, but it will ensure you guys are seeing what we're seeing as soon as we arrive – for however short a time it is that we arrive there."

Lucy turned to hear someone in the conference room whose voice wasn't being picked up by the microphones. She turned back to see Peter's queried expression.

"Sorry, guess a mic is out. That inspires confidence, eh?" Everyone chuckled. "You were being asked by the astrometry team if your fellows could include real-time information on the position of a series of stars and Station as you are moving through the gravity stream. I guess this is something they don't usually do?"

"That's right. Never been an issue, but I think I see where they are going," Peter said. "Are they wondering if this anomaly we're picking up might wobble the stream a bit?"

Apparently that was it.

"Alright, Station, *Shackleton* is going to check out this suddenly interesting section of nothing."

+++

As the connection dropped, Lucy sat back in her chair even as everyone else in the room began moving. She smiled at two colleagues as she did the one thing she never did: she checked to see if Chris Stoddard was on Station. Not only was he on Station, she learned, but his location registered as just outside the executive suites, down the hall.

She called him. "If you aren't busy, would you like to visit missions control with me in a couple minutes?"

"I'd be honored. I bet you haven't called your dad, yet, have you?"

She checked her watch and realized she had not. "Are you trying to cause a panic attack or a guilt trip?"

"Neither one. I may or may not have mentioned to him

things were a little crazy up here. Want me to grab you a cup of coffee?"

"Sure. I'll be out there in two minutes." She grabbed her things and turned to go. On the wall was the only official photo of her father on Station. Not in the main entrance hall, but here in this conference room that was once his personal apartment. And even this photo he only begrudgingly allowed because it was a personal favorite, flanked as he was by Jason Roberts, Chris Stoddard, his wife Jessica, and sister Teresa on the day Station become operational. Yet when Lucy looked at it, on this particularly morning, all she saw was her dad.

She should give him a call. She knew he and mom would be home in Texas, putting him on the same time zone as Station. But it would have to wait until after the *Shackleton* made its jump. She didn't want to worry him; he was retired, after all.

CHAPTER 15

Near Seminole, Texas, U.S.A

No one thought Ian MacGregor would retire. No one thought he would step away from his company. No one thought he would leave to anyone else the oversight of Quantum Advantage, and especially the orbital Station he created.

That included Ian MacGregor himself.

That decision was made for him, and he had accepted it. It had come in the form of a near-death experience in one of the first test flights of a more compact version of a ship using the second-generation engine. The idea was to try to cheat a little distance out of engines.

The physics were shaky, but it was a fun project. Jason Roberts, though only a few years younger than Ian, was not about to let someone else take out first a ship he helped design on a lark.

So they strapped in... and things went very badly. The *Shackleton* had come to their rescue, but not soon enough to save Jason Roberts' life. He become the first – and so far only – QA casualty in space.

Ian's injuries were severe. He vividly remembered Jason saying, "Punch it" but nothing else until awakening in a hospital near Houston. His days of being a man of Earth and sky had ended.

Curiously, he found his desire to be a man of the sky had ended, too. In what seemed decidedly stereotypical, Ian's time in the hospital provided him an opportunity to examine his life through the death of his friend. He found it lacking. Laying in that bed, he wanted nothing more than to spend his days with Jessica, spoiling grandchildren, and enjoying life.

He maintained a deep and abiding interest in QA, but he was confident that Lucy had it capably in control. And, just as Teresa had kept him in line, he was certain Samantha – the oldest of the children – would do the same for Lucy when the time was right.

Lucy and Samantha were very different than he and Teresa. They had different needs, different strengths, different attitudes. But different was good. QA needed different.

While many in the business of business gossip would occasionally point out that Samantha was the "rebel," the one child who had nothing to do with the company, it simply was not true in the ways that mattered most. A purposeful decision had been made along the way to let the perception persist. It was not an entirely false, or even unearned. She was not involved in the business in a classic sense, but she certainly understood it and kept abreast of its various successes and failures. But, more importantly, she had very specific opinions on how it should be run.

All of which the baby of the family, the star pupil, Lucy, very much appreciated.

Truth be told, it was Peter who was the rebel – though none outside the family would have believed that to be true.

While dutifully employed by QA, he had no interest whatsoever in the business of the business.

Ian had seen from the boy's first steps that he had the heart of an explorer. That the family's business just happened to end up having a component in the space exploration business was a nice bonus. He would have escaped Earth one way or the other.

At 74, Ian was glad he was around to watch it all.

But, at this age, he got much more nervous for them than he had ever been when they were children flying around the grav-plating test facility. The stakes were higher now.

On this particularly morning, he had the rough outlines

of what his middle-child, Peter, and his youngest, Lucy, were dealing with out there, beyond the thin blue atmosphere. He regretted that his ego-driven joy-ride meant he could not actually be on the *Shackleton*, that he could not even be at Station. He was suddenly, and most profoundly, shaken by the thought that maybe he should have warned them.

Ian MacGregor had never second-guessed himself about anything until now.

But what, exactly, would he have warned them about? Nothing. Literally, nothing.

When he had finally told Chris Stoddard, his friend had been angry, perplexed and confused. Sitting in Ian's office, Chris reeled at what this revelation had meant, peeling back the curtain on what had actually driven everything the two of them had done together. They had built a globe-spanning business enterprise... there were the untold trillions of dollars in wealth created and expended... whole new fields of science sprouting up from nothing... All to answer the nagging question of an arrogant 22-year-old.

"They will build monuments to your obsessive-compulsive ego," Stoddard had said, very much not wanting it to be kind. "But we've gone this far, so let's keep going."

Ian hoped his children would be at least as charitable... when he finally worked up the courage to tell them.

CHAPTER 16

Station, HEO

As she greeted Chris in the hall, and gratefully took a coffee from him, Lucy realized she was about to miss her scheduled call with Charlie. It was supposed to be in eight minutes. She checked her watched and did the math.

"I can do it," she said out loud.

"I'm sure you can, never doubted it," replied Stoddard.

"Sorry, I need to call Charlotte Smith-Davies. But I'll have time when I get to missions controls."

They walked in silence for several minutes, neither really noticing the way the people in the hallways parted for them like Station royalty.

"Have you ever thought about that nickname?" Stoddard asked.

"It's her dad's name," she responded. "Literally. He's Charles, so he named his daughter Charlotte, despite having two sons. I never quite..."

"No, not *that* nickname. But that is funny. Her dad is a real piece of work. Some people say your dad and me are eccentric, but – whoa – Charles Smith-Davies is really out there. Got stuck in an elevator with him a couple years ago. Wow. Anyway, I meant the way everyone calls the Space Operations Center 'missions control,' like you just did. Obviously it is supposed to harken back to NASA's glory days and such. But no one says 'mission' singular here; we all say it as a plural. This thing which shouldn't exist, because of a technology that's impossible, somehow manages to operate dozens of missions of various kinds on two planets and three moons, not to mention these two missions at the very edge of the solar system, all while being but one part of a major corporation creating all sorts of fun gizmos." He glanced over. "Still making the gizmos, right?"

Lucy arched her eyebrows. "I don't recall you being this, uh, homespun before. Are you what I have to look forward to becoming?"

Stoddard laughed, "Yep, it's all peaches and cream, and getting up to pee three times a night. You're gonna love it!"

They entered the Space Operations Center; missions control. The room had been cleared of everyone not working on the *Shackleton* and *Henson* mission. Those teams were sent to make-shift control rooms in other parts of Station. With fewer people, the cavernous room felt larger, more impersonal – almost ominous.

"Yes," she whispered in his ear before anyone noticed them. "We still make the fun gizmos."

A clock informed everyone there were 20 minutes until *Shackleton* initiated its drive. At any other time, this would have been considered a trivial piece of information, and as such would be displayed on a small monitor somewhere in the room with rows of workstations.

Today, it was front and center on the big board.

Lucy went to make her call, updating the *Henson*.

CHAPTER 17

The Henson, *Kuiper Belt*

"You need more rest, young lady," Charlotte said to Lucy.

"Thanks, mom," the younger woman replied. "I need to be quick." She quickly explained what had transpired with the *Shackleton.*

"Right now, everything appears to be an anomaly with that region of space, and not a problem with the ship. That said, I would feel better if you guys sat still until Peter gets eyes on whatever it is."

"Thanks for that update. In the meantime, I'll have my crew run a series of diagnostic tests. If my quick math is right, I think the *Henson* has made maybe 30 more jumps in its life than the *Shackleton.* So your idea of some sort of space-anomaly is plausible, for as strange as that is to say out loud. Peter is absolutely the right man to be captaining a ship confronting something new like this. He'll do marvelous."

"I appreciate that, Charlie. Really needed to hear it, in fact. That might even be why I called, now that I think about it." She checked her watch. "I need to run. Will update you as soon as I can."

The screen went blank as Lucy cut the channel.

Charlotte stood from the desk in her cramped private office and walked into the bridge. She leaned against the main desk, across from where her first officer was doing paperwork.

"We've been cleared to do our little jump out of the solar system," she said, bringing a smile to Adriana O'Neil's face. "But before we do it, I want to run system checks on everything onboard. I want our most recent diagnostics transmitted to missions control, as well as the results of these new tests. Once those are complete, we'll go ahead and start our drive sequences to catch up to Voyager."

"Yes, ma'am," answered O'Neil. With an arched eyebrow she asked, "Have you talked to Prasadh?"

Charlotte laughed. "No, but I understand he had quite the late-night call."

"Yes. I presume we're not tossing him overboard?"

"He made a very good impression, apparently." Charlotte pushed off from the desk, intending to go below and grab coffee. "Two things. First, Prasadh needs to be reminded that if he is going to talk about our poker tournaments, he needs to mention I came in second. Second, can you think of anything in nature that would emit something that looks like the signature of artificial gravity?"

Adriana, who had led the life support design teams for the internal gravity systems, titled her head and said, "No, which is why we call it 'artificial' gravity. It feels real, but it isn't."

Charlotte shook her head with a grimace. "It's not Prasadh, but I'm thinking maybe someone needs to be tossed overboard."

O'Neil laughed, "Go get your coffee, so you'll be less grumpy. I'm rather funny, and if you kick me off the ship you'll be stuck doing this paperwork. So, I know I'm safe."

+++

After she ended the connection with Charlotte on the *Henson*, Lucy grabbed her coffee mug and and walked back into the main room of missions control.

"Charlie doing alright?" Stoddard asked.

"She is." Came the clipped reply. "She and the *Henson* are dashing out to check on Voyager."

"One minute until *Shackleton*'s scheduled drive activation," said someone in the darkened room.

"That should be interesting," Stoddard absently. "The first humans to leave the solar system. One for the history books."

The big board changed to show the bridge of the *Shackleton*. Peter was seated at his desk. If someone didn't know what they were looking it, it could easily be confused for security footage at a mid-sized call center somewhere in Iowa. Space travel was simultaneously more exciting, and more boring, than most people thought.

"Ladies and gentlemen of the *Shackleton*," Peter was addressing his crew. "You know the drill. We need everyone on duty to keep their eyes glued to their stations, and everyone else watching them. We don't know what we're going to find when we get out of the gravity stream, but we will be the first people to see it. When Ernest Shackleton was putting together his ill-fated trip to Antartica, hundreds or maybe thousands allegedly applied to go. It was because he had the finest crew possible that they made it safely home. But if he had had you people, this crew, with him, they would have made it to Antartica and then back home. You people are the best."

Lucy smiled at her brother's attempt to bolster his crews' shaky nerves. She was pretty sure she saw him wink at his first officer when he quickly added, "All hands, prepare for drive initialization." The audio clicked, as the ship-wide communication system was turned off, and the ambient bridge sounds filled missions control.

"Mr. Stuenkel, are you ready?"

"Aye, sir," came the German crewman's reply.

"Let's go."

The big board went black. All of the other screens, which had been mirroring data streams from the *Shackleton*, likewise went black. For the very briefest of moments, Lucy felt panic rise in her throat. *They're gone!*

But then her rational mind kicked in. It was alright. This was normal. She glanced quickly around the room, and saw the same rush of irrational panic flashing across the faces of everyone else.

"The gravity stream interferes with quantum communications equipment," Chris Stoddard was saying, to no one and maybe only to himself. "It's a product of the bubble the drives create, shoving the ship into the stream. Ian has theorized it might just be possible to..." he stopped. "Sorry," he said, looking at Lucy.

"No, me too." She checked her watch, which seemed to be her most common action. "We have a couple minutes. And, before you say it, I'll call Dad as soon as Peter's connection is restored."

CHAPTER 18

The Shackleton, *Kuiper Belt*

Peter MacGregor asked, "Mr. Stuenkel, are you ready?"

"Aye, sir."

"Let's go."

And, as was always the case, nothing seemed to happen. Out here, one didn't even get the thrill of seeing the Earth, Station, the Moon, or Mars receding quickly in the rearview mirror – or monitor, as it were. The comparatively short distances involved meant even the stars didn't shift enough for human visual perception. Out here, there was only empty space, and they were going to more empty space.

Not really, of course.

Space is actually quite dirty. Rocks, dust, and radiation, swirling around and mixed with ancient shards of galactic ice. The wispy remnants of failed stars, and pieces of moons and planets ripped apart by incomprehensible forces.

From the earliest days of space travel, it was understood that micro-meteors and space junk were existential threats. When a spacecraft orbits the Earth at five miles per second, and it comes into contact with a micro-meteor pulled into the planet's gravity well, they met at speeds far faster than a bullet leaving a gun's barrel. And so spacecraft were designed to withstand those up to a certain size... and everyone prayed they didn't encounter anything bigger than that assumed size for that particular craft's mission.

The faster one goes, the more damage even small things can do to a spacecraft – especially one hurdling through space at – almost – the speed of light. And yet, the *Shackleton* wasn't truly in space, it was in a gravity stream.

If the *Shackleton* plotted a gravity-stream course through a moon, an asteroid, a sun, everyone's trip would indeed be over really quick, as Han Solo said in that old movie. Yet every single course included space dust, rocks, ice bits, and other materials. So, why no boom?

Even the rocks and dust remained untouched by the "passing." Peter MacGregor knew this because QA had actually tested it years ago by sending one of their first test engines through a small asteroid; it created a rather impressive explosion. A second engine was sent through the debris field. It survived for six more tests until it, too, was destroyed by passing too close to the Sun's gravity field.

"Interestingly," Jason Roberts had said in reporting on the experiment to the board a day after the experiment, "the Sun has survived the encounter without so much as a blemish."

It had to do with the peculiar interactions between the gravity stream and the gravity field of the objects. Yes, even a speck of dust has *some* gravity. Enough specks of dust get close enough and their gravity pulls them into rocks, and so on. But the gravity of a small rock, even, doesn't interfere with the gravity-drive. Or, at least, it isn't supposed to. The gravity divot in space-time of an asteroid, a moon, or a star, most certainly do, and in rather predictable ways. The generated field, the mass of the ship, and the mass of the object which the gravity stream passes through, are among the variables in a tedious calculation as to the survivability for any particular jump.

When the drive initiates, on-board sensors are able to detect variances in the gravity-stream. If there are ripples that will cause trouble, alarms sound. Different ripples cause different alarms. All the alarms are a notification of an action the ship's systems take in the milliseconds after drive initiation, but before the ship is actually inserted into the gravity-stream. Far faster than any human could react, when a ripple is detected in the stream the ship is prevented from jumping in. So the alarm is not telling the crew to stop, but rather telling them why they never started.

But then there is the problem of the things one does not know about. Of course, any unknown ripple sounds an alarm. But there was always the possibility, however remote, of ripples the sensors were not programmed to notice.

Which is part of the reason why the brains at Station, and the brains on board, were wanting the astrometric readings. They knew precisely where the stream was supposed to go. If there was something out there messing around with their gravity-stream in a previously unknown way, it was possible it would impact the gravity-stream in unknown ways.

Unknown unknowns are generally avoided in space travel. Even garden variety unknowns are potentially incompatible with staying alive in space.

Peter hoped he and his crew would be able to have a discussion about all these newly known unknowns. The reality was that once the drive was initiated, and the ship entered the gravity stream it created, one didn't get to just "jump out early." If you were in, you were in. Any attempt to do otherwise would have disastrous consequences. That's why those first several milliseconds after initiation were so important; that's when the systems kept the ship from entering a rippled gravity-stream.

In the worst possible way, Peter's father – Ian – had learned practically about the effects of dropping from a gravity-stream prematurely. It cost the life of his friend and test pilot, Jason Roberts. It's not a surprise that the forces involved resulted in the death of Jason Roberts; what was perplexing was those same forces only *almost* killed Ian MacGregor. The largest recovered piece of their test ship was 2.3 meters in length – and happened to be 2.3 meters that included most of Ian MacGregor.

Every model indicated that if a ship like the *Shackleton* were to drop from, or be forced out of, a gravity-stream, it would be cataclysmic. Future search teams might find tiny bits and pieces of the ship if they looked hard enough. *Maybe*.

Space travel, Peter thought not for the first time while drumming his finger on the command desk on the bridge, was both a hundred times more boring, and a hundred times more terrifying, than anyone wanted to imagine.

So, to sum up, while space is very big and very empty, it is also full of very small things and if those small things unexpectedly become bigger things, then you will become space dust.

Kids, sign up for an exciting career in space travel right over here. That's why my sister doesn't let me design the brochures, Peter chuckled to himself.

"We have ninety seconds," said Stuenkel.

"Astrometic data is holding steady and as predicted," Bletchley reported.

"Sixty seconds."

And then. "We have arrived," said Bletchley. "All stop. Dumping transit data to Station, along with real-time observations."

"What does anyone see?" Peter asked.

A chorus of "nothing" sounded from around the bridge. Someone was missing in saying "nothing." Peter did a quick census in his head.

He turned to look at Linda Bletchley. "Well?" he asked. Everyone else had been looking at data sets from the active and passive sensor arrays. She, however, was watching the external video feeds.

"Well," she began, and then stopped. "Peter, I... well, that's not a usual kind of nothing."

He stood and walked to her desk. The screen was on, but it was blank. It should not have been.

"Well, you're right. That's definitely not nothing."

CHAPTER 19

Missions Control, Station, HEO

"Well, you're right. That's definitely not nothing," Captain Peter MacGregor of the *Shackleton* could be heard saying.

"What are they looking at?" Lucy asked the flight director, Yua Saito.

"I think Bletchley was going to be watching the visual spectrum feeds," the woman said. She raised her voice, "Who here is watching the ship's exterior cameras?"

A hand in the corner of the room shot up. "I'm seeing this too. It's unbelievable. One second." Then, "I'm putting it up on the screen."

On the big board, the scene from the *Shackleton* bridge was replaced with the blackness of space.

"You're going to need to help us out here," said Yua in the direction of the scientist. "We're seeing nothing."

"Yes, ma'am. That's right. Nothing. This is the lower forward-facing, port camera feed we're looking at." The woman grabbed a laser-pointer and aimed it at the screen. A red dot steadied just off from center. "And right there," she checked her tablet, again, "yeah, right there you should be seeing the Sun."

Silence descended on the room... and then everyone started talking at once.

It took several minutes before order returned.

"Whatever is eclipsing the Sun from their vantage point is big enough it should be on their sensors," said Paul Brightmer, the frustration evident in his voice. "I can't explain why they aren't seeing it. Everything checks out. The *Henson* sent over their most recent diagnostics, and the results of a ship-wide systems test. Everything is operating identically to the *Shackleton*. Whatever it is that's out there, if it was something we could detect, we'd be detecting it."

No one wanted to speak next; everyone was at once confident their particular systems were operating correctly, and terrified it was something they missed.

"Light," Lucy said, the word surprising even herself.

"Excuse me?" ask Chris Stoddard.

"We don't have an outside light on the *Shackleton*, do we? We found this because it was interfering with the gravity-stream. We found this because it was blocking out the light. Right now, we're looking for it with everything but our eyes. The one indication of something being there is that it stopped us from seeing the Sun's light. Since we're seeing other stars around the edges..." She trailed off, with others around the room groaning. Everyone got it at the same time.

Yua Saito thumbed the communications pad. "*Shackleton* Actual, flight director." She paused, as the signal was confirmed. "This going to sound silly, but we need you to use the maneuvering rockets to move around a bit, keeping the forward port camera locked on the relative position of where the Sun should be." She paused again. "High school geometry was a long time ago for all us, Peter."

Within moments, everyone could see the display on the big board slightly shift as *Shackleton* began moving. A moment later, the screen blazed when the sun appeared as if rising over a horizon. The view shifted and the sun disappeared again.

"We see it, too. Hold there." Yua muted her microphone. To the missions control room she said, "Alright, we're making progress. Now what?"

The decision was easy enough. Both the *Shackleton* and *Henson* carried a compliment of small probes – landers not dissimilar to the early days of NASA's planetary exploration – meant to be sent one-way to any objects of interest that might be encountered. The probes could perform basic drilling, spectra-graphical analysis, and the like. They were designed to be launched at anything that hadn't yet been discovered, with the data made available to astronomers, researchers, and whoever else wanted to see it. Anything interesting that warranted study could be explored the next time a ship was close enough.

If it was exotic or profitable enough, the next ship to visit it could be a QA vessel out to make some money. For years, it had been theorized that massive diamonds could be at the center of some gas giants, and therefore those exotic planetary cores might someday be found lurking in space.

Each probe was equipped with light assemblies on the devices' landing struts and mounted on the forward manipulator arms.

Four probes would be launched from *Shackleton*, lights blazing, manually controlled by the ship's flight crew. Not only would the probes' own cameras see what could be seen, so would the *Shackleton*'s now-indispensable cameras.

Only when the probes got close to the object would anyone know exactly how far away it was from the *Shackleton*, or how big.

"It's going to take an hour or so for the packages to be prepared," Peter informed the missions control center. "We'll let you know when we're ready to launch."

Lucy MacGregor Hyde turned to her shadow. "Now, Chris, I am going to go call my dad."

CHAPTER 20

The Shackleton, *Kuiper Belt*

It didn't take quite an hour for the probes to be retrofitted and prepared. Peter MacGregor simply wasn't in the mood to wait; neither was anyone under his command.

"Linda, please notify missions control we're launching the probes," he said, then gave the command. "Let 'em fly."

The main display in the bridge was divided into four quadrants, providing a feed from each probe's landing approach cameras.

First, each probe was maneuvered until the Sun was eclipsed by the object. Then the probes moved along the X-Y axis relative to the *Shackleton* – north, south, east, and west. Each stopped when the Sun was fixed on the horizon of the object, and began moving toward it – keeping the Sun in that position.

"It's huge," said Sophia Scott. One of the junior navigators, she was scratching out numbers on a pad of paper.

"How big is huge," Peter asked.

"It's almost as big as Station, maybe bigger."

The probes kept moving closer to the object. It presented almost as a rectangle, though that was unlikely. But, then, everything about this was so unlikely that anything was now likely.

Peter looked around the room and saw better than half his senior staff hunched over pieces of paper, calculating the angles and known distances.

"So it is definitely a kilometer on what I'll call the Y axis," Sophia Scott said confidently. "And call it... 500 meters on the

X. My gut tells me this thing is sort of cylindrical."

As the probes got closer to the object, their lights seemed to play off the pitch black. The surface, which had been uniformly black, now appeared uneven if still inscrutable.

Linda Bletchley immediately thought of 'Oumuamua, an interstellar astroid believed to be an ancient planetary fragment from elsewhere in the galaxy that decades earlier had hurled through solar system. It wasn't even spotted until it was on its way out. Some publicity-seeking astronomers posited that it could have been alien visitors. They were, eventually, roundly mocked.

"If this is the big brother of 'Oumuamua, I call dibs on naming it," she said to the bridge crew, bring out an even number of raised eyebrows as light chuckles.

But before she could explain, Fritz Stuenkel said, "Probe 2 appears to be almost even with the object now." His voice was, as always, calm and measured. "Slowing and approaching."

Silence fell as the monitor displaying the probe's video feed filled with inky, uneven blackness, which seemed impervious to the brightly shining lights.

"Something is happening," said Andrew Todd, the lead communications technician. No one responded. "Can't you see it? The blackness is... moving."

Peter tilted his head and squinted. "Maybe...?"

The gentle swirl of black and less black became more pronounced as the probe lightly fired braking thrusters to slow itself relative to the object. The inkiness dissolved into a cloud of... dust?

As the *Shackleton*'s probe advanced, a uniform, reflective silver emerged.

With a level of excitement no one had thought Stuenkel was capable, the German exclaimed, "It's no planetary fragment. This is a ship!"

CHAPTER 21

Near Seminole, Texas, USA

"It is not a ship."

Those were among the first words Ian MacGregor wrote in his first set of notes to summarize his early findings. He was not yet 30 years old, but the void in the data from the edge of solar system had already become an obsession. His evenings and weekends were spent for years trying to tease more details out of the data he had glimpsed at the JPL.

His notes began:

> The phenomenon is highly localized and appears to be in a stable orbit, where it has remained so for at least the last eight years. If this is a craft of extraterrestrial origin, they are the most boring aliens ever. I suppose it could be an observation outpost.
>
> It is not a ship.
>
> Until I can see the gravitational waves being produced there, I refuse to entertain the idea that this is an artificial object.
>
> Whatever it is, it must be incredibly dense. For the distortions I believe it is causing in the local space, it cannot be Planet X. I suppose it could be a miniature black hole, but the theories there do not predict what I'm actually seeing. Or what I think I'm seeing, anyway.
>
> Besides, I know the guys doing that work. They're morons, so it should not surprise anyone their theory would be stupid. A grapefruit sized black hole seems more like a lazy McGuffin than an actual theory.

I do not think it is a black hole, but I will not rule it out completely. And, no, those guys aren't morons. Their work is moronic. I'm sure there is a difference.

If it is not a ship, not a planet, not a miniature black hole, could it be some exotic, ultra-heavy materials? Which I guess sounds like a miniature black hole, if you squint at it. Could I be the moron?

Nothing shows up in the visible light, nothing shows up in radio spectrographs I've been able to get my minds on.

Whatever it is that is sitting there, it is almost like it is not there at all. Nothing is there.

Maybe I sent it from the distant future to mock myself?

In the following pages, Ian MacGregor had catalogued the various source materials. He had organized the data he knew was available, what he hoped was available, and what he would want that no one would have and so he would have to create a clever way to get.

It never once occurred to 30-year-old Ian MacGregor to ask anyone for help, or even to look over his initial findings. His arrogance and pride hated the mocking he had received for questioning the established orthodoxy of the Church of Albert Einstein. The scientific community, those allegedly open-mind researchers of bias-free facts, were more rigidly opposed to anyone challenging their comfortable orthodoxy than the most dogmatic of fundamentalist priests in the Middle Ages. You were a quack, or worse, if you did not toe the line saying the speed of light was the universal speed limit. Albert said it, there were beautifully written equations to go along with it, and if you disagreed then you were a heretic, an idiot, someone unworthy of professional respect.

So, when he stumbled on the beyond-strange readings from the edge of the solar system, Ian chose not to share what he was thinking.

If he was wrong, he would learn it all on his own. If someone else saw what he saw and publicly solved the puzzle,

Ian would be happy about it. And if no one else did, he would enjoy poking at it all by himself.

For years he kept a journal of all his thoughts and suspicions, cataloguing the data, and eventually – of course – there was the holographic representation of all that data turned into a hyper-precise map of that region of space. He would go weeks without viewing it, and then spend days looking at nothing else.

Some forty years later, a more measured, thoughtful, and even mellowed, Ian MacGregor was still shocked and embarrassed by the arrogant young man he had been. His eyes darted between his wife, Jessica, and the view screen featuring his daughter, Lucy. He had just spent an hour detailing how he had come to notice the gravitational divot at the edge of the solar system. He explained the decades of gathering data. He explained the development of his heterodox views on gravity, so that he could understand what he had been seeing at the edge of the solar system. How his fascination necessitated the power of quantum computing, which basically then resulted in everything that had happened with QA.

"All I wanted, Lucy, was to solve the puzzle," he said.

"All of this... Everything..." she grasped at it all. "Dad, when did you tell mom and Chris?"

"Dad told me before Samantha was born," Jessica answered. "I'm embarrassed by this now, but I actually accused him of cheating on me. As it turned out, his mistress was a massive spreadsheet of data, and stacks of old astronomy photos."

"I finally let Chris in on it a few years back. Just before the gen-2 tests, actually. Your mom wanted me to tell you, but then the accident happened. I decided I didn't want you or Peter, or even Samantha feeling some burden to pursue Moby Dick as a way to appease your old man."

"But knowing there was a gravity divot out there would have saved a little heartache."

"Maybe, but that's why the sensors exist, why the gravity

stream is tested before a ship slips in."

Lucy again shook her head. "Literally everything has been about this?"

"Not exactly everything. And as your Aunt Teresa tells me, this is how the free market is supposed to work. One man's crazy infatuation becomes the employment engine for thousands of people, creating happiness for millions. It's really rather cool." Ian chuckled. "Yes, I am being careful not to hurt my arm as I pat myself on the back for that bit of self-aggrandizement and personal justification."

"Do you want to tell Peter, or should I?"

Ian glanced to the fireplace in his study, where recent photos of the children and grandchildren were placed. The photo of Peter depicted him in Station utility overalls, standing alongside what Ian knew was an exposed section of the *Shackleton's* gravity drive core.

"You tell him," replied Ian. "He'll be more likely to vent, and froth, and get it out of his system so he can get on figuring out what that thing actually is. If he hears it first from me, he'll no doubt hold it in and then be distracted for a while."

Lucy nodded even as she looked away. "Hold on, Dad." Her eyes widened.

"Play that back for me, will you?" Her eyes got bigger. Ian had never seen his unflappable daughter look so astonished. She wiggled her fingers and a disembodied hand gave her a tablet. "They launched their probes early. This just happened."

The tablet's screen faced the camera on her end, and she pressed play. It was a view of the *Shackleton's* bridge.

A crewman could be heard saying, "Something is happening. Can't you see it? The blackness is... moving."

Of course, neither Ian nor Jessica could see what the man was seeing; they were only seeing the bridge. They heard Peter say, "Maybe..."

And then the crewman at the helm exclaimed, "It's no planetary fragment. This is a ship!"

Lucy put the tablet down. "Dad, Mom, I need to go.

I'll keep you updated, but probably through Uncle Chris." She started to stand, and leaned her face back into view of the camera's lens. "I love you both."

She left the room without severing the communication. Jessica and Ian stared at the place where she had been sitting. Neither spoke for a long moment.

"I was wrong," Ian said with a smile. "I dismissed what it was out of hand, from day one."

"You were also pretty right," Jessica replied, before cutting off the call and giving her husband a reassuring kiss on the forehead. "The void was there. It was something."

CHAPTER 22

Missions Control, Station, HEO

"So I'm not the only one who felt their stomach drop?" Lucy asked Yua Saito and Chris Stoddard when she left the small communications room where she had been talking to her parents.

"All of us, here and on the ship, are still in shock," said Yua. "Let me update you on what we have."

The latest calculations from the *Shackleton*'s crew and the missions control team set the object as roughly cylindrical, with what they were calling the "top" more narrow than the rest. It appeared to be a kilometer long, roughly 450 wide in diameter, and 500 meters deep. All approximations.

"Station is the size of the Pentagon, plus another twenty-five percent, in terms of square footage," Chris Stoddard was saying. "The biggest thing ever put in space, we thought, until... Well, it appears, this thing."

Lucy wasn't sure where to begin her questions. "Is the dust what was keeping us from seeing it?"

"Possibly," Yua Saito responded. "Everyone on the *Shackleton* is jumping in to see what's what. They just began moving closer to the object. Probes two and three have landed on the surface, while one and four are starting to orbit around it. We'll hopefully have a better sense of what this thing is in an hour or two."

Lucy felt that was highly optimistic. "This thing has been sitting there unnoticed for at least a half-century while the human race has been pulsating every kind of electromagnetic wave we can in every direction, and measuring every beam of light and radio wave coming in. And no one saw it. We're going to need to help."

Chris put his arm on Lucy's shoulder.

"I urge we take a moment," he said. "The revelation that this thing is sitting on the edge of solar system is going to be profoundly disruptive. Let's be careful here."

Lucy wanted to push his hand from her shoulder and shout, "You have known this secret for years, said nothing, and would now lecture me!" That would be unproductive.

And he was right. Nothing would be harmed by gathering more data before they unlocked the doors and started letting information out.

Paul Brightmer, who oversaw the external sensor technology feeds, waved over Flight Director Saito.

"What do you have, Paul?"

"Getting a feed from Probe Four," he said. "Probe One was put in an east-west orbit, while Four was set on a north-south orbit. Both of them are definitely registering the gravimetric waves. If the math is right, we found this only because we were literally aiming for the bottom quarter on that first drive initialization. We'd have probably never seen it otherwise. That is crazy lucky."

Lucy and Chris shared a quick glance.

Brightmer went on. "The surface is unnaturally smooth. The crewman who called it a ship may have been premature in his pronouncement, but it doesn't look like he was wrong, either. But this is the most interesting thing so far." He pointed to a computer model being created in real time from the probes' LIDAR and other sensors. He twisted his fingers in the air to move the model for them, pinching and squeezing at invisible lines.

They all immediately saw what he meant.

The bottom – if it was the bottom – was a mess. The smooth surfaces looked like wreckage, perhaps the result of a collision or explosion.

"Some portion of the object is missing. I don't know if it

was bashed, or exploded, or some combination of the two. But this thing is a floating accident site."

"So you're saying this thing is dead in space?"

"I don't know if I'd use 'dead,' or not. It is definitely still producing artificial gravity, which means something is still working internally. As long as this thing makes artificial gravity the way we do, something is powering it." He took a deep breath. "A couple of my team members have been analyzing the data coming off the probes as it relates to the dust. It's a pretty crazy mixture of the gunk we usually see out there, as well as something which looks like, well, fuel propellent mixed with other materials. All that combined out there to create a coating that accomplished what the military's stealth tech does, but only a whole lot better."

Lucy nodded. "So, you are saying this thing being invisible was a product of dust collecting on it, not an intentional act of camouflage?"

"I'm not going to necessarily assert *that* with just an hour with the data, but it's looking that way. I mean, this dust is very, very, very fine. Almost like talcum powder. The gravity being generated by the object wouldn't be noticeable to any of us if we were floating beside it, but it grabs that powder and pulls it in." He pointed to a section of the model.

"This is where our first probe disturbed the dust," he said. "And already we're seeing tiny flecks being pulled back down."

Chris Stoddard tapped at the screen with one finger and smiled. "Paul, do you mind figuring out a way to see how fast the dust accumulates?"

The technician nodded in understanding. "I see what you're thinking. That is a really good idea."

CHAPTER 23

The Shackleton, *Kuiper Belt*

"They're measuring what?" Peter asked Linda, not certain he heard her right. She had just informed him that they would need to angle the Shackleton's approach so as to not disturb the site where Probe Two set down.

"The dust," she said.

"We are staring at a massive alien spaceship, and missions control is worried about measuring dust?"

"They want to get an idea of how long this thing has been out here."

"Fine." He stared at his tablet. "I'm supposed to be on a call with Mrs. Hyde in 10 minutes." He called his sister that when he felt put upon, which he did – most unreasonably – at this minute. Her message said to allow an hour. It had better be good. "If little green men start popping out of the hatches, let me know."

"I'm not sure this thing has any hatches," Linda replied.

He scowled as he walked to his cramped office for the call.

Linda turned to Fritz Stuenkel. "So where are you taking us?"

"I'm heading to southern portion. According to the scans being created, that's where the explosion or collision occurred. Either way, it should give us something to look at, and keeps us away from Probe Two."

The *Shackleton* – and her sister explorer-class ships – were the largest spacefaring vessels created by humanity, not counting Station which generally did not count since it just sat in orbit. The explorer-class ships each measured 225 meters from bow to stern, 70 meters tall and 75 meters wide. If the ship were able to enter the atmosphere of a planet, and if they landed it stern-side down, it would look for all the world like strange office building.

Compared to this object, the *Shackleton* was puny. A couple hundred copies of their ship could fit inside, Linda realized. Maybe they should be watching for hatches and little green men.

"Have we seen anything that looks like hatches, doors, or windows?" she found herself asking out loud.

"Not yet," came a quick reply from Jennifer Stokes. "I've been looking, but there is still too much dust. But now that we know what the dust is made of, I'm thinking we can see through it if we re-calibrate the external sensors."

Linda Bletchley examined the woman. "Not bad for a life-support tech?"

Stokes glanced at her boss' boss, and took a deep breath. "We still have breathable air and gravity, so I figured I'd help out."

"Keep that up and you'll find yourself promoted." A pause. "How long would the calibration take?"

"Ideally we'd have a physical sample in our lab to look over, rather than taking the probe's analysis. The probes are good, but the lab is better."

"Please don't tell me you are asking for a space walk."

"Me? No way. Thank you, though. No, I'd rather someone else did a space walk and bagged some of this stuff."

Linda tapped a note on her tablet. "I bet we can find someone willing to go out there."

"Me!" said an overly eager Andrew Todd, the lead communications specialist. "I'll go." He truly loved his EVA excursions at Station, was one of the first people in QA's space division certified in extravehicular rescue, and one of the few on the *Shackleton* with a masters-walker designation on his file. And, besides, he really wanted to impress Jennifer Stokes.

"Hold up, cowboy. Don't go putting on your fancy clothes just yet. The captain will need to decide on this one, but you'll be at the top of the volunteer list."

Stuenkel, who got queasy at the thought of a spacewalk, muttered, "It'll be a short list."

+++

"Dad knew all along?" Peter was incredulous. "He planned the entire beacon navigation system from these particular coordinates? He knew this was here?" He shook his head. "So, even with the whole 'I'm-super-arrogent-and-won't-tell-you-anything-so-you-validate-my-hobby' deal, why not start here instead of making us hopscotch around the solar system for all this time?"

Lucy was letting her brother vent. She paused to be sure this wasn't a rhetorical question before he started up again. He just stared at her.

"Because the beacon system is a legitimate mission, and because if you and Charlie both came home right now, the beacons already established would be sufficient. Not complete, but sufficient, for the need, for now."

"So just how manipulative has this been? Is this why I captained the *Shackleton*?"

Lucy had expected this. "No. Absolutely not. The mission routes were handed out randomly; I know, because I am the one who set it up. There was an equal chance of either *Henson* or *Shackleton* getting the assignment. And every single person on Station and both ships know you and Charlotte were the two best candidates for leading these missions. And if you will recall, you almost lost out on captaining one of these when you were flirting with sticking with the Mars run so you could have more time with the third-gen engine team. And that decision was all on you."

Peter let out a long sigh; she knew he was winding down. "I mean, it was cute when he kept stowing away on test flights. But, wow, this is beyond... And mom and Chris, keeping it to themselves? I just... Fine." He stared hard at her through the computer screen, then blinked twice and refocused his attention.

"You keeping communications shut down?"

There it was, Lucy saw. Dad was right. Venting complete, now Peter was working the problem. Peter didn't wait for answer.

"That can't last, or families will get worried. You get some time because the *Henson* is due to approach Voyager any minute now. That'll draw attention to the other side of the solar system from us, but eventually parents, spouses, and kids will wonder why they haven't heard from us." He paused. "For now, I'll have everyone send messages saying our quantum communications systems are having glitches. Might be a little bad P.R. for the Quantum Advantage, but I figure your guys can come up with some decent excuses?"

Lucy smiled. "I don't think you've ever used the company's full name before... but I am sure they can."

He stole a glance at his tablet's message queue. "I'm going to let my guys do an EVA. There is some idea about getting more dust samples so we can re-calibrate our equipment and get a better look at this thing."

Before she could respond, Peter asked, "Any other surprises out here Dad didn't mention?"

"Not that he mentioned." They both smiled. "But, remember, for the record, he was sure that it wasn't a ship."

"That's something, I guess. Chat soon."

When he left his office, Peter MacGregor addressed Bletchley, Scott and Todd before anyone could speak. "The EVA is approved. Mr. Todd, get two others. I want you all three tethered to the *Shackleton* at all times. Ms. Scott, you are off the life-support team and are officially in charge of figuring out how to see through this dust. And, my dear Linda, I want to you to figure out how we can get a look inside this thing."

CHAPTER 24

Between the Shackleton *and the Object, Kuiper Belt*

Andrew Todd had been terrified of heights. As a child, he refused to play in the tree house with his siblings. His parents had to medicate him on flights. Even the thought of being more than few feet off the ground made him queasy well into his teens.

"I am now 25 meters from the airlock," he said. "Carlson, you're next."

"Stepping out now," came the reply.

His visor display, showing the view behind, confirmed Carlson was snapped onto the tether and stepping out. Andrew tapped lightly on the thrust and his suit moved ahead.

His fear of heights changed, ironically, watching a school news video about the early work constructing Station. One of the construction crew members described seeing the entire world in a single glance. "I want to do that," he whispered to his twin brother, Alec.

"Dude, you couldn't handle it," his brother said. "Trust me."

The next day, at 16, Andrew climbed into the old treehouse for the first time. The next day, he pulled the ladder from their shed, and forced himself up on the roof of the house. From there it was a short trip to the U.S. Military Academy at West Point, followed by four years of active duty as an Airborne Ranger where he had fallen in love with communications technologies. But those images of the Station being constructed never left his imagination.

"Hernandez, you ready?" he called out.

"I'm locked on to your tether," she replied. "And my secondary safety is clipped to the side of the airlock."

Andrew nodded, then remembered he need to speak. "Great. We're ready to engage the programmed flight. Just relax and enjoy the ride."

With that, all three of the walkers ordered their suits to follow the program Sophia Scott designed. The primary and secondary tethers were almost a kilometer long, more than they needed. They would all three touch down on the object about 75 meter apart from each other, with *Shackleton* 250 meters back.

Andrew Todd's fingers were the first to touch the object. "Definitely metallic. Even through my EVA suit, I can tell the dust is very fine."

Jack Carlson and Felicia Hernandez let Andrew Todd do the talking as they, also touched the ship. Carlson executed a 90 degree turn and engaged the boots' magnets. "Magnets work." He closed his eyes and forced his brain to accept a new paradigm. No longer was he face to face to the thing, now he was walking on it. His training kicked in. "Walking 5 meters."

Hernandez had already bagged two samples of the dust. "I agree with you, Andrew. The dust is going to make quite a mess in the airlock." She removed a small chipping tool and hammer. She lightly tapped the dull silver hull, and could see minute shavings on the chip. After bagging it, she removed a small round puck. With a tap, it glowed green and she attached it to the hull. They would now be able to measure any vibrations inside.

Andrew set a similar device in place. With the two sensors attached to the hull, the science labs on the *Shackleton* and Station would be able to start figuring out what was inside.

"Alright, team. Everyone ready to head back in?"

"Hold," came Carlson.

"Is there a problem, Jack?"

"One second." A slight grunt. "As I was walking, my boots

kicked up some dust. I think I just found an airlock."

+++

In all, the EVA took 15 minutes longer than planned, but that was due to Carlson's discovery of what everyone on *Shackleton* immediately began calling an airlock.

Andrew and Felicia had made their way over and helped Jack clear the pervasive dust. Whether or not it was an airlock, it was definitely a hatch. It measured roughly 2 meters tall, and a meter wide. Essentially, the size of a door. A surprisingly simple mechanism was set next to the door frame, less than halfway from the "bottom" of the object. One needed only to pull the ring up, and twist.

"No," the captain had said. "Not yet. Get back over here with the samples. We'll discuss what to do with the airlock when you arrive." Felicia pulled an emergency magnetic tethering point from her gear pouch, secured it to the side of the door and strung her tether cable through it.

As predicted, the dust made a mess of the *Shackleton* airlock. The filtration system easily handled it, but the smell was... smokey.

The three walkers, along with Peter and Linda, were sitting in the galley watching video recorded from the ship's cameras. This would pass as their after-action review.

"You three did an amazing job. Right by the book. Felicia, tell me why you took a temporary tether."

"When I was putting my gear together I remembered one of the training simulations for doing repairs on Station. The idea was to have a temporary hook so if your main tether line somehow snapped, you could re-tether your team to your workspace. Not my idea, but it beats flying off. So I shoved it in my bag. I assumed we'd want easy access to that airlock, so I attached the tether point to make a future EVA over there a little easier."

Peter nodded. "That's great thinking. Linda, make sure

Hernandez gets a special commendation in her file for that."

The young woman beamed. "Thanks, Peter."

"In fact, all three of you are now in the history book. First people to touch an alien object. Congratulations. Now, let's figure out what to do next."

That involved yet another meeting with the flight director back on Station. At this particular moment, Peter started thinking that maybe an intermittent disruption in their communications wouldn't be such a bad idea.

CHAPTER 25

The Henson, *beyond the Heliosphere*

For as old as Voyager I was, and as far as it had traveled, the craft was in remarkable shape. There was some scoring along one side, no doubt a brush with a micrometer. Everything that had been white when it launched was now a dingy gray, covered in the soot of space.

Around the world, people were glued to coverage of the *Henson* – the idea that humans had now left the solar system had somehow connected in ways no one imagined.

It turned out actually getting to Voyager was harder than Charlotte Smith-Davies and her crew let on. After the *Henson* made its final gravity-stream jump to Voyager's proximity, it still took several days of careful maneuvering to get in position for the viewing. All without disturbing the Voyager itself.

Over those days, Charlotte's husband, Thomas Newcome, and several crew members gave dozens of interviews to the global media about the trip. No one even brought up the *Shackleton*'s communications problems. The most common question was whether the galaxy looked different from outside the solar system.

Charlotte giggled to herself on more than one occasion as Thomas tried to answer without being condescending. The struggle was real, because "condescending" was an innate attitude British academicians exuded without thought, something she knew all too well from within her own family.

For three painstaking hours, the *Henson*'s lead navigator tapped carefully at the controls of the probe they had launched to observe Voyager. At no time did it get closer than 75 meters, but the high resolution cameras made up for it. The markings of the craft, the proud American flag, the golden record of the sounds of Earth – all visible.

Thomas narrated the entire thing, giving the international audience a sense of the Voyager Interstellar Mission's importance while describing the lengths the *Henson* crew was going to examine the probe without disturbing it.

"As it turns out, these so-called space scientists, who are in fact the cowboys of the galaxy, would make the most stodgy archeologist proud," he had said – a quote that became an international meme within minutes.

The broadcast finally ended as the *Henson* let itself drift further away from Voyager.

"Truly remarkable," Thomas Newcome said to his wife. "Thank you."

Catching up to Voyager had been difficult on the crew, but as they slid away everyone onboard knew it had been a successful side-trip for themselves, the company, and the history books. But, now, it was time to say goodbye. There was still work to be done back in the solar system.

"Captain," junior comms tech Jeff Prasadh said, "there's an incoming call for you from Station. It's marked confidential." No one said it, but there had been an awful lot of confidential traffic coming from Station. No one could remember a single one, until a week ago. Now, they were regular occurrences.

Jeff couldn't help but wonder if it concerned the intermittent communications problems their sister ship was having.

In her office, Charlotte Smith-Davies opened the link. Yau Saito's face filled the screen.

"Good afternoon," she began. "Everyone here is incredibly proud of how you, your crew, and your husband especially, represented the mission and this trip to Voyager."

"Thank you for that."

"So, I'm sorry to have to do this, but Lucy wanted you updated on the *Shackleton*."

"Thank you. What's happening now?"

The sensors set on the object after that space first space walk revealed the hum of electrical activity inside, as well as the sounds of a rushing liquid, and the circulation of gases. In other words, it was active.

But the next discovery made the first all the more surprising. Monitoring the dust accumulation on the object, and even on the *Shackleton*, a preliminary estimate was made of how long it had been there. Accounting for a variety of factors, the time was set at ten millennia.

"We think it is probably closer to thirteen-thousand years," Saito said casually. While this was new and shocking information for Charlotte, the flight director herself had accepted the dating and moved on. She now considered it surprising only in that it meant the internal power source was incredibly efficient and long-lasting. "The company's R&D guys will want to get their hands on it as quickly as possible."

"So what makes you think the object hasn't been, um, replenished in the intervening years? Couldn't it be an observational post? Why assume an efficient power source lasting ten-thousand or more years?"

"It's a good point. Mainly, it is because of that dust. The only places it has been disturbed is where we have been." Yua Saito explained. "Nothing has gotten into or out of this object basically since it arrived in the Kuiper Belt."

"Arrived from... where?"

"On that, there is no idea until we get inside. Metallurgical analysis on the *Shackleton* shows the object's skin was basically a martensitic form of stainless steel. Nothing exotic or special."

"Did you just say, 'get inside'?"

"That's why we're talking. In just over an hour, a team is going in. By which I mean, Peter is leading a team in."

Charlotte considered that for a moment. "I understand

that." She saw the quizzical look in Saito's eyes. "Seriously. I never believed it before, but there is something to being the 'captain' of a ship. I never got it until we pulled the *Henson* out of Station and started our mission. I'd like to think that if something ever happened to us on the *Henson* that the first person to come on board would be the captain of another ship – someone who would be respectful of this place, of this property, of this home, of the work done here."

Her voice trailed off. "Sorry, but I'd never put those thoughts into words, but I mean them. So I support Peter in that."

Yua smiled, and said, "None of us will argue the point of how you guys feel – though as you can imagine, Lucy did try." Both women laughed and Yua glanced down, probably at her tablet's to-do list. She explained that the *Shackleton*'s captain and crew would not be entering through the hatch they found. Instead, the engineering team had printed small drones that were released into the damaged area at the "bottom" of the object. They discovered what appeared to be the exposed bottom of an elevator-style shaft, providing the safest entry.

"Going through the open backdoor rather than risk a boobytrapped front door?" Charlotte asked, rhetorically.

"Probably a good way to look at it," Yua said. "A couple other things you need to know, since your crew might see this in news feeds, emails from friends, and the like. If it hasn't yet gone out, it will shortly, that the *Shackleton*'s communications interruptions have been caused by the discovery of a small dusty object – yes, that's what we're having someone in the P.R. office call it on purpose – that they are exploring. It seems the substances play havoc with our various equipment. The release is going to note that, like so much of what we're finding in the Kuiper Belt, we're excited to see what it holds."

"So you're hoping people assume you mean 'giant rock'?"

"Yes, that would be correct. And, still be true, since the substances did prevent us from seeing it. Obviously, the higher ups think that releasing this on the heels of the big Voyager coverage means it will go mostly unnoticed. They just gave four days of coverage plus three straight hours of *Henson* being the first out of the solar system, so this will seem like trivium."

"I guess you want my people to play it up?"

"On the contrary, we're hoping you're people will say, 'We knew nothing about that, but then we've been very focused on being the first people to leave the solar system and visit the Voyager. We haven't had time to learn much about rocks in the Kuiper Belt.'"

Charlotte smiled. "Easy enough. Anything else?"

"No. When do you plan to start back into the solar system?"

"It'll be a day. We need to put more room between us and Voyager before we activate the drive. And then it'll be a couple of days until we're back on task."

"Very good. Again, please express the thanks of everyone here for the crew's – and especially Thomas' – outstanding work."

The call switched off, and Charlotte composed herself. Peter was walking into an alien object. Unbelievable. Given the way the assignments were handed out, there had been a fifty percent chance she would be the one whose mission-set included those coordinates. All things considered, she was pretty glad to be where she was and not where he was.

Charlotte Smith-Davies left her office, surprised to see Thomas still on the bridge. She went to her chair, grabbed the microphone, and thumbed it to address the crew.

"Everyone, a couple things. The company is beyond pleased with how our little trip out here went. Everyone on Earth loved it, and they expect it to be major headlines for days to come. So, congratulations." She paused for dramatic effect. "I was briefed on something you'll be hearing about pretty quickly, perhaps. While we have been making history leaving the solar system and all these, uh, cowboy activities –" she smiled at Thomas "– our colleagues on the *Shackleton* have found some interesting rocks and dust that've messed up some of their instruments. Carry on."

She could literally hear laughter and groans echo around the ship. Job done.

CHAPTER 26

The Shackleton, *Kuiper Belt*

Peter MacGregor groaned when he realized he had not correctly secured the backpack to his EVA suit. He could have asked for help, but he chose not to; he'd have to do it again.

"Are you sure I can't help you?" asked an overly earnest Andrew Todd.

"I screwed up, so I need to fix it," Peter replied.

Jack Carlson and Felicia Hernandez would be rounding out the away team. While this would be Peter's first time to the object, the three others had been on two more trips since their first excursion, and three other crew members had made one trip each.

No one had yet complained about the communications gag order. Yet. Peter hoped the amount of work being dumped on everyone would keep that at bay a while longer.

Sending the drones had been Carlson's idea. The probes originally used to explore the outside of the object were too big to approach the wreckage area. That's when Carlson thought of the toy quadcopter drones he had played with as a boy. It didn't take long for Chief Engineer Benny Hathaway and his team to 3D print space-borne versions that could fit in spaces as small as air-conditioning ducts.

A swarm of the drones had gone over the wrecked area, and deeply enough into the ship, to realize human exploration was viable... and probably safe.

Once Peter's backpack was secured, the foursome made their way to the airlock where Linda Bletchley was waiting. "The drones' radios faded off the deeper they went in. Your gear is better, but not much. So you four need to promise that as soon as the communications start to get sketchy, you come back."

All four nodded. "I need a verbal agreement from you, MacGregor."

"Aye, aye, captain!" he said, earning an eye roll from his subordinate. "We will be back before you've had time to move everything out of my office."

"Get into the airlock," she said.

Leaving the ship's gravity sent Peter back to his childhood, when he and his sisters would get to make clandestine trips to their dad's facility so they could play in the artificial weightlessness. The trip from the *Shackleton*'s airlock would only take a few minutes, thanks to the cable and harness system the engineering team had devised.

Despite the time they had now spent in proximity to the object, this was the first time Peter had seen it with his own eyes and not through a camera. The sheer size took his breath away.

As they approached the mangled wreckage, he found himself wondering if it had been caused by a small impact, an internal malfunction... sabotage? And, he wondered, who had brought this here, anyway? Had they come to observe the earthlings, or were they just passing through?

"Alright, Captain, this is the elevator shaft we identified," said Andrew Todd, who had the lead on this walk. "Once again, we're going up in single-file with me in the lead. We'll be tethered to each other, but not to the cable. I'll be controlling our ascent to where the drones saw the first set of doors. We'll try to enter there. Good?"

All concurred, again, with the plan they had discussed a dozen times.

Within moments, they were slowly moving "up" through the elevator shaft. Peter marveled that, yes, it really was an elevator shaft. The rails on the walls, the mechanisms on the door they approached, all of it was exactly how an elevator shaft would appear.

"Observation note," he began, using the phrase that would trigger a recording for later review, rather than the idle conversation. The comms system automatically lowered the volume of his voice for the other walkers, though they could hear him. "This shaft is not analogous to an elevator shaft, it is one. This shaft looks like the elevator shafts in buildings around the world, and even in the *Shackleton*."

"The doors are opening easily enough," Andrew Todd said. He wasn't using any tools, just pushing the double doors apart with his gloved hands.

"Remember," said Peter, "we are here to look and not touch."

Each of them stepped into... a very plain hallway. Their headlamps illuminated the pitch black corridor. But it was a corridor. As their lights played down the hallway, it curved following roughly the lines of the object. And, it would appear, the "up" and "down" designations given to the object were accurate. Where they stood had a pleasant pattern, like tile, while the walls and ceiling were painted an institutional white. At regular increments along the ceiling were recessed light fixtures.

"Away team to *Shackleton*," said Carlson, who was the last into the hallway. "We have entered the object proper and are moving down a corridor. How do we copy."

They were moving, but not walking. Whatever artificial gravity the ship had, it did not extend to this hallway. And since the floor was not magnetic, they pushed themselves gently along.

"Away team, this is *Shackleton*. Good copy. We read you five-by-five."

"Observation note," Peter said. "We need to improve the drones' range, and send them up the elevator shaft to see how high it goes, and how many levels it opens on to."

Andrew Todd was already moving down the hallway, playing his helmet and wrist-mount lights along the walls.

"There's none of the dust in here," he observed. Ahead, as the corridor jagged further into the ship, creating an alcove where his lights did not quite reach.

Peter looked back on where they had come, motioning to Felicia Hernandez. "You agree that those are lights," he pointed up, then motioning down, "and this is the floor?"

"Yes, sir. Frankly this looks like the tile in my bath–"

She was cut off by a loud scream filling their headphones. It was Andrew.

The two swung around in time to see the spacewalk enthusiast swing at a figure wearing a bulky suit – Andrew's action in the weightless environment spinning him in circle as the – thing? person? – enveloped him.

Peter and Felicia pushed bounded across the way to help him, followed by Jack Carlson.

"Away team, *Shackleton* – what is your status?" They had heard the scream over the open microphone.

MacGregor leapt at the bulky figure attacking Andrew. He and the object exploded past, colliding into the wall. It was then Andrew realized it was an empty... pressure suit?

"Away team, *Shackleton* – respond. What is your status?"

"*Shackleton*, this is MacGregor," he replied, panting heavily. "We're fine. Repeat, we're fine. But we just had a scare. Give us a minute."

Peter turned toward Andrew Todd, who was floating in the middle of an alcove – even through the visor the younger man still looked terrified. Peter killed the broadcast, so only his away team members could hear him. "Andrew, you alright?"

"I will be. That thing..."

"We're literally on an alien ghost ship, so there is nothing for you to have to explain." He clicked the radio. "MacGregor to *Shackleton*, we came across what appears to be a discarded pressure suit. It scared the tar out of us."

Hernandez and Carlson moved closer to it. To their eyes, it passingly resembled the old U.S. and Russian spacesuits of the 1950s and 1960s. It wasn't that, but similar. There were no patches or insignia of any kind – but it was clearly some sort of protective gear.

Felicia was the first to speak. "Observation note: the item appears to be designed for a mid-sized adult, no more than than 5-foot-8, or 1.75 meters," she forced herself to sound far more clinical than she felt. "It has an attached hood and face mask." She pushed at the garb so it rotated. "It appears one steps into the suit from the rear and it is sealed by a..." her lights reflected off it, "by a hook-and-loop system. I'm not sure this would be airtight, but it could also be some sort of fire suppression gear."

Carlson had moved from the garment with Hernandez, giving space to Todd and MacGregor. He began playing his light around the alcove, and was immediately blinded by a reflection. It should have been the outer wall of the object.

"Observation note," he began, knowing the system would be able to simultaneously record all four of them making notes should the need arise. "The question of windows has been answered. I have found one here, though it is clearly covered by dust on the outside. Turning right, there is another wall of what appears to be glass." He toggled off his wrist light, and adjusted the angle of his suit to cut down the reflection. "This appears to look into a... maybe a bay of some sort."

Peter and Andrew joined him at the window. It was set a little lower than they would have considered normal – but perhaps just right if 1.75 meters was at the tall end of a population. They could tell the corridor in which they stood was at the "ground" level of the bay on the other side of the window.

Carlson continued: "The corridor appears to dead-end just past this point. There might be a door there."

Andrew Todd played his light through the window and into the larger room what Carlson had called a bay. It was perhaps 10 meters across, and at least 10 meters high.

"What was that?" Peter asked Andrew. "Swing your light back to the left a little."

CHAPTER 27

The Shackelton, Kuiper Belt

"Tell me again what you see there?" Yau Saito asked from the Space Operations Center. Lucy Hyde among twenty others thinking the same question as they tried to make out the fuzzy photos taken at the edge of the solar system onboard an alien object.

Standing back at the command desk on the *Shackleton*, Peter MacGregor would have laughed except he had the exact same reaction – and he had been the one standing there and saw it.

"That is a giant wrench, and what appears to be rope playing up the far wall, along the ceiling, and then connecting to the outer hull. In the photo you have in front of you right now, you can see a handle for the gear." He used a stylus to circle it. "There." He then highlighted the rope. "See?" He advanced to the next series of photos, demonstrating what they saw through the corridor window.

"That is most definitely the outer hull. You can see there a seam running lengthwise from the ceiling to the floor. We sent a probe out, dusted that area off, and we found the seem there. It is a door."

"And what about the outward facing glass from that alcove?"

"We had a probe clear the dust away while we were in there." Peter paused, and sent a photo taken by the probe, showing Peter, Andrew, Felicia, and Jack looking out the window.

"Nice group photo," said Hyde. "Let's go back to the door.

What does that mean?"

"I have no idea," Peter said. "Except that perhaps this was like an emergency door? We have numerous systems on the *Shackleton* for which far more advanced versions exist at home, like the air conditioning, but we use the simplest version. The design-thinking has been that in case it breaks we can fix it easily. Our main-use airlocks are state of the art, but our emergency escape airlocks are basically the same kind of hatch you'd find on an old submarine. Tried and true."

Chris Stoddard stepped into the video. "Captain, not to be the stodgy old man, but we should also be careful about assuming things about what we're seeing. I remember years and years ago, this is like when I was in high school, people were passing around a clip from a century-old early silent movie that showed what appeared to be a woman on a cellphone walk through the background, long before cellphones or even mobile radios existed. Well, it was actually a tube device people with hearing problems carried to help hear conversations. But in the early 21st century, we saw something from the late 19th century, and applied what we knew to what we saw. So, yes, maybe this is a gear and pulley system to open and close a bay door. Or maybe it just looks that way. In either case, I think you and your people need to get a better look at it."

Peter smiled. "I like the way you think, stodgy old man."

"Alright, alright," said Lucy. "First, how soon can you guys get back over there. And, second, what's the status of improving the range of your drones?"

"Engineer Hathaway is testing a new version now. He thinks he can have a dozen printed up by the time my next away party goes across. Which, to answer your question, would be as soon as I get off the call."

"Then get to it, mister."

+++

The away team grew from four to a dozen, which was

almost everyone on ship rated for extravehicular activity.

Peter looked at the massive sets of boxes they would be towing across the chasm. "What's all this?"

"The red box is your drones," began Hathaway. "I included charging bases. Basically, these can sense how far they are from their base, fly back, recharge, and then take the most expedient route back to their last position, without doing any data recording, or the like. You'll get two hours of use per charge, and base stations offer about 10 charges per bird before you need to get them refilled. The case also has a massive radio signal repeater that can run for a couple weeks. Obviously we cannot guarantee it will reach around the monster, but it will make sure you, the team, and the drones can talk to each other and the ship."

"Great work, man!"

"Thanks, boss. The second box is medical supplies, extra EVA gear, patches, and the like. You guys poking around that wreckage made me nervous the whole time. Instead of that empty suit floating around, it could have been jagged glass that ripped into your suits and caused an air leak."

"Again, great thinking."

"And the third and fourth boxes are some basic all-around tools – handsaws, wrenches, pliers, and some more exotic stuff like laser cutters, and, last but not least, I put a repair shed in there with a couple extra air systems."

That last item was a unique touch. The repair shed was designed to create a temporary bubble on the hull of a ship. It was primarily used for work that was too detailed to be done wearing the EVA suits' gloves. The shed was set up like an oversized backpacking tent, the crewman would enter, activate the atmosphere, and be able to work comfortably in shirtsleeves.

That is, if one could ever be said to be comfortable in a situation where a thin layer of plastic, some heavy magnets and adhesive, were all that separated you from the instant death of space. Peter had spent exactly 20 minutes in one, four years earlier, in order to get fully EVA rated. It was an experience he hoped not to repeat.

With all the suits sealed up, the airlock cycled and the away team was taken across the void to the object.

Four of the engineers were assigned to begin exploring the area of wreckage. They would map what they found and see if they could understand what had been down there.

The remaining eight entered the elevator shaft and rose quickly to the corridor where they had started their exploration. Two of the engineers stayed in the shaft, and went up to explore what appeared to be an elevator car.

Uncle Chris had been right, Peter thought. They needed to be careful about assuming that what they saw was, indeed, what they were seeing. As he helped position the last of the carts in place with the crewmen in his detail, Peter wished they had had an archeologist or two onboard.

Not that anyone up until this moment thought they would be exploring ancient ruins on this trip... "Even Dad had rejected that," Peter muttered to himself.

The alcove was established as their base of operation. Half the drones were released, to be controlled by the engineering and communications teams back on the *Shackleton*.

"MacGregor to *Shackleton*, we have established Alpha Base."

"*Shackleton* to Alpha Base Actual, we copy."

And, with that, Peter MacGregor and his team went to work getting into the object's bay.

CHAPTER 28

Alpha Base, Object, Kuiper Belt

That was easier than they had thought, Peter realized with satisfaction.

Andrew Todd and one of the engineers in their group walked up to the door at the end of the corridor, which presumably led to the bay... and turned a door knob.

"See, you guys didn't need us," said Engineer Second-Class Paul Bratton.

The entered the space. What they had failed to notice originally were the markings on the floor. These seemed to each of them like highway painting stripes, creating lanes for traffic. Each lane had a complex series of designs, which repeated up the lane, from the outer hull leading straight to the opposing wall.

In this room, their magnetized boots worked – unlike in the hallways. That made movement a little more natural.

It was Paul Bratton who noticed that the "wall" was actually another massive door. Whatever mechanisms operated that door were most definitely not in this chamber. Each of them played their lights around the room, when Peter MacGregor noticed, 20 meter up, a window like the one they had peered through on this level.

"Maybe the operations happen from up there?"

"One way to find out," said Bratton. He and his colleague, Tim Nelson, turned off their boot magnets and pushed up in the weightlessness towards the window.

Back on the ground level, Peter had already headed to the gear and pulley system. He looked it over, and gave the wheel a tug to the left. Nothing. He pulled to the right... and felt a slight give. Increasing the hold of his boots' magnets, he leveraged himself, and pushed again. The wheel moved more easily. As he turned it, a vibration filled the room.

"Boss," began Andrew Todd, "uh, the big door into outer space is opening."

Peter stopped and looked. Sure enough, a crack almost two feet appeared.

"Observation note. Tell Uncle Chris that sometimes, things are what they appear. But his wise words are still true." He paused for the system to register he was done, and then called the ship.

"Linda, I got the exterior door working. I'm thinking we may eventually want to move the ship so that we enter and exit over here rather than through the wreckage."

She responded, "Great idea. We'll plot that out and make the arrangements for the next round."

"Captain, you need to come up here," called Tim Nelson over the microphone and from 20 meters overhead.

"Be right there." He looked at Andrew Todd. "You mind closing the door for me? Don't want to let the air conditioning out."

"Will do," he said. "I got pictures of all these floor markings."

"Thanks," Peter said as he pushed up to the observation window.

Joining Nelson and Bratton, he asked, "What have you got?"

The man pointed through the glass. "That, sir."

Inside the window was a workstation, a desk with papers stacked neatly in organizing boxes. But it was the chair that Peter noticed. It was... a chair. Just, a chair. It was like the pressure suit when they entered the object; two arms, two legs. And that was a chair, four legs and two armrests – clearly designed for bipedal beings to take a load off and relax while doing paperwork. The desk, the chair, the papers, were all angled in a way that sitting at the desk, one would be looking down into the bay. That indicated gravity plating, or its analogue here, to Peter MacGregor. The construction bays at Station back in Earth orbit had very similar set ups, positioned with gravity plating to allow an observer to look "out" while also looking "down."

As it turned out, however, none of that is what Nelson and Bratton had intended for Peter MacGregor to see.

"Any idea what that could be," Nelson asked, unaware of what was drawing his captain's attention. "I mean, I swear that's a glass of water sitting in that box."

Now Peter saw it. It was a glass of water. It was in a box. The box emitted a faint blue glow that did not, for some reason, seem to extend beyond the confines of that box. That water was in a glass meant the gravity plating was, indeed working in there.

That water – *if it was water* – was in a glass, and not vaporized away, meant there was atmosphere in that room. Or, at least, in that box. And, to all of them, it looked like the glass of water was... sweating... like it had been sitting there for just a couple minutes.

The clock was formally ticking on this walk, and Peter MacGregor wanted to get in that room.

"Mr. Bratton, Mr. Nelson... you guys know how to set up the repair shed?"

CHAPTER 29

Dayton, Ohio, U.S.A

Max Prasadh knew he wasn't going to run out of storage space, but every time he froze the image and made a screen capture, he expected to get a warning message. He never dreamt his son would be at the center of a defining moment in human history. Or that he would be able to watch it.

Jeff's interview with India's largest news network was now its most watched story – ever. Max felt like sending a big "I told you so" message to his son about forcing the boy to learn Hindi those many years ago, and then keeping it up.

"But, daaaaaad," he could still hear his son saying all those years ago, "I'll never, ever need it."

"I know, but you have family there, it is half of your heritage, and India is a massive trading partner with the United States," Max had said more times than he could count. He was relatively certain, though, he had never said, "And one day when you are the first Indian-American to leave the solar system, you'll be able to give an interview that nearly two billion people – half of whom are women – will watch."

Since the interview had aired, distant relatives had come out of the woodwork claiming they had the perfect Indian or Indian-American girl for Jeff. Would Max kindly provide the appropriate contact information?

Instead, Max had merely sent his son well wishes and hearty congratulations. He may have mentioned the courting and marriage offers, a couple of times.

Right now he was capturing images from the replay of the *Henson*'s approach to Voyager. He knew, from his son's occasional messages, that the communications crew adhered to a very strict shift schedule – no matter what else was going on. They were responsible not only for live, recorded, and text messages between "ship and shore," but also the intricate data relays within the ship, and the navigation beacons being established around the solar system.

This particular image had captured Jeff perfectly. Frozen at the bottom of the screen grab was the annoying crawl text, this one noting that the sister ship to the *Henson* had found an intriguing asteroid to climb on. A part of Max felt sorry for that crew and their families. He cropped out the news crawl, and sent the photo to a couple family members and friends.

He keyed the video screen to the message he had received from Jeff a day before the big newscast.

"Hey, pop – sorry I missed you!" The message had been received during Max's lone lecture of the day. Despite the miracle of quantum communications, the ship's bandwidth was limited. Every member of the crew, Max knew, from the captain on down, had the same "ration" of live messages in a particular week. "I'll send a note later but wanted to let you know my Hindi is going to come in handy. I'm doing a live one-on-one with India TV. I can't remember the guy and gal doing the interview, or the name of the network, but I'll send those details so you can tell –" he did an inappropriately exaggerated impersonation of his Indian grandfather "– the extended family on the subcontinent when I can be seen." The young man resumed his normal accent, a mixture of Louisiana drawl, Texas twang, and hopeless midwestern. "I'm doing great out here. Hope you're being nice to the students. And, really, you need to take that English professor on a second date. Love you, dad!"

Max Prasadh was now a tenured professor of medicine at the Boonshoft School of Medicine, a part of Wright State University. He had left research behind a number of years before, moving into a teaching position focused on aerospace medicine. Now, he used his seniority in the department to grab undergraduate courses for pre-med students. Needless to say, he didn't have to grab that hard.

Boonshoft had recruited him heavily, and were glad to have him on staff. The dean had, only once, inquired about his teaching load.

"These kids want to help people," Max had answered. "It's invigorating. They haven't yet learned about overbearing hospital administrators, insurance bill schemes, narcotic-seeking patients, or the need to publish regularly, spring after academic fashions, or answer silly questions from their deans. They just want to save lives."

Tenure, after being heavily recruited, had allowed Max Prasadh to find his voice.

The "second date" jab was his son's reminder that he knew his dad wasn't dating, and had not been, for some time. Max had accidentally let it slip he and the assistant dean of the Department of English had shared lunch together. They ended up spending three hours discussing Shakespeare. It was perfectly innocent; it was not a date. But the more he denied it, the more his son acted like... well, like Max had acted when Jeff was in high school. The child becomes the parent, and the parent becomes the child.

"I love you, son," he said to the frozen video message on the wall display screen. He waited a moment and then clicked over to the live news.

He felt a wave of nausea rip over him.

CHAPTER 30

Dayton, Ohio, U.S.A

"Details are just now coming in, but QA sources at Station tell us the *Henson* has suffered a catastrophic malfunction in its gravity-stream drive," reported Angela Crompton of the World News Network.

Max could not believe he was watching. This could not be real. The incoming message indicator showed 30 new messages and more were coming in. If any had been from Jeff, or from the QA family notification center, his system would have overridden the newscast.

The news anchor continued. "It's unclear right now if there are casualties, or if there are indeed any survivors. I am joined right now by physicist Carlo Gianotto of the Massachusetts Institution of Technology. Dr. Gianotto, you're one of the leading experts on gravity-drives who is not, though, affiliated with QA. In your estimation, what could have happened?"

Max screamed at the display, "Why are you asking him? He doesn't know!" He could not believe a professor of anything would even agree to be interviewed when there were definitionally no facts.

"Well, Angela, it depends on when the malfunction occurred," Gianotto began. "If it occurred before the ship entered the so-called gravity stream, then there were likely few if any casualties. On the other hand, if it occurred after–"

"I'm sorry, Dr. Gianotto, we will come back to you but right now we have World News Network's Jim Summerland, who broke this story about 25 minutes ago, back at our bureau on Station, with a QA Space Operations briefing about to begin. Jim, has anyone responded to your inquiries?"

The scene switched to a podium in front of a blue curtain. Jim Summerland wasn't on screen, but could be heard saying, "No, they instead stonewalled and have asked the media to stand down on what we first reported from a source inside Space Operations. We just got word that Yau Saito will make a statement any moment. She is the director of flight operations for QA's Space Operations Center, which is often referred to on Station as 'Missions Control.' Yau came to QA from JAXA, the Japanese Aerospace Exploration Agency and is most known for her... Oh, she's walking to the podium now."

Saito appeared on screen. Max Prasadh remembered meeting her, briefly, at the launch ceremony when the *Henson* began its current mission.

"Inappropriate rumor mongering by the media has caused a great many families a great deal of anguish in the last half-hour," she began. "Rather than allow us to get facts about the situation on the *Henson*, some irresponsible media agencies began reporting rumors and innuendo. So I am, unfortunately, here with fewer facts than I would like to have had when addressing this situation for the first time. Because of the recklessness of the news organizations in this room, this will be the last *media* briefing on the subject. The rest of the communications about this issue will be made directly to the public. We will not answer any questions from the media organizations in this room until they prove themselves better than gossip tabloids." Indignant mutterings sounded, but Yua Saito wasn't slowing down.

"First, no crew member on the *Henson* is now, or ever was, in any danger. Second, before attempting the third in a long series of jumps back into the Kuiper Belt to resume their planned mission, the gravity-drive suffered an overload. Third, every system worked as it should, with drive control systems flashing a series of warnings on the ship and at the Space Operations Center, indicating there had been an overload and a burn out.

"Fourth, a now-former low-level employee saw the words 'overload' and 'burn out' and ignorantly decided that meant every one was dead. Fifth, that employee called Jim Summerland of the World News Network and repeated that misinformation. Rather than allow us the opportunity to explain what happened first, Summerland and his reckless network created a false story and let others offer their own breathless misreporting."

Saito took a deep breath, then continued. "Families were placed in anguish by this recklessness. Therefore, going forward, any media entity that employs Jim Summerland will lose all access to all of the Quantum Advantage products and services. Any entity that advertises on a news site, network, or station that employs Jim Summerland will be barred from all QA services and products. Summerland and all the employees of the World News Network now on Station have exactly five minutes to catch the next earthbound shuttle. After that time, they will be treated as criminal trespassers. No one gets to terrify the families of QA's brave space explorers with lies and innuendo."

Saito turned from podium and was out the door before stunned reporters could shout any questions.

With only the podium and blue curtain now on screen, a confused Angela Crompton back on Earth began asking for Jim Summerland to offer any comments... but none were forthcoming.

It would later be reported that Summerland, his producer, cameraman, sound engineer, and make-up artist were last seen rushing through Station to make the shuttle departure.

But at the moment, Max Prasadh was taking deep breaths of relief and weeping tears of joy.

+++

A short while later a message from Yau Saito arrived in Max Prasadh's queue. It was substantively similar to what he had seen on the newscast, but included additional information.

The *Henson* was by no means dead-in-space. It had traditional propulsion, which it was already using to keep the vessel headed into the solar system proper. Such a trip would not take as long as Voyager, but would be many years. The *Henson* did have enough provisions and emergency rations to last almost that many years. They would not be needed; QA was already preparing emergency operations to get the crew back to Station. And, lastly, crew members would be sending text-based messages to all families and friends within the hour.

In just under that time, Jeff's message home appeared. It began, "Exciting day for us, but I hear more so for y'all at home. Sorry about that, sounds like Saito kicked butt as usual. Hey, what ever happened to that second date?"

Max Prasadh had never been so happy to be harassed by his son.

CHAPTER 31

Alpha Base, the Object, Kuiper Belt

"Mr. Bratton, Mr. Nelson... you guys know how to set up the repair shed?"

"I can do it in my sleep," said Bratton as he and Nelson pushed off to grab the utility box. "I know exactly what you're thinking."

"Forgive me, but... um, is that a good idea?" asked Andrew Todd, who was still down on the bay deck. "I mean, it's one thing to walk through exposed shafts and unlocked doors, but going into a room with atmosphere? No telling what the air would be like, contaminants, or any of that."

"Good point, Mr. Todd," seeing the two engineers re-entering the bay. "But the suit protects anything in there from me, and vice versa."

Within minutes, the airlock was established over an area larger than the window itself. MacGregor and Bratton remained inside as the tent expanded with air pressurizing it. "We're staying in our suits."

"Understood," the engineer said as he began working on cutting the glass. Again, it did not take long. It was definitely pressure-treated, but it wasn't anything exotic. Even through their suits, they could feel air from the room enter the portable airlock tent; the air pressure in the room was slightly higher than in the tent.

"Can the airlock withstand this?"

"Absolutely, we didn't fully pressurize it in the first place since we were staying suited up." Bratton checked his equipment. "Appears we've already hit   equalization and holding steady. We're at one atmosphere. Basically, the pressure in there is what you'd get at sea level back home."

With the glass out of the way, Peter took a small screw driver from his utility belt. He pushed it towards the window frame. It floated in the weightlessness to the window sill. Just over... and then the handle dove for the table, striking it with an audible bang. Gravity.

"Alpha Base Actual to *Shackleton*, I am going into the bay observation room."

"What did you just say you're doing?" replied Linda Bletchley, notably not following protocol.

"Mr. Bratton will fill you in. Will report back shortly."

And, with that, Peter MacGregor found himself entering the small room like a clumsy cat burglar. The gravity pulled him to the floor.

Suddenly, Peter was looking down at a sharp angle into the bay, even though his senses told him he was upright. He closed his eyes and took a deep breathe to reorient himself with the sudden pull of gravity. Meanwhile, Bratton efficiently described the operation. Bletchley had recomposed herself and seemed far from pleased.

"Observation note. The gravity in this room feels, for all the world, like... normal. I have a whole series of questions arising for some exobiologists back on Earth. I thought aliens were human-sized and bipedal only in science fiction. Cannot wait for these explanations."

He walked across the room. The glass of water, sitting in the device emitting the blue glow, looked like it had just been poured. There was condensation on the side. He stiffened. What if the calculations about the dust were wrong? What if this place was occupied? What if...

No, there would have been a response. The water in the glass... Something wasn't right about that.

He took in the room, turning in a full circle where he stood. The papers were filled with incomprehensible squiggles and other markings. He looked, but did not touch. As he looked at the small office, he had the impression that whoever had last been in here had, actually, completed their work and left the room – the job done. The water in glass was... something else. He walked to the windowless door. It was on the wall leading deeper into the ship. This would be in line with the inner doors of the bay.

On the door itself, and on the wall next to it, was a symbol, like a circle whose top quarter cut away, with the two pieces set back together but slightly off.

"I'm going a little further in." Like the door in the corridor leading into the bay, this door's knob was a little lower than he would have expected. Just enough to be noticeable.

Before he took a step, his head spun with the new angles his eyes registered. A staircase led down, sort of, away from the room he was in, to a floor that would have been even with the bay floor. He closed his eyes, took a breath... and stepped onto the staircase. Gravity grabbed him and everything was correctly situated.

Peter's lights barely pierced the darkness. He was looking into what he could only describe as a massive warehouse. He was closer to the ceiling than the floor, and could make out the basic contours of the airlock doors on this side of the bay. They were, indeed, more complicated... he assumed. At least, he did not see any more pulleys, ropes, or gears.

What struck him were the rows and rows of cabinets all emitting a soft blue glow.

"Alpha Base Actual to *Shackleton*. I want to de-prioritize exploration of the wreckage. I want all EVA qualified personnel to join me." He flipped on the video feed, so that Linda had a sense of what he was seeing. "I need you to move the ship closer to the bay, and send someone with life sciences over here with some of their toys. If they aren't EVA qualified, get them trained up fast."

CHAPTER 32

Space Operations Center, Station, HEO

Lucy Hyde was dealing with her own set of disorientations. The *Henson*'s grav-drive was dead, leaving the ship to push along on propellent fuel at the edge of interstellar space, while the *Shackleton* was parked alongside an ancient alien object whose first floor looked for all the world like a third-world shipping warehouse.

Meanwhile, Quantum Advantage was preparing to launch its newest line of handsets despite the software still being buggy. One of the Martian colonies was exploring independence from the Martian Atmospheric Trade Union, which was their right, but she wished not right now.

It was a lot to handle.

Fortunately, the *Shackleton* was silo'd. Anyone who might have been asking questions about what it was doing, was not – for now. All eyes in Missions Control, and on Earth, were focused on the *Henson*.

Meanwhile, her brother had become a space-faring Indiana Jones.

"Honestly, I cannot believe I am about to say this, Yua, but I think Peter and his crew have things under control there. Give them orders to *only* explore this first level. We need to expand the bubble on that. We need an archeologist advising here. We may need to get some out there."

"Forgive me, but I cannot even begin to imagine what kind of pathogens and disease they could be exposed to," Yua Saito said, before realizing she was talking about her boss' brother. "Though, in reality, I think..."

"No, you're right. But I think for now we have to roll with where they are and deal with that later. But, to your point, let's find someone who is an expert in, I don't now, space alien diseases? They are about as quarantined as is possible, without being on the *Henson*."

Yua nodded to her assistant, who understood precisely what the nod meant: *Find real archeologist, hire expert on pathogens, find theorist on alien diseases.*

"So, speaking of the *Henson*," Yau said, "we're almost complete with the re-tasking of the *Powell*, *Byrd*, and *Freuchen*. The *Powell* and the *Byrd* had been configured for equipment runs, but fortunately the *Freuchen* had just set in dock for a passenger configuration. It will be ready in a week, and the other two will be about three weeks – but only after they drop their cargos at Mars and return. Unloading there will be done later this week."

"So, what's our timing?"

"It will take a week of fairly hard jumping to get to them, so the *Freuchen* can be there in two weeks. The other two will be a month out. We need to talk some numbers here," Yua's assistant handed her a piece of paper. "The *Henson* has 123 souls on board. The *Freuchen* can be there the fastest - delivering fresh supplies and returning 27, leaving 96 on board. The *Powell* and *Byrd* would get there a couple weeks later. The maximum they will be able to carry is 42 each. That will leave 12 individuals left on the *Henson*."

"At some point," Lucy said, "people might ask about the *Shackleton*."

"Yes, but here is the easy answer. The *Shackleton* is currently further away than these three boats, and has nearly a full complement on its own. Yes, they could pick up those dozen remaining folks without any strain on the ship resources. However the *Shackleton* would still arrive after the *Powell* and the *Byrd*, but not much sooner than a return trip from the *Freuchen*. The *Shackleton* and her crew are eager to help with the retrieval of their colleagues, but right now their assistance isn't needed."

Lucy took a deep breath and looked around the room. That made sense, both in terms of reality and in terms of what could be said publicly. Everyone else was nodding. She looked specifically at QA's lawyer, Hanson O'Donnell, and Peter Torres, the Vice President for Media and Communications. They were nodding in agreement.

The circle of trust regarding the *Shackleton*'s discovery had expanded. And yet, in accordance with his wishes, the fact her father had discovered this anomaly and plotted the course of his entire company around uncovering it was not known to any of the people in this room.

CHAPTER 33

The Shackleton, *Kuiper Belt*

Chief Engineer Benny Hathaway was pleased with his crew. In a matter of days they had constructed with the onboard 3D printers a sturdy umbilical between the Shackleton's primary airlock and the Object's bay. Inside the bay, the tent-like airlock engulfing the observation office window had been itself engulfed by a far more sturdy structure.

By using surplus gravity plates, one could walk from Shackleton, into the Object bay, up some stairs and into the small room. There were still the vertigo-inspiring gravity shifts, but it wasn't too bad.

A series of ultraviolet decontamination and sterilization stations were established in the bay itself, on the staircase, and inside the airlock tent. For now, the ship's doctor was not letting anyone leave the *Shackleton* without a full EVA suit.

An infectious diseases expert and an exobiologist back on Earth were working up protocols for detecting viruses and other pathogens. The problem, of course, is that it is hard to look for what one doesn't know exists.

While the *Shackleton*'s medical officer would not admit it, she was enjoying the change from minor bumps and bruises and space sickness. With a crew of 135, everyone knew each other – but with all the new things needed for this operation, Dr. Dana Regan and Engineer Hathaway were spending more time together than ever. Both were pleasantly surprised to find their respective disciplines were more similar than not.

With each new set of ideas and recommendations from

Earth, Regan needed Hathaway to adjust settings, change out equipment, or build tools never before contemplated.

"Rob was asking about a triage bed, but wasn't sure which configuration you wanted," Hathaway said to Regan, referring to her nurse Rob Beckett. In what had become a routine, they were sitting in the galley just after breakfast service had concluded.

"It'll be the same as we have in the main medical bay. This isn't meant for surgical use, though, just basic examinations. We're going to set it up in that alcove that was originally 'Alpha Base' when your team has it sealed up."

"Then we'll get working," he replied. "The alcove is now connected in with our hamster tubes in the bay."

"Excellent, thanks."

"You going over there today?"

"Only if Rob needs help, otherwise I'm supposed to be on a conference call with the disease squad," she explained, using her personal designation for the infectious diseases expert, exobiologist, and flight doctor from Station. "I think today I'm going to be told to make sure everyone is washing their hands before eating."

Both laughed. They were the second furthest set of humans away from Earth, light took six hours to get here from the Sun... but the power of a committee to create busy work could not be stopped.

"Well, if either of you need help, let me know and my guys can jump on it."

They looked over their respective to-do lists, and were satisfied they had covered what needed to be done.

"See you around, Benny." Dana gathered her papers, coffee mug, and headed for the medical ward.

Hathaway was staying put. His next coffee meeting was with the life support team.

+++

"We have what we hope is a good solution, with supporting rationale, for your crew," Yua Saito was saying during the call of the disease squad. Dana Regan had been surprised by her presence on the Station side of the video feed. Usually it was just Senior Flight Doctor Antonio Perez with the two experts. Today's expanded attendance list was either actually good news, or bad news being dressed up.

Saito nodded to Perez who picked up his tablet. Dana Regan liked Perez, he tended to summarize and assume his staff – which included her – were smart enough to read the documentation for details. The meeting would go faster. It was already a good meeting.

"We've reached the conclusion that wearing EVA suits into the Object itself isn't necessary for anyone but you and Nurse Beckett. In fact, we'd rather the two of you avoid entry into the Object as much as possible excepting what you call the Alpha Base and the emergency medical station you are establishing. The bottomline is that it is highly unlikely diseases that evolved on other worlds will have much effect on human physiology. Just like we probably won't be tasty to their versions of lions and tigers, so would their viruses not be that interested in us. But while their lions and tigers might attack out of preservation, they wouldn't be able to stomach us. More so for viruses and bacteria. The pathogenesis just doesn't work out."

Dana Regan nodded along. Ironically, this is what she and Captain MacGregor had been discussing over dinner the night before.

Perez was continuing, "There are millions of strains of bacteria on Earth, but the number that are actual pathogens runs just a few hundred, and just a tiny number infect healthy humans. And we have all grown up together, so to speak. The chances of any alien diseases infecting a human approaches zero."

The exobiologist interjected himself. "On the other

hand, you are on a space ship. There is the possibility this object visited Earth before being stranded. The occupants could have wandered around, collected samples, and shoved things in that warehouse you found. My only concern is that maybe there are Earth pathogens lurking around there."

"To that end," Perez continued, "You are already tracking who goes on and off the object, how long they are there, etc. Add in a weekly blood draw, a temperature check for everyone. Also, we want detectors set up around entry way – the observation office, whatever you call it – and around the *Shackleton* looking for the tale-tell signs of various viruses and bacterium."

He looked at the infectious diseases expert, a woman from Canada, who nodded and added, "We'll be sending the base markers to check for small pox, polio, mumps, the various coronaviruses. We have a pretty good idea of what existed on Earth 13,000 years ago and in what forms."

Dr. Regan agreed with the assessments. Her tablet had begun chirping, letting her know the sensor schematics and other information were loading in. She would need Hathaway to print some new tools tonight, which would make the engineering crew grumble.

But, finally being able to ditch the suits... The crew would be happy about that.

CHAPTER 34

The Shackleton, *Kuiper Belt*

Peter MacGregor was not happy about this. Charlotte Smith-Davies and nearly a dozen members of her crew were going to be waiting more than a month sitting, almost literally, in the middle of nowhere for the final retrieval.

They were both sitting in their respective captain's offices. Identical rooms, on identical ships. The only discernible difference was that she had a small painting of her family hanging on the wall behind her, with personal items visible on the desk. He, on the other hand, had brought several family photos that were, these months later, still in boxes in the corner.

"We've profiled out carefully who is staying. And everyone will be sliding into their own rooms. It won't be that bad," she tried to reassure him. "Everyone will have something like unlimited ship-to-shore transmissions, so it will be in many ways more enjoyable."

"So is it true Thomas is staying on board?"

"He is, the dear. Our son's semester doesn't end for two more months and then he is going straight off to a backpacking adventure with my oldest brother and his sons in Australia. So if Thomas went home, he'd have less human interaction than he would here." She smiled. "The Royal Society even gave his office to a visiting fellow for the time he was to be away. He's able to do some very intense work out here cataloging and observing stars from this slightly different angle. He's convinced he'll get a couple decades worth of publishable papers out of this."

"That's great news. So it will be the dozen of you after the final forty-two get picked up. And that happens... next week?"

"Just under, but ours won't be too far behind." She raised both hands into the field of the camera's view, showing her cross fingers. "So, if you need to lose a round or two of chess, my schedule is very open for a fortnight."

They both laughed, as Peter said, "I'll call regularly, but I've got a ship full of people who enjoy besting their captain at chess. It turns out my childhood *au pair* wasn't particularly interested in teaching me how to play chess to win."

"Yeah, your parents really should have deported that one," the former *au pair* to the MacGregors said haughtily. "Sorry to jump off, but my communications chief and ship doctor are buzzing in to see me."

CHAPTER 35

The Henson, *interstellar space*

Captain Charlotte Smith-Davies gave her counterpart on the *Shackleton* a smile as she terminated the connection.

She stood up and unlocked the door to her small office. It was unusual to ever receive a visitor in here, let alone two at a time. And it was the first time Dr. Enzokuhle Nkosi, the ship's physician, had ever stopped in.

"What can I do for you?" she ushered them in and pointed to the two guest chairs.

"We need to put Jane on this next departure group," Dr. Nkosi began, his eyes imploring the captain not to ask too many questions.

Unfortunately, she had questions. "I don't understand, why?"

Jane Leach was the head of communications, and as such would be required to stay with the ship – like the chief engineer, like the captain, like the doctor – until the final retrieval.

"I can't do it," the woman began to sob. "I'd hoped no one would need to find out, but my husband has..."

The doctor put his hand on her shoulder. "She came to me a few weeks ago. Her husband was in an accident, and he's taken a turn for the worse. Because of his position in Canada's government, this has been kept quiet. I've spoken with his doctors and..." His voice trailed off.

"I'm very sorry this is happening for you and your family," Charlotte looked at the doctor. "I should have been notified. Immediately."

"I made the decision as the ship's doctor. At no time did I feel her performance would be impacted, and it hasn't been." Nkosi looked at Leach, who was struggling to regain control of herself.

Charlotte Smith-Davies was sympathetic, but was aware of the new set of headaches this would be causing. After a moment she nodded and paged her first officer, Adriana O'Neil. Adriana, Comms Chief Jane Leach is to be considered relieved of her duties. We need to get her things packed so she can be on the next transport home."

O'Neil acknowledged the change, and Charlotte looked at the doctor. "And you and I will chat later." Her face softened as she looked at Jane. "Again, I hope you get home soon enough." Leach and Nkosi knew they were being dismissed.

When the door closed behind them, she called O'Neil again. "Now, I have to break it to her remaining staff that one of them will have to fill in."

A small department anyway, Smith-Davies knew only two comms technicians were left on board: Aaron Hill and Jeff Prasadh. "Can you ask them both in here, when their schedules align?"

A couple hours later, Charlotte delicately explained the situation to the two men. Before Hill could say anything, Prasadh spoke.

"Ma'am, if it is all the same, I'd like to stay. Aaron here has a wife and a kid, while all I have waiting for me is an empty refrigerator and a father trying to marry me off. So, basically, hanging around out here is a lot more appealing than you might think."

Hill began to protest, but Smith-Davies cut him off. "Jeff has made a persuasive case. This will go down in my logs as a random draw and that Prasadh lost. Now, Aaron, you have work to do. Jeff, stick around for a moment."

When Hill had left, Charlotte gave Prasadh a small smile. "Thanks for doing that. When they leave in four days, you'll be promoted to chief, with a few extra bucks waiting for you to fill that empty fridge."

"Thank you, I appreciate that," he paused. "As I think about it, I might have a bag of popcorn and a half-bottle of wine still in my apartment."

"You know, Jeff, that somehow sounds even more pathetic."

CHAPTER 36

The Shackleton, *Kuiper Belt*

Peter's to-do list had grown to the extent that in the last two weeks he had not had a chance to play chess with Charlie. Though, despite the burdens, he wouldn't trade places with her; at least he was busy.

Setting up the new medical scanners had taken longer than anticipated, but Peter knew it was worth it both in terms of peace of mind and productivity. In EVA suits, certified crew members had been slowing walking through whatever it was they called the warehouse. They had not yet covered everything. Once they could walk through in their regular clothes, it would be easier.

As he had seen from that first view, the warehouse was full of small cubes, with one side open and emitting that blue glow. They were stacked three or four high, in tight rows. They thought of them as lockers. Each held what appeared to be closed sacks or covered clay pots. The contents remained a mystery, because no one was allowed to reach into the boxes. Every attempt to place a handheld thermometer or other probe into the boxes met with the equipment shorting out in a fiery display of sparks as it made contact with the blue light.

A wooden spoon was secured from *Shackleton*'s galley, to chef's extreme annoyance, and used to probe into the first of the boxes they had come across – the one found in the observation office holding what appeared to be a fresh glass of water. The spoon actually entered the open space, but then froze in place. It could not be moved. Eventually, the handle broke cleanly at the invisible line marking the edge of the box.

Dr. Regan was certain she knew what it was. "It's a stasis field. Whatever is placed in there becomes essentially frozen in place. Not frozen, but frozen." She had looked around the faces of the senior officers when she made the suggestion. "Seriously, none of you people watched science fiction as kids? I'm on a ship full of nerds, and yet I'm the only one who watched any science fiction?"

Finally, all begrudgingly admitted that they had. The meeting briefly devolved into a debate over the merits of various entries in the genre, until Peter MacGregor brought them back to focus. "So, the lockers, the stasis boxes...?" he said, "How do they keep things so perfectly preserved?"

"How do they even work?" asked Benny Hathaway, the engineer, looking at the Dana.

"I'm a doctor, not an engineer," she replied with a smirk, earning a roomful of laughs. "You and your team need to figure it out."

But Peter MacGregor wasn't laughing now, in part because the chef was really mad that his wooden spoon had been sacrificed to the experiment and refused to use anything in his kitchen that had been "built" by the 3D printers. The man could act like haggis was a treat, but he wouldn't stir pasta sauce with a printed spoon.

It all gave Peter a headache.

+ + +

Peter was pulling on his EVA suit when his comms device went off. It was resting on the cabinet shelf in the airlock where his suit was stored. He tapped to answer as he kept pulling the suit over his clothes.

"Sir, it's Rob Beckett and Paul Bratton from the Object. You available to chat with them? They said it is urgent."

"Patch them through," he told Susanne Billings, one of comms junior techs manning the desk. A moment later, Bratton's voice filled the room.

"Sir, you are going to want to see what we've found."

"I'm almost suited up. What do you have?"

"Well, we found one of those boxes but the blue light was out. You said to call if anyone came across a dark box. We did. We haven't reached in, of course, but it is one of those with a bag in it. Well, the bag is slumped over and it opened up, and the contents spilled out a little."

"And..."

"Well, sir, it looks like it was corn."

CHAPTER 37

Docking Bay 2, Station, HEO

Christopher Hecht paced around the bridge of the *Freuchen*. It was a nervous habit he had had since entering the United States Navy's submarine service nearly 30 years ago. The anticipation of the departure. The moment the sub was free, his nerves became as still as the pond in his granddaddy's backyard. He thought that would have changed when he was recruited into QA's fleet.

As it turned out, the attitude and mindset for being a submariner paired nicely with being a captain of a spaceship. While he still struggled with "captain of a spaceship" as an actual job, the similarities to his previous career underwater were strong. Both operated in an environmentally sealed bubble, kept alive by barely believable technology, knowing that at any moment the hostile environment around you could terminate your life. Just as the submarine fleet was composed of those who wanted to be there, the QA's ships were staffed with the absolute best and brightest.

Yet, there were differences that forced him to learn new ways to manage a crew. Despite his title, QA's "fleet" was anything but martial. They weren't trying to make the spacefaring vessels into a private military; no one saluted anyone, there were no real uniforms. He had a certain amount of power, of control, as the captain, but it wasn't the same as he'd had in the Navy. In fact, he had initially been apprehensive about working in such an unforgiving environment without the safety of discipline and a firm chain of command. Yet it all worked for the simple fact no one on board wanted to be doing anything else; to a man and women, they were consummate professionals.

Hecht toggled the secondary display view. The nearby *Powell* was already being re-fitted back to a cargo configuration after returning its share of the *Henson*'s personnel. And he knew everything was set for the incoming *Byrd* to do likewise. The fledgeling colony on Mars was getting desperate for both of the ships to be back in service. Not life or death, yet – but, desperate nonetheless.

The *Freuchen* was preparing its second run out of the solar system. On their first trip they had collected 27 of the *Henson* crew, the most they could carry with so little preparation. The *Powell* and *Byrd* made the trek out getting 42 each. And so now, he was returning for the remaining dozen individuals.

Hecht and his crew should have left four days ago on this little trip, but a redundant sensor on the backup to the secondary system air-scrubbers kept tripping a life sciences alarm. Station personnel had worked double-shifts to find the problem and get the *Freuchen* up to standards. The maintenance chief described the source of the delay as a "47-cent piece of rubber."

But, finally, now they were leaving.

If the shipyard scuttlebutt was to be believed, he would in a couple months be making a third trip out of the solar system. For that voyage, the *Freuchen* would be in a cargo configuration and carrying a repair team. The hope was to fix the *Henson*'s problematic gravity drive and bring it home. Hecht hadn't been told this officially, but it seemed likely. The *Freuchen* had been scheduled for a re-fit to start carrying visitors between Station and Mars, but that service would not be starting for more than a year. There was plenty of time to do both.

"Station to *Freuchen*. You are cleared to cast off moorings on your mission to retrieve the captain and crew of the *Henson*. Godspeed."

"Copy, Station. *Freuchen* out," replied Hecht's communications chief.

"Well, people, you know the drill. Let's go bring those people home," he moved to the command desk. "Clear moorings."

"Moorings clear, captain."

"Ahead, quarter speed."

A moment later came confirmation of the order. The ship was moving outside the interaction area of Station's artificial gravity. It would be approximately 18 minutes. Hecht could feel his nerves calming.

"All hands," he called on the ship-wide. "In about 15 minutes, you might want to check the forward starboard video. Just before we jump out, we should get a show of the *Byrd* making her return."

Due to the nature of the gravity drive systems, someone onboard never got the sense – even when watching a video monitor – of the beginning or ending of the jump. There was, internally, nothing special to see or feel. It just happened. But if you were in the right position to observe an incoming ship, the view was something else altogether.

As the clock ticked by, Hecht's first officer – also a former Navy submariner named Brown – said it was four minutes until their own drive initialization.

"Thanks, put the starboard video feed up," he said.

They were about 50 kilometers from where the *Byrd* would arrive. From this distance the ship would not be visible, of course, but it really wasn't the ship everyone would see.

A small burst of blue light begin to shine from nowhere. It grew, shifting to a pure white, and became brighter than any source in the sky except the sun. The white light intensified and then began pulsing. Without warning, that small section of sky exploded with the colors of the rainbow. And then, if one looked very carefully, the running lights of the *Byrd* would suddenly be visible.

"Captain, the *Byrd* has arrived and we're clear of their

gravity interaction area," reported Mr. Brown. "Engineering reports the gravity drive is ready for initialization."

Christopher Hecht thumbed the ship-wide. "All hands, prepare for drive initialization." Out the corner of his eye, he could see a series of yellow indicators flashing at the life sciences section. He started to tell the helmsman to "punch it" when he felt his whole body punched from something overhead.

His head was swimming as he felt himself being pushed down into his seat... and then nothing. All the lights flickered off as he felt himself go weightless. All the little noises one gets so quickly accustomed to hearing were gone. None of the clicks and beeps, not even the slight rustle of the air circulation system.

"Life support systems have crashed," he could hear someone yelling. The battery-powered emergency lights flickered on, washing the room in a dull, tepid red.

From behind him, Hecht could hear the communications chief calling out "Mayday, mayday, mayday, this is the *Freuchen* declaring an emergency. Mayday, mayday, mayday."

There was no way to know if the main radio was even working.

Hecht shook his head and leaned across his desk. The only other source of light in the room came a button, settled under a clear plastic housing. It was the emergency locator beacon which operated independently of the main communications system.

He became the first person in the brief history of QA's fleet to use it.

CHAPTER 38

The Object, Kuiper Belt

Despite having attended a university that was part of the 19th century federal land grant system for higher education, and had once had "agriculture" in its name, the most Peter MacGregor knew about corn was that he liked it popped with hot butter, or served as bread using his maternal grandmother's recipe at family meals. And that was about it.

As he stared at the bag sitting slumped in the box, the items that had slipped out did, indeed, look like corn.

"So while we were waiting for you, boss, I did a search on the history of corn," Paul Bratton began, as if this was something he did. "It wasn't believed to have been domesticated until maybe nine thousand years ago. So that creates a conflict if we think this ship has been here for almost thirteen thousand years."

Peter wasn't sure how he was supposed to respond, so he just decided he was supposed to offer his opinion on if this was, indeed, corn.

"No idea, Paul. Until we can test it, all we know for sure is that it looks like what corn should, maybe, look like." Bratton turned his tablet's display screen towards Peter. "Alright, so it looks a lot like what corn looks like. It could also be something completely different that to our eyes looks like corn." He flipped his eyes back and forth between the screen and the bag. "But it does look like corn."

Peter MacGregor looked around. "I don't guess you guys stole another spoon from chef?" Both gave him a "are you crazy" look that he obviously deserved.

Nurse Beckett pulled a telescoping rod from his medical kit. "Hathaway said this would probably have the same inert properties as the wooden spoon without the side effect of being murdered by the chef."

Peter took it from him, glad the man hadn't even attempted to do what he was about to do. Rank does have privileges. Or something.

Peter extended the rod to its full length, took a step back – and was amused to see the two men beside him both take two steps back. He gently extended it into the box, past the point where the wooden spoon had became stuck. He paused. Still no "grab" of the rod, so he knocked at the bag, disturbing its contents even more. More of the substance, the "corn" spilled out and several kernels trickled to the floor. He pushed the bag more upright and the trickle stopped.

Beckett already had a medical specimen kit out and was scoping the kernels into it. "I can get this into the lab at Alpha Base if you'd like."

"Get to it," MacGregor agreed, then recorded the event for the observation notes.

His comms device chirped. "*Shackleton* to MacGregor."

"Here, Linda. I think the boys may have found corn. Thinking about ordering up some butter and a movie."

"Peter, the *Freuchen* just declared an emergency. Their gravity and life support systems shut down just as they were about to initiate the gravity drive."

He stood straighter, the joviality gone from his voice. "Were they at the *Henson*?"

"No, they had been delayed and were just leaving Station."

What else could go wrong, Peter wondered. "What do we need to do?"

"Missions control wants us to go get the *Henson*. We're now the only the ship capable."

"Absolutely," he said. "Tell the crew to prepare to depart. How many do we have on the Object right now?"

She checked her logs. "We have twelve souls in the warehouse, and six on the outer skin. It's probably thirty minutes before the extravehicular teams can get onboard."

"Start recalling everyone. Acknowledge the request and prep for departure. I'm heading that way."

MacGregor clicked off communications and called out for Paul Bratton, "We need to get back to the ship."

"Yes sir," the man replied, from what sounded like the next row over. "But you should come see this first."

Peter knew he had time, so he rounded the corner and found Bratton and another crewman – Tina Olson – staring at a box whose mysterious glow was flashing between red and yellow. "What's that?" He asked.

Inside was what appeared to be a cactus. With each shift in the color, the plant seemed to... move?

"That is peculiar, but not critical," said MacGregor, explaining the situation with *Freuchen*. "Take some quick video and we have to leave."

Yet, the movement of the cactus was hypnotizing. Like it was shaking in a wind that did not exist. He leaned forward for a last look, when his foot slipped. He fell forward, reflexively shooting his arm forward – into the box – to steady himself. The glow settled on the familiar blue, and his arm was immobilized.

+++

Linda Bletchley reluctantly found herself agreeing with Engineer Hathaway and Dr. Regan. Peter's life was not in immediate danger, and his mental state was sound. And, so, she still had to follow his orders. She just really didn't like them

That meant not calling Yua Saito at Space Operations Control. It meant not notifying Charlotte Smith-Davies on the *Henson*. It meant leaving a handful of crew members on the Object while Bletchley and the *Shackleton* went to retrieve the crew of the *Henson*. They were to communicate the situation only after they completed their first step into the gravity stream. And they were to leave now.

Meanwhile, Hathaway and several of his best engineers would remain on the Object to try getting Peter MacGregor unstuck. Nurse Beckett would remain to monitor the captain's vitals. They had tried to make him comfortable, setting up a chair so he could sit – sort of. He was, after all, stuck in the position of falling forward and there was only so far he could twist his body without causing excruciating pain throughout his arm.

"Remember the wooden spoon, captain..." Paul Bratton had, unhelpfully, said several times.

The box was now glowing steadily blue. Everyone agreed it must have been malfunctioning and that his arm – perhaps by simply jostling the mechanism – somehow restored it to normal operation. The cactus was again as immobile as Peter.

Two weeks of supplies – including food, water, and a waste reclamation system – were quickly pushed from *Shackleton* to the Alpha Base. As the ship moved outside the gravitational interaction area of the Object, Bletchley made a last call to MacGregor.

"Your sister is going to be furious."

It was, Peter reflected, the first time he could remember Bletchley referring to the fact his younger sister was the head of QA. "Then it's a good thing her comms won't reach me in here, and you can take the verbal abuse."

"Thanks. We'll see you in two weeks. *Shackleton* out."

MacGregor and the team on the Object were effectively more alone than any human had ever been. While the *Henson* had maintained full quantum communications with Station, and therefore Earth, the system at Alpha Base had just a standard radio. They would know when the *Shackleton* returned only when the radio chatter started again.

In the meantime, Rob Beckett was examining the area around Peter MacGregor's arm.

"The good news is that nothing is looking necrotic. Everything seems perfectly healthy. However this thing works, it doesn't appear to be harming the tissue where it is touched by the... whatever it is."

CHAPTER 39

Space Operations Control conference room, Station, HEO

All things considered, Lucy MacGregor Hyde took the news in stride. She had wanted to demand why Bletchley obeyed Peter's order, but she knew it was useless. Bletchley followed the protocol by seeking the input of the doctor and other senior officers. Everyone agreed the order was reasonable.

That's because it was reasonable. Most of the crew on the *Shackleton* could do nothing to assist Peter's condition, so they might as well go help their colleagues on the *Henson*. It was reasonable.

Everyone who could help get Peter unstuck would be with him on the Object. Again, it was perfectly reasonable.

Of course, that it was her brother stuck inside an alien artifact on an ancient spaceship, on the other hand, was in her estimation the furthest possible point from "reasonable."

At the moment, Lucy was more concerned with the status of the *Freuchen*. It had been delayed due to what everyone agreed was a sensor error triggered by a faulty seal on a backup subsystem relay. Now, it appeared the problem had been more serious.

Except for some bumps and bruises, everyone on *Freuchen* was fine. It was easily hauled back to Station, to the chagrin of the ship's captain. She had never seen someone so thoroughly disgusted as he did when he disembarked. His problem, of course, was that he did not know who was at fault, if anyone. All he knew was that he and his ship were not able to complete their mission.

A full investigation was already underway, with Hecht on a review board along with the captains of the *Byrd* and the *Powell*, and several outside engineers. The problem would be uncovered. She just hoped it wasn't affecting the other ships.

For that matter, the failure of the gravity drive on the *Henson* was still unsolved. Until the system could be pulled apart, they would not know what had caused the overload.

Two ships with two very different problems; forty percent of her grav-drive fleet, incidentally.

Lucy used the conference room terminal to call Charlotte on the *Henson*. It would be up to the *Henson*'s captain to tell everyone still onboard that, (a) they were being picked up by the *Shackleton*, (b) they would not be coming straight home, and (c) no one had been told the complete story.

" know this will be hard, I need you to wait until you are onboard the *Shackleton* before you tell them about the Object, and the secrecy around it. I want everything for them to proceed as normally as possible right now. We're already notifying the families that the *Shackleton* is doing the pick-up and that they will be away a bit longer."

Smith-Davies agreed, reluctantly. Truth be told, she was as ready as everyone else for her camping adventure on the *Henson* to come to an end. If that meant a quick visit to an alien craft, so be it.

CHAPTER 40

The Object, Kuiper Belt

Hours had gone by, and the shock of his situation had been replaced by boredom. One of the crew who stayed behind, Felicia Hernandez, brought Peter a sandwich and water. Dr. Regan's last decision before the *Shackleton* departed, and consulting the baseline numbers, was to let the crew staying behind shed the EVA suits. Not that it did Peter any good. Though he was glad not to be wearing the helmet; he was hungry.

"Felicia, how did you get stuck at this little party?"

"I was walking the surface of the Object when everything went down. So I volunteered to stay."

"What did you find?"

"Well, what we knew. This thing is massive. You going to eat all your chips?" she asked as she picked one off his plate without waiting for a reply. "It's wider at the bottom than at the top. I think we've found three bay doors at this level."

She stood, stepped on a stool to get her bearings, and then pointed. "There, and there." As she stepped down, she added, "But those don't seem to have the observation rooms or offices or whatever they were. If we had gone in one of those, instead, you wouldn't have found the warehouse and be stuck here."

"I'm so glad you stuck around, Felicia. What else?"

"We found another set of three big bay doors just above these, but off-set. Also found a couple smaller hatches, a ways up, like the size of a double-entry door at a store, if you can picture what I mean. We also found a few nozzles further up that we think are probably for navigation, but won't know until we get a better look."

From across the bay, sound could be heard of someone coming down the staircase. It was the engineer.

Benny Hathaway and his team had begun dissecting the box which had brought Peter to the warehouse in the first place – the one that had stopped working. That was the one containing a sack of corn.

When staffing up the *Shackleton*, Peter tried to follow his father's own hiring philosophy. He hired the people he thought were the best to lead departments – not the people he necessarily liked – and then let them hire whoever they wanted to work underneath them. That's how Benny Hathaway became the *Shackleton*'s chief engineer. He had worked on the vessels since just after they came off the drawing boards. He could probably take one apart and put it back together by himself, in his sleep.

With that said, Peter didn't enjoy Benny's company, and he was fairly certain the engineer felt the same way.

And so, when Hathaway walked up with a scowl on his face it didn't seem that odd. It was usually the expression he had when approaching the captain about anything.

"How hard is it going to be to figure out the workings?" asked Peter.

"When you guys first came over, you found the rope and the pulley and the gear that opened the door. Remember that?"

"Hard to forget that, Benny."

"Well, how this stasis field thing works is beyond me. I'm sure some life sciences people could describe it, or someone smarter than me. But the wiring for it is, well, second-rate at best. It's old-fashioned. It's amazing more of these things haven't shorted out. It's like something out of an old 'how not to wire anything' book. Everything is connected to the power sources through poorly insulated copper wiring. It's cheap and poorly done. How you could have a vessel like this, yet this kind of basic sloppiness, is beyond me."

"I'm sorry the little green space aliens' electricians didn't meet your standards. How does that help us here?"

"Well, you said that when you stumbled here, you steadied yourself by throwing your arm into the box. I've been thinking a lot about that. And about the wiring."

Peter nodded. The whole thing was actually less intentional than Hathaway made it sound, but that wasn't really the man's point, Petter assumed.

"If you will trust me, Peter. I think we can get you out." He pulled a tape measure from his utility belt, finding a mark just over halfway along the top frame, and a few centimeters back. He placed a small piece of tape on the spot.

This is when Peter MacGregor expected the engineer's brilliance to shine through. In his mind's eye, Peter could see the engineer produce an intricate device that somehow reversed the effects of the field long enough for Peter to – just barely – extricate his arm from the grip of the field.

Instead, Hathaway wiggled his fingers and one of his assistants placed a hammer in it.

Peter became very worried. "Now, Benny, careful here."

"Get ready, boss." The engineer took careful aim and slammed the hammer on the mark. The blue light twinkled to yellow. Peter felt his arm start to slip out. The light shifted to red, and then blue. Stuck, again.

The engineer gave it an angry look, shifted his weight, and slammed the hammer into the box frame with enough force that sparks flew from the point at which the hammer connected with the surface. The blue glow, dazzled brightly, shifted to red and yellow, and then went out.

Peter quickly moved his arm out. "Not what I was expecting, but thank you, Benny!"

"As my mother said, sir, sometimes you just have to hit the damned thing." This might have been the first time Peter MacGregor had seen Benny Hathaway look totally, completely, and perhaps even a little childishly, pleased with himself.

CHAPTER 41

Alpha Base, The Object, Kuiper Belt

It had taken Engineer Hathaway and his crew just thirteen hours to determine that the best way to free their captain from the grip of ancient technology was to bash it with a hammer and break it.

On the one hand, Peter MacGregor mused, if he had not been so impatient (driven perhaps by a bit of embarrassment) to get the *Shackleton* on its way to retrieve the stranded *Henson* crew... Well, they would have only been thirteen hours behind.

On the other hand, this meant he and his dirty dozen volunteers – or volun-*tolds*, in the case of several of Hathaway's engineering team – could explore the warehouse, and perhaps upper levels, at their leisure and without the... helpful?... oversight they had been getting from Station.

As a man approaching 40, Peter MacGregor was at peace with his limitations and shortcomings. Serving as captain of the *Shackleton* was an honor bestowed on him for his critical work in flight testing... and because his father invented the whole blasted technology and owned the company which made it happen. Peter was also at peace with that.

He now had begun to suspect he was chosen as captain because his father wanted to make sure his son was the one who found out what the mysterious void was at the edge of the solar system. Peter was at peace with that, also.

He also understood that this career in the captaincy was not what he wanted to do with his life. He admired men like Christopher Hecht of the *Freuchen*. In some ways, he desperately wanted to be a man like that, a captain who wanted to be a captain. A devise-protocol and inspire-educate-cajole-train-men-to-follow-it kind of leader.

But it was a struggle. Yes, Peter was a fine engineer in his own right, but he was not an inventor or innovator like his dad. He did not possess the ability to coolly, calmly, and rationally prioritize thousands of small details like his younger sister. He did not have the determined self-control and passion for the civic good like his older sister. He actually thought he'd wanted the captaincy. Now, he wasn't so sure.

What he had, and had most definitely inherited from his father, was a highly refined sense of "what is that?" and "why has no one been there?" and "surely that's not the limit?" to everything he saw around him. He was not content being content. He was most content when he was doing something neither he nor anyone thought could be done. He was restless. He was a test pilot. He was an explorer.

Taking the captaincy for this mission had been just another challenge. The newness of it was wearing off. Too much of his time was spent watching and reporting on what other people were doing as they pushed boundaries and did new things.

Yet, here he was. He was told only to explore the warehouse. But... there was so much more to see. He was not going to miss the opportunity.

"We're not archeologists," Nelson Timms protested. "We need to be so very careful. If the back-of-the-envelope math is right, this thing is older than the Egyptian pyramids, older than basically any structure on Earth."

Peter called together his Object team, the Dirty Dozen, for a meeting on how to use these two weeks productively.

"I'm not opposed to exploring this place, but I just want us to be as careful as possible." Timms looked pointedly between Peter MacGregor and Paul Bratton.

"Point well taken, Mr. Timms," Peter said as everyone laughed, including Bratton.

Dion Coleman timidly raised her hand. She was

a payload specialist, who understood the workings and placements of the navigational beacons at the heart of their original mission, more than anyone else on the ship. She had also designed the probes used in the initial exploration of the Object's exterior.

"Ms. Coleman, you don't have to raise your hand," said Peter, "but I do appreciate the decorum. What do you have?"

"I, of course, agree with Nelson's point, but I didn't work two jobs going through undergrad and graduate school, to get a job with QA's space operations, to play it safe. I want to see more of what's on this ship." That earned her a round of here-here's.

"Where do we start?" This came from Hathaway, the chief engineer. "I can dissect anything and put it back together, but that requires a plan. And, as Timms pointed out, we're not archeologists."

A brief silence fell over the assembled group, which was broken by the throat clearing of Garrett Brandywine. Peter could not have been more shocked. He had literally never heard the man utter a single word. Not once. Ever.

"I am," he said quietly.

"Excuse me, Mr. Brandywine?" Peter asked. "You are, what?"

"An archeologist. Well, that was my undergraduate degree. I did two summers in Egypt, and one on a dig in rural England. Fun stuff."

Peter revised his earlier sentiment. *This* was more shocking. Brandywine had studied archeology?

"I'm sorry if this offends everyone else, or even you, Garrett, but, could you walk me through how you went from an archeological dig in rural England to serving in life sciences and being the assistant chef on our little space ship?"

The man laughed nervously. "If I said, 'it was a bad divorce' would that answer all the questions?"

"No," the group said in unison.

He shook his head. "I'm not good with stories, but

basically my dad was kind of a celebrity chef back in the day. He did this show where he did unique spins on every day foods and then, because of the last name, had a part of the show devoted to what wines worked best with it."

"'Cooking with Paul'?" asked Andrew Todd. "That was your dad? I think my parents watched that show more than they talked to me. Seriously?"

"Yeah, so Dad wanted me to be a chef. I didn't, and he gave in. So I studied archeology. Actually, I first studied nautical archeology, but found that actually required getting into a small little craft, away from fresh air, and open sky and no chance of seeing the sunlight for extended periods of time." He smirked. "Who'd wanna job like that, right?" Everyone chuckled. "Well, so I applied to every internship there was. I got noticed by the Fund for Excellence in Research."

Peter MacGregor raised an eyebrow. "That's the charitable trust run by Charlotte Smith-Davies' family."

"Yes, sir. That becomes important in a second. But, basically, after I'm accepted into their program, Charles Smith-Davies figures out who I'm related to. He was like this crazy fan-boy of my dad's show. So, he connects me with some top-notch folks in the field. It was while I was in England that I got married, too soon, too young, too fast. That was really, really bad, and it made me question every decision I had made. So I saw QA was hiring chefs on Station. Decent pay, good people, and the guy who was going to be chef – now our chef on *Shackleton* – had been the sous-chef in one of my dad's restaurants. Small world, thing. He hired me on to Station, and that was as far into space as I wanted to go, but I found I really liked the commute. Well, Charlie – um, Captain Smith-Davies – had kept up with me and knew I was working Station, so when this project was starting she suggested I tell chef that I was interested in the gig. What she later told me, like the day before we left, was that she really didn't want me to take this gig. What she hoped was that I'd see I was kind of dead-ending in a way, that I had made a huge mistake in leaving archeology, and would go back to it." He took a deep breath. "And, so, apparently I have."

Dion began clapping first, followed by Hathaway, Timms, Nelson, and the rest. Soon they all broke into laughter.

"Alright," Hathaway said as they stopped. "What do we do."

CHAPTER 42

Alpha Base, The Object, Kuiper Belt

As it turned out, as a chef and archeologist, Garrett Brandywine was able to speak engineer – in tone and methodology, if not actual words. The engineers approved of his very disciplined approach to meticulously looking-not-touching approach to cataloging everything they found.

First, he deployed the small airborne drones to get a physical map of the warehouse floor. This put Dion Coleman and her assistant, Stephanie Porter, to work. Any spot they found that showed a broken stasis box would get a human inspection look. *Touching nothing!*

Meanwhile, the engineers were to focus on the walls of the room, and the support structures around it. Specifically, they were looking at mechanisms and anything that hinted at operations. *Do. Not. Touch. Anything.*

Hathaway wanted to deploy a couple of his crew back on the Object's exterior, but was overruled by Stephanie Porter. On the *Shackleton* she was the backup in life support sciences, and would have never dreamt of saying no to the ship's chief engineer. But here, she was responsible for keeping them breathing air instead of vacuum.

"Your team did an amazing job with the airlock structure, but the fact remains it was 3-D printed and not manufactured to the standards of a reusable airlock. I really don't want us pushing it beyond its limits and creating a sub-optimal situation."

Hathaway relented. No space walks until *Shackleton* returned.

As it turned out, despite what the engineers had labeled as shoddy workmanship on the electrical wiring for the still-mysterious stasis boxes, very few of them had seemed to break down. In all, perhaps four percent of the total in the warehouse.

"It's all plants here," said Rob Beckett as he slid the last sample out from his microscope. The best he could tell it was the remains of what had been palm tree seeds, but he could not be sure. "I mean, doesn't it seem strange that everything we are finding is definitely from Earth, but are just plants?"

Peter MacGregor had to agree it was strange, but there was a lot more Object on top of them without a particularly visible way of accessing any of it just yet.

Now at the halfway mark in their expected stay, they had all but finished mapping and categorizing the flora. It was on the verge of being monotonous.

Interestingly, it wasn't the engineers who started noticing *it* everywhere. In fact, all of them had ignored it. Almost all of them, anyway.

One could not turn around without finding white markings on things. Andrew Todd, the *Shackleton*'s communications chief and erstwhile EVA enthusiast, had been the first to photograph and categorize markings on the floor in the bay. Those markings were set inside what for all intents and purposes appeared to be lanes. But they were everywhere.

Some of those markings repeated on various aisles inside the warehouse, on the ends, on the floors, and on the walls.

"This is the language of the people who built the Object, gentlemen," Andrew Todd told Peter MacGregor and Benny Hathaway over lunch the third day of their stay. He had now photographed every symbol and marking he could find. He had even carefully – with Garrett Brandywine's assistance – photographed the neatly organized papers that had been found in that initial office.

It was all gibberish to their eyes, but Todd had had the

system render every unique marking, and the frequency in which they appeared. There were a lot.

"My guess is that this is no different than the markings on the *Shackleton*. Sometimes we use the word 'Danger' spelled out. Sometimes we employ a triangle with an exclamation mark, or a triangle with a lighting bolt, and so on. But it all means danger, though sometimes with the specific kind of danger if you know the cultural connotation of the markings inside the triangle. Another example, we have bathrooms that read 'men' and 'women' but also have little stick figures representing 'men' and 'women.' Your cabin is marked by a room number, a deck location pictograph, and your name. My guess is that this is what we are seeing here."

Between bites of meatloaf, Hathaway asked, "And so what does any of it mean, Andrew?"

The man chewed at his tongue the way Peter had noticed him do when he was thinking. "I do not have a clue. Except that the more I look at, the more alien everything here feels. I mean, everything in that warehouse is from Earth. I mean, appears to be. But it is. From Earth nearly thirteen millennia ago. So this language obviously is... not. This is the language of the beings who built this thing."

The three of them smiled, and Hathaway said, "Any chance our little motley crew has a linguist in their midst?"

Peter put down his glass of water and smiled. "No, but as soon as the *Shackleton* returns, I know quite well one of the world's best linguists and I bet she'll be excited to put her brain to this little puzzle."

He was, of course, referring to the world's richest missionary, employee number two at QA, in the company founded, in part – without her immediate knowledge – to solve the puzzle of the gravitational divot in space. His aunt, Teresa.

But before he could verbalize that, Paul Bratton called for him on the radio.

"Sir, you are going to want to see what we've found."

CHAPTER 43

The Henson, *interstellar space*

"You are a sight for sore eyes," Charlotte Smith-Davies said as Linda Bletchley emerged through the Henson's airlock. The two ships were mated, in what would ordinarily ensure the rapid transfer of dozens of crew members and cargo.

"Glad to be here, Captain," answered Linda. "My own captain sends his regards."

"I hear he got himself kind of stuck?"

"That's the long and short of it."

The corridor in which they were standing was deserted. "What's it like?" Charlie asked.

"I haven't been inside."

"Seriously?"

"No, too much to do on my end, though I hope to get a look around when we get back. Speaking of which, your crew...?"

"Still in the dark. My orders were to wait until we'd transferred over to tell my team."

"Understood. Let's get you moved."

The *Henson*'s skeleton crew had their belongings packed in footlockers, and the computer drives had already been backed up with Station. It was just a matter of setting the ship into a low-power, un-crewed mode.

"This setting was originally designed for a ship waiting for a re-configure at Station, not floating in the middle of nowhere," Bletchley said. "Will be interesting to see how it fares over the next couple of months."

"We made some modifications over the last few weeks,"

the *Henson*'s First Officer, Adriana O'Neil, said with some pride. "Based on the Voyager observations, we've configured the ship to do a series of small attitude adjustments that we hope will let it avoid stray strikes out here. Plus, we're going to keep the internal life-support systems running as if we're here. That will make it easier for the repair crew when they arrive, and keep some of the structures from operating outside their design specs."

Linda nodded approvingly. "Tell me how I can help."

Within four hours the last of the Henson crew were off-loaded, including Charlotte's husband, Thomas, and his battery of astronomical gear. Each of the airlocks between the ships had been sealed, save one.

With Linda Bletchley standing on the *Shackleton* side of the remaining connection, Charlotte would be the last of the crew to leave the *Henson*. She looked back down the corridor, resisting the urge to call, "You're about to be left behind." Instead, she reached over and tapped the last of a series of commands on a terminal by the airlock.

She paused for a moment, looked across at Bletchley, and said, "When this ship took its maiden voyage, the late Jason Roberts quoted Matthew Henson. 'It'll work, if God, wind, leads, ice, snow, and all the hells of this damned frozen land are willing.' That seems an appropriate quote with which to leave this fine vessel. She'll return to service, better than ever."

With a final tap on the terminal, internal lights began dimming as Charlotte Smith-Davies of the *Henson* stepped onboard the *Shackleton*. "Requesting permission to board?"

"Welcome aboard, ma'am."

+++

As soon as the ships separated, Charlotte Smith-Davies called her remaining *Henson* crew together in the galley to brief them on where they were going, and on what they could expect.

Jeff Prasadh listened intently, suddenly making sense of the half-conversations he heard over the last several hours. Everyone had been led to believe the *Shackleton* had fallen prey to communications glitches driven by some confounding space dust. Now that he knew the truth, he was surprised the powers that be on *Shackleton* and Station had kept the ruse up as long as they had.

"Fewer than two hundred people on Station and Earth know about this discovery. The *Shackleton* crew has kept it secret, and now so must we," Smith-Davies was saying. "Some of the best minds are at work unraveling what this is, what it means, and how to break this news to the people of Earth. The answer to the question of 'are we alone' seems to have been answered, but the answer itself opens up more questions than I think anyone realized. I apologize that I had to keep this from you, and I hope you can forgive me in understanding the orders I was under."

She took a couple questions and everyone departed to their assigned quarters, to wrap their heads around what they had been told. Within a few minutes, she was left alone with the one person she had most dreaded keeping the secret from, and then having to admit she had done so.

Thomas Newcome, astronomer, smiled and reached for her hand. "I understand," he said before she could even begin her apology.

"And, for the record, this is now the coolest trip we could ever take in a thousand lives," he said, with a raucous laugh. "We left the solar system. I've made observations no other astronomer has ever made. I got to host a global broadcast of our visit to humanity's first interstellar probe, and now I get to see an alien spaceship. Baby, you don't need to worry about Christmas presents ever again."

Charlotte laughed, suprised her husband could be so giddy.

CHAPTER 44

The Object, Kuiper Belt

There was nothing giddy about the tone in Paul Bratton's voice. He was nervous.

"Sir, you are going to want to see what we've found."

"The last time you said that, I ended up stuck in one of those stasis boxes for half-a-day," said Peter, in reply. "So, if I'm going to set my lunch down, I want to be sure something like that doesn't happen again."

He intended it as a joke, but Bratton didn't seem to get it. "Sir, this is... It's... You just need to come over as soon as you can."

Peter MacGregor, Benny Hathaway, and Andrew Todd finished their meals in a quick gulps and then rushed into the Object's first-level warehouse.

"Where can we find you?" he asked.

"I'm flashing my signal light," Bratton replied. "And my location should appear on your tablet."

Okay, we see you."

Bratton appeared to be near one of the support beams scattered around the warehouse.

What they found waiting for them was a staircase that hadn't been there before. Their survey maps showed a support column, but definitely no staircase. Peter MacGregor himself had walked past this spot a day earlier, and there had been no staircase.

He could see that Garrett Brandywine was two-thirds of the way up the stairs, so that his head was in the dark shadow of the ceiling.

Bratton began speaking. "So me and Garret were measuring the bay. Basically, we've realized there is about fifteen percent of the space on the inside missing from what the outside of the Object says should be here." This much everyone had already agreed upon. "We wanted to see if we could determine where the space was missing. Was it uniform, or out of a chunk on side or the other. Anyway, we didn't answer that question but we were standing here thinking of ways to test the question. That's when we noticed a yellow light."

"A yellow light?" Hathaway asked.

"Yeah, it was a strip of coherent light, like a laser, maybe, going from the ceiling to the floor, with the light running the length of the column. Anyway, it was a light. Because it made a bright dot on the floor, and there was the bright dot on the ceiling, we couldn't tell if it was coming from the floor or the ceiling."

"Get to the point, Paul," MacGregor said, impatiently. He wondered what Garrett Brandywine was seeing up there.

"So, I put my hand into the light. That's when we found out the beam originated above us. But it is also when a mechanism began creaking and this staircase emerged from the ceiling," he pointed to the Brandywine's torso, which was disappearing into the ceiling.

Peter asked, "What do you see up there?"

"It's a menagerie," Brandywine replied loudly, his voice echoing slightly. "Just turning in a circle and... this is unreal."

Peter MacGregor mounted the steps two at a time, pulling a flashlight from his own utility belt. As he stepped through the ceiling, he gasped and then swore under his breath when he came face to face with a pair of... saber-tooth tigers? They were frozen, asleep, in a larger version of the stasis boxes below holding seeds and plant life.

Garrett Brandywine was already on the deck, and three men below were queueing up to follow MacGregor.

Resting in smaller boxes above the pair of extinct

tigers were smaller boxes containing sparrows, another with pigeons, and other birds he could not identify.

"Rob," called Peter as he looked around, "you were wondering about just finding plants? Well, now we have animals." The nurse appeared next to the captain, and then started moving down one of the aisles while letting out a low whistle.

"Some of these animal I've only seen in museums," said Bratton.

Within minutes the rest of Object Dirty Dozen were heading up the staircase, bringing the small mapping drones to release into this level of the warehouse. The first thing they all noticed was that this level was more tightly packed than the one below with which they were more familiar.

When Garrett Brandywine described what we saw as a "menagerie," he only scratched the surface. There was no animal anyone in the group could think that they did not find over the next three days. That included more sets of extinct animals, like the saber-tooth tigers.

A quick census revealed not just pairs of animals, but seven of all the mammals and reptiles, and a dozen or more of the birds. The visible evidence of a particular monkey, on what their map labelled aisle nine, created a theory. These monkeys – none of them knew what kind – were very obviously three males and four females. One of the females was very obviously quite pregnant. That pattern seemed to repeat among the various mammals.

They quickly identified the observation office for this level, situated next to an identical set of massive bay doors, offset by a third around the Object, from the bay doors in the horticulture level below. This version of the observation office was larger by an order of magnitude. It, too, had its gravity plates set askew from the perspective of both the loading bay and the warehouse... the menagerie? the zoo?... The effect here, as the level below, was to provide a comfortable, if initially jarring, view onto the loading area, which was also slightly larger.

It was this level's observation office, however, which proved the most interesting. It had the same desks, chairs, and table-top stasis box. It also had stacks of neatly organized papers. What this one had was a series of wall-mounted diagrams detailing these first two warehouse levels. The aisles and locations of stasis boxes on the diagrams were matched with the team's own observations and mapping of the two levels they had already explored. The locations of the stasis boxes contained small symbols, which everyone agreed must be the representations of the contents – be it flora or fauna – in the alien language.

Through the observation office window they could make out, across the bay and at floor level, a large window. It appeared to be leading into another alcove and access corridor leading to an elevator shaft. Not knowing the extent of the damage to this (assumed) elevator shaft, if any, and therefore the availability of breathable air, it was decided they would not attempt an entry until the *Shackleton* made its return.

"Someone went to a lot of trouble to collect animals from Earth," observed Hathaway. "It reminds me of stories of the Roman soldiers returning home from campaigns, bringing with them animals from faraway places. They'd parade them through the streets and then display them in the Coliseum along with the people that had been defeated."

"Does this mean these aliens thought they had conquered Earth?" asked Bratton.

CHAPTER 45

Alpha Base, Object, Kuiper Belt

Rob Beckett was having decidedly more fun on this second level than the one below. Before becoming a human nurse, he had had plans to be a large-animal veterinarian. It was being drafted into the Australian Army and sent into the medical corps that changed his focus. He loved being a nurse, as evidence by continuing the profession when the Sino-Australian War concluded, but he maintained an abiding love for patients who didn't talk back.

"I can tell you, without a doubt, that in every case where I have made a visual examination, the seventh animal of the kind is a female and is pregnant," said Beckett. "Obviously, it's a little hard to tell with many of the species in here, but a lot of them are like the monkeys we saw, and are very pregnant – to the extent that if they are actually really alive behind that stasis field, they will be giving birth in a matter of hours or days."

He looked around at his colleagues as they ate dinner.

"Seriously, this doesn't interest you? Think about it. Let's assume the pattern holds. All these animals have different mating cycles and terms of pregnancy. That these females were impregnated, allowed to nearly reach completion of gestation, and put into stasis points to an incredible amount of planning, organization, and even time."

Helen Lee, the payload specialist, swallowed the last of her green beans before saying, "I think only a male could find the scientific and organizational beauty of being pregnant for ten thousand years."

This brought laugh from everyone, but especially Benny Hathaway, whose gruff demeanor had mellowed over their twelve days on the Object.

"My ex-wife would shout 'amen' if she was here, so I will do so in her honor," he said, raising his cup of coffee in a salute. "Of course, she would also then tell you all how our children have had to overcome the horrid legacy of bearing my genetic material, and suggest that – perhaps – I might be more closely related to either a dog or the devil."

Before anyone could respond, the radio sitting in the corner of the alcove off the loading, where they were dining, piped a hailing tone.

"*Shackleton* to Alpha Base, do you copy? *Shackleton* Actual to Alpha Base Actual, do you copy?" It was the unmistakable voice of Linda Bletchley. A cheer rose up among the dozen of them.

Peter MacGregor grabbed the microphone but kept the audio open for everyone to hear. "Alpha Base Actual to *Shackleton* Actual, we copy five-by-five. It's great to hear your voice. No complaints on this side, but it seems like you might be a day early? Out."

Dropping the radio protocols, Bletchley replied, "As it turns out, having a dozen extra senior ship crew who'd had a month of boredom thrust upon them can be an amazing thing." She paused. "And tell Engineer Hathaway that his constant tinkering with the ships systems is most definitely what saved *Shackleton* from experiencing the same gravity drive problem that hit the *Henson*. I hereby, officially, regret ever having made fun of his tinkering."

Hathaway nodded, with a bit of pride.

It was another several hours before the *Shackleton* was docked back with the umbilical system leading to the Object. The ship's doctor, Dana Regan, established a link with Beckett and described a series of tests recommended by Station to be run on everyone before the airlocks connecting the two would be opened.

When the *Henson* crew had boarded the *Shackleton*, these screenings had been performed as a baseline and replicated by everyone in Space Operations Command – including Lucy MacGregor Hyde. The *Shackleton* crew was then tested, with the results showing there were no unexpected illnesses or antibodies – though in the case of Lucy Hyde it had revealed she was pregnant.

Now, those same tests would be conducted so as to ensure no one who had been on the Object for the last two weeks picked up anything new, nasty, or surprising. No one had.

Linda Bletchley and Charlotte Smith-Davies were waiting at the *Shackleton* airlock as the seals were finally released allowing Peter MacGregor to re-enter his ship.

"Welcome back, Captain," Bletchley said, "nice to see you have all your limbs attached."

For her part, Smith-Davies gave Peter an almost maternal hug. "It is so good of you to have sent your ship for us," she said after pecking him on the check.

"Great to see you, Charlie." To both of them, he said, "We need to schedule a call with missions control." In the hours between the first radio contact and opening the airlock, the Object crew had downloaded their reports and data to the *Shackleton*, which in turn uploaded it all to Space Operations.

"Already set. Three hours from now. I thought maybe while you and your team reacquainted yourself with the *Shackleton*, Captain Smith-Davies, Dr. Newcome, and I would take a look at your botanical gardens and zoo?"

"Have at it," he peered around the airlock with a bit of exaggerated movement. "Though I fail to see Thomas, anywhere."

"He'll be right along. He left his camera in our quarters."

Peter passed the man in the hall, where they warmly greeted each other and then as quickly parted ways. While they had had a rudimentary shower set up in the Object, which had been put in the make-shift infirmary to wash off contaminates rather than clean up, he was very excited to take a long, hot shower in his own cabin.

The rest of the Object crew had a similar objective, which meant the warehouse levels were mostly clear as Charlotte, Thomas, and Linda made their way around. The map on their tablets guided the way, and all three were impressed by the lighting system Hathaway's engineers had put in place. It made the massive chamber slightly less foreboding.

"I guess they couldn't figure out where the lights were," Thomas muttered.

"They took the 'touch nothing' mantra rather seriously," Linda said. "Though we'll see if our superiors decide interrupting a beam of light to make a staircase appear counts as touching nothing."

And there was the matter of the remains that Beckett had disturbed. The four percent failure rate of the stasis fields had held on the second level. He had found what were most definitely two penguins that had been released from stasis. That they had not moved from the box itself had caused them to wonder if the animals were, in fact, stored at the moment of death. That did not explain the pregnant females, though...

The trio mounted the stairs of the fauna section to its observation office. Inside, Charlotte was drawn to the schematics of the two levels. She had flipped past them when running through the mission reports, but now – having had the context of seeing the place – looked at them more carefully.

"Not possible," she muttered.

"What, dear?" asked Thomas, who was struggling with the shifted gravity.

"It's just that this symbol. It..." she trailed off. Linda and Thomas joined her at the wall. Charlotte pulled a ballpoint pen from her pocket and made sure the lid was sealed. She pointed at several places on the fauna level map, where the symbol was repeated over a series of other symbols. "My dad has, for my entire life, doodled *that* symbol. I wish I could remember what language it was from, or what part of the world, but he said that symbol meant 'danger.'"

She looked out the window into the warehouse, with its stacks of glowing blue boxes, then back to the map.

"That one," she jabbed at the map. "That's the saber-tooth tiger. And that one is the grizzly bear. And that is the crocodile. Those three we walked past from the stairs getting here." She took her camera and took close up photos. "We need Teresa Schultz to see these. Now."

CHAPTER 46

Portland, Oregon, U.S.A.

Hank Schultz didn't want to be a missionary to Mars. He had been content with his ministry in central Africa. He and Teresa had gone to the grand opening of Station, and he had even offered a nice ecumenical prayer to start the ceremonies.

"As 'to whom it may concern' prayers go, it wasn't so bad," he had said to his wife later. They had also been there for the christening of *Henson* and *Shackleton*, but they preferred keeping their feet on *terra firma* as a matter of daily life.

It wasn't disease, war, or tribal crime that took Hank Schultz from Teresa. Instead, it had been a car accident in London. A careless cab driver had run a light, slamming into the vehicle ferrying Hank to a conference where he was to be the keynote speaker.

And so Teresa had moved four years ago to Portland, where their oldest son practiced medicine. The other two boys were career military and moved frequently, so Portland seemed like a good choice to be near family.

For the first time in decades, Teresa now actually lived a sliver of the lifestyle which many assumed her wealth generally guaranteed. In fact, though, she preferred to live modestly. After all, most of her married life had been in tents and huts. Because she used Hank's last name, most people in her upper middle class neighborhood had no idea who the kindly widow was that owned the nicer of the homes. That was just fine. When she told them her husband had been a missionary, and she was living in Portland to be near her son the neurosurgeon, they just assumed whatever they assumed.

She lectured on linguistics at the University of Portland, and did guest seminars around the country, though to suggest she was an academic would make her laugh.

Sitting now at her desk, with a series of screens surrounding her, she had to agree that, yes, Charlotte had been right. That was, absolutely, the same symbol she remembered her friend Charles Smith-Davies using for danger. She remembered him telling her once he had come across it at several different dig sites, but for the life of her she could not recall what sites. He had said it just struck him as "danger" – but hastened to add he was no linguist.

In all, she recognized several dozen symbols that were duplicates of, or clearly related to, the glyphs or pictographs of a series of highly disconnected ancient peoples.

But the overwhelming majority of the markings that had been sent to her were, on their face, about as meaningful as chicken scratchings in the dirt. What would eventually, she knew, make the task of translating these glyphs easier would be the sheer amount of information she had – all set in the context of their use.

There was no rhyme or reason to those recognizable symbols in regards to the languages, peoples, or places from which they were... what? Borrowed? Taken? Donated?

The symbols seem to be used consistently throughout the Object, based on the detailed records taken by the *Shackleton*'s Andrew Todd. It appeared – a word she used lightly – that the symbols retained a passing resemblance to the meaning with which the academic record accorded them – at least of the half-dozen for which there was a consensus of meaning. In all, this gave Teresa Schultz a head start on almost any translation project ever recorded. It wasn't the Rosetta Stone, but it was close.

She wondered briefly how long it would have been to get to this point had Charlotte not immediately recognized her father's long-standing doodle.

Teresa leaned back in her chair and checked the large

grandfather clock in the corner. She had another five minutes until the conference would start. For not the first time, her mind wandered to the theological and philosophical questions raised by the presence of the Object, this alien language, and the cargo hold full of biological specimens from Earth. She would have trusted Hank to have thoughtfully begun to frame the questions in the context of all he knew to be true.

She hoped the system she had designed, driven as it was by QA's latest quantum processors, would have rendered something by now. The repeating symbols and markings in the "stasis boxes" of the same kinds of animals helped immeasurably. But, still, it was not a certainty that the writings corresponded to the animals. It was a decent bet, but not a sure thing.

The computer chimed and Teresa self-consciously adjusted her silver hair and sat up in her chair before initializing the call.

On the screen was her brother, whose hairline had receded and grayed, but whose eyes danced and flashed with an almost scary intelligence. They were joined by his daughters, Samantha and Lucy. Yua Saito was on the screen, and a moment later Chris Stoddard appeared, as well.

This was Lucy's meeting, and so after everyone greeted each other – and offered Lucy congratulations on her pregnancy – they debated the point over which Teresa had no clarity: when to tell the world, and how. Not even world leaders – presidents, prime ministers, monarchs, or premiers – had been brought into the circle of trust on this most Earth-shattering discovery. That likely is what had accounted for the sustained secrecy. In her experience, politicians saw secrets as a form of currency to be traded for their own benefit.

"At this point," Chris was saying, "we've found a giant biology lab. A real-life catalogue of the flora and fauna of Earth, circa thirteen thousand years ago. Could this thing have been set up as a kind of 'in case of emergency, open' sort of thing by aliens wishing to preserve life here?"

"Forgive me, Uncle Chris, but we need to stay focused on the question of expanding knowledge of this discovery, up to and including full public disclosure. We can't debate what we cannot know," said Lucy, trying to keep the time productive.

"No, this is exactly my point. All we have is a menagerie. No little green men, nothing pointing to where they are from or where they were going, or even if they were going anywhere. For all we know, this was an abandoned science experiment. By staying silent, we are not depriving humanity of any special knowledge... except that full-size, possibly still-alive – in the most generous definition of the word – set of wooly mammoths and saber-tooth tigers are at the edge of the solar system."

Teresa, who had been silent for the last twenty minutes, spoke up. "But, Chris, there is the problem of the language. It would appear that whoever collected these animals did so meticulously over a period of years. And in doing so, they seem to have interacted with our ancestors to the extent that some of their symbols became ingrained in the earliest cultures of men. This affects everything."

"That's what I'm trying to say," he said. "But it doesn't affect anything right now. We don't know what questions to ask, let alone have any answers. Until we have some answers, I think we'd start ripping apart the fabric of society by revealing what little we know."

That brought a smile to Teresa's face. Her oldest friend in the world was making a surprisingly humanistic case for secrecy. Twenty years ago he would have been insulted by the charge of being a "humanist" who kept secrets for other people's own good. After all, he was the one who demanded the gravity drive be revealed the moment it was safe, who demanded that as soon as products were past the "imagination" phase that they be revealed. He felt collaboration, and especially criticism, always made things better.

"I think I agree," said Ian MacGregor. "At least, insofar as we keep this among us and no one else except as a matter of necessity. As soon as we bring in too many people, reporters will start spinning stories that will get out of control very fast."

CHAPTER 47

Washington, D.C., U.S.A.

Jim Summerland was now unemployable in his chosen profession as a journalist. His source in QA's Space Operations Center had burned him well and spectacularly. He had been blackballed by one of the world's largest companies, and easily its most important.

His lawyer, who was usually highly combative, made it clear no one would find sympathy for a journalist who had rushed to be first with a story claiming the deaths of a highly popular space crew. It reeked of what it was: crass, irresponsible self-promotion.

"The First Amendment has freedoms, but also responsibility. You can say whatever you want, but other people can act on that as they wish," the lawyer had said each time Summerland tried to argue journalistic shields.

On that lawyer's recommendation, Summerland had written a carefully worded apology to the senior leadership of QA, Space Operations, and the *Henson*. He sent similar apologies to the spouse or parent of every *Henson* crew member. And he even sent one, through the school's headmaster, to the son of the ship's captain.

Not a single one had been answered, except from the mother of a crewman who wrote that his reporting had made her father – the grandfather of one the *Henson*'s youngest crew members – suffer a heart attack. He had survived, but she argued persuasively, it was Summerland's fault and his letter was trash.

The World News Network, highly chastened, had

groveled sufficiently to be given the possibility of a review, in three years, so that they could have access to QA properties and events. The network bought out Summerland's contract and pointed him to the door.

Meanwhile, all of the notoriety had worked to in network's favor; their viewership jumped 10 percent.

Summerland himself was now selling shoes in a department store in Alexandria, Virginia, by day and running an anonymous news aggregator by night. The world headquarters of "Space Industry Reviews and News" was an anonymized server farm off the coast of Ireland, which he accessed by way of a masked network, from his apartment not far from the Capitol of the United States.

Something was up with the *Shackleton*. He knew that.

Summerland, based on what few sources who had not gone completely silent, thought it was either a black-op mission for the U.S. government – though what that could possibly be in the outer edge of the solar system was unimaginable – or that QA had found a hunk of... something valuable beyond measure.

Years ago people had theorized Jupiter's core could be a diamond. It still could be, Summerland supposed, but more recent discoveries of burnt out white dwarf stars had – indeed – been confirmed as diamonds. That meant it was possible hunks of a diamond-like star or the remnants of an exoplanet had made their way into the Kuiper Belt. That would be valuable for any number of reasons and uses, especially for a company building colonies on Mars. And, it would explain the secrecy. They could be trying to figure out how to move the thing closer in to exploit it.

Summerland thought about it, and considered poking the bear. And then reconsidered it. After downing the last of his second glass of whiskey, he re-reconsidered it and decided to send in a query using a *nom de plum*. He thought of that smug Yua Saito trying to answer this question.

The thought of a massive diamond in space inspired

inclinations towards mischief as Jim Summerland poured another finger of whisky, added a block of ice, and went to typing.

+++

Unbeknownst to Jim Summerland, his message was never going to reach Saito – at least not in the way he intended. Milliseconds after he pressed 'send' on the inquiry, the artificial intelligence algorithms at QA had achieved a ninety-nine percent certainty that – based on years of writing samples – "Carla Suntner" was actually Jim Summerland.

And, for what it was worth, QA knew that the mostly unread "Space Industry Reviews and News" was his attempt at a clandestine publication. They could have shut it down – the server farm he used was a distant subsidiary of QA – but instead kept the account active to ensure he did not cause additional grief or too much mischief.

+++

Across the North American continent, Lucy Hyde had finished her conference call and was sending a report to her brother, letting him know what had – for now – been decided. "For now" were the operative words, because it was agreed this decision would need to be regularly reviewed.

Lucy's message indicator flared; the special projects team within the QA communications office had received another message for Yua Saito from one of Jim Summerland's aliases. She could see Saito was copied on the notification and was considering their options when a second indicator flashed. This one from Yua.

"I think Mr. Summerland may have just given us an out," the flight operations director wrote, presenting the outline of an idea. Lucy responded, copying both QA's general counsel, Hanson O'Donnell, and Peter Torres, the Vice President for Media and Communications.

Within a few minutes, all four were on a call. O'Donnell

cleaned up Saito's original language to ensure it was legally truthful, while Torres gave the legal truth a slightly more elegant feel. The lawyer changed two words, and Torres edited one back.

+++

"Ms. Suntner, thank you for your inquiry," began the message. Jim could barely believe his luck; Saito was finally responding to an inquiry from one of his aliases.

It is only because it is from a woman's name, he thought as he set his drink aside.

"As director of flight operations, I cannot comment specifically on your question. You will need to go through QA's Media and Communications office. However, this is a very exciting topic pushing the boundaries of space sciences. I woud recommend to you for background reading a series of papers on super-massive carbon structures. If, which is a word I must strongly stress here for reasons you can surely understand, *if* such an object – from Pluto-sized to Moon-sized or bigger, as has been hypothesized – the implications for space construction would be considerable. It is a fascinating topic, and one which has long interested me. Again, thank you for writing and please contact Shawn Overstreet, who heads the M&C desk during these hours. Cordially, Yua Saito."

The message included links to a series of papers, and instructions on how to reach Shawn Overstreet directly.

She literally just confirmed it. Those greedy QA guys are mining a diamond the size of the Moon, Jim thought as he typed the next message – making sure it also was coming from Carla Suntner. But in his mind, he had already composed two-thirds of the article. This would be more fun to do as a video, but – he had to remind himself – he couldn't do that. Not yet. Not as himself. He could deep-fake it, though…

Two hours passed after he sent a note to Shawn Overstreet, seeking an on-the-record comment. His article was ready to publish, when the response arrived.

"Dear Ms. Suntner, QA has yet to publish any statements regarding the nature of the discovery by the *Shackleton* and has not yet determined when any public statements will be forthcoming. I will make sure you are contacted when any such statement is imminent."

Summerland opened his ready-to-publish article and inserted a single sentence between the second and third paragraphs: "A spokesman for QA refused to confirm the discovery, which has been hinted at and all but confirmed by numerous high level sources."

CHAPTER 48

The Shackleton, *Kuiper Belt*

Peter wished he had an opinion about the decision made to continue the secrecy surrounding the Object. On the one hand, it meant his crew had to keep their families in the dark about what they were doing. On the other hand, no one had yet really raised any concerns.

There had been minor complaints about the reduced access to live conversations with family, but those had been resolved simply enough: giving everyone more access to live conversations by increasing the comms rations.

It was a testament to the professionalism and temperament of the crew that no one wanted to act rashly in regards to the situation. And the fact of the matter was that they still had at least another month on the books before they were scheduled to be back at Station anyway. No one was really inconvenienced... yet.

Now, with the *Henson's* trouble, there was an implied but unspoken assumption they might have to be out here a little longer to take up the slack. *Implied, never said.*

The most interesting part of the message came at the end, where Lucy related that Teresa hoped Peter and his crew would "soon find" a third warehouse level. If the pattern of symbols and glyphs that had corollaries to other ancient languages held, that is where they would find fish.

Because, *of course* they would.

So now Peter MacGregor – the intrepid spaceman and archeologist in the stars – was also a fisherman. "Too bad I left my fly rod at home," he typed in a reply note to Lucy, on which he copied his aunt.

He checked the time, and realized if he was going to get whatever lunch offerings chef had prepared he would have to go now. He closed out his terminal, grabbed his tablet and headed out of his small office.

Peter had just reached the galley when his message alert sounded. It was Charlotte calling from the Object. Even as he answered, he had a sneaking fear doing so would cause him to miss lunch.

"So I'm over here with Paul Bratton, and he was insistent that it be me who called you and not him," she began. "He seems to think you would be put out with him. For my part, I think you will want to see what we have found before we start touching things."

"Will head right over," he said. He then added, "Any of you want something from the galley?"

+++

Peter finished the sandwich as he approached the Shackleton umbilical to the Object. Through the windows he could see Hathaway's engineering crew members exploring the wreckage. He knew they were looking – so far, unsuccessfully – for other exposed elevator shafts or entrances to the other side of the Object. They knew those had to exist, but the jumble of metal and debris – combined with the knowledge that there was live power flowing through the ship – made too much excavation too risky. But they could look.

Along the way, they had discovered that this lower portion of the Object seemed to have housed a gravity drive system not unlike the first-generation device his father had demonstrated so long ago – and which still transported people around the Earth gravity well and up to Station. Similar to, but structurally different and on a much larger scale.

The gravity plating inside the ship achieved the same ends as that developed two decades ago by his dad, Chris

Stoddard, and their team, but operated on a slightly different set of principles and assumptions.

He heard hurried footsteps come up behind him. It was the *Henson*'s acting communications lead. Jeff *Something*, Peter thought.

"Captain, I'm Jeff Prasadh from the *Henson*," the younger man helpfully said. "I was walking over to the Object and saw you crossing the bridge. Mind if I walk with you?"

"Not at all, Jeff, please do. Anything in particularly you are coming to do?"

"Actually, yes. Mr. Todd just asked me to help with a project." He pulled a virtual reality headset from his bag, "We're looking for a very specific set of symbols on the second floor. The headset will help with that, and we can put them in context faster than drone footage."

Peter nodded. He knew that had to be coming directly from Aunt Teresa, who was now running Andrew Todd like a graduate assistant in the most meaningful lab experiment of all time. "Well, I'm heading up to the second floor. Let's go."

Into the Object's bay, up the stairs, into the observation office, out the door, down the stairs, through the maze of aisles, up the stairs... right into the unblinking eyes of the larger of the two saber-tooth tigers in the stasis box straight ahead.

Jeff Prasadh gasped. He caught himself and mumbled, "Sorry, captain."

"Don't be. I do the same thing almost every time I walk up here."

Jeff Prasadh and Peter MacGregor parted company. Prasadh stopped to put on the headset and began exploring the area for the symbols being tested, while MacGregor continued on down the aisle to where he knew Charlotte and her husband, Thomas Newcome, were waiting with Paul Bratton.

Paul did, indeed, look sheepish. "Sir, there was no way I was calling you again. I just happened to be with Captain Smith-Davies when *she* found it. This is not on me."

Peter laughed and slapped the crewman on the back.

"Got it, man. So, what did you guys find."

"Well," Charlotte began, "we've been looking for a bright yellow projection, almost laser-like, light between the ceiling and floor that would trigger stairs coming down from the ceiling like I understand happened before."

She pointed up. "Several of us have been walking through here like turkeys in the rain, trying to catch a glimpse of the little dot of light. Nothing. Well, as you know, you and your delightful crew went about making it a little less dreary in here by placing temporary lighting atop the stasis boxes. Yellow lights. That's why no one noticed, until Thomas and I were standing here having a spirited discussion about which of us had gotten us lost, when I spotted this."

She pointed, a little dramatically, Peter thought, to the wall.

He didn't see anything. "I'm sorry, Charlie. What are you pointing out?"

Before she could reply, an excited voice came from behind them. It was Jeff Prasadh, wearing the VR headset, shouting, "Fish! You found the fish!" He came to a stop, staring at the place where Charlotte Smith-Davies hand was pointing. He was shocked they weren't as excited as he was, and the group was convinced the young man was space-happy.

Until Peter got it. The message from Lucy. Teresa working with the *Shackleton*'s comms teams. Prasadh's tasking. It all came together.

Jeff pointed to the hand-sized symbol. "That is a symbol that has something to do with fish."

Charlotte, still not completely clear, said, "No, that is the light trigger for the entrance to the third level of the warehouse. Without asking, she waved her hand and the ceiling opened, with stairs folding out of it.

"Oh, sorry about that Peter," she said. "I didn't mean for..."

"No worries," he said. "Let's go fishing, shall we?"

The third level did, indeed, contain aquatic life. Massive

stasis boxes, and tiny jars inside small stasis boxes.

Thomas and Charlotte went down an aisle that seemed to contain varieties of freshwater fish – something Thomas knew something about as an avid fisherman back home.

Still standing at the stairs, Jeff Prasadh had sent the findings to Andrew Todd before joining Paul Bratton in going in the opposite direction from Charlotte and her husband.

This left Peter to walk... forward. Immediately, he could see this level of the warehouse was different. The two lower levels were, with the exception of support columns, wide open spaces filled with stacks of stasis boxes. Unlike those, this level had a wall cutting off what he estimated to be a quarter or a third of the available space.

He tried to call up on his tablet images the schematic of this warehouse level they had found in the second-level's observation office. The connection to the ship database was not strong enough for him to access them, and he cursed himself for not having downloaded them. He then tried to contact Bletchley, hoping she could send the maps across. He was intensely curious about what was behind the wall.

There was no response, except a bit of static. He knew Prasadh had gotten through, a hundred meters back at the staircase. He decided to see what he could see, then head back and try again.

His headset crackled. "Bratton to MacGregor. You read me?"

"I do."

"Sir, we seem to be cut off here from the radio relay to the ship."

"Yeah, I found that out myself just now." He approached the wall, letting his flashlight play along it. "Paul, do you happen to have the image of the third-level schematic handy?"

"Yes, sir. I saved it to my tablet. Let me pull it up here."

Peter kept walking. His light caught the glimpse of a hatchway or portal.

"I got it here, sir. What were were you interested in?" he

asked. Then added, "Funny, looks like maybe a wall cuts this section into two parts. The part we're in is the bigger part, maybe two-thirds of the space."

"That's exactly what I was calling about. Does it look like there are stasis boxes in the other side?" Maybe this was a hub point to access the rest of the ship?

No such luck, apparently.

"It looks like stasis boxes. I mean, the drawings are the same." He paused. "That's funny."

"What do you mean, Paul?" The portal had a set of doors that were closed. He played his flashlight further down the wall and saw two more sets of doors further along, all of which were roughly set off from what he estimated to be the center of the wall. He pushed against the first door. It didn't budge. "So...?"

He could hear Jeff Prasadh was saying something to Paul Bratton.

"Well, what we have seen up until now is that every stasis box has slightly different markings, which we have come to believe those marking represents the species of the animal in it. On the other side of the wall, the stasis boxes all have the same repeated symbols. Strange, huh?"

Peter pushed on the next door. It moved a little. "Yeah, that's odd. So, maybe this is a whole lot of one kind of fish?" He pushed harder and the door swung inward.

More stasis boxes, but none were stacked. They all seemed to be the same size. Rectangular and under two meters tall. He moved through the door and could finally see inside the first aisle of boxes.

Peter MacGregor stumbled backwards, gasping.

"Paul," he began, the words catching in his throat. "Get Charlotte and Thomas. Have Prasadh radio for Dr. Regan, fast. You are all going to want to see what I've found."

CHAPTER 49

Washington, D.C., U.S.A.

For someone who didn't actually exist, "Carla Sunter" was getting regular requests for interviews from major networks around the globe – including Jim Summerland's own former employer. He loved it.

The article on QA secretly mining a space diamond had, in his own estimation, rocketed through the stratosphere. It was like someone had juiced it with advertising and pushed it onto every social network and news feed.

By this point, Summerland had become so consumed by the story that he forgot he had basically created it from thin air. There was no set of facts actually in evidence that the *Shackleton* was actually mining a space diamond, or that one even existed. He was riding the exhilarating wave of anonymous fame.

In each case, Summerland – using yet a different pseudonym, posing as "Carla's" editor – replied to inquires that she was incredibly shy and would only conduct interviews in writing. He was shocked by how many agreed; he never would have.

In fact, the actual number of stories generated by Summerland's post was relatively small by the standards of any network or major news site. Minor celebrities reviewing their latest ice cream purchase would get a dozen times the coverage, but Summerland was the lone occupant of a small island, so the steady drip of attention felt like a tsunami.

And so the story had become, in his own mind, real.

For the rest of the world, it was a curious datapoint.

The denial from QA certainly sounded like a "confirmation," but it did not mean anything, as experts discussing the "Carla Sunter" story on late-night shows were quick to point out.

Yes, there could possibly be a diamond – but it would not be a diamond most people thought much about. It would be of the industrial variety, perhaps. It would probably be unsuited for anything on Earth, but perhaps of great importance for future construction projects on Mars. Maybe.

It was marginally fascinating. It made good filler content. It gave the family members a talking point if asked, which no one was. The story subconsciously explained to everyone why the *Shackleton* was not in the news, despite the fact it had never actually been in the news in the first place. The minor story about a diamond in space had the effect of making, in the mind of the public, the *Shackleton* disappear into the background of noise known as "the news."

Jim Summerland did not realize how badly he had been played, nor would he ever. Without knowing it, he had done the leadership of QA and the crew of the *Shackleton* a great service. He had given them the most important of gifts.

He had bought them time.

INTERLUDE 2

The written history of anatomically modern humans extends barely more than 5,000 years, while the fossil record suggests the species has existed for barely 200,000 years. For much of the time in so-called pre-history, physically modern *Homo sapiens* existed with its various genetic cousins.

The species calls itself, with no sense of irony, *Homo sapiens*, Latin for "wise man." A designation coined in 1758, long after Latin died as a language.

In the early days of the 21st Century, archeologists at Grotte Mandrin, a cave in the Rhône Valley, found evidence of modern humans and their neanderthal cousins living side by side. Of particular interest in the find was a baby tooth belonging to an anatomically modern human nestled in between layers of clay that contained the teeth of baby Neanderthals.

Sometimes the cousins got friendly; sometimes they got very friendly. Even now, bits and pieces of genetic code from those other species are floating around in modern humanity's DNA.

Often times, the relations were less friendly, more strained. Even deadly.

It has not been determined exactly when, how, or why those other branches of humanity stopped existing. They apparently left no monuments, no structures. There remain no books of poetry, no cultural totems. They were not eulogized.

They simply ceased to exist.

In some cases, it is theorized, those cousins of modern man could not adjust to new climates or changes in the food supply. Others, despite wandering the planet longer than this newer branch of *homo sapiens*, found themselves succumbing to new diseases. Still others, it is thought, were hunted down and killed by their upstart cousins.

Neanderthal. Denisovans. Cro-Magnon.

Homo habilis. Homo rudolfensis. Homo erectus. Homo antecessor. Homo heidelbergensis. Homo floresiensis. Homo naledi.

But of the lot, the last man standing has been the self-proclaimed *Homo sapiens sapiens*. The wisest of the wise man.

For now, anyway.

PART III

Awakening

CHAPTER 50

Third Level, The Object, Kuiper Belt

It was a mostly naked woman. As best Peter could tell, she was in her early thirties. In the next box was a man, completely naked, and perhaps in his mid-twenties. And so it went down the aisle.

By the time Dr. Regan and First Office Bletchley had arrived, Peter and the others had covered five aisles. The stasis boxes all contained people, ranging from infants to the elderly. The males were all naked, the females had simple skirts wrapped around their midsections. Most of the adult men were clean-shaven, with long hair pulled back in ponytails. The women all had their hair cropped slightly below than their ears.

Every single person was wearing three bracelets. There was a uniformity to the pattern of colors down each aisle.

There were so many people. At some point, it struck Peter and each of the crew that these people had been here for a staggering long time.

"The thought of how long all this has been here didn't hit me emotionally when we were looking plants, dogs, and fish," said the doctor. "But seeing all these people..."

So far, each of the warehouse floors measured approximately 400 meters by 450 meters. This was smaller than the external measurements of the ship would indicate, but then the same was true for the *Shackleton* – or any vessel under, on, or over, the sea. Space ships like these had massive equipment needed to generate power, preserve life, and move. The processes by which this particular vessel did those things was not yet known, but those undoubtedly accounted for the missing space.

But setting that aside, and considering the visible space, this created 180,000 square meters of floor space. There are 4,046 square meters in an acre, so each of these three levels of the Object had slightly better than forty-four acres of floor space. On this level, two-thirds of the space was taken up by aquatic life collected from ancient Earth. That left one-third, or thirteen acres, to be filled with humans.

All the stasis boxes in this section were of uniform size, regardless of the size of the person inside. Each aisle had the same number of boxes. So far, no stasis box had more than two people, though a number of women – girls, really, in their late teens – did appear to be pregnant.

"If the math holds, we're looking at maybe twelve thousand people here," Peter said. He wanted Charlotte, Thomas, Paul, and Jeff to confirm his math. The number still felt unreal.

"That's the size of my hometown," Linda said in stunned disbelief as she took a step down an aisle. A wave of embarrassment washed over her, like she was invading their privacy.

Dr. Dana Regan set in place her clinical face and approached the stasis boxes. She examined the man in it briefly, and moved to the next box, and then the next.

"This one," she said, not exactly expecting anyone to join her. Speaking to her computer, she began, "Observation notes. Visual examination. Subject appears to be an adult male, early twenties, maybe 170 centimeters or five-foot-five, weighing 120 pounds or 54 kilograms, slight, muscular build. Appears to be of European ancestry." Her voice stopped as she considered that, perhaps, Europe was actually descended from him.

She continued. "He has reddish-brown hair, a broad nose. Teeth appear clean. No tattoos or other markings. The index finger on the left hand appears to have been broken and poorly reset. On subject's right wrist are three interconnected bracelets. The one furthest from his wrist is alternating blue and green fabric. The middle one has red and yellow fabric. The third, set closest to the wrist and therefore the fingers, is a set of beads in a pattern with reds, blues, white, and possibly yellows. The significance is unknown." She continued with a few more observations and then signed off.

Paul Bratton asked, "What made that guy so special?"

"I could see his teeth," she said. "It was almost like he was smiling. Teeth are a good indication of health." Regan looked down the aisle. "I'm not a anthropologist, so I cannot tell you what health conditions looked like thirteen millennia ago. But with just a visual exam, if that man walked into my office, my only reservation about signing him off as fit for duty aboard the *Shackleton* would be that his hair is too long."

Peter stepped back, into the intersection, so he could view several rows of glowing blue boxes. He felt the hairs on his neck stand and, inexplicably, his heart began beating a little faster. He slowed his breathing in an effort to push back the primal panic that had started to churn in his gut.

+ + +

Later, after a radio repeater was installed on the third level, drones were assigned to map the space. Interest in the aquatic life quickly vanished. This latest discovery significantly darkened the mood of the crew. Just entering the walled off section of the third level seemed invasive, inappropriate.

These were people. Thousands of them. All collected and stored as if for sale.

"This all had the feeling of an expansive zoo. It was fun. But this..." Linda Bletchley's voice trailed off. She and Charlotte Smith-Davies were back in Peter's office on the *Shackleton*. They were on a call with what seemed like everyone from Missions Control. This was news Peter decided needed to be delivered in person, not packaged in a report.

"You will forgive me," Peter's father, Ian MacGregor, said. "But this is still a zoo, it is just one that very uncomfortably includes... humans."

Teresa Schultz moved quickly, knowing where her brother was heading, and wanted to cut him off.

"That's a good point, Ian. I think this changes the face of this mission, almost literally. But let's think about what we think we know. On this ship we have found large samples of every kind of life found on Earth. They are not pinned to poster board, but it would seem are alive in those stasis boxes." She could be seen peering at her screen. "Peter, there, on your desk. What is that?"

Peter knew what she was asking. "It's the cactus that I shared a stasis box with for a few hours."

"And it is alive?"

"Yes, ma'am."

"So, who or what collected everything from sea algae to prairie grass seeds to lions, tigers, and humans, seems to have wanted to keep them alive."

"Alive, for almost thirteen thousand years, in a state of suspended animation... What kind of alive is that?" This came from the lawyer, Hanson O'Donnell. "Don't we have a moral obligation, a human obligation, to free these people?"

Charlotte spoke up. "Let me point out something uncomfortable. These people are from our very distant past. Turn back the clock thirteen thousand years, and humans were still six thousand years from writing. They had not yet settled into anything we think of as cities. They were hunter-gatherer nomads. If memory serves, this thirteen-thousand year mark from which we are operating is important. We got that number based on the dust collected on the Object's exterior and seems confirmed by some of the animals we have found in our exploration. But thirteen thousand years ago also corresponds with the Younger Drays extinction event." She paused. "You will all forgive me. As you might know, this is an era which my father held the least controversial of his views."

This drew a chuckle from those who knew Charles Smith-Davies, which she had intended. Charlotte continued. "These people might as well be as alien as little green men, practically. If we 'released' them, we would be releasing them into a world more alien than almost anything we could imagine. We need to exercise caution."

The conversation continued. Finally, Lucy Hyde announced they needed to close out the meeting. "Peter, what do you need from us?"

He looked at the list he made for this meeting. Only one major item remained unaddressed.

"We need some more people out here. Specifically, we need an anthropologist, a forensic scientist, and maybe a medical doctor or two. The four-percent failure rate for these boxes seems to hold pretty steady, and our guess is that there are between 450 and 500 sets of human remains in there. Dr. Regan tells me we could learn a lot with some specialists and specialized equipment."

Lucy nodded. "We'll take that under advisement."

"And two more things," said Peter. "First, there could be a lot more people on this ship. We've looked at three levels of what potentially could be a hundred levels of warehouse space, each with up to thirty or more acres of floor space. So, we need to be able to see more of what this ship has hidden from us."

On the screen, Peter could see both his father and sister nodding in agreement. "And second?" Lucy asked.

"Second, we need a plan for letting some of these folks on the *Shackleton* go home. Every single one of them signed on for hard work a long way from home. But this isn't what anyone expected. No one was prepared for this." Not that anyone could tell, but Peter was looking at the little box in which his father was sitting. After all, almost no one else on this call knew what his dad had known, and Ian betrayed nothing.

"This went from exciting and fun, to depressing and heart-wrenching pretty quickly. I don't care that these people are basically cavemen. They're people."

213

CHAPTER 51

Near Seminole, Texas, USA

"If I had even suspected this was a ship or other form of alien technology, I like to think I would have told you and others much sooner," said Ian MacGregor, sitting at his desk and looking earnestly at the screen. "I know over the years I wasn't the nicest guy to a lot of people, and my reputation from my twenties and thirties haunts me today. In some ways, I still fight that guy. I am repulsed by him, in more ways than you can know."

Ian watched his son fidget. A couple hours had gone by since the group call ended, and Ian could not shake the feeling that his son blamed him for having put the lives of twelve thousand or more ancient strangers in his lap. Not to mention re-writing humanity's understanding of its place in the cosmos.

"I was certain it was some kind of natural phenomenon. A process that was creating gravimetric waves differently from the way we thought of gravity." He shook his head. "I mean, researchers have now unequivocally established the so-called 'grapefruit-size' black holes floating around in space. We can now find them. But those also don't do what I was seeing then." Ian stopped. He was in self-defense mode, with his son, who was at the edge of the solar system.

He wiped away as his right eye. Something was in it. He hoped it was not a tear. He didn't want to be *that* old man. And he did feel responsible for putting the lives of twelve thousand ancient strangers in his son's lap.

"Dad, I don't blame you. I may have sounded like I did,

but I really don't. Unless you are the oldest man on Earth and witnessed your family being scoped up by E.T., then there is no way any rational person would have thought this was a ship containing human specimens," he tried to smile, and hoped it wasn't condescending. "When the alarms went off on the ship, I was absolutely certain it was a malfunction. I never in thirteen thousand years would have guessed an alien artifact was causing the problems."

Ian rubbed again at his right eye. Something was making everything look funny. Eyelash, dust, something.

"I appreciate that, son. Thank you. You and your sisters are what I am most proud of in this, followed very quickly by those men and women with you out there." He smiled, a headache coming on, probably from all this. "Your mother and I simply cannot stop talking about the way you're leading these people, the way Samantha is keeping Lucy in check, and the way Lucy is juggling the millions of details of the crazy business Chris and I gave her."

"Thanks, Dad. By the way, that old paper you gave me to read when you were cleaning up... the one by the doctoral candidate about wormholes, remember it?"

Ian smiled; Dr. W.J. Williams' work from two decades earlier. He'd almost forgotten he'd given a copy to Peter. "Yeah, I gave digital copies to you and to Charlotte, on the off chance this might have been a different kind of wormhole. Her husband gave it a dubious endorsement in a message a few months back. Seems he dislikes the temporal displacement ideas." *What is that?* He thought, smelling something unfamiliar as he rubbed his eye once again.

"Well, I've been reworking some of the assumptions he made. When I catch a break, I'll digitize them and send them your way."

"Alright, son. That sounds great. I need to get off. I'm pretty exhausted, and I bet you, are, too. Please, and I mean this, thank everyone on the *Shackleton*. They, you, are doing history proud."

They ended the connection. Ian sat there a little longer, closing his eyes and wishing the headache away. He just needed to go grab a glass of water and then collapse in bed.

He stood, feeling a little dizzy, steadied himself, and made his way toward the bedroom.

He did not get there.

CHAPTER 52

The Shackleton, *Kuiper Belt*

"Please, and I mean this, thank everyone on the *Shackleton*. They, you, are doing history proud."

"Love you, Dad," Peter said and reached to terminate the connection at the same time his dad did. Immediately his door chimed. "Now what?" he asked the air. Louder, "Come in!"

It was Dr. Regan. This couldn't be good.

"Can I sit?"

"Of course," he said. It really could not be good.

"You like puzzles, don't you Peter?" He blinked his eyes, uncertain where this was going. "I mean, we all know about that ongoing math problem you've been working since we started this trip."

He smiled. "Not math, exactly, but theoretical physics. I'm not a physicist, but my dad has been working the math off and on for years with a professor from New Mexico. It's some pretty obscure wormhole theory stuff. I'm just a starship captain, but if I was going to be a decent starship captain I figured I needed to learn about the physics related to all this. Why?"

Her face softened. "You're not a physicist, and I'm not a pathologist or a forensic scientist. You're a starship captain, and I'm an old-fashion general practice doc."

She smiled. "I just happen to be a very good general practice doc in a spaceship that operates on some pretty outlandish physics. I tell you all of that to let you know what I am about to say may or may not mean anything. So, as soon as we identified each of the 473 human remains from the failed boxes, I had them tagged and sealed. I am going to assume for now the conditions in that room have been exactly the same for as long as they have been in there."

She waited for Peter to nod in understanding.

"I could not tell you how fast a corn seed is supposed to decay, or a dead fish in a vat of water. I'm sure there are other people back home who can tell you such things, but not me. But human bodies, though I know a bit more about. You do physics puzzles? I do flesh and bone puzzles. In some of those places, we found the dust to which we return. That happens. It's a real thing. In most, we found varying degrees of decay. Here is what I think I know: Half of those humans died within the last hundred years."

She let that sink in, then continued. "So the first half died from whatever the malfunctions are in those boxes in the first thirteen thousand years of them being stuck here, the rest occurred in the last hundred years. It makes me think that the stasis process, or just those boxes themselves, have a failure rate that is going to be increasing."

Peter leaned back and nodded. "So being here means we have a chance to save lives?"

"Yes, maybe. But you can also look at it like this: if we weren't here, if we'd never come to this spot in space, they would all be dying anyway. You shouldn't feel the weight of their lives as your personal responsibility," she said. "I know this is hard on you, Peter. It's hard on everyone. On the other hand, there is not a man or woman on this ship who wouldn't trade their own right arm to save lives. You know that, because you picked these people. You know that because you and I both read through every single one of their psychological profiles before we let them get near the ship in the first place."

"Dr. Regan, are you telling me to man up?"

"Peter MacGregor, I am a medical doctor who is almost old enough to be your mo... your older sister." She stood up. "And I am telling you, you have about six hours to mope about this mess being shoved in your lap. After that, it is time to man up and get over there, ignore the second-guessers a solar-system away, and start thinking up how we are going to save lives now that the opportunity has presented itself."

She turned and left his office, pulling the door shut as she went.

Peter looked at his little ancient cactus. "Have I mentioned you have a nicer bedside manner than my doctor?"

CHAPTER 53

The Shackleton, Kuiper Belt

Jeff Prasadh had almost gotten over the fact he was on a live chat with Teresa MacGregor Schultz. She was a living legend, and she was proving it yet again.

As she explained it to Jeff and his new boss, Andrew Todd, within seconds of the massive group meeting about the discovery of humans on board, the translation detection software she had written started spitting out content for review. That content, in turn, she tried to put into context with what she knew from the reports and pictures they had sent to her.

She now had the basics of the written language for the aliens who built this ship.

"Of course, I have no idea how to pronounce anything I'm about to start talking about, but I think we're going to jump from the 'babbling baby' stage of language comprehension to 'toddler.' You boys ready?"

The written language was a hybrid, she explained.

There were aspects that seemed to scream out as being a predecessor of sorts to the still undeciphered Vinča language. Yet she had a context. As the detection software spit out translations, those markings being translated ran the gambit of basic pictograms and signs, to semanto-phonetic compounds more closely aligned with Chinese script.

An early point of contention had been why there seemed to be no "biological relief" stations on the three levels for the people who worked the Object. Did these aliens not have to pee, as Paul Bratton had asked.

Yes, they probably did, was the answer. They now knew this because Teresa had found signs explaining where to find the bathrooms. "This set of markings says, 'Biological relief stations on' a word we don't know, 'deck one and above.'" And so it went.

Andrew was most intrigued by those first markings he had found on the floor of the bay – which had been covered up later while making the *Shackleton* umbilical and Alpha Station airlock. As it turned out, each were indeed intended as lanes of travel, indicating which general type of flora was to go where. As he started moving through his own pictures, he saw now what he had missed before, the same sorts of markings repeating through the bay lanes, to the aisle markers, and then to the individual stasis boxes.

He used his stylus to mark a picture on their shared display. "This lane includes what seems to be 'edible plants,' it leads to aisles which include vegetation that could be safely consumed." He paused. "Could the aliens eat our plants?"

Each of them agreed it was a good question, but probably not knowable at this time.

"It could also mean something like, 'these plants are edible by the alpha hunter-gatherers on this planet,'" Teresa offered. "The point is, we don't know exactly what they meant by what they wrote, but we do now have an idea about what they were writing. Let's keep going."

Their task now was to load the translation matrix into the *Shackleton*-based VR headset and go see if predictive theory held with reality. If so, there might be doors they had missed leading to elevators, offices, equipment... and, yes, even easy ways to the "biological relief stations."

Possibly, it would eventually lead them to the aliens who had established this menagerie in the first place.

CHAPTER 54

Alpha Base, The Object, Kuiper Belt

Peter MacGregor needed to clear his head, and for that he decided to take a walk. That, in turn, led him to the Object. But now, here he was, just standing in what had been a loading bay and was now tied via an umbilical bridge to his ship.

"Captain, can I help you?" asked Andrew Todd, who emerged from the alcove in which they and ten others had used as a living room when the *Shackleton* had retrieved the remaining members of the *Henson*'s crew from their ship.

"Uh, no. What, um, what are you doing?"

"Your aunt, um, Dr. Schultz, she has me and Jeff Prasadh doing some tests with the translation work. We think we have a good working model of the written language."

"Wait... Translations?"

"Yes, sir. It looks like we have a pretty reliable–"

"Why wasn't I told?"

"Well, sir, I figured Dr. Schultz or Station messaged you..."

"Well, they didn't," Peter snapped back. He took a deep breath. "Or, maybe they did. I'm sorry, forgive me." He pulled out his tablet. There were a number of messages waiting for him, most offering thoughts and concerns about his father. One, however, from Yua Saito, was labelled "Translation Success."

Andrew Todd looked his captain over. "Is everything alright?"

Peter looked around. "I got word an hour or so ago that right after a call my dad and I had, he collapsed in his bedroom from what appears to be a massive stroke. It will be a while until there is more information. And so, I..." He should not be telling this to Andrew Todd. "I'm sorry."

"No, sir. I get it. No worries."

"So, tell me about this." Peter nodded to the headset. The younger man took the hint.

"We loaded the translation matrix into the headset to give a real-time translation for whatever text we're looking at." He handed the pair in his hand to Peter, who slipped them over his eyes. The computer scanned Peter's retinas, took spatial measurements, and immediately rendered the world just as it had looked a moment before. He knew he was wearing the headset only because he could feel the weight of wearing the device.

Andrew continued. "We're just going around comparing what we see written to what, well, we see."

"You have an extra set?" Peter asked before taking them off.

"Sure."

"I'll join you guys."

Which is how Peter MacGregor, Andrew Todd, and Jeff Prasadh found themselves together on the second level of the Object. Andrew pointed to the staircase leading to the observation platform. "I forgot to mention it earlier, but did you notice the rendering of the funny symbol on and around the doors?"

MacGregor looked over. The symbol was faintly visible under the rendered words. "Uneasy planet," he read out loud. "That makes a strange sort of sense."

"I think that it should be something like, 'Warning: Gravity Shift.' What do you think, sir?" asked Prasadh.

"I agree. Can you update that?" In seconds, the change was done. "Cool."

As they walked past a series of stasis boxes, holding rabbits, the translations shifted rapidly. "Unknown" appeared in large letters in the field of view. Under it, "small, fast, coastal" which then flipped to "sylvilagus bachmani" then "western bush rabbit" and back to "small, fast, coastal." Peter didn't know his rabbits, but it seemed plausible.

"I don't understand. How is this rendering names?"

"It's not," Prasadh said. "As Dr. Schultz described it, what we see happening is the system is reading the name, which it shows in the VR as 'unknown.' If you took off the headset, what you would be seeing are characters that mean nothing to us, and then under them more characters that mean nothing. Well, for us, the system is reading the written text, and then extrapolating. That's where the 'small, fast, coastal' is coming from. This rabbit is obviously being described that way under whatever the name is. So here, we find some word that the matrix simply cannot render, so it renders 'unknown' and that is visible. Next, it renders the next set of text, whatever short description is being used. Lastly, the system recognizes this as a 'western bush rabbit,' so the matrix renders that and the scientific name."

"Okay, thanks. That makes sense."

"In fairness," added Todd. "We were warned by your aunt this all works much better when we're looking at things without names."

They walked out of the aisles and looked at the walls. The difference was immediate. What in the real world looked like meaningless splashes of paint, were in VR suddenly rendered as helpful warnings or informational notifications.

These included: Keep Objects Neatly Organized When Loading, No Breathing In Of Poison, Keep Drink From Deck, Fast Abandonment Access.

The last one intrigued them all. "Fast Abandonment Access" also rendered an arrow pointing right. Peter dialed up the transparency, letting him see the arrow was being translated from a long horizontal line with a block on the rightward end. The staircase to the observation room had a line at 45 degrees with a block on the upward end. He shook his head. The directions were staring them in the face.

The group followed the "Fast Abandonment Access" until they reached a section of bulkhead where nothing was written except the words "Fast Abandonment Access." They looked and finally found a dim light running left to right that was pulsing blue, compared to the steady yellow that they had found with previous doors. Opening that door was out of the question, since it was obviously air-tight. They would have to explore that another time.

Andrew Todd reacted to something. He nodded. "Sir, I fed my comms into my VR headset. We're being asked to come upstairs and check out a translation on what appears to be a drop-down staircase like we have seen in the past."

They walked through aisles of naked and mostly naked humans, heading for the location they had been given. Peter stopped at one intersection.

"Do you guys see this?" He pointed at a yellow line on the floor. The VR headset rendered the writing on the line as "Unknown" followed by "House Only" and an arrow. He walked across the yellow line.

He looked carefully at each of the humans in stasis. And then he saw it. Everyone over the age of... he walked the aisle checking both sides. Well, it seemed like starting at puberty everyone had two bracelets made from fabric. By the late teens, a third bracelet of beads was added, closest to the wrist. For everyone on this aisle, the fabric bracelet furthest from the wrist was red and blue. The second bracelet, therefore closer to the wrist, were all the same pattern of green, red, yellow, and white. The third bracelets, made of beads, were of a variety of colors and patterns.

Peter checked the yellow line and moved to the next aisle. Again, the fabric bracelet furthest from the wrist was red and blue. Approximately half of these people had a second bracelet a green, red, yellow, and white matching the other aisle. The other half had a second bracelet with black, yellow, and white. The beads were different... but some were the same.

He then crossed the yellow line. The bracelets furthest

from the wrist were no longer red and blue, but now green and yellow. He cross back to the original aisle, where his colleagues were staring at him.

"The first bracelet refers to the House of whatever. This line says, 'Only our humans go here.' These people are slaves."

Andrew spoke without thinking. "I think you are making a leap. For all we know, these people are the 'House' of whatever." He then caught himself. "Sorry, a little out of line."

"No, please don't apologize. Maybe you're right. I have a gut feeling, but you should never let me just state my opinion as a fact." He paused. "Observation note. The floor in the human stasis box area seems to be marked up by 'houses,' whatever that means. Need a scan and map of theses so-called houses, cross-matched with the color of the bracelets. Focus on the bracelet colors furthest from the wrist, and see if there is a correlation with the house names."

They continued on to where Thomas Newcome was standing with several of the *Shackleton* crew. Among them was Nelson Timms, who had been on Object with MacGregor when *Shackleton* went to *Henson*'s aid.

Timms greeted his captain and said, "We think this is another staircase, but we figured that now that the translation software exists, it would be good having the translation team look before we started opening doors."

Apparently the entire crew knew there was a translation test going on, Peter realized with a bit of barely concealed embarrassment.

The three men with the VR headset looked at the pinpoint of light originating from the ceiling, running along the support beam and down to the floor. The ceiling had nothing, but the support beam was a treasure trove of words, messages and warnings.

And an arrow was pointing up, with a hazard symbol that the translation matrix rendered as a falling object. That was appropriate enough. "Fast Access To Deck We Who Are The People." In smaller text were the words, "Moving Room" and an arrow that pointed towards the exterior of the ship.

Jeff Prasadh said, "I'd wager next week's pay that 'Moving Room' is really 'elevator.' The rest is straightforward. There is another level up, and it has more people."

As everyone moved out of the way, Peter tried to remember what the translation matrix had displayed for the markings on the door leading into the human area. He asked Andrew if he recalled. "I didn't even think to look, sir. Sorry. I'll make a note to check it when we head back."

Peter had a thought as the stairway assembled itself. He pulled out his tablet and flipped to the series of drone photos of that level, first flipping too far one way into the pictures of the people, and then too far the other way to the aquatic life boxes.

As he did so, Thomas Newcome and Nelson Timms mounted the stairs first, flipping on their lights. Andrew Todd followed, aware his captain was standing still. He looked back and saw MacGregor staring at his tablet. He could tell it was an image of the doors leading into the previous chamber, the one with the humans. The captain wasn't saying anything, just staring.

Andrew Todd took a step back down and walked up beside his boss, allowing his own headset to render a translation for the wall markings. As he did so, he heard Thomas Newcome and Nelson Timms both issue forth a series of startled profanities.

The translation on MacGregor's tablet read: "Those Who Serve Us."

CHAPTER 55

Level Four, The Object, Kuiper Belt

Taking the stairs three at a time, Andrew Todd and Peter MacGregor both pulled off their headsets and raced to the top. The rest of the group was crowded at the head of the staircase. The captain pushed through them, and barely stopped himself from gasping. He forced down whatever emotion he felt. Fear? Horror?

Standing before them was a man, holding a device that looked like a gun but had no obvious trigger. On his head, worn like a hat, was a human skull without the jawbone attached to a shimmering fabric cover that revealed only his eyes. He wore a long jacket which ended at the knees, just above high boots. This person was standing rigidly at attention. It took a moment to realize it was a statue.

Everyone collected themselves as they processed what they were seeing.

The group began turning carefully, getting a view of what was around them. The level seemed more like the first two than the third. It was wide open, with only aisles of stasis boxes and support columns in the way.

The biggest difference was that the blue of these stasis fields was more intense. It was almost impossible to see details of the people inside. What was immediately obvious was that these people were clothed – though at first glance no one seemed as garishly dressed as the statue which had greeted them. For the moment, no one strayed too far from the staircase.

"These stasis boxes seem more sturdy." Thomas

Newcome was the first to say anything. "The people inside all seem to have a human form, and are wearing clothes." As an afterthought he added, "Which is an improvement, I guess."

Peter was still studying the statue. On inspection, the skull used as a hat seemed... fake. There were none of the lines and marks of an actual skull, from where the plates fuse together in the early teen years. The statue itself was shorter than Peter, like nearly all the men in the level below, but he was of a much stockier build. The jacket was lined with metal threads woven into a dark fabric. The boots were functional, with what appeared to be rubber soles.

Unlike the lower chambers, each of the stasis boxes were set on what appeared to be pedestals from which the person could step out, pause, and then step down onto the floor. It was Nelson Timms who noticed the pedestal contained a drawer. Another drawer was on top of each box. The stasis boxes were all slightly larger than the boxes for the humans below, and none of the boxes in their immediate area contained more than one shadowy figure.

"MacGregor to Alpha Base. We need drones to meet us outside the human holding area."

+++

A rough census by the artificial intelligence matrix, using all of *Shackleton*'s improvised drone imagery, took about three hours. It found close to 20,000 "We Who Are The People" stasis boxes on this fourth level of the Object. It identified what appeared to be 381 – two percent – dark stasis boxes; all of them would be checked for signs of remains that could be studied.

Peter was now joined by Linda Bletchley, Dana Regan, Charlotte Smith-Davies, and Thomas Newcome, next to one of the dark boxes closest to the staircase. An engineering team had just begun installing lights.

This particular stasis box had malfunctioned long

enough ago that very little remained besides bones and articles of clothing. The person – creature? alien? – had rotted away a long time ago.

Peter knelt down, pushing fabric away with a stylus, and opened the drawer with a gloved hand. The space had been vacuum sealed, requiring a little more of a pull than he had expected. Inside, he found and removed easily identifiable things. Two shirts, two pairs of pants, two pairs of shorts which might have also been undergarments. A pair of low-cut shoes, and several articles of jewelry. All of which he placed in a carry-all box that had brought up from the Alpha Base staging area.

He then stood, and pulled on the upper drawer. It also had an air-tight seal. Inside were a series of papers, more pants, a shirt, shoes, and small leather case. All of which he set in the carry-all.

"I'm now going to purposefully disturb these remains," he announced, as he riffled through the jumble of bones and fabric. He pulled a bag that had apparently been draped over one shoulder and across the torso. It was almost indistinguishable from the messenger bags people had now been wearing for nearly a century. If he slipped it on and walked down a boulevard in Anywhere Europe, no one would have noticed.

Inside the bag he found several coins, papers bound by a leather strap, and what appeared to be a pocket knife. He examined markings along the bag's strap, which he had not noticed at first. Like the bag itself, the strap was leather – but the entire length of the strap alternated between two inches of red and blue fabric sewn into the leather, a six-inch strip of exposed leather, followed by two more inches of red and blue fabric.

Peter dropped the bag unceremoniously into the box, and said, "Follow me." His confused party did so without hesitation as Peter strapped the VR headset back to his head, looking down at the floor.

"Gotcha!" he yelled. Two yellow lines ran down the aisle. On side, with an arrow pointing to where they had come, was the same unknown symbol he had seen downstairs, probably a name, with the words "House At This Place." The other yellow line had an arrow pointing the other other way, a different symbol, and the words "House At This Place."

The red and blue fabric on the bag's strap. The red and blue fabric on the bracelet.

"The people up here are clothed, they have belongings. Personal items, trinkets, even some reading materials. I'll bet you guys a steak dinner back on Earth that was basically a thirteen-thousand-year-old brain-candy novel I pulled from the bag. That rotted away person there liked to advertise that he or she was from the Red-Blue House. It's on an accessory. The naked person down below? He had that tight-fitting bracelet on his hand. I suspect it was a sign of ownership. Those people downstairs are called 'Those Who Serve Us' while this group is called 'We Who Are The People.'"

Everyone was nodding in apparent agreement. Peter hoped that it was not because they thought he had lost his mind. He, in fact, hoped he had not lost his mind.

"These people are the masters," he pointed ahead of him. "And those are either indentured servants or slaves. Who put them here and built this thing? I have no idea, but it seems clear to me there is a master-slave relationship between the seventeen-thousand naked humans down there, and the twenty-thousand clothed people up here. My guess? We haven't yet found the last of these 'We Who Are The People' on the Object."

CHAPTER 56

Executive Offices, Station, HEO

"The ship doctor tells me Peter has thrown himself into work like a madman," Lucy MacGregor Hyde was saying to her sister, Samantha, over a video chat.

"Mom says he checks in with her every other day, to see about Dad, but I haven't heard anything from him," Samantha MacGregor Porter added. As the oldest of the MacGregor siblings she had developed a matriarchal view towards her "youngers" long before she had children of her own. Some, specifically Lucy and Peter, would claim she had had that attitude since they were all three children. In fact, in their teens, Lucy had had a slightly different – and more profane – word by which to describe the oldest sibling. Whichever word was used, Samantha thought, it was probably true after a fashion. "What about you? Anything?"

"Only his mission reports, and then every time with one of his staff present. I've decided not to press it," she said. "My read is that he feels guilty over being the last person with whom Dad spoke."

"Mom was listening to the whole thing. She said it was a sweet call. I think Peter is overreacting, irrationally, if he blames himself." Samantha paused. "And I fear it is going to affect his work. Based on what I'm seeing, he's basically ignoring the archeologists' recommendations on how they should proceed. He's tearing through the Object."

Lucy nodded, but then shook her head. "I think 'tearing through' is a little strong, but not much. He's definitely pushing the envelope on what the archeologists would like for him to be doing."

"Well, since one of those archeologists is my brother-in-law, I would appreciate it if we could figure out a way for Peter to take a deep breath. Maybe he should come home?"

Lucy laughed. "I may be his boss, but I don't think I'll be suggesting that. Looks like Dr. Regan has basically had to force a third of the crew to agree to leave, for the relief-rotation we've set up."

"She could force him to leave."

"She could, but then she's also not on the rotation," said Lucy. "Basically, the only people returning are those who have spouses and children back here or on Mars. And even those *Shackleton* crew members are demanding to know when they'd be back. One minute, Peter is demanding a rotation schedule be established for his people, and the next, like just after Dad's stroke, he and the rest of the crew have gone maniac about the work. Is obsessive-compulsive disorder an infectious thing?"

An alert chimed on the display Lucy kept set to a financial news site she preferred. It was, of course, about the latest war engulfing the African continent. While both countries denied it, India and China were using Africa as a proxy for their latest round of economic fights. The death toll was rising, which meant the world was focused on it. Buzzing questions from a few weeks back about a QA diamond mining operation on the edge of the solar system had evaporated when images of the newest Chinese tanks bearing the Kenyan National Unity Party emblems were seen rolling across Egypt's southern border.

It was hard to imagine anyone on the planet cared about what the *Shackleton* was doing. Maybe, Lucy thought, if they knew what had been found...

In those weeks, a ring of elevators had been discovered by the *Shackleton* crew that ran from the fourth level – the first level of "We Who Are The People" – to the eighty-second level of the Object. That fourth level, it turned out, had two sets of exterior doors next to each other opening into a massive bay.

In the bay itself, a single bay door led into the warehouse. The ring of elevators began on either side of that. Each elevator was marked with deck numbers and bands of colors – apparently a representation of "houses." So far, at least, Peter's theory about the House or clan division had been adopted by the small team of reputable experts assembled on Station as a council of advisors.

If the coloring system was correct, there were ten houses. Yet no House occupied a single deck. Instead, all ten Houses seemed to be represented on each deck. Maybe the colors had nothing to do with Houses at all. But it made sense, based on the facts.

Like the original exterior bay doors, the elevators were of a strange hybrid of designs. The elevator doors opened and closed like accordions, without any mechanical or electric assistance. Every part of the ancient ship felt like a combination of 19th century and 21st century technologies. One of the Station engineers, in reviewing images, said it looked like it had been designed by Jules Verne.

The original review of the fourth deck had been accurate. The warehouse space was smaller. That continued as high as they had yet been, to the eighty-second deck. Each of those decks was laid out exactly the same with the exception of a loading bay. That meant each of these decks had approximately 20,000 stasis boxes. In all, one and a half million "We Who Are The People" were on the Object.

The remaining space they could access on each deck was composed of storage lockers filled with furniture, clothing, desks, tables, tools, farming equipment, and assorted materials – fabrics, metal ingots and the like. And books. A lot of books. The Station-assembled advisors successfully pressed on MacGregor the importance of leaving the books untouched until special scanning equipment could arrive on the promised relief vessel.

There were also massive stasis boxes filled with food, some easily recognizable fruits, vegetables, and breads. Some of the foodstuffs appeared particularly unappetizing. Between samples of every conceivable seed, plant, insect, fish, and animal, these stasis boxes included food ready to eat.

On the first three decks, the four percent failure rate for the stasis boxes held, as did the recognization the boxes had begun failing more rapidly. On these higher decks, the rate seemed to be about two percent, though they had not yet found evidence that any had failed recently... whatever "recently" meant on an Object that had been floating at the edge of the solar system for thirteen millennia.

When the boxes failed, though, the living creatures inside seemed to die without a struggle. They just collapsed against the wall of the box, which implied there was something else at work besides the still-unexplained stasis system.

+++

"Well, speak of the devil," Lucy said to her sister. "Peter is calling me. Want to be on?"

"Absolutely," replied Samantha as Lucy tapped her keyboard. The screen split in two, Samantha on one side, and the other a blank box. For a moment it was filled with the logo of the *Shackleton*, and then Peter's face resolved into focus. He was in his ship-board office. The small cactus still there.

"One call, two sisters. Were y'all talking about me?" he said by way of greeting.

"Yes, Peter," Samantha said. "Because we can only have conversations that involve you."

"Good," he said. "Well, I've got Dr. Regan with me." Lucy shot a barely perceptible *see-I-told-you-so* glance at her older sister, who immediately got it; Peter didn't seem to notice. The screen split again, because Regan was not actually in Peter's office. She was in the make-shift medical facility on the Object.

"Dr. Regan," he introduced, "would you mind explaining?"

Three hours earlier, while exploring the seventy-seventh deck, crew members were just down the aisle from a stasis box when they saw the now-familiar blue shimmering glow suddenly begin flashing yellow and red. They got to the box in time to see the color shift back to blue and then fade as it died. The man inside fell against the back of the box and slid to the floor. He remained unconscious even as he appeared to be struggling to breath. The two crew members rushed to administer first aid and call for medics.

The man opened his eyes wide for a moment, seemingly focused on the two men helping him, and cried, "Oo'pub?" He passed out again, and then he died.

Regan rushed him to the examination room and begun an autopsy.

"The bottomline is that he is human, but not the way we are," said Regan. "I've consulted every record I can access, but before I talked to the advisory team, Peter and I wanted you to hear the results, first." She paused and looked down. Lucy was thankful the body was out of the camera shot, and hoped it stayed that way. Knowing she could be heard, Dr. Regan said, "I'm not in the practice of making surgeries or autopsies a public spectacle. You can get the video if you want, but let me describe a couple things.

"The eye orbits are rectangular, and the brain capacity is about a quarter to a half again as large as is typical for us. This man was in his early thirties, finger and toe nails were manicured, no evidence of any physical trauma except x-rays revealed evidence of a broken arm in his youth," she paused. "I ran his DNA through our databases. Some related matches show up. He's human. Except... he is not exactly our kind of human."

CHAPTER 57

The Shackleton, Kuiper belt

"Are you some kind of quack? Do you really expect us to believe that the Neanderthals built the Object and flew it out there?" asked an incredulous anthropologist of Dr. Regan. This massive meeting had been hastily arranged to discuss her shocking findings. Close to two hundred people were taking part, and it appeared some number of them felt the anthropologist might be right.

For his part, Peter MacGregor wanted to beat the man to a bloody pulp for challenging her findings and interrupting her presentation.

"I have suggested no such thing," Dr. Regan replied with a kind of calm Peter frankly had not expected.

"Let me repeat for the slow or the distracted. The genetic testing I have done on the recently deceased man from the upper levels of the Object show elements of Early Anatomically Modern Humans, some of which are known as Cro-Magnons. And, yes, there is an even stronger genetic relationship to the profiles researchers have established for Neanderthals. Elements. A relationship. I cannot tell you exactly what this person is, but I can tell you what the genetic testing tells us," she paused. "I am not an engineer, an archeologist, an anthropologist, or a duck, so I cannot speak to who built the Object, but I can tell you without a shadow of a doubt is that this man appeared to be a modern human, but with DNA that includes... well, much stronger connections to Neanderthals than most of the people on this call."

Teresa Schultz, who had been silent up until this point,

spoke up rather than laugh. "Hopefully I can say what I want to say without being accused of being a quack, but I think that Dr. Regan has done an excellent job of chasing the data where it leads, not to where our biases or the biases of our colleagues would rather us go."

No one challenged her.

She continued. "Up until now, we have operated on the assumption, without anyone explicitly saying it, that extraterrestrials had collected a wide variety of plant and animal samples from Earth. This may or may not have been the case. I would like for us to be open to all of the possibilities." She paused.

"Let me offer three observations. One, this Object exists where no predictive model of established science said it would. Two, the Object itself is evidence that some thirteen-thousand years ago there was a space-faring population that did indeed gather samples of life on Earth. Three, the Object with its collection did go to the very edge of the solar system," Teresa took a deep breath. "Why is it easier to believe that an alien intelligence would gather up a large number of the intelligent species on Earth, rather than a previously unknown terrestrial intelligence? I do not have the answers, but what I know is that we should follow the facts without bias. I personally would expect those of us who are scientists to practice that, and appreciate Dr. Regan for having done so."

No one spoke for a long moment.

Peter MacGregor, addressing the attendees from his small ship-board office, then spoke. "The equipment coming out to us on the *Byrd* will be important for a great many reasons. As you all know, we think there are five or as many as ten levels remaining, but we haven't found how to reach them yet. We expect we might find the operational controls for the Object, and perhaps that could contain the answers we're looking to find. And to Dr. Schultz' point, I suspect if nothing else that is where we will find out more about who was actually running the show."

A pathologist, who was participating from her cabin aboard the *Byrd*, heading for the *Shackleton* with the relief personnel and requested equipment, spoke up. "Dr. Regan, the blood work on the man shows some strange chemical compounds. Any idea what those could be?"

"Add 'ancient pharmaceutical expert' to the things I am not," said Regan, eliciting a chuckle from numerous participants. "Whatever it is, it started breaking down fairly quickly when the stasis box failed, but I'm still looking. Maybe the equipment you're bringing can tease the results out better than what we have here."

One of the consulting engineers asked about the lack of information available on the basic mechanics of the Object. "You'll forgive me for changing topics, but I had hoped by now we'd know what was powering the Object systems, and by what means it got to where it is."

The *Shackleton*'s engineer, Benny Hathaway, chimed in. "Javier, Benny here. I know what you are saying. I feel the same way. Right now, about 25 percent of the space between levels four and eighty-two has not been accessible to us. The mapping we have done puts the space like a massive spine running along the inside of the Object. For obvious reasons, we have not wanted to start cutting into bulkheads. With the equipment coming on the *Byrd*, we hope to be able to peer through the exterior skin to see what's in there. My guess? That's where we find powertrain and mechanical sections." He paused. "And let's not forget about what we will never see: the mangled area that was destroyed at some point in the past. For all we know, that's where the primary engines were."

Questions went back to the various humans found on board, to the chemical compounds in their blood, and lastly to the efforts taken to ensure viable samples for testing remained. Teresa Schultz asked to visit with the crew members who found the man, so she could hear from them what they had heard him say.

The conference only ran two hours, and Peter was

thankful when it ended. By pre-agreement, he met Benny Hathaway, Dana Regan, and Andrew Todd in the Galley as soon as it concluded.

"Your sister, Samantha, sent me a note saying she wanted to punch the guy. I think I like all the women in your family, Peter."

He smiled. "I think Teresa put him in his place."

"That she did."

Andrew Todd spoke up, his mind not on what was being said by his colleagues. "Remember that very first elevator shaft we found on that first trip?"

"I do," replied Peter, uncertain where this was going.

"Well, I've been thinking. We haven't come across that shaft anywhere else on the ship. There was that one access point to the first level. It was blocked the rest of the way up by an elevator car." He called up a three-dimensional rendering of the Object, "Where that elevator shaft runs is right next to the 'spine' Benny mentioned. With everything else we found, trying to get up that shaft, and around the stopped elevator car, never seemed like a priority. But I just wonder where it goes."

"Mr. Todd, are you suggesting a walk?"

CHAPTER 58

Near Seminole, Texas, U.S.A.

After the conference ended, Lucy Hyde had spent thirty minutes on follow up calls with her various department heads – making sure everything the *Shackleton* needed, it would be getting. Her last call was to her general counsel, Hanson O'Donnell.

"I want that guy off the project, off Station, and unemployable unless he sends a personal apology to every single person on the call, and especially to Dr. Regan. The people on the *Shackleton* don't deserve that kind of nonsense. It may fly in seminars on college campuses, but not here, and not now."

"Hope you don't mind, but I already put that in motion," O'Donnell said. "He'll be sending me a copy of the apologies."

"Thank you, Hanson," she said. "One more thing. I need you to track someone down for me and arrange a meeting, preferably for today."

O'Donnell looked a little confused; he wasn't usually called on to set up meetings. Though, of course, he would... "Who is it?"

"That's the problem, I don't know for sure. Do you remember when I was working in your office?"

"Yes, like yesterday, and you absolutely remain my favorite college intern," he said with over-done sincerity.

She laughed, and added, "You had me reviewing all the pre-patent research QA had bought and then shelved."

He nodded, "Yes. We have interns and first-year associates do a regular inventory of those. Keep the records updated for easy retrieval by our research teams."

"Right, so I probably looked over hundreds that summer, but I think one is going to be really important. I want to find the researcher, but the patents aren't available for me to search."

"We keep those locked down and the records air-gapped. Most of the patents we acquired, especially prior to your time, we did through third-parties or with tight non-disclosures. Chris Stoddard and your dad didn't exactly want to advertise they were buying, so as to avoid being constantly pitched. Tell me what you remember, and I'll get someone on it."

"Thanks, but I need this to actually be you, and I need the utmost discretion in setting up the meeting."

CHAPTER 59

Dayton, Ohio, U.S.A.

Max Prasadh slipped his tablet into the beaten up leather briefcase he had carried for thirty years. He checked around his office to be sure he had everything, then checked his watch. He had plenty of time to get home, relax, and change clothes before his date. This would be his third date, actually.

"Jeff would be so proud," he giggled like a school boy, and caught himself. That would be undignified for a man in his position. Tonight's date would feature dinner at a restaurant just off campus, followed by a production of "The Tempest" put on by the theater department.

He reached down to message his assistant that he was, indeed, leaving, when his office intercom chimed. He answered, "Yes?"

"Max, this is Justine, I'm sorry to do this, but can you come to my office?" the Dean of the College of Medicine, his boss, asked. "It's urgent."

He did not actually need to rest before the night out, and he was dressed appropriately enough for a quick dinner and the theater, if it came to that.

"I'll be right there." He grabbed his briefcase and hat. He vowed to make it clear to her he was done for the day, and this "urgent" meeting should also be brief.

Fortunately, her office was one floor up. He took the stairs, as he always did, and was in the receptionist's office two minutes later. Two beefy men were occupying the visitor chairs, but the receptionist herself was nowhere to be seen. Both men looked as if they were expecting him, which was a strange feeling. One stood, a concealed handgun briefly visible as the man's jacket flapped, like some sort of police officer.

"Dr. Prasadh," the man said, "they are waiting for you inside."

Max nodded and walked to the door, which was not quite closed. Inside he saw his friend and boss, Justine Martin. She had just started as the dean of the college when she recruited Max years earlier to move to Dayton and take a position at Wright State College. Her offer had not been the most lucrative, but he liked her and her staff. It was also nice that thee college's aerospace medicine program, his field of accidental speciality, had been one of the best in the country for several decades.

Justine was sitting not at her desk, but in one of the soft chairs placed around a small table she used when conducting personnel reviews. He immediately recognized the guest. It was the chief executive of QA, Lucy Hyde. His heart skipped a beat.

"Has something happened to my son?" he asked in horror. It had to be bad if Hyde herself was delivering the news.

"No, absolutely not," said Lucy Hyde, embarrassed she hadn't considered that as his response.

Max's eyes darted to the dean of the college. "So this isn't about Jeff?"

"No, no, Max. I'm sorry. I don't think so..." her voice trailed off, looking to her guest.

For her part, Lucy Hyde was trying to push past her embarrassment. She had not realized, until entering the dean's office ten minutes before, that Dr. Max Prasadh's son had been on the *Henson* as part of the communications team, and was now on board the *Shackleton*.

She stood and extended her hand.

"No, Dr. Prasadh, Jeff is doing very well. You'll forgive me, until just a moment ago I hadn't made the connection." She made a mental note that, in the future, participants in every meeting would be checked to see if there were immediate family connections with the company.

Max dropped his hat and briefcase with a heavy sigh in an empty chair, and took a seat himself. "Old men don't need scares like that," he said with a smile.

Justine Martin stood. "I'm going to leave the two of you to your discussion. I'll be down the hall if you need me."

Well, Max thought, this is strange.

It was no secret QA had been a supporter of the college. A few weeks ago, one of his colleagues – a woman he did not know well – took a sudden leave of absence, reportedly to do a project with QA.

Lucy took a folder from her briefcase, opened it, and removed a thick stack of bound papers. She handed it to him.

"Dr. Prasadh, do you remember this?"

The letterhead was from the University of Kansas' School of Medicine. It was a copy of a letter from more than thirty years earlier letting him know about the approval of a research grant. He took the tabbed folders from her and flipped through the pages.

It was the executive study of his research findings, then a patent application, and, lastly, a letter from the private science foundation which had been the ultimate funder of his work. The foundation had offered to buy from him the research results and data for an unheard of sum of money. All for a project that would not deliver anything of value any time soon.

"Well, the last several pages are the original non-disclosure agreements I signed about this entire thing with the McKenzie Foundation for Scientific Research, which states I am not to disclose knowledge of any of this," he paused. "I'm an intelligent man, so I am going to assume because you have the original signed copies, that the McKenzie Foundation was somehow connected to QA?"

"Yes, McKenzie was my grandmother's maiden name. The private research foundation was established in her honor by my father. Dad said when everyone else thought he was just a crazy kid, she set aside money to buy him books and telescopes. So he decided to set up a foundation that would, in her name, keep doing that."

"I was sorry to hear about your father."

"Thank you," Lucy said, shifting in her seat. These last several weeks of pregnancy were less comfortable than the books and her friends had let on. "As it turns out, you had some really interesting ideas about how to help people survive the rigors of space travel."

He smiled. "That isn't actually what started me down that path. But the joy of scientific research is we sometimes we end up in places we don't intend. I was looking to help people suffering extreme pain from accidents. Turns out, some non-addictive medicines were developed just after I began my initial research. I was ready to toss the project aside when a friend suggested I look at other applications."

He shuffled through the papers. "We had our first big breakthrough the day of QA's first grav-drive launch." He looked up. "At the time, I wasn't sure if that had again killed my research, like those drugs had, but the offer to purchase the data and related work made me think someone thought it wasn't too crazy."

Lucy nodded. "Not too crazy, indeed. Dr. Prasadh, it turns out your research was more important than you or anyone realized, even if not for reasons you'll be able to guess. I'm going need to ask you to sign some new non-disclosures, and then tomorrow we'll have transportation to take you to Station for a briefing, if you're willing."

CHAPTER 60

The Object, Kuiper Belt

"Why, Benny, that suit looks very nice on you," Peter said through the EVA suit radios. For this excursion, it would be just the captain, his chief engineer, and the always-ready-to-EVA Andrew Todd.

"Don't think I won't just turn around and hop back over to our ship," Hathaway said with a gruff laugh. He wasn't a fan of being outside. One had a ship, he often said, precisely to avoid being outside it.

Now that they had something by which to compare them to, this elevator shaft was a tight fit – the others accommodated cars intended to carry dozens or even hundreds. By contrast, the cars traveling in this shaft – such as the one blocking the way above them – would hold no more than ten people. There also wasn't an easy way around the elevator car that seems to have been wedged into the shaft, probably a result of whatever had mangled the bottom of the Object.

"If you can't go over it, and can't go around it, then you gotta go through it," Hathaway said. He pulled a cutting torch from the case that was floating behind him on a tether and went to work.

In a few minutes, the ring of smoldering metal was floating free. The heat quickly dissipated in the cold of space. He entered the elevator car, and immediately went to work on the ceiling. When that was done, Peter and Todd pushed through the openings and joined him on the roof. All three men craned their necks as far as the EVA helmets would allow.

Peter let out a low whistle. "How is it that we are in outer space, surrounded by infinity, and yet a kilometer looks like a really long way?"

While the engineer put the cutting device back in its box, Peter and Andrew took careful readings and found nothing else in their way. In minutes, all three had their suits' miniature thrusters engaged and were moving up the shaft.

As predicted, there were no doors to be seen; this was an express elevator.

"We're passing the seventh level now," Hathaway said, checking their position against the Object maps that been had created over the last several weeks. The three men slowed their rate of ascent. Up ahead, their lights played against a door. Another door was above it. By agreement, they passed both and went to the top of the shaft – flying by three more sets of doors.

"We're about 10 meters from the top, give or take," observed Hathaway. "I counted only five sets of doors."

"Me, too," said Todd. "Which one should we try?"

"Let's go back to the first one. That's worked well enough," said MacGregor.

They moved back down the shaft, where Benny Hathaway gave the door a careful review. "It appears airtight. We should assume there's atmosphere on the other side."

He and Peter began assembling the portable airlock while Andrew contacted the *Shackleton* with an update. Once assembled, they all squeezed into the tent-like structure, sealed in, and went to work opening the elevator door. In moments they could feel the air pressure building in the portable airlock. With almost no effort, the door slid open.

They came out onto a hallway, which curved following the exterior of the Object. Their lights pierced the darkness. On the left side of the hall was the solid exterior wall; to the right, doors and what appeared to be passageways.

The first door was set several feet from the elevator. Benny Hathaway pushed it open, revealing several dozen stasis boxes set in the middle of the room. In addition to the soft blue glow of the stasis chambers, lights in the ceiling softly emitted a gentle yellow-white light. This was different from everywhere else on the ship, which other than the stasis boxes had been draped in complete darkness.

But that made sense; there was no need to leave the lights on if everyone was going to be asleep.

"So what makes this room special?" Peter asked out loud.

"You should turn on your helmet's VR and translation matrix," Andrew said to his captain and the ship's engineer. His was already active.

The stasis pods contained more of the same kind of people as below. No little green men. Even through the nearly opaque blue shimmer, it was obvious these people were all dressed more uniformly. Indeed, they appeared to be wearing uniforms.

The room itself had several work tables, where tools – some obviously hammers and screw drivers or their analogues, and others of unknown purpose – were affixed to the walls. At the far end of the room was a set of sliding doors. It was marked, according to the translation matrix, "To Holy Temple." Looking back, the other door from which they had entered the room, was labeled "Elsewhere To Visions."

"Mr. Todd, you and my sister are the champions of this translation matrix. Do we go with visions or the temple."

"Well, Captain, I say we visit the temple, first."

The "temple" turned out to be what Benny Hathaway immediately recognized as the main engineering level. He began taking pictures, and promised not to leave.

Andrew Todd and Peter MacGregor walked back through the original room and into the hallway. They decided to walk as far as they could, only peering into rooms along the way. The hallway did indeed follow the curve of the Object. They came to a dead end, approximately seventy-five percent of the way around. Here, they confronted not an elevator shaft – the one on which they had arrived seemed to be the only one – but a large door. It was labelled "Holy Temple." Entering, they could see Benny Hathaway's light bouncing off equipment. They had come, literally, full circle.

"Just us Benny, we found a different way in," Peter said over the EVA suit radio, aware of its bulk. "I think we can shed some of this gear."

"Hold up, Captain," Hathaway said. "Some of the readings coming off this equipment are a little troubling. I'd suggest staying in the suits when you're in here. Doesn't seem to be a problem past the doors, but in here it is. Radiation levels a little higher than we'd like."

"Thanks. We'll stay suited up for now. Andrew and I will backtrack around and see you in the room where we entered."

They had found three sets of doors labeled "biological relief station" on the long walk, each next to a hallway leading to the ship's center. At the halfway point in their walk, they turned to walk down one of the halls.

Andrew Todd stopped and pointed to the floor. In the real world, complex symbols were embedded in the tile. Superimposed over those symbols by helmet's software was the word "Visions."

As it turned out, each of the hallways on this level led to a single large room in what seemed be the center. Tables, desks, and chairs filled the space. Sprawled across the tables, and posted on walls, were star charts. Andrew marked the location for further research as Peter walked to a section of wall. This was a photograph of Earth. Not exactly Earth as Peter knew it; large glaciers extended from the poles. But it was Earth.

There were drawers full of maps of Earth, small print on which the translation matrix was trying to read without success. And lots of pictures.

Dead-center on the wall of the large room was a double-door. It was labelled "Holy Temple." No need to go back in.

"Hathaway to MacGregor. You guys heading this way?"

"We are Benny, got distracted on the way. Everything alright?"

"Just noticed that all the stasis boxes in this room we first entered, they all have what I assume are name-plates." He paused. "The names don't render as anything, but under all the names are the words translated as 'Temple Servant.' If the engineering room is the temple, then whoever these people are hanging out in the blue light are surely the engineering crew."

"I bet you're right. We will be right there."

They left the room, intending to take the main hallway back to Hathaway's location. It was Peter's turn to stop their progress just two steps in.

"What is it?" Andrew asked.

Two large doors faced into the "Visions" map room. The markings were translated as, "Priests-Rulers. Actions."

With a translation like that, of course they felt the need to open the door. Inside they found themselves at the base of an ornately decorated staircase, which disappeared into the shadows.

CHAPTER 61

Alpha Base. The Object. Kuiper Belt

"Of course, you finally find something that interests me twelve hours before I am being forced to leave," complained Fritz Stuenkel, the *Shackleton*'s lead navigator, to his captain.

"Wait a second, out of everything we have found here. All of it, and the 'something' that interests you is the map room? Not the million-plus people frozen in boxes, the animals, the fact there are boxes holding people, but maps?"

The German arched his eyebrows. "I'm a navigator. On most days, I prefer maps to people." He was looking at the pictures Peter MacGregor had taken. "But maps can tell you a lot about people. Like, the fact that these maps are geocentric." He tapped the image on the screen, and showed it to Charlotte Smith-Davies' husband, Thomas Newcome.

The astronomer had been in the Alpha Base helping other crew members make room for the arriving *Byrd*. He and his wife had tried to blend in with *Shackleton*'s crew, rather than stand apart as the displaced leaders of the *Henson*. Well, she would have been a displaced leader; he was the displaced consort.

Stuenkel and MacGregor had waved him over, and he glanced at the screen.

"This is a map of the constellation we know as Camelopardalis," said Newcome as Peter nodded. The astronomer did not mention that the picture was actually of a satellite image of an old Earth. The star map, while in focus, was not what Peter had thought was the most important thing to document at that moment.

"Well, in order for this star map to make sense," Newcome pinched and squeezed at the image to bring other portions into view. "Of all the star maps I see in these pictures, for any of them to make any sense, you have to be on Earth, or at least in our solar system." He flipped through the images and grimaced at how few were of the star maps.

"From what I can tell, every map in this room was drawn with the idea you were starting from Earth," added Stuenkel. "Think of old maps of the world. The Greeks drew maps where Greece was at the center. Same goes for the Chinese. Christian Europe did something strange, they put Jerusalem at the center of their maps." He looked at Peter and Thomas, "Maps can tell you a lot about people."

Peter nodded. "I promise to send you a scan of every map we find."

The German nodded. "You'd better." He and MacGregor shook hands, expecting it would be at least a year before they saw each other again.

"*Shackleton* to MacGregor," came the voice of Jeff Prasadh. "The *Byrd* is on final approach."

"I'll head that way," he responded. To his navigator, Peter said, "Give my best to your family and try not to spend all your time looking over our maps."

"Can I walk with you?" Thomas Newcome asked Peter MacGregor. "I have a proposal."

+++

Peter felt he had spent very little time on the *Shackleton*'s bridge, in large part because he had not been needed. It seemed his days were divided between his office, Alpha Base, and the Object's interior.

"*Shackleton* Actual to *Byrd* Actual," he said after activating the comms. "Welcome to our part of space."

"*Byrd* Actual to *Shackleton* Actual," came the voice of Conrad Oscar. "That's quite the salvage job you've taken on."

"Just wait until you get inside it, Conrad. We're extending our secondary docks."

"Copy. *Byrd*'s navigator has everything lined up and ready for coupling whenever you're ready."

Peter switched his own communications to intercom mode. "All personnel, this is the captain. We're about to join up with the *Byrd*. Since we're using our secondary docks, this is a little more complex than usual. Secure yourselves."

He looked to his reliable first officer, Linda Bletchley, who indicated that the umbilical to the Object was closed at both ends. After each of the *Shackleton*'s departments reported in, she stated that all personnel were in place.

In the end, the docking went smoothly. Personnel and cargo began flowing in both directions almost immediately. This would not be a long visit; as Stuenkel had noted, the *Byrd* would be leaving in less than twelve hours.

But it would be leaving with one fewer person than had been anticipated. Newcome wanted to stay.

While Navigator Stuenkel was interested in maps, Thomas Newcome was an actual astronomer. Besides, once *Byrd* got to Station, his wife would be heading immediately to the *Henson,* and his son was already preparing to go back to school. He would probably see both wife and son more using the *Shackleton*'s priority comms system than if he was sitting at his office in London.

Walking to the receiving bay, Peter could not tell which of the department heads gathered there were more excited.

Engineering was getting a slew of equipment that Hathaway simply could not manufacture even with the *Shackleton*'s state-of-the-art printers. Medical and life sciences were getting additional personnel, including archeological specialists, as well as forensic devices more suited to dusty digs on Earth than the edge of the solar system. And the kitchen was being stocked with fresh fruits, vegetables, and meats. He knew that would make the rest of the crew happy.

He and Conrad had gone to college together, and so they

caught up briefly on old friends as they made their way to the umbilical connecting the *Shackleton* to the Object. The man deserved to see what the fuss was all about.

MacGregor, Hathaway, and Todd had only finished their brief exploration of the Object's command levels a few hours before the *Byrd*'s arrival. Hathaway already had his team designing a way to seal off and access the express elevator shaft without resorting to an EVA walk through wreckage. It might take a couple days, so Hathway promised to develop an interim solution as well.

For now, Conrad Oscar was overwhelmed just by what he could see in the warehouse levels. Peter thought how quickly accustomed he had become to walking through here, surrounded by the glowing boxes and frozen animals. They had not yet reached the section of humans.

"So any words of wisdom regarding Captain Smith-Davies?" the Byrd's captain asked. "Is she a good passenger or does she expect to be co-captain?"

"No, she's great. She helped Hathaway clear out the cargo hold, and took the shifts of various crew members to give them a break," said Peter. "Fact is, I think my crew will miss her more than they would me." Both men laughed.

"I know you've got background with her. She was a babysitter?"

"More like a nanny."

"Whatever. So, any idea why she's going back but her husband is suddenly staying?"

"Well, she wants to oversee the refit of the *Henson*, which I completely understand," said Peter. "And we got a hint of something upstairs just before you arrived that will put Mr. Newcome to good use."

Conrad nodded as he pondered a great white shark suspended in the tank in front of them. "So you really think if the blue light was turned off, that thing would just start swimming around?"

"Well, we don't know. The cactus on my desk is thriving,

but for some reason the remains of animals and people we have found seem to basically die in place. Maybe that's because the boxes have stopped working, rather than been turned off. Maybe plants are different. We just don't know yet."

"Incredible," the captain of the *Byrd* said, not for the first time. "Thanks for bringing me over." He glanced at his watch. "Can I see some of these, uhh, people?"

They crossed the warehouse, and into the area of "Those Who Serve Us."

"For what it is worth, based on the reports I was allowed to read coming out here, I think you're right about all this," said Conrad. "About the relationship between these people and the, uhh, other people."

He stopped at a box where a blond man in his mid-thirties stood frozen, naked except the ever-present bracelet. "They all seem healthy," he said, looking back down the row of stasis boxes they had passed, "but healthy in the way you keep your best dogs or horses healthy."

They walked on to the staircase. "Not sure we've ever talked about this, Peter, but you know my family – one hundred percent of it – was in the slave trade. Ironically enough, half of it as slavers and half of it as slaves. My guess is that if sets of families from the late eighteenth century suspected their descendants would eventually marry up, they'd all be furious."

Conrad looked at Peter. "What? You're thinking right now how I could possibly have *any* white blood in me?" He laughed. "You never did pay close enough attention in history." As they mounted the stair case, leading to the fourth level he added, "This place is a reminder that the last two hundred years is the aberration in history. In five thousand years of recorded history... in thirteen thousand years of history, apparently... slavery was the norm."

"Didn't know you had become such a philosopher," Peter said to his friend.

"Running people and cargo between Earth and Mars has given me a chance to catch up on a lot of reading," Conrad

Oscar said. On this level, the first one of "We Who Are The People," the *Byrd*'s captain was also struck by the obvious differences in the stasis boxes.

"I don't know where all this is headed," he finally said, "but you need to remember that whether these people are from Earth or wherever, they come from a different world. And they may not like the world we now have."

CHAPTER 62

Station, HEO

Teresa Schultz had never enjoyed the feeling of artificial gravity. She didn't like the feeling when Ian first demonstrated the gravity plates for her. Like her nieces and nephew, and two of her own children, she could feel the lurch when it activated. Not everyone felt it, but almost everyone who did said the feeling quickly disappeared. That was not Teresa's experience at all. It made her feel vaguely nauseous the moment she stepped on gravity plating, and it never went away until she stepped off. But the moment she did, she felt better.

Yet, this is where she could get real-time access to the scans being made of the documents on the Object. *The good news is*, she thought, *I could stand to lose a couple pounds*.

Without a doubt, the language they had uncovered was at the root of many of the languages on Earth. The stilted translations were the result of the matrix she designed predicting meanings based on the analogies found in long-dead languages. Ancient human languages, which were no doubt drawing from half-remembered sounds and symbols they had previously learned from... others.

Peter had told her about the conversation he had with his navigator regarding the geocentric nature of the maps. Based on the few pictures of the maps so far available, she was forming a hypothesis about the language.

For years, it had been common in academia to dismiss oral traditions. More and more research had led to a complete reversal of that view. It was believed now that there had been more growth in language in the last thousand years, than in the history of language combined. The world, or at least culture, had moved much more slowly in the past. Someone from colonial America would have trouble following modern language, and vice versa. Yet someone from ancient Egypt, pushed forward three hundred years, would have been able to carry on a conversation without missing an Egyptian beat.

So what if ancient people forming their languages, used symbols and words handed down to them hundred or thousands of years earlier? Things that had been heard and seen by their fore-bearers?

Can an engineering center become a temple? It's not the deification of science, but rather the application of seemingly similar activities. An uneducated, illiterate man might see an engineer crouched down working on a device, and in his mind make the connection to someone knelt in prayer. He knew it wasn't the same thing, but the words worked. If one thinks of language just as a tool to be employed, one employs the tools available.

She went through imagery scans and matched them with the presented translations, and then began reassessing the expectations. She created a separate matrix, which she would eventually push over for the *Shackleton*'s Andrew Todd to review. Were she not so old, she'd consider bullying her way on the next transport and seeing this thing for herself.

But she wasn't sure she could take the artificial gravity for that long.

CHAPTER 63

The Shackleton. *Kuiper Belt*

Even before *Byrd* was beyond the gravity interaction zone, the *Shackleton*'s crew was renewing their focus on the Object. Those who were departing had not been exactly replaced. Most of the new crew were individuals with specialties or skills that would help in uncovering the secrets of the Object. There simply had not been a need for exobiologists or archeologists when the *Shackleton* began her initial mission setting up navigational beacons.

But not all of the new team members would ever actually set foot on either the *Shackleton* or the Object. Among the items brought over was a new conference facility to be set up in the cargo hold that had previously held those navigation beacons.

That nearly-forgotten mission of the *Shackleton* – placing beacons around the edge of the solar system to provide real-time positioning for ships and probes – would now fall to *Byrd* – after, of course, taking the departing *Shackleton* crew to Station to be debriefed and reunited with family.

This cargo hold was the largest space on the ship, and it was being divided into four meeting spaces. These would allow for greater collaboration with teams back on Station and Earth. The first of the conference rooms went live almost immediately, so that Dr. Regan and her expanded team could meet with their colleagues – literally over the dead body of the man recovered from the Object.

Before it began, however, the young communications officer newly assigned to the *Shackleton* was given the opportunity to test the equipment by talking with the newest member of Station's Object Medical Task Force – his dad Max.

"Jeff, Jeff, Jeff, what have you gotten yourself involved with?" asked the life-size projection of his father with a smile. The system required users to be fitted with either special glasses or contacts, so as to render the three-dimensional objects. Without them, the room would appear as a dizzying array of flashing colors and partially coherent beams of light. For his near-sightedness, Jeff was always wearing contacts anyway, while his dad's own omnipresent glasses had been retro-fitted for the display. It was hard to remember they could not actually hug, the rendering was so complete.

"Yeah, well – surprise! – no diamond mine out here," he said. "So how did you get pulled into this?

"I did some research into hibernation before you were born."

"It put me through college, as I recall."

"True. Well, apparently Mrs. Hyde had seen it in some archives, and reached out. So, of course, here I am about to consult on an alien artifact."

"Speaking of which, Dr. Regan and her team are waiting outside," Jeff said, seeing them gathering at the glass door. Until they had their glasses on and actually entered the space, all they could see in here was Jeff standing in a pool of light talking to himself. He waved them in. "It was great to see you, Dad."

"My team is here, too. It was great to briefly visit in person," he said as the *Shackleton* team began filing in – pushing two large tables that – from Max's perspective on Station – began shimmering into existence as they entered the room. For Jeff, members of the Station task force began shimmering into existence through the fake door on the other side of the room – all giving the illusion of real collaboration. Just as Jeff reached his own door, his father called out. "By the way, son. The third date was a play, and next week will be dinner here on Station."

The younger man smiled as he waved and exited the room. He was surprised to see Andrew Todd waiting for him. "My dad has a more active social life than I do."

"Well, your dad isn't stuck on a spaceship with less than two hundred other people who are contractually forbidden from having romantic interludes," said Andrew as they stepped out of the way of the last of the medical team.

"What about your little interlude with the lab assistant from engineering?"

Andrew gave Jeff a sideways glance. "That was hardly an interlude. But, hey, junior employee, changing topics, Peter MacGregor is wondering if would you like to walk up a staircase designated for rulers and priests?"

"This feels like the start of a bad joke about my Indian heritage..."

+++

Back inside the conference room, the quick round of introductions had concluded.

"I read through your autopsy and other reports," Max Prasadh was saying, holding his own tablet. "The thoroughness, given the lack of equipment you have had, is remarkable." Others echoed his praise.

What Dr. Regan had found followed exactly what his research from so many years earlier had predicted. Specifically, the negative results if someone was awakened from an induced metabolic slumber without the appropriate counteragent at ready.

If the counteragent had been available, the man would most definitely have survived. One of the devices that had been brought into the conference room was a multi-purpose medical compounder. Limited only by the supply of base chemicals, it could produce almost any medicine known to man as either a pill, liquid, or aerosol.

Over the course of the next 30 minutes, Regan and her

team pulled out the man's dissected organs and examined them with the new equipment.

"I think I have the counteragent identified," Dr. Prasadh said from a stool he had brought in. "It's simpler than what we were working with, but there is nothing else it could be."

For her part, Dana Regan was shocked by the speed with which he had worked. "You are kidding, right?" Her own tablet chimed, and she could see the formulation. "I guess you weren't kidding."

CHAPTER 64

Alpha Base, The Object, Kuiper Belt

"You're kidding, right?"

Jeff Prasadh was looking at the monstrosity at the end of the hallway. "We're going to ride in that?"

For all the world, it looked to Prasadh like a tent set up on a platform. That's because it was a tent set up on a platform.

"One of the engineers came up with this," said Peter MacGregor. "They removed the broken elevator car from the shaft and set this up."

"A temporary airlock, on an oversized grav-plate?"

On the one hand, Jeff wasn't EVA qualified, which meant a spacewalk was technically off-limits to him – so therefore the highest levels of the Object were otherwise inaccessible until a the shaft was sealed and retro-fitted with a new elevator car the engineering staff was designing.

On the other hand, it was a tent. "Let's get it over with."

"That's the spirit," said the *Shackleton's* engineer, Benny Hathaway, as he slapped the junior comms officer on the back.

"So, how many times has this gone up?"

"This will be its maiden voyage."

"If I vomit, it's not my fault, and Andrew has to clean it up."

And so the Vomit Lift was christened in name, though not in actuality. For as strange as it looked, Jeff had to admit it wasn't so bad in practice. But, for good measure, he just kept his eyes focused on his boots and tried not to think about what they were doing in a tent strapped to a sheet of high-tech metal, situated in the elevator shaft of a derelict, ancient vehicle, millimeters from the deadly vacuum of space.

He almost vomited, but didn't.

The four men stepped through the interchange of temporary airlocks and into the hallway. Benny Hathaway and Andrew Todd went in different directions; immediately pulling on their radiation-resistant EVA gear so they could explore the engineering section in greater detail after three more engineers came up on the platform. They would be followed by a team from the life sciences department, who were going to begin setting up the scanning devices to record the pages and pages of maps.

This left Peter MacGregor and Jeff Prasadh to head for the staircase.

"So, why did you want me to tag along? Not that I'm ungrateful for the experience," asked Prasadh.

"Honestly, because Benny's review of the engineering section requires Andrew Todd's expertise with the translation matrix. And because I promised my bosses I wouldn't go off half-cocked exploring the ship by myself." He looked at Prasadh. "So I'm going off half-cocked exploring the ship with you. Congratulations."

They came to the doors marked "Priests-Rulers. Actions."

"One second, sir," said Jeff then established a direct link to Andrew. "Hey, Andrew, my copy of the new alternate translation matrix didn't fully load. Did yours?"

He paused, listening to the response in his earpiece. "Okay, great. Thanks. Getting it now."

It was only then that Peter remembered that the young man had his comms gear "fully loaded" as contact lenses, with a dual-function hearing implant and microphone. For some reason, the set-up reminded Peter of his father. He felt a pang of regret that he hadn't talked to his mother in a couple days to check in on the old man. He was beginning to accept his dad's condition as the new normal.

"What was that about?" he heard himself asking

Prasadh.

"Dr. Schultz sent me and Andrew a draft version of a new translation matrix. The data-packet didn't fully unpack on my tablet, so Jeff re-sent it." He pointed at the door. "The old matrix reads 'priests' hyphen 'rulers' period 'actions.'" Peter looked at his tablet and nodded in agreement.

Prasadh continued, "Well, this new version renders it as 'officers and staff' followed by 'command center.' Not quite as poetic, but probably more accurate."

They entered the room, and started climbing the staircase. They came to landing, on the wall was painted a rather gaudy star scene. To the left and right were more stairs. Stenciled in gold lettering to the left was "Command Center" and to the right, "Officers and Staff."

They went left to the Command Center, climbing twice the distance they had on the first flight. Looking back, they could see the "officers and staff" staircase rose only half as high as the one they had taken.

Their stairway opened into a large room not entirely different from the *Shackleton*'s own bridge. A simple guard rail separated the staircase landing from the room. In the center of the room was a desk and chair on a platform that appeared able to turn. Various work stations were set facing that chair. There did not seem to be a "front" to the room. It seemed to the Jeff the arrangement meant everyone looked at the captain, who, in turn, could look at everyone else.

Based on the chairs, the room held twenty-five people.

"You think 'officers and staff' went to their quarters?" Prasadh asked.

"Seems reasonable. Remember, look but don't touch." They started looking around the bridge work stations. Peter went straight to the chair and could see it was, indeed, set on a swivel. It looked fairly comfortable, if perhaps a little small.

He pointed his flashlight light around the room, seeing a reflection come off screens – the first he had actually seen anywhere in the Object. Embedded in the work stations were buttons and keys. Built in keyboards and controls? he wondered. He leaned in close examining one of the screens and certain it was a cathode ray tube.

"Captain," said Jeff Prasadh.

"Yeah, what do you have," he responded without looking back.

"Um, no, sorry, I was reading this door plate."

Door plate? Peter turned and saw Jeff standing at an open door.

"The door was just standing open, and I saw the plate. It reads, 'High Priest of' something. But my bet is that this would be the captain."

Peter craned his neck. There was a straight shot to the center chair. He walked past Jeff and entered the room.

A small desk was built into the wall, with an attached chair. For some reason, Peter couldn't help but think it looked custom-made for the person who would be sitting in it. Papers were neatly stacked in trays, and another screen was embedded in the wall.

Opposite the door they entered was a simple bed, and then a door leading to a bathroom. Nestled in the corner of the room was the familiar blue glow of a stasis box. The heavy blue glow shrouded the occupant, but Peter could not help but notice that – unlike the other million-plus individuals in the seventy-eight levels of "We Who Are The People," the person – the woman – inside this box was completely naked.

Prasadh had moved across to the bathroom. It had a metal sink with polished steel mirror. A sliding door divided the space, protecting behind it a toilet and what was probably a shower head. Privacy? Water containment? On the other side of the sink and mirror was an alcove-like closet. Hanging inside were identical sets of uniform-style clothing.

Despite the "no touching" rule, Jeff Prasadh grabbed one and held it out for the captain to see. With his free hand he pointed to bands on the cuff of the shirt. A repeated pattern of green and blue. Green. Blue.

Peter nodded. The "House of Green and Blue," he said. "I wonder how many of those human slaves down there belong to her."

Prasadh put it back and they turned to leave the quarters and continue their exploration. As they did, for the briefest moment, the heavy blue of the stasis chamber flashed yellow and then back to blue.

"That doesn't seem like a good thing, Captain."

"We need to get Dr. Regan up here."

CHAPTER 65

The Object, Kuiper Belt

If there was anyone less interested in traveling up the Vomit Lift than Jeff Prasadh, it had been Dr. Dana Regan.

It took three trips in the kilometer-tall elevator shaft for her team and equipment to reach the presumed bridge and captain's quarters. Fortunately, they did not have to hike up the stairs. One of the "express" elevator shaft's upper outlets was found to open in an alcove on the bridge level. A temporary airlock was quickly erected there.

"Let's see her," Regan said. The medical team, and Benny Hathaway, had crowded into the small room and began looking at the stasis box's occupant. The color had not shifted since that one time, but everyone agreed – based on what had been previously observed – it wasn't a good sign.

For his part, Peter MacGregor was just outside the door, leaning against a wall and looking at the reports from the teams crawling through this section of the Object.

On the "Officers and staff" level they had found forty versions of the same little apartment as the captain – though only three had had private bathrooms. Each of these cabins had alcove-like closets, and the uniforms had different colored bands at the cuffs. Only one color set – green-red – was not present.

"What do they have against Christmas?" Jeff Prasadh had joked within earshot of the captain.

"Well, they predate Hanukah by ten-thousand years," said a straight-faced Phyllis Levin, "so its a safe bet they wouldn't have a clue what to do with a decorated tree."

On the level immediately above the bridge were what could only be medical exam bays, surgical suites, and storage rooms in which vials of liquids and powders were stacked neatly in stasis boxes.

The top level proved to be the most fascinating. It was an observatory. Like an eyelid, shields could be lowered allowing powerful devices to look through what the engineers decided was a type of transparent metal – possibly a form of aluminum.

Thomas Newcome should be brought up immediately to review the equipment, Peter typed on his tablet in a note to Linda Bletchley. He was glad she opted to stay with the *Shackleton*.

Peter wasn't sure when he had done it, but he was now seated on the swiveling captain's platform, making his notes, when Dr. Regan cleared her throat. "I guess you captains just naturally gravitate to the big chairs, eh?"

"Tell me about your patient."

"Not much more than you could see. That heavy blue fog-light makes a visual exam nearly impossible. Female, obviously. Maybe five-three, with indeterminate weight, hair color, and skin tone. Benny says that flash you fellows saw is definitely problematic. His team knows that their priority is to understand how to purposefully deactivate those devices. I'll keep someone up here with the counteragent ready to administer in case we need to undo this hibernation state she is in."

Peter squinted his eyes up. "Is that safe? I mean, injecting these people with an untested drug?"

"Safe? We know there is a hundred percent death rate when these things fail. In such a situation, my medical ethics are slippery enough to allow me to try something a little radical." She paused. "Meanwhile, under Dr. Prasadh's guidance, we're going to be forcing some small mammals out of hibernation to try the treatment. So that should be fun. All creatures great and small, and all that."

"Well, keep me updated."

CHAPTER 66

Residence, Station, HEO

On the same day Lucy MacGregor Hyde gave birth to a healthy son, the High Priest or Captain (or whatever she was) of the Object was awakened.

Lucy did not know that, of course. She, her husband Robert, and their son Ian, were completely exhausted. She only learned about it the next day, when her mother and aunt arrived to see the boy.

Jessica MacGregor knew better than to keep either her sister-in-law or daughter from talking about work. While she and her son-in-law marveled at the baby, Teresa gave Lucy the details.

"So had they even tried the counteragent on the guinea pigs?" Lucy asked, knowing the creatures weren't actually guinea pigs, but also not feeling particularly precise at the moment.

"Yes, about six hours earlier," said Teresa. "Meanwhile, back in Dayton, Dr. Prasadh had back-engineered the chemical formula of the knock-out drug and put a monkey to sleep. With the counteragent, the animal woke up without any problems."

Lucy looked up. "I thought we discouraged research with primates?"

"We do, but Chris and I gave the go-ahead for this one attempt. Successful attempt," she added.

Lucy frowned. "I'm glad it was a success, but I want to be careful about cutting corners on our research policies." She look at her mother, cuddling her infant son. "Back to the woman. What's happened with her?"

"Yes, so she woke up, was highly confused and a little agitated. Dr. Regan made the decision to lightly sedate her for now."

"Was that wise?"

"I think so. The trauma is immense here. They've kept her under, monitoring vitals and the like. Dr. Regan says the medical bays on the Object are very comfortable."

"So now what? We can't keep her sedated forever?" She considered for a moment that, in fact, the woman had been sedated for something like thirteen thousand years.

"My recommendation to Flight Director Yua Saito and the working group has been that we follow the protocols we drafted a month ago, and stick to them."

Lucy nodded, thinking back on what that would entail. "Who is making the first round of calls?"

Teresa Schultz smiled. "Well, Chris Stoddard is a big donor so he managed to get fairly quickly on the president's schedule later today. I'm speaking with the prime ministers of the United Kingdom and Australia tonight, Yua is visiting with the Japanese and Taiwanese leaders tomorrow."

"Do you think any of them will say anything?"

The older woman looked out the Station window, then back at her niece. "The last several months have been the most theologically challenging of my life. My beliefs are not dependent, exactly, on science, and science has had a way of confirming much of what I believe, after a fashion. But, like your dad, I never truly expected to find intelligent life out there. And now, especially, we are confronted with the possibility of..." her voice trailed off. "The possibility of space-faring intelligence having arisen on Earth twice? Of intelligence from out there coming here thousands of years ago to train ancient astronauts? So many big questions."

Teresa Schultz' eyes focused on a distant point, and then came back. "So, no, Lucy, I don't think these people will go public. At least not yet. At least not for a while. They will need to process all this. They will need to come to their own peace about it. And even then, there is still a lot to understand."

CHAPTER 67

The Object, Kuiper Belt.

Until they could finalize a system of communication, the captain was kept in a state of induced hibernation, though in a medical bay and not in a stasis box. The good news was that the *Shackleton* engineering team – with help from experts on Station – had figured out how to turn the stasis boxes off and on. While the basic mechanics of the boxes were now mostly known, the principles under which they operated were still a complete mystery. Everyone was comfortable with it remaining that way until a doctor or engineer was awakened from one to explain things.

No one thought that would happen any time soon.

QA's former Chief Operating Office, Chris Stoddard, had been an acquaintance of the president of the United States for many years. Their conversation went better than Chris had expected. Among other things, he learned the president had long been of the unsubstantiated belief that space aliens were regularly visiting Earth, so news of an ancient derelict floating at the edge of the solar system didn't surprise him much. The details did.

The president's only condition for remaining silent, and letting QA continue to run the operation, was that they respect the laws and customs of the sea. The Object, the ship, was no longer a derelict. The master of the vessel had been located and should therefore control it, its passengers, and cargo. In other words, all invasive exploration needed to stop. Passive observation, and the preservation of life, was acceptable until communication could be established.

Otherwise, everyone should get off the ship.

The Object was now designated a ship. Everyone had known that for a while, but now it was decreed.

In very little time, Thomas Newcome and his team deciphered that the ship was intended to be heading for a star in the constellation known as Camelopardalis. The star was not particularly interesting, no exoplanets had been detected there, but it seemed to be their destination. In fact, if the constantly updated translation matrix and star charts were to be believed, that star was only the first of hundreds of destinations for the Object. That information only added to the mysteries of the ship and its occupants.

Nothing they yet found explained why. Nor, for that matter, did they find anything explaining how this technology came to be in the possession of primitive hunter-gatherers, or how those same primitives came to be running it.

The man who *Shackleton* crew members witnessed die in the failure of his stasis box had been what Dr. Regan and the various Station-based scientists called an "Early European Modern Human." He shared many DNA characteristics similar to the so-called "Cro-Magnons," which had been so named because of the French cave where their remains were first discovered in 1868. Many of the characteristics, but not all.

As it turned out, he had as much genetically in common with the *homo neanderthalensis* as with the modern humans. But the Neanderthals had gone extinct between twenty- and forty-thousand years ago, not thirteen, which was the Object's almost definitive age. Yet another mystery.

The ship was to fly through space by means of what Benny Hathaway called "the single most inefficient gravity-drive system ever built." It was massive, occupying most of that interior spine and taking up a quarter of the space of each deck. The radiation he had detected when they first stumbled into the engineering room was part of the gross inefficiency.

Yet, in engineering, size can compensate for inefficiency. No matter how inefficient Engineer Hathaway and a team of engineers might think it was, the gravity-drive on the ship would qualify – in terms of output, if not design – as what the men and women of QA would begrudgingly recognize as at least two generations ahead of their own speculative work. In other words, the Object was faster and more powerful than anything that had actually yet been built.

Or, rather, had actually been built on Earth.

Or, built *recently* on Earth.

At a minimum, it was faster and more powerful than anything QA had built or even had planned. Metallurgical analysis, bio-testing, atmospheric testing – indeed, every kind of analysis and testing that could be done, all gave the same results. The Object had been built on Earth. Another mystery.

What was not a mystery about this, the fastest and most powerful space-faring vessel that was known to exist was that, if its gravity-drive had been enabled, it would have absolutely violated Albert Einstein's speed limit. It would absolutely arrive at a place faster than light. Exactly how "fast," or for how long, was not precisely known. But faster.

The power source for the ship remained a mystery. They knew where it was, they could see it, detect it, and they knew it was powering everything... but it was a completely closed system. Since it was keeping untold thousands of people alive, they could not risk opening up the equipment.

Like the stasis boxes, the power generation system would remain unknown until they could speak to one of the sleeping engineers, or they found and translated a copy of "ancient super-tech for dummies" somewhere in the ship's collection of books.

Which was massive. Each level of the "We Who Are The People" sections of the ship was found to contain books and scrolls. Most were made of thick paper, though some appeared to be animal skin. Nearly all of them were in stasis boxes.

This is where knowing how to turn the boxes off and on became helpful. Following instructions by an archival team on Station, the library boxes were turned off long enough to have the contents scanned, and then turned back on. Nothing was touched.

Peter MacGregor was happy to note that the book he had discovered in the messenger bag was, indeed, some sort of novel. "The Structure Over Water" was how the translation matrix rendered the name. He had tried to read the translation, but it was tedious. Someone was in love with someone who lived across a lake, maybe. He gave up after three chapters. He thought they were chapters, anyway. His comms lead-turned-linguist, Andrew Todd, on the other hand, had devoured it.

By this point, Peter had begun to think of leaving his work on the Object for a brief vacation. He still had not met the beast of a nephew his diminutive younger sister had birthed – a fact she needled him about on occasion. The next crew relief would arrive in two months. If everything went as planned, it would be the *Henson* arriving from her refit. The damage to the drive system had been substantial, but ultimately repairable.

He and Thomas Newcome had become friends. They spent many evenings playing poker in the galley with Andrew Todd and a rotation of crew members. It turned out that Mr. Newcome had been the organizer of the *Henson's* infamous poker games, though Mr. Todd was the reigning champion on *Shackleton*.

It was at one of those games, as Peter was deciding whether to continue his bluff or fold, that the room's intercom rang out. "Captain, you are needed on the bridge." He tossed his cards to the table in relief.

"Thomas, I hate you and never want to see you again." He stood up as several crew members chuckled. "See you later."

On the bridge, he saw Yua Saito on the main screen. "Sorry to keep you waiting, Flight Director. Everything alright?"

"We are having ongoing discussions with our new partners in this venture," began Saito, diplomatically. "It has been decided that the status quo is not sustainable. You and your crew need to open a dialogue with the Object's commander."

Peter nodded. It was the right thing to do. There were so many questions, not the least of which being what should be done with the more than one and a half million sentient beings held in those slowly dying stasis boxes.

CHAPTER 68

Medical Bay, The Object, Kuiper Belt

Kaziok Tar'lol did not know why she was waking in a room on the medical deck, instead of her quarter's stasis box. She looked down at the strange blankets covering her and the even more strange clothing in which she was draped. Her head hurt. Rather than the built in lights, strange devices illuminated the room.

She had a momentary flash of memory. She had been surrounded by several oo'Pub. They were dressed, and dressed strangely. There had been noises coming from their mouths but none of it made sense. She seemed to remember the sounds of those voices fading in and out.

Tar'lol, captain of the House of Kaziok's designated ship, took a deep breath in through her nose. The headache began to subside. She was certain everything was under control. Everyone in leadership had been warned that, because of the travel times and the differences in the exploration patterns, things might have changed during the sleeping periods.

Perhaps these new bedsheets and robes were part of whatever had changed during the journey? But why had she not been awakened before now?

She did not quite feel like moving. A doctor or attendant would soon come around. Another breath. "Doctor?" she called lightly. No response. She tried again, a little louder. Her arms and legs were stiff. She moved them, even as she stayed in the bed.

Someone entered, finally. Very little was visible about the person, who was pushing a device in – a pole on wheels with a video monitor of some sort attached. How curious.

The person moved... like an oo'Pub? Tar'lol took a another deep breath as the person left and images appeared on the screen.

A voice came from the impossibly thin screen. "Greetings. Friend. Understand?" The pronunciations were wrong, but she could make out the words.

Tar'lol nodded. Then said, "Yes."

"Friend. Say. Yes."

"Yes."

"Friend. Say..." Pictures of animals, shapes, and familiar came on the screen. Each image paused until she said the name. And then came written words, usually of the same animals or objects she had just seen pictures of, but not always. She read the words, beginning to understand that – perhaps – these people did not speak her language. An even more disconcerting thought entered her mind; perhaps they thought she was unable to speak her own language, perhaps something had gone terribly wrong with...

She pushed down the fear and concern. She kept going.

The screen went black. A moment later it was filled with the blue orb she had left several weeks earlier, by her internal sense of time. How long had it been? She felt her mind drift, before snapping back to the picture on the screen.

"Dar'Eq," she said.

+++

Andrew Todd was just down the hall, in a room exactly like hers. There were as many cameras monitoring him as there were her, he thought. Among those watching across the millions of miles of space was Teresa Schultz, sitting in her home office. The test was of her own design, creating a baseline of words and sounds. While the Object's captain had been sedated, the *Shackleton*'s medical team scanned her vocal cords and larynx so her throat could be modeled. A team of specialists on and around the third planet from the sun poured over the results, examining the muscles in an attempt to predict the sounds this woman would make.

All of this provided Teresa and the linguists working with her the opportunity to build phonetics, quickly, for this language.

In the academic sense, for Teresa Schultz more than almost anyone else, the most important word uttered so far was the one used for "Earth." It had tantalizing hints of a word long-suspected from the proto-afroasiatic.

"Start with the simple words, and see what happens," came her typed suggestion to Andrew Todd, Peter MacGregor sitting next to him. "Just follow the script. Resist the urge to go beyond what we think we know."

"Hello, friend," he said into the microphone. A moment later, a computerized version of his voice uttered foreign sounds. The woman smiled. She repeated the words – a mesh of constants. The system updated the pronunciation and repeated it.

She smiled.

He started with several of the same pictures. "Elephant," he said, with the computerized voice seemingly getting the sounds correct. For another thirty minutes he said words which were translated, and she spoke them back. He checked the prompts from Teresa, who believed there was now enough data from which to work.

Andrew handed the microphone to Peter MacGregor. "You're up, boss."

Peter thought for a moment, looked at the script, and said, "Greetings. I am Captain Peter MacGregor. My crew and I found your vessel." He could tell the computerized voice rendering her language was meant to mimic his own, and was different from that used to represent Andrew. Aunt Teresa paid attention to details.

The woman crinkled her brow at the odd names. "You are Captain Petermacgregor," she said, attempting to repeat his name. "You found my... water ship?"

A picture of the Object was rendered on the screen in front of her. He said, "What do you call this?"

She said two words. The system registered the word "seventh" but lacked context for the other.

"Seventh," he repeated and paused. "Could you explain the other?"

She considered his question. "It is a large craft that protects life, and carries it to its new home. This is the seventh one."

The computer rendered a series of words, searching through the database of possible translations.

"Could you tell me again what you call this?" asked Peter , pointing again at the Object.

"Led by the House of Kaziok, it is the seventh ark."

CHAPTER 69

The Shackleton, *Kuiper Belt*

Peter MacGregor slouched in his office chair. The language lesson lasted more than two hours, before Kaziok Tar'lol began nodding off. Dr. Prasadh and Dr. Regan were not bothered by it. For that matter, Peter was ready for nap himself.

The translation matrix was learning on the fly during the conversation, so that something like a normal conversation was almost possible when they ended. Sitting across from his desk was Andrew Todd and Thomas Newcome.

"So if this was the seventh ark, does it mean the other six are flying around out there?" asked Newcome.

"If I understood her correctly, there were maybe ten or up to a dozen of these sent out," Andrew replied. "Maybe there are others lurking here at the edge of the solar system?"

"There aren't," Peter said with a confidence that surprised his colleagues. "There aren't. The signal beacons and gravimetric surveys haven't found any others."

"So the others took off and left this lost ark behind?"

"It would appear so."

Everything said during the first conversation had been recorded and was being analyzed by Teresa Schultz and her team. Usually, given his unique place, Andrew would have taken part in what was surely an interesting discussion. But like his captain, he was exhausted – yet he knew sleep would be elusive. He needed to unpack the questions banging in the back of his head.

The equipment trained on Kaziok Tar'lol had monitored

not only her vitals, but peered under her skin to see her musculature at work during the conversation. In communication, spoken language was just a small part of what was taking place. Therefore, the system read her eye movements, the tilt of her head, her back, watched for muscle strain, even the circulation of blood to her lips and checks. All of that was correlated to the questions she had been asked, the words used in response, and any hints of emotion – all in service of building a more accurate translation matrix.

Thomas Newcome looked at an image on his tablet. It was a photo taken at a Christmas dinner several years ago, at the home of his wife's family. "As you know, my father-in-law has maintained some unorthodox views on our ancient ancestors. He has been certain Neanderthals and Cro-Magnons were more advanced than they had been given credit. He has held out that they had an expansive culture, and built large structures."

He paused. "But never, not once, has he ever hinted that they were capable of anything like this."

"We still aren't sure they were," Peter said. "We know they piloted this. We know this vessel was assigned to them. We think we know this particular one was built on Earth. But did they originate the plans? Were they following the blueprints given to them by alien visitors? All of it seems equally unbelievable."

"Maybe we'll know more tomorrow," Andrew suggested, hopefully.

"Maybe we will, but talking through a disembodied screen has its limits. I need to speak with her, directly. Captain to captain. Human to... whatever."

CHAPTER 70

Medical Bay, The Object, Kuiper Belt

Dana Regan had enjoyed her conversation with Kaziok Tar'lol. Of all her patients over the years, this one seemed the most willing to follow orders. Stay in bed. Drink water. Eat the foods that seem appealing. Do not remove the head, arm, or finger sensors.

She learned that the family name came first, and is how someone was to be addressed in formal settings, not even by a title. For Tar'lol, Kaziok was her family name but it was also the name of her House. Many in the House of Kaziok had different family names, and so Kaziok was their second name.

In professional settings, the family name was the only name to be used even by one's closest friends or family. In any such professional setting, the correct protocol was to begin a conversation with a greeting that used the individual's title and family name. These professional titles seemed to run the gamut of those not dissimilar to English.

Yet, in a more casual affairs, even a businesslike setting among regular colleagues, such as among the crew in conversation with their captain, the title and given name could be used. And in the most casual of situations, even when individuals were strangers, the given name would be appropriate.

And so *Dana* found herself visiting with *Tar'lol* about her health and life.

Since the woman had been awakened, everyone entering the room remained in heavy surgical gear. They were concerned about the ancient woman's ability to fight off their diseases... and vice versa. Tar'lol seemed to understand, saying that her crew had been inoculated against everything known to the Pra'oo – "We Who Are The People."

The arrangement helped conceal from her the strikingly different features of Dana and the other doctors and nurses. They had simply not been sure how she would react.

Tar'lol now knew the ship had been *almost* dead in space for approximately thirteen thousand orbits of "dar'Eq" – Earth – around the Sun. If she was shocked or surprised, she internalized the news well – or Dana and the others simply were not yet able to read her facial expressions well enough.

On the other hand, she captained a vessel and oversaw the lives of more than a million people. That would require nerves of steel, Dana reflected. And no doubt the possibility of very long hibernation had been part of Tar'lol's training.

When Peter MacGregor walked in Dr. Regan's makeshift office, she was finishing her notes – dictating them for the computer. She held a hand up.

"My patient asked again about status of her crew, passengers, cargo, and ship. She should be updated as soon as possible." The doctor closed out the recording and looked at Peter. "You arrived just in time."

"I was planning on visiting with her today about, well, everything. If you agree, but it sounds like you do."

And so Peter opted to enter Tar'lol's room without any protective gear. He promised the medical team he would keep his distance.

When Peter walked in the room, Tar'lol had been staring at the ceiling. He stayed just inside the door, when she began to speak in her native language. The sounds had become familiar.

"I had assumed you were all... Those Who Serve Us," she said, her words coming from the tablet still hanging in the middle of the room. The word sounded like 'oo'Pub.' She looked him over. "In the way you walked and move. There is a gracefulness among the oo'Pub, a fluidity of movement, that we Pra'oo simply lack."

"I'm Peter MacGregor. Or, as I understand your language and customs, I am MacGregor Peter. We have spoken over the intercom, but I thought you and I should speak in person. As fellow captains and leaders."

She smiled appreciatively and nodded. "The doctor, Dana, has been quite helpful. As I would expect of a medical professional, she would not answer questions about my crew, passengers, and cargo. I assume you now will?"

"Yes," he began to describe the wreckage at the bottom of the ship, noting that it had not appeared to impact any of the occupied levels. He lifted his tablet so she could see a rendering of the ship's exterior. Peter could see the technology represented by the tablet was new to her, but that she adapted quickly to it.

She explained that section had, as suspected, housed both the traditional propulsion engines and the system for moving the ship off and out of the Earth's gravity well. It was considered the most dangerous part of the ship's assembly, and a series of blast-proofs had been established in case of a catastrophic explosion.

"We assumed if any such explosion would occur, it would be later, or further away."

"Are you surprised none of the other vessels came looking for it?"

"No, especially if we are where you say we are." She paused and looked at him evenly. "Every captain, everyone in leadership, everyone who boarded an ark, understood that we could never return to this system. The Great Master was adamant on that point. No one could ever come close to this system once we left. Therefore, any ship that did not make it to our first or second rendezvous," she said something which the system could not translate. It chimed, and repeated in her language what she had said, asking for clarification. She paused, "This device is remarkable," and then continued. "Our second rendezvous was to be at the tenth star system in our jump set. Any that did not make it there would be presumed lost. A failure to rendezvous at any subsequent intervals would result in a search."

"Yours was the seventh to leave?"

"No, this was designated as the seventh ark but the Great Master ordered that departure to be randomized over a period of ten years, on specific days. Mine was the last to leave. Now, please, the status of the passengers and cargo?"

"Of what we presume to be your crew members, only one stasis box seems to have malfunctioned besides yours, and that happened many years ago. The remains were not identifiable to us." He showed her a picture of the name plate.

She looked away. "He was a distant member of my family, and was the second in command of the engineering section."

"I'm sorry for you loss." He gave her a moment before continuing, "Among the people like you, the passengers, there was a failure rate of approximately two percent." He paused. "Though it appears the rate at which the devices are failing has increased in recent years."

She nodded, clearly doing the math in her head as he continued. "For the rest, the failure rate appears to be about four percent." He felt only the hardness in his voice.

She locked eyes with Peter. It was unnerving. In that moment, he saw the flash of an apex predator. She was a master of the master race, and he was a slave. The moment was gone quickly, if it had ever been there at all. But he was certain she had read into his words the charge he not-so-subtly leveled.

"There it is. I had wondered how long until the topic would be broached. May I be direct, Captain Peter?"

"I would appreciate that."

"It is a tenant of my people's faith that the oo'Pub would inherit *dar'Eq* – as they appear to have done, as the Great Master said. But the reality is that despite the innate gracefulness of the oo'Pub of my day, most are not yet much more than animals themselves. Smart animals, clever, to be sure, but not yet very social with a great deal of effort. They need our care, and thrive under the structure we provide them. It is true that they have begun to work together, in community, but they are too stubbornly individualistic. I mean all that from my perspective, from my time."

She paused, looking carefully at Peter. "Does that offend you?"

"I am not here to offend, or be offended. You are the product of your culture, which has been dead on Earth for thirteen thousand years. Because of my crew of oo'Pub descendants, you, your crew, passengers, the oo'Pub, and cargo have been rescued."

Tar'lol nodded.

"I am grateful for the rescue, and it is proof my people were right to leave so yours might flourish. By the end, all of us knew my people were dying. Some wanted to fight it. The reality, is that we had been dying as a people for generations. The Houses represent what is left of those original," another word that could not be translated. "The Houses were what were left of the clans of the old people. The Houses tried to remain pure, but even today," she paused. "Well, today for me, the today I remember from just before entering the stasis, even the most pure of families like mine were less than they had been."

Peter let her talk. If he was understanding, she was telling him that this was what was left of the so-called... What? Neanderthals, the Clovis, or some other early version of humanity.

"Ours had been a great society, if the legends and stories were true. We built great cities with amazing technology, perhaps even rivaling your own. But all that was a thousand years ago..." she smiled. "Again, from my perspective. But we lost the drive for growth. We resumed simple ways. But then, four generations ago, the Great Master appeared and said what was evident but none wanted to admit: the world was changing, it could no longer be our home. It would be the home of the oo'Pub. We would have to die, or leave. My father's grandfather was among those who met the Great Master. Because of the Great Master, my people left their simple lives and went to work creating technologies even our ancestors could not imagine. My own grandmother, the matriarch of the House of Kaziok, had never ridden in a self-powered carriage, and I am the captain of an ark designed to fly through the stars. As a people, we became solely focused on leaving. Every action, every day, by everyone in our society, was focused on that goal."

She reached for the glass of water sitting beside her, took a sip, and set it down.

"So why bring the slaves?"

She cocked her head as she listened to a complex rendering of Peter's simply sentence.

"Slaves?" she finally said with exasperation. "The oo'Pub were not slaves. They were weak creatures, and we cared for them. They entertained us, and we loved them even as we resented the knowledge they would eventually surpass us."

"So then why bring them?"

She looked away, taking a deep breath. "Too many of my people simply could not part with their favored pets. It was a compromise."

CHAPTER 71

The Shackleton, *Kuiper Belt*

"And so they went off and created a new world safe for human pets," said Peter MacGregor, back in his Shackleton office. He was talking to his aunt and both sisters ahead of a briefing with the larger advisory group. "Sure, it was for the betterment of the humans, but right now, somewhere in the galaxy, is a world with saber-tooth tigers and enslaved humans serving a planet trying to reclaim its Neanderthal heritage."

"You're assuming they found anywhere to go," said Teresa. "Those other vessels, those, uh, arks, could have met the same fate as this one."

"Now you're just trying to make me feel good."

Samantha laughed. "Well, I was watching, and I thought you handled it well, little brother. And you were right. The culture she is operating from is thirteen thousand years dead. Let's say they found a new home. In those years, her people could have ended slavery and seen its culture radically shift. She could show up on their world seeming as foreign to them, as she does to us."

"That," said Lucy, "is an excellent point. I think I feel pity for her. She'd planned to awaken in a whole new world, or, at least, on route to one. Instead, she's been jarred into an unbelievably different life. Maybe even a version of a nightmare. This is not what she signed up for, everything is vastly more different than she imagined. In my reading, I suspect more than ever that what we know as the Younger Dryas event was the looming disaster they were fleeing. A comet strike in Greenland shifted the ecological landscape, killing many of the species you found preserved on the Object."

They all had a hard time calling it an "ark," for all the various implications.

Peter nodded. "You're right. She is very cool, very collected, and this is a lot to process. I cannot imagine how crazy all this must seem to her."

"It is, but it isn't," Teresa chimed in. "She seemed to indicate their 'Great Master' warned them it was coming. There seemed to be the implication this last 'Ark' had to leave by a specific date. Are you curious who this Great Master was to have forecasted this and motivated their societal shift? He must have been very persuasive."

"I meant," said Peter, "that this current circumstance must be crazy. I don't think her Great Master told them they'd spend thirteen thousand years frozen on the edge of the solar system. As for who it is, I just assumed it was a translation glitch. Some title we haven't seen. Maybe a scientist, researcher, or other innovator? You think it's more?"

Teresa looked tired. "I don't know. The questions are piling up faster than we can keep track."

CHAPTER 72

Medical Bay, The Object, Kuiper Belt

"Do you mind if we walk while we talk?" Tar'lol asked Peter as he entered her room the next morning. "I need to move." She was wearing one of the clothing sets from her closet. The cuffs of the long sleeves lined with the alternating green and blue of the House of Kaziok. Her tunic was tucked into pants, which were in turn tucked neatly into laced boots.

Peter MacGregor looked back down the hallway, where Dr. Regan gave a half-hearted thumbs up. "Let's go."

Tar'lol walked slowly, but for the first time he realized how differently she moved. It wasn't stiffness or injury. The range of motion was different. Her hips sort of rolled as she walked, her proportions were just enough different from what one expected in another person. But then, was she "another person"? She was sentient. She was alive. She thought and had feelings. But... what was she, to him? To all of them? Peter decided "re-define personhood" wasn't anywhere in his mandate out here.

They went to the stairs leading down to the command center, through a passageway, and down another staircase, into the series of officers' quarters. She stopped in front of one. It was the berth of the dead engineer, one of her distant family members. She looked in and shook her head, then kept walking.

"You may not believe this, but my people hold that life is sacred. All life. It is why we brought life from all over Earth. And we brought it ten times over."

She took a step back, and looked thoughtfully at Peter

MacGregor.

"I hope it is not inappropriate, but Dr. Dana has told me about your father and the affliction from which he suffers," she began, taking Peter by surprise.

He wasn't sure, though, which surprised him more: that the doctor had talked about his father, or that Tar'lol wanted to discuss it.

"This medical situation is one with which I am familiar. My own father had what you call a stroke, but it came after the adoption of" she said a name and was asked by the translation matrix to explain further. "I am sorry. Your machine is asking me to define these things, but I am not a doctor. So instead, I will say that my father's stroke came after we developed methods to repair such damage. In fact, what you call stasis boxes were part of that treatment. You are welcome to bring him here, or take the appropriate dosage of medications and a box to him."

Peter stopped walking, as did Tar'lol. "Why would you offer this?"

"I told you. We hold all life as sacred." She allowed a slight smile, showing her teeth. "And, if I understand correctly, everyone under my command and protection here owes our lives to his lifetime of diligence. So if my general respect for life is not enough a reason, perhaps simple repayment is?"

As he considered her words, she opened the door to one of the rooms that contained a dozen stasis boxes. She stopped. "I thought you said only one of my command crew had died."

"That's right," he said coming up next to her. Three of the boxes were occupied and lit with the dark blue light, nine stood empty. "There were no remains in them, so we assumed they were extras or unoccupied."

Tar'lol looked more closely, then stood with a furor in her eyes. "Were there other boxes you presumed to be empty on this level?

"Yes, only one. In one of the cabins like yours."

She let out low growl. "Take me."

Back up the stairs, through the passageway, to the left. "This one," he said. Andrew Todd and Dana Regan had left the medical bay and met them there. Tar'lol entered the small room. She mumbled a series of words that did not translate, but their tone suggested a series of invectives. Apparently even the artificial intelligence running the translation matrix knew not to ask. She emerged from the room, "Was there anything in here?"

"Nothing," Andrew Todd answered. "No one in the stasis box, nothing in the closest or drawers. Again, we assumed it was an empty berth."

She responded in her vowel-heavy language, with the translation taking an extra moment to translate.

A beat later, "Were any of the scouts missing?"

MacGregor, Regan, and Todd looked at each other. "Who?" they said in unison.

"Not a who. The scouts." Tar'lol paused. "Small craft."

It was not a surprise that they had not yet discovered all the secrets of this vessel, the Object, or Ark, but this was a big one. Everyone knew the dimensions they had of the explored levels did not add up; they still did not have a handle on the total space taken up by the grav-drive equipment, life support, or power generation. Nearly twenty percent of the overall kilometer length of the Object was missing in the *Shackleton* crews' measurements.

Following her down staircases and into a hitherto unknown elevator, a significant percentage of the "missing" space was revealed.

Between the first crew level and last passenger level was a launch bay for small craft; it was accessible only from special elevators on the command and engineering levels. The enclosed bay itself measured 55 meters in height, 200 meters in depth, and 100 meters in width. The *Shackleton* itself could almost fit in here; not quite, but almost.

Tar'lol explained the craft were designed to explore any potentially habitable worlds in the systems to which the Ark came. The scouts could carry a crew of four. While the Ark waited at a system's edge, these would go in for a closer reconnaissance.

Standing in an alcove and looking through heavy glass, Tar'lol said, "There should have been six scouts in here. Three are missing."

The hanger bay was, indeed, almost empty. Large, single-panel doors sat flush with the exterior wall. In the back corner of the cavernous room, farthest from them, were the remaining vehicles. The curves suggested an ability to cut through atmosphere despite being designed with gravity-drive technology in mind.

"Need you to slow down," began Peter. "What are you thinking happened?"

She closed her eyes, clearly in an attempt to calm herself. "After we cleared the orbit of–" a series of small clicks came from the translator, she answered a question, and then continued.

"After we cleared the orbit of our moon, the protocol was to make a series of small verification jumps. Our gravity drives could only make three such jumps before being locked into regular jump configuration. The third verification jump brought us to the orbit we now occupy. From here, we would have left to our first destination star. Before that happened, most of the entire crew was placed in stasis. When we got here, my first officer and I drew lots as to who would stand watch until our propulsion system could get the Ark into position for the first major jump. The winner would go in to stasis and be the first to be awakened when we arrived. I won. He stood watch and I went to sleep. It was his box that was empty, and the crew members that are missing all came from his–" again, the translation matrix tried to understand her word.

She and the automated system went back and forth, but the translation finally rendered as "cultish political party."

"So you think they abandoned ship?" Peter was incredulous. "Why would they have done that?"

Tar'lol responded with a string of words. The translation was chilling: "Sabotage."

CHAPTER 73

Command Level, The Object, Kuiper Belt

It took thirty minutes for Tar'lol to get her ship's ancient computer system online. Not only was the system ancient in actual years, it was antiquated by the standards of QA's quantum-based computers.

Lines of code flickered across the screens in the command level. "This is the archives station. It records orders entered into the Ark's mechanisms."

As she waited, Tar'lol explained – with no small embarrassment in her voice – that not the entirety of Pra'oo culture had agreed with the decision to leave Earth. And so the Council of the Ten Houses had decided that those who wished to remain could do so, provided they were stripped of all technology, manufactured tools, and materials which exceeded those found among the semi-wild oo'Pub – those early modern humans who had only recently begun assembling themselves into self-governing townships and conclaves. Recently, compared to the Pra'oo, anyway.

Those found to be aiding recalcitrant Pra'oo by providing materials, tools, or resources would be subjected to an even more harsh form of exile, which included what Dr. Regan understood to be something like a lobotomy.

For whatever reason, the House of Zoptu – of which her first officer's family was a part – seemed to have an outsized number of individuals opposing both the departure and the rules for staying.

A cult-like sub-group calling themselves the Pleydon dar'Eq – the Friends of Earth – rejected the teachings and prophesy of the so-called Great Master. They engaged in a campaign for the Council to reconsider the decision to leave, and gathered supporters from other Houses.

It seems her first officer – a man named Frean Zoptu Um'vat – had been an outspoken member of the group in his youth, though he publicly renounced the tenants and applied for crew status. The House of Zoptu, of which the Frean family was among the most prominent, tried to salvage its reputation ahead of the first Ark's departure. They attested to Um'vat's commitment to the mission, to the sincerity of his reform, and lobbied for him to be a First Officer – proving the Frean family's loyalty to the cause.

"He clearly had not rehabilitated," said Tar'lol. "There were rumors the Friends of Earth intended to disrupt Ark operations, but those were discounted as fear-mongering. Wrongly, it seems."

She stopped speaking, and began reading the words scrolling quickly across the screen. "Frean Zoptu Um'vat seals Kaziok Tar'lol for sleep. Frean Zoptu Um'vat accesses crew quarters. Releases..." she murmurs a series of names, and slowed the page scroll. "Frean Zoptu Um'vat disables emergency release systems. Frean Zoptu Um'vat seals engine houses and engages propulsion on delay. Scout bay doors opened. Scouts one, three, and four depart. Bay doors close on departure. Propulsion system engages."

A new page appeared. She looked up. "The system read the explosion as a catastrophic failure, locked down the Ark, and set itself in system preservation mode. That is how we were when you found us."

"Well, that preservation mode worked," remarked Andrew Todd.

"Indeed," she replied. "The remaining command crew should have been awakened when we entered preservation mode, but I suspect we will find those subroutines were violated by Um'vat."

"Does this mean he and his conspirators went back to

Earth?" asked Peter.

"It is possible," Tar'lol answered. "The scouts had that range. It was their purpose, after all. I imagine they thought overloading the propulsion system would destroy the Ark. And I would not be surprised that if we checked the inventories, we would find the scouts had been filled with whatever forbidden supplies they could get their hands on."

CHAPTER 74

Alpha Base, The Object, Kuiper Belt

It would be a long time, if ever, before they knew what – if anything – had been taken by the saboteurs. The manifest was the responsibility of each vessel's first officer, in this case, the conspirator Frean Zoptu Um'vat. Things could have been brought on board and not recorded. Things that had been recorded and catalogued could have been erased from those records and catalogues. He had had both the time and the ability to do a lot of damage.

Still, Tar'lol was pouring over the archived records in hopes of finding some clue. It was literally all she could do.

It was the fifth day after being fully awakened, and Tar'lol was finding herself vaguely wishing the ark had never been discovered, that she had not been pulled from her induced slumber. To learn that she had been betrayed, even if nearly thirteen thousand years ago, was demoralizing enough. But for that realization to have been made in front of the oo'Pub – even these advanced and civilized descendants of her time's oo'Pub... Well, it served only to enflame her anger.

According to the oo'Pub doctor and engineer, her stasis box had been in decline for some time. This had caused minor health deterioration, but nothing serious. She felt less physically sharp, and more easily tired. Those would pass as her body healed, the kind doctor assured her. It was akin to a couple bad nights of sleep. The body just needed to catch up on its rest.

But that rest proved elusive as she worked to make sense of the options available to her and her people.

Tar'lol had moved from the medical bay into to her own quarters. Her rooms had been designed for use during the planned periods of activity when arriving at a star. The mission profile alternated which crew members were to be awakened at each star for cataloguing before joining the rest of the fleet at the various intervals. She had once imagined sitting in this room and reading the report that indicated her crew had been the one to find the expected new home for their people promised by the Grand Master. She imagined sitting in this room and getting word one of the arks had found that world. But she had never imagined any of this.

Dr. Regan had agreed to the relocation on the condition Tar'lol continued wearing the unobtrusive bands around her forehead, left arm, and left index finger. These monitored her vital health statistics, she was told, and would allow them to be certain the damage caused by the failing box was not more severe. Tar'lol suspected the devices might be doing more, but she kept those particular thoughts to herself. She had yet to discover guile among these people.

Her reverie was interrupted by a slight tap from the wall of her doorway. She knew she had left the door open and was annoyed by the sound.

Among her people, an open door would have meant anyone could enter, at any time, and begin speaking. These oo'Pub paid too much deference to privacy, she had already decided. It was ironic, she thought, given they had entered her ship without permission, had begun experimenting on its systems without permission, and had rifled through her passengers' and crew's personal effects without permission. Yet they looked away when she dressed, and knocked on her door when it was open.

On the other hand, she knew, they had stopped all of that when they found her alive. More importantly, they seem single-mindedly focused on helping her. Helping her do *what* exactly, neither she nor they yet knew.

"Yes?" she asked, hearing the frustration in her voice and

briefly wondered if the almost magical computer translation system rendered the tone in addition to her words.

"Captain Tar'lol," came the actual voice of Andrew Todd, not the synthesized version of his voice to which she had become accustomed. She looked up and realized he was attempting to speak in her language. "Am I able to be a burden to you?"

She smiled. "I am honored you are trying my language." She then repeated the sounds she had heard the oo'Pub make, "Thank you."

He entered her room. A small device hung from a lanyard around his neck. He held a small box, which he presented to her. She opened it and found a similar necklace inside, as well as a small round device that she intuitively knew would fit in her ear.

"I've configured these devices with the translation matrix," he said. "It will allow you to speak softly in your own language, with the translation coming out of the speaker. Meanwhile, the earpiece should allow you to hear every conversation around you, but in your own language. This is my own design," he said with a modest smile. She noticed that he was, indeed, speaking more softly with his own voice, allowing the device to project the sounds for him. And it seemed the translations were coming faster and in a more natural tone.

"I remain amazed by your ingenuity," she said. "This feels very comfortable."

"Some off-the-shelf technology, with a few modifications," he said, then wondered how that actually translated. "Does that phrase, 'off-the-shelf,' actually translate for you?"

"What I hear you saying in my language is 'Some available tools have been modified for slightly new purposes.' Is that what you are intending to say?"

"Yes, thank you," he said, amazed again at the matrix's capabilities.

"It seems to me you are being too modest," she said.

She watched his checks flush red. It was a reaction she remembered among the oo'Pub who had lived in their home when she was a child. It was a physical manifestation of embarrassment. "I do not mean to embarrass you, only that I appreciate the accommodation."

He nodded. "Well, it is a little self-serving on my part, because it will make conversation a little easier. Thank you for allowing our research team to scan the Ark's collection of maps and books, I have some questions if you don't mind?"

"Of course not, and I thank you for understanding my reasons for not allowing you to scan the personal documents of my passengers and crew."

"Absolutely. So I want to ask you about a book I have read twice now. The first time was before we had revived you, so the translation was very rough. I've re-read it now with the better translation and I am hoping you can confirm I am understanding the literature."

Tar'lol laughed. "Well, I have never been one for literature, most of my reading in recent years has been devoted to technical manuals and the like, but I will certainly try to help."

Andrew pulled the book, one from the Ark's library, from his satchel. "The first copy we found, before we found you, was with the remains of a Pra'oo. We have since returned that copy to the person's resting place. At first we thought the title was *The Structure Over Water*. Now, we think it is *The Bridge of Love*."

Tar'lol smiled as she thumbed the book he handed to her. "I think you have the title correct. This is actually one I know, I should confess. It has long been a favorite of young men and women."

"So here is what I think I know. It's a book of poetry, that weaves together the story of a young woman and young man who fall in love despite coming from warring houses. How am I doing?" He felt like he was giving a book report.

"You have it right so far," she closed her eyes and recited

a passage:

> *Klir'lat had found his love, the maiden Nic'cal.*
> *Even if it cost his life and honor, he*
> *would have her. He would toss his soul*
> *against the Moon before denouncing their love.*

Andrew was impressed. "I've seen that phrase a time or two in other books of what appeared to be poetry, that idea of being slammed into the Moon. Where does it come from?"

"I do not know," she said after a moment of consideration. "It's a phrase that is very old. It represents dealing with the deepest anguish by ending one's life in the most spectacular of fashions."

Andrew nodded. "I guess crashing into the moon would make quite the statement. So despite everything, Klir'lat refused to renounce Nic'cal. He was ready to end it all, but he was saved when the families of both houses made peace and then threatened to overthrow the ruling elders who opposed their marriage. And they did it all for the purity of the young couple's love."

"Yes, your summary is sufficient. I believe you understand it quite well." She gave a genuine laugh. "I never imagined I'd talk about poetry and literature with a...." Tar'lol stopped herself. They both knew what she was going to say. "But this is a welcome diversion."

He nodded in agreement. "If you liked this, you might enjoy *Romeo and Juliet*, though the ending isn't as pleasant." He paused. "May I ask you a personal question?" She nodded, a hint of skepticism in her eyes, so he continued. "Do you have family onboard?"

"In terms of my immediate family, only my husband and our two children. They are in the passenger section, of course. I visited them earlier today; they appear to be sleeping well. The rest of my siblings are scattered among the other Arks. No two offspring of any Heir of House can be on the same Ark, unless a particular heir had more than ten offspring, which I do not believe to be the case with any of the Houses."

"So as captain of the Ark assigned to your House, does that mean you are the head of the House of Kaziok?"

"Oh, no, that would be my sister, the second-born, she was on the third Ark to depart." She understood the inquisitive furrow of his brow, as a question forming. "The first born of the Heir of the House sees after the primary businesses of the House and its families. The second born of the Heir makes the decisions about application of House resources, sits on the Council of the Ten Houses, and eventually becomes the Head of the House. Both the first and second born rotate in various posts of the House's businesses until they ascend to their particular role. They are expected to develop leadership skills and relationships with House members of various stations. The third born of the Heir of the House, me for example, is allowed to pursue any career, but must marry the third or fourth born of one of the other Houses."

"So your husband...?"

"He was of the House of Kaln."

"Was of? As in, not anymore?"

"That would be correct. When any child of the Heir of a House marries the Heir of another House's offspring, the male becomes part of the female's House."

Andrew shook his head. "I have a lot to learn about your culture."

"I know less about yours, or even you," she said. "Do you have a spouse on Earth? Children, perhaps?"

"Tried marriage, but it didn't work out. No kids. My twin brother, Alec, is married with children."

It was then that Andrew learned from Tar'lol that the Pra'oo did not have a word for "divorce" or "twins" because, apparently, they did not have either. This, in turn, was how he learned he should not be giving lectures on either biology or genetics any more than he should ancient love poetry or modern civil law.

CHAPTER 75

Eisenhower Executive Office Building, Washington, D.C., U.S.A.

The head of the U.S. Geological Survey had never been on the White House grounds, except for a field trip in junior high school. This was now his second visit in as many days.

Technically, of course, Fred Vanover wasn't in the White House, he was in the adjoining Eisenhower Executive Office Building. More precisely, he was underneath it in a highly secured briefing room. And even more precisely, according to the president's chief of staff, none of these visits ever happened.

His official schedule, should anyone inquire (which, no one ever had), indicated he was going for a jog around the monuments, and then having lunch with an unnamed friend.

"We have found nothing, in any database or live scan, matching these schematics," he said. "Wherever those ships went, they either aren't anywhere on Earth, or they were completely dismantled and scrapped."

He had thought it was joke, an ancient spaceship and all that. It was not. He had been told to look for concentrations of certain metals in certain parts of the world. For as impressive as the satellites facing out towards the universe were, the resources suddenly available to the USGS looking down were even more so.

The USGS had long operated under the Department of the Interior – an agency known jokingly as the Department of Everything Else because things like land, programs, and even minor agencies, all collected there when they had nowhere else to go. Like everything else at Interior, the USGS was allowed to exist without too many interruptions, provided that it operated efficiently and quietly. In exchange for being left alone by meddling politicians in Congress and career-climbing bureaucrats from other parts of the executive branch, agencies and organizations within Interior found themselves occassionally asked to provide cover for activities no one else in the federal government could be seen doing.

"In the last twenty-four hours we've identified every lost airplane and fishing boat between the California coast and Prime Meridian. But we haven't found these 'scouts.'"

Sitting across from him was a woman he had only ever seen on television, Lucy Hyde of QA. She had sped through his written report. "Even if they had been scrapped or crashed in the Atlantic, the specific composition of these materials would have flashed on your surveys, there is no doubt. Maybe they didn't actually make it this far?"

The other person in the secured room was Special Assistant to the President Karen Baxter. Shortly after the president had been briefed, she had been read into the situation involving the Object – the Seventh Ark – and became the administration's point person. She had the authority to move any agencies of government necessary to help understand more about, and what to do with, the Object discovered by QA.

Fred first met Karen Baxter years earlier when he was USGS' liaison to Congress and she was the legislative director to the congressman who was now the president. She had been likable back then. The weight of her job made her less so these days. He figured the same could be said of him, at times.

"So we wasted a day and valuable resources looking for something that isn't there?"

Lucy looked up at Karen. "No, Karen, we spent a day and valuable resources finding where these things are not located. That's useful. It means that twelve-thousand-eight-hundred years ago these scout ships did not land on Earth. They went somewhere, but not here."

Fred Vanover had known only "ancient," he had not been given a specific age. "Did you just say, 'twelve-thousand-eight-hundred years ago'? Because if I heard you right, there might be a reason why the ships haven't been found, or didn't land here at all."

That reason was Younger Dryas, a cataclysmic global event. Within a matter of days, the planet's temperatures plummeted, and stayed there for almost a millennia. The mammoth, the mastodon, and other species died off across the North American continent. Some theories blamed the great cooling on ice dams collapsing in North America, releasing vast amounts of fresh water into the Atlantic ocean, altering its hydrology and the planet's weather patterns. Fred Vanover, like a majority of scientists who studied the period, had come to believe Younger Dryas actually resulted from an astroid or fragment of a comet slamming into Greenland.

No one knew for sure, of course. But however it happened, Younger Dryas had changed the Earth dramatically for everyone and everything.

"If they had parked their scouts in North America, Europe, or western Asia, they could well have been obliterated by the impacts. Conversely, if your guys showed up as it was happening, they may have decided to go somewhere else." Fred Vanover wondered why she didn't seem surprised by this.

Lucy smiled briefly; her aunt's hunch about Younger Drays was just seconded by an actual expert. She quickly opened the messaging tool on her tablet and sent a group query to Linda Bletchley, Andrew Todd, and her brother on *Shackleton*. "Are there any wooly mammoths or mastodons on the Object?"

Bletchley responded within seconds. "Inventory translation shows seven of both."

Lucy looked out the window for a moment, thinking. What they knew was that Tar'lol's vessel – the last of ten to leave – had made it off planet just ahead of the prophesied cataclysm, very likely this Younger Dryas event.

What if Tar'lol had literally left just before it, as in weeks? What if, because her society was following the commands of a religious-like leader and no one knew what form this altering of the Earth would take, some wanted to see it? What if some wanted to confirm the prophesy? What if some doubted? What if her *Great Master* wasn't just trying to save the oo'Pub branch of humans from the Pra'oo branch of humans, but rather saving the Pra'oo from the devastation of Younger Dryas? And what if the First Officer and his fellow saboteurs came back to find the Earth's climate collapsing as predicated, from this impact... what would they have done?

"The scout ships had enough power to get to Earth and back, but no more," Lucy said out loud, surprising Baxter and Vanover. "Their batteries had to be recharged by the Object."

"Excuse me?" the president's special assistant said.

"The scouts would not have tried to go back to the Object, to the Ark, because they believed they had destroyed it. So, they come all this way and they find Earth is being pummeled by a planet-altering comet. They have nowhere to go, so where would they go?"

+++

"They plowed themselves into the moon," said Yua Saito. The moon had been under constant bombardment by all sorts of unsavory collisions over the years. The small craters near the north pole on the far side of the Moon had never stood out as remarkable. Until now.

"We're seeing trace elements of materials from the scouts," she said, then corrected herself. "And by 'trace,' I mean enough to make three of these scout ships."

The decision to check the Moon came after Lucy Hyde left Washington. She made a voice call to her brother from the car, using Station's quantum link. As it happened, Andrew Todd had been in her brother's office. She laid out what she had learned about the timing.

"They killed themselves by crashing into Moon," Andrew had said immediately and with absolute assurance.

"Come again?" Lucy and Peter had asked in unison.

"That was a huge poetic device in their culture. I've come across it in the works of Ma'len, and even in speeches from their top politicians."

"I now really wish this was a video call, because I'd like to see my brother's face right now."

"My expression says that Mr. Todd has lost his mind, but at this point he is the undisputed expert on the Pra'oo culture."

And so, since it would cost nothing, Lucy Hyde had instructed Yua Saito to order a moon survey team to scan the Earth's natural satellite. Within forty-two minutes, they had been given their answer.

CHAPTER 76

Command Level, The Ark, Kuiper Belt

It wasn't fair to say Tar'lol was relieved. Even for all her anger directed at Um'vat and his band of saboteurs, she hated the idea of suicide even more. She would have rather learned they had died any number of ways – at the hands of wild oo'Pub, or from famished animals preying on Pra'oo flesh. But suicide?

No matter what the poets said, there was nothing romantic about it.

"It was a long time ago," she said to Peter MacGregor, who delivered the findings from his colleagues. "But, not for you."

"No, not for me. But, in fact, it was a long time ago."

The Seventh Ark's command level fell silent. Several moments passed before the quiet was interrupted by an insistent whistle from Peter's tablet. He ignored it.

"Tar'lol, how has your review of the systems gone?"

"The damage from the explosion was severe, and the years have not been kind to the independent systems and backups keeping the Ark alive. Engineer Benny has been an astute pupil, thanks in large part to Andrew helping with the translations."

"Anything you need from us we will try to–"

His tablet whistled again. Peter picked it up, and saw a text message from Linda Bletchley. "Urgent from Station. Request Actual, secure message incoming."

He excused himself, leaving Andrew and Tar'lol on the Ark. He made his way down the kilometer-long elevator shaft, through the sealed passageway to Alpha Base, across the umbilical, and finally to the *Shackleton*'s own command center.

Linda gave him an apologetic shake of the head as newly minted Communications Lead Jeff Prasadh keyed in the codes to bring Flight Director Saito on the screen.

"Sorry to keep you waiting, Flight Director. Everything alright?"

It was not. Three hours earlier one of the stellar cartographers at Station, using data from the navigation beacon system, had flagged a massive and previously unknown rock in an orbit perilously close to the Object.

"We now estimate a ninety-five percent or greater chance it will strike the Object," she said. "You either need to move it, or get *Shackleton* out of harm's way. You have ninety-two days and some change."

And at that moment Peter MacGregor knew Tar'lol, and Tar'lol alone, had to decide what to do about the one and half million lives under her command.

CHAPTER 77

The Shackleton, *Kuiper Belt*

"A decision tomorrow?" asked an incredulous Karen Baxter, the special assistant to the President of the United States. "What sort of decision is this? We move your ship out of the way of the massive rock bearing down on it, or you and everyone onboard will die. What am I missing?"

As soon as he had ended his call with Saito, Peter had gone back to the Object and briefed Tar'lol on the situation. She said she would need to think about the options. She promised a decision within two days.

"With all due respect," began Charlotte Smith-Davies, from her office on the *Henson*. The vessel had received a patchwork of repairs in interstellar space, and then given a clean bill of health after a refit back at Station. Now, it was waiting for a Station berth to load crew and provisions. Charlotte had not wanted to leave her ship alone, even in high Earth orbit, even tied off to Station.

"After nearly thirteen-thousand years, she has a lot to decide," continued Charlotte. "From what we're learning about their belief structure, she cannot come back to Earth. We certainly do not know of any viable planet to point her toward. For all we know, the other ships are still bouncing around the stars. And even if she accidentally found their people, the Seventh Ark's crew and passenger would be as different as we are from... well, from the cavemen she's transporting. I say she has a lot to consider."

"Moving the ship doesn't change any of that," said Baxton. "It just gives her more time to think about the options.

What am I missing here?"

While this briefing was larger than Peter would have liked, it was only a couple dozen people. Yet from his perspective, it was made up by an outsized number of opinionated people certain they were smarter than anyone else participating.

"Forgive me for interrupting, Ms. Baxter," began Peter. "Is it the position of the President of the United States that we should simply move the Object without the consent of its rightful captain? I thought we slowed down our work researching the Object and its contents at the behest of the President and the British Prime Minister precisely because they felt that since the rightful decision maker was conscious, we needed to respect that right of ownership. So, as the guy who has to put all these things into motion out here, I would appreciate some clarity."

The presidential appointee started to speak, and then stopped herself from replying twice.

So Peter continued. "You'll forgive me, I'm a pretty black and white guy. If there is a lack of clarity in terms of what you are being asked to communicate, I'd be happy to chat with your boss. Even way out here, the re-election committee's urgent requests for money still find me. I'm pretty confident, given my financial situation, that I could get on a call real fast. Would that be easier? Maybe I'll just sign off here and call his personal number? Does that work?"

Lucy could see her brother building a head of steam. She had never once, in all her life, ever heard him bring up their family's financial resources. She stepped in to defuse the situation.

"I think, for right now, a delay of a few hours in getting an answer is more than acceptable for an event that is months away. The clock is still very favorable."

It would not be that long. When the call ended, Peter had two messages waiting. The first was from Andrew Todd's comms device, but the message itself was Tar'lol.

"I would like for you to try to move the Ark," she said. "I have said this before; my people hold that life is sacred and I have a responsibility to use every means at my disposal to preserve the lives of those in my charge. Despite everything else, my mission objective remains the same. I must always err on the side of life."

He felt a sense of relief wash over him, and he immediately forwarded the message to his sister Lucy, and Flight Director Saito.

He then remembered the second message. It was a text message from Chief Engineer Hathaway. As always, it was crisp and to the point.

"The Ark cannot be moved by *Shackleton* unless you want to destroy both ships."

CHAPTER 78

Conference Room, The Shackleton, *Kuiper Belt*

After all these weeks, this was Tar'lol's first visit to the *Shackleton*. Despite its diminutive size compared to her own vessel, she was nonetheless in awe of the technology in such varied uses. Before they went in, Andrew Todd explained the conference room technology.

It seemed the young communications expert-turned-linguist had developed a comfortable advisory relationship with the woman. Andrew had spent more time with her than even Dr. Regan, and was now speaking bits of her language with increasing degrees of success.

Peter was sure it was somewhere in the personnel files, but he had not realized Andrew Todd possessed an incredibly well-trained eidetic memory – perhaps even close to what was commonly called photographic.

Coupled with speed-reading, Andrew Todd was absorbing much of the cultural materials being scanned from the Object's libraries. He was the closest thing they had to an expert. He did not have the knowledge base to understand the technical manuals – ranging from operations of the Object to basic farming techniques – but the books on history, literature, and religion were accessible to him. And, as Tar'lol had pointed out several days earlier, Mr. Todd was actually very helpful in serving as a translation go-between on the technical issues with the Hathaway's engineering team.

Tar'lol put on the special conferencing glasses, and was amazed when the bare room with a simple table transformed before her eyes into a more finely appointed version of itself from Station. Like most first-time users, she pulled the glasses down to see the room in which she was standing – awash in incoherent pinpoints of lights – and then watched the enhanced version re-materialize as she slid the glasses back in place.

A moment later Lucy Hyde "entered" the room, followed by Teresa Schultz, Flight Director Yua Saito, Flight Doctor Antonio Perez. Two more figures appeared in the room: from her berth on *Henson* was Charlotte Smith-Davies, and from the White House was Karen Baxter, on behalf of the President of the United States.

Peter saw two more people were entering the meeting space: Hanson O'Donnell, QA's general counsel, and his sister, Samantha.

Andrew Todd spoke first. "The translation matrix has been doing an excellent job, but it will be important – with so many of us – that everyone speak deliberately and take care not to speak over each other." He introduced everyone in the room.

"Teresa Schultz," said Tar'lol. "Andrew tells me I have you to thank for the ability to hear and be heard despite the differences in language. It is amazing."

Teresa smiled, "I am glad it has been of use, but Mr. Todd there seems to have made it all the more practical. Well, done, Andrew."

Andrew blushed, mumbled his thanks, and looked at Peter MacGregor and Benny Hathaway. They were up.

Hathaway began, "As it turns out, the structural integrity of the Ark will not withstand a push from the *Shackleton*. The damage caused by the explosion to the propulsion system was severe. It is a testament to the engineering prowess of the Pra'oo that it survived the incident at all, and then for some thirteen thousand years in space."

Karen Baxter, who had become a fixture in the briefings, had a scowl on her face. "Is there nowhere else from which you can push, pull, or otherwise move this thing? It's massive."

"We can, but at none of those places would we be able

to provide enough power to move the Seventh Ark out of the way in time without risking its structural integrity. Tar'lol's ship was absolutely designed to withstand massive structural forces, just not in the way we would be applying them."

"So we're dooming these people?" she asked.

"No, we have a plan," said Hathaway, who turned to Peter. "Boss?"

"You just heard Engineer Hathaway. There's nowhere *on* the Ark that can withstand the pressure we would need to apply to move it out of the way in the time we have. But as it turns out, the Ark can actually move itself." He let the murmurs stop.

"The *Shackleton*, the *Henson*, the *Powell*, and the rest of the ships in our fleet have – just like the Object, excuse me, the Seventh Ark – they all have three types of engines. The first is good old-fashioned rocket propulsion. The second is the gravity-drive system that works by manipulating the gravity fields of larges object within its interaction radius. And, the third, is the drive system that allows us to create and move into a sort of subspace gravity stream. Each of these systems are independent of each other. So while two of the Ark's systems were destroyed by sabotage, the third was not."

"Are you suggesting the main gravity-drive system is working?" asked Yua Saito.

"Not suggesting," he said. "Informing. Our engineering team says once the system is warmed up, in under a week it could be operating. What's more, we could have it operating at an even higher efficiency than Captain Tar'lol and her crew could have expected."

"So, why this call?" asked the lawyer, O'Donnell. "We've given permission for the Object to be moved. Why do you need oversight here?"

"It's because the main mechanism on my ship was not made for short jumps," said Tar'lol. "Once it is powered up and activated, we will make a jump that is the equivalent of five light-years. And, by oath, the Ark of the Kaziok's cannot return here."

Silence fell in the room.

Finally, Lucy spoke. "Captain Tar'lol, let's set aside the distances involved, and forgive me for being frank. It's been almost thirteen thousand years. What is the reasonable expectation you will find your people? Will they be recognizable to you, or you to them? Isn't there a time limit on your oath? Surely we could find a way to integrate you and your people back here on Earth?"

Tar'lol listened thoughtfully to the translation. She stood from her seat and walked around the table to where the holographic image of Lucy Hyde was sitting. She knelt before the projection and spoke in a low voice.

"For me, for every single man, woman, and child, Pra'oo and oo'Pub alike, it was yesterday, not thirteen thousand years. We have staked our lives on leaving, our beliefs about ourselves and the universe. Your people have heard me explain the value we place on life, so I hope that will give weight to what I am about to say. If you will not let us leave, then I know each of the people on the Ark of Kaziok would rather die in the cold silence of space than betray our oath. As for those waiting for us among the stars? I do not know what difference the years will have made, but I would hope they would even today honor us for honoring the oath we all made."

The room again fell silent.

Andrew Todd was the first to speak. "I know I'm the low man on the totem pole here, but how in the world is there even a question about the right thing to do? Shouldn't the answer simply be, 'Thanks for the information, now get to work moving that ship'?"

"I appreciate, and agree, with your enthusiasm Mr. Todd," said Lucy Hyde. "But I feel like there might be more hanging in the air as it relates to this plan."

There was.

Benny Hathaway took a deep breath. "I hope that what I am about to say is not offensive, Captain Tar'lol, but I need to be frank with my colleagues."

She nodded, so Hathaway continued.

"I'm an engineer, and as such I have studied the history of engineering. Always thought maybe I would finish my doctorate and teach on the subject. I bring that up because this ship follows no single standard for technological progress. Generally, when you find a complex system, everything in the system is of similar progress. Not here. They have exterior bay doors that open and close with manual gears, on a ship with a sort of gravity-drive we haven't yet built, but operated by computers barely deserving the name. I don't even know where to begin on their power generation system... They have these stasis boxes we cannot even begin to understand, but the ship's lighting is barely a step ahead of Thomas Edison's first light bulb. As Tar'lol explained it to me, everything in the Pra'oo culture was aimed at getting off the Earth and to a distant star. They got aspects of technology only to the point critical for that to be achieved, and nothing more."

"This is fascinating, Mr. Hathaway, but where are you heading?" asked Saito.

"It means that for the Ark to be up and running in the time needed, and for them to continue on their mission, we would need to interface some of our technology with it. And we would need to crew it."

More silence.

Then, Hanson O'Donnell said, "You want permission to send some people on a one-way trip aboard a thirteen-thousand-year-old ship that is held together by duct tape and baling wire? I'm pretty sure we can't do that."

Before anyone else could speak, Andrew Todd cleared his throat. "I've already volunteered. Benny and Dana are ready to go. I know this language better than anyone, and I think I am getting a handle on their culture to an extent no one else here has or will. And I know the translation matrix well enough to be able to modify it when we find their people. After all these years, there will have been some language shift." He added, "If this is the price of saving more than a million people, it's worth it."

No one on Station could hide their shock. Lucy Hyde said, "I would like for everyone on *Shackleton* to leave the conference room except for my brother."

As they filed out, Tar'lol could be heard asking Andrew, "What is this 'totem pole' on which you occupy a low position?"

CHAPTER 79

Executive Conference Room, Station, HEO

Lucy's communications board indicated her brother was, indeed, the last man in the *Shackleton's* makeshift conference room.

"Why have you allowed that conversation to go this far?" she demanded. "Letting people think they can just…"

"Because more than a million lives are at stake," Peter replied. He turned to his aunt. "Teresa, you and Samantha, more than anyone else, should understand this. This is what you two have hard-wired into QA's corporate culture. The people on board the *Shackleton* simply cannot be told to stand down from a chance to save lives. You always ask, what is QA doing to better the lives of people? Well, we've come into contact with people who will die if we do nothing."

There was a long period of silence.

"I don't want to lose you to space," said Lucy. "I haven't been able to introduce your nephew to you, yet." She hoped the projection system did not render her eyes swelling with tears.

"No, I'm not going," Peter said quickly, the matter already settled in his mind. "I want to come home with what may be a way to save Dad, to bring him back to us. But for all this to happen, there a few more parts of this plan you need to understand and buy into. And you can't let the *Henson* leave Station just yet."

Charlotte Smith-Davies laughed nervously. "What, you want to send the *Henson* along with them?"

"No," said Peter. "Of course not. I want the *Henson* to come out here with a skeleton crew, and transfer everyone not going on the trip on to it... so we can tuck the *Shackleton* inside the Seventh Ark's gravity field bubble."

Lucy narrowed her eyes. "So, we're giving away a ship, now?"

This part of the plan was straightforward. With Tar'lol's guidance, the wreckage underneath the Ark could be cut away, he explained. Some could be kept to reuse as raw materials for the *Shackleton*'s 3D printers, the rest bundled and hauled back to Earth for study.

Meanwhile, the *Shackleton* would be coupled to the Seventh Ark in the newly cleaned out space, sitting within the bubble created by the much larger vessel's gravity drive. Using a bay full of probes, like the ones that the *Shackleton* crew created to originally explore the Object's exterior so many weeks earlier, star systems could be explored more quickly and efficiently for signs the Pra'oo had been there.

When deciding to leave Earth nearly thirteen thousand years earlier, after an initial pre-set series of 10 jumps to nearby stars, the Arks were to rendezvous at a common star every fifth jump. When the first Ark arrived at any particular rendezvous system, a timer was set for two standard years, at which time the leadership would be awakened to see what others had arrived. They would agree on their next jump series and leave a message buoy for stragglers.

"This means from the second rendezvous point on, there will be a message buoy waiting, since this Ark never made the meet up," explained Peter.

"So you first have to make it to that first rendezvous, and you still have an almost unlimited number of stars to explore in finding that buoy," said Saito. "How do you expect to find them?"

"We have three advantages. First, we know what kinds of stars they were looking for, but didn't have the ability to detect at distance. We do. We can cross off every star outside those parameters. Second, the *Shackleton*'s computers are armed with several decades of exoplanet surveys and stellar analysis.

We can significantly reduce the number of systems to explore based on that. Third, after this many years, the radio messages from the buoys will be all over the place. Faint? Yes, but now that we know what to be listening for, *Shackleton*'s equipment should be sensitive enough to pick them up from a distance – a capability the Ark doesn't have." '

Lucy Hyde spoke again. "So you want to donate the *Shackleton* and a large number of probes and equipment to this cause from which several of your crew may never return?"

+++

When the meeting ended, Lucy and Teresa sat alone in the conference room.

"Is it wrong that when Peter said he wasn't going, I immediately decided I didn't really care?" Lucy asked her aunt.

"The draw of family is very strong. It's why Tar'lol is willing to keep looking for her people. Even distant family is better than no family."

"Do you think he will regret his decision to come home, and not go trekking through the stars?"

"I'm sure that thought will cross his mind, but like you and Samantha, he has enough of his father in him to make me think he'll figure out a way to make both things happen."

At a chime, Lucy looked at her tablet. She smiled.

"Looks like this alleged treatment for dad might work," she said. "Dr. Prasadh and his team have been looking over the initial data Dr. Regan transmitted from the *Shackleton*. His message to me makes a rather enthusiastic case for it being the greatest medical breakthrough in our history. So I think it's a good start."

CHAPTER 80

The Ark, Kuiper Belt

Explaining a totem pole to Tar'lol had taken Andrew longer than he would have expected, in part because he realized that he didn't fully understand them himself. He knew what the expression meant, but not what a totem pole actually represented in real life.

By the time they reached the elevator shaft that would take them the kilometer to her command level, she had also begun regretting having asked.

"Do you think Engineer Benny would be able to secure the elevator shaft before we depart?" she asked, changing the subject to his great relief.

"We can ask. I suspect this is on his list of items to address in securing the Ark for grav-drive travel."

Imperceptibly, the elevator began moving.

He turned to her and said something that had been on his mind.

"You have more than a million people onboard – Pra'oo and oo'Pub. Why wasn't your First Officer to able recruit anyone else?"

Tar'lol nodded thoughtfully.

"I have taken some solace that he and his fellow cultists didn't have a bigger following. I doubt any of the people who boarded as passengers did so expecting their lives to be ended while in stasis. They would have simply stayed behind and waited." She smiled ruefully. "On the other hand, it would have been structurally impossible for him to get any sympathetic passengers out. While the crew can be individually awakened, the passengers can only be awakened by House, except for a select few individuals."

She added, "With the exception of the crew and senior members of the Houses on each Ark, the passengers were to only be awakened when we reached our final destination."

They were greeted at the top of the elevator shaft by a beaming Benny Hathaway. "Just got word from the Captain. We're going."

CHAPTER 81

Abingdon-on-Thames, Oxfordshire, England

While his physical health was failing, Charlotte Smith-Davies took comfort that her aged father was mentally as sharp as ever. Some detractors might challenge how sharp that mind had ever been, but she knew her father had been proven more right than anyone else.

Indeed, the discovery some ten months earlier had vindicated her father's ideas more than they had those of Ian MacGregor. And did so in ways he never would have imagined.

She had fond memories of this home. It had been in their family for generations, and she felt the warm embrace of each of her ancestors here. After her mother had died in France, Charles Smith-Davies had returned to England to live out his final years. The last time she had been home was just before taking command of the *Henson's* mission.

With Lucy Hyde's permission, and at the encouragement of Teresa Schultz, Charlotte had not only told her aged father about the Object and shown him pictures, he had been given the chance to have a brief conversation with Captain Kaziok Tar'lol of the Ark of Kaziok. "I never, in all my life, dreamt that..." his frail voice trailed off. He smiled at his daughter as she squeezed his hand. "I wish I could go."

"It was your doodles that made it possible," she said, reminding him of the 'danger' sign he had drawn for so many years. "With that single clue, that reference mark, Teresa was able to build out the language translation matrix."

He nodded. "I'm glad you are doing it. You will be missed, but I am glad you're going."

Charlotte lifted her eyebrow quizzically.

"Come, now, Charlie? Just how dim do you think I have become?" he smiled. "You tell me about this fantastic discovery, about the things and peoples on board, and the plan to help them continue their voyage thirteen millennia later. You are here, now, and your son cuts short his semester... You think I can't connect the dots?"

"I guess I had hoped to tell you myself."

"Little girl, you did, and did so in the most glorious way imaginable."

She could not have quite placed her finger on the feeling she had when the meeting ended on Station that resulted in the plan being approved. She just knew, deeply, that she needed to talk to her husband, Thomas, who had been an accidental crew member aboard the *Shackleton* and the Seventh Ark for months. Before saying it, they both knew they wanted to go. As an astronomer who had specialized in exoplanets, Thomas Newcome was certain his skills would add immediate value to the search for the Pra'oo's new world.

Of course, they would only go if their son Grayson would be allowed to join them... and if he wanted to go. What would likely be a one-way trip across the galaxy for their family was equal parts terrifying and exhilarating. He had agreed without a moment's hesitation.

Preparations for the trip had been easier than imagined. The *Henson* was being loaded with everything, including a couple spare kitchen sinks. Foodstuffs from around the world were procured, items of personal or professional interest to the crew volunteering for the mission had been gathered.

Thomas, Charlotte, and Grayson would be the only family going.

Apparently, the lanky 17-year-old had quietly entered his grandfather's study. The old man looked past his daughter to the youngest of his grandchildren. "This will definitely beat that backpacking trip around Australia you had with your uncle and cousins."

+++

In Washington, D.C., the President of the United States was standing in the situation room, which had long utilized the remote-conference capabilities developed by QA. Tables and chairs had been removed, so it matched the configuration of what the president had been told was the configuration of the makeshift conference room in the *Shackleton*'s hold.

The president was headed for an all-but certain re-election. This meant, after years seeking and holding public office, he could focus on governing rather than politicking. That had not always been the case. During his first years as a Member of Congress, he skipped as many committee hearings and floor debates as possible so he could he engage in retail politics. At some point in there, his interests changed. He kept his "hand-shaking and baby-kissing" muscles in practice, but they interested him less. He was convinced that the only reason he was elected president was because he had developed a deep love for the act of governing, which he hoped was ultimately visible to the electorate – and more winsome.

In his own mind, the difference was most noticeable at a party. For a long time, like all politicians everywhere, he had been focused on his own words, not those of the person he was talking *at.* When the other person spoke, he would scan the room to see who else might be a step more important to greet or speak *at.*

That had changed. Now, he realized, that when he was in a room full of people, he simply focused on the person who was talking to him. He did more listening now, engaged in more conversations. It was refreshing.

At this moment, he was talking with the projection of a young man on the edge of the solar system and charging him to be America's first ambassador in space. He was not actually going to be an ambassador, per se, since that would require senatorial confirmation – and not a single member of the U.S.

Senate knew about any of this.

The Attorney General, herself a former member of the Senate, had found a clever way to work around the problem. Mr. Todd would be direct-commissioned as a colonel in the U.S. Army, nominally assigned to the White House and then tasked as a foreign liaison officer to the Secretary of State. Andrew Todd had left active military duty five years earlier, and remained a terminal first lieutenant in the inactive ready reserves. He was about to jump four ranks and back into active duty. Not bad for a Tuesday.

"Mr. Todd, do you understand what has been requested of you?"

"Yes, sir, I do."

"Then please raise your right hand and repeat after me. These words should be familiar," said the president, who glanced at the small notecard he held in his left hand. "I do solemnly swear... that I will support and defend the Constitution of the United States against all enemies, foreign and domestic... that I will bear true faith and allegiance to the same... that I take this obligation freely... without any mental reservation or purpose of evasion... and that I will well and faithfully discharge the duties of the office on which I am about to enter. So help me God."

And with that, Col. Todd would be the senior representative of the United States of America on the Seventh Ark of the Pra'oo. No longer would the expedition be a private enterprise of QA but a joint mission of the United Kingdom and the United States. By agreement, in several hours, the Prime Minister would be commissioning Charlotte Smith-Davies as a roving ambassador in service of the crown.

She and Todd would jointly represent humanity – if they found anyone, that is. Whether these Pra'oo had survived wandering through the stars was anyone's guess. The president was irrationally optimistic.

"I understand the *Shackleton* will be fitted with the latest quantum communications devices and relays, as well as some powerful traditional radios?"

"Yes, sir. I'll make weekly reports, as long as we're able and then send them along the relay."

The first jump would take them five light-years from Earth. A message sent by traditional radio would not arrive until a year into his successor's first term. While the quantum communications devices theoretically have no range limit, in practice it was presumed the signal began degrading a couple light-years or so out. Therefore, the cluster of navigational beacons set in place by *Henson* and *Shackleton*, would now double as interstellar repeaters. They could only hope the signal reached the five light-year distance between jumps. This interstellar communication system hadn't even been a gleam in someone's eye three weeks ago, the president thought with a smile. Necessity is the mother of invention.

The president had made rhe mistake of asking why repeaters would not simply be dropped along the way. He had been given a mind-numbing explanation that would have been better answered with "because things will go boom."

"My understanding is that *Henson* will begin its trip to your location later this week, Colonel. If there is anything you realize you might need, please let me know and we'll add it to the cargo."

CHAPTER 82

Alpha Base, The Object, Kuiper Belt

Nearly seventy-five percent of the wreckage had been cleared away when *it* happened.

Two Shackleton crew members, one from engineering and one from life sciences, had been in EVA suits cutting out a twisted support beam. As it came free, a gaseous bubble of propellant that had been trapped for nearly thirteen thousand years spread out and touched an active cutting torch. The fireball consumed the two individuals, killing them instantly.

Fearing additional loss of life, Engineer Hathaway and his advisors on Station devised a new method for detecting and releasing gaseous pockets. This, in turn, lead to the discovery of a dozen unexploded bombs that had been placed under the blast shield of the Seventh Ark. The shield had been designed to handle a possible explosion of the liquid propellent. The Pra'oo designers of the Ark had made sure that the entire engine assembly could explode – as had happened – without endangering the passengers, cargo, or crew. It had exceeded expectations. What the shield had not been designed to absorb, however, was the force of Um'vat's directed explosives.

Tar'lol had thought she could no longer be shocked by the treachery of Freon Zoptu Um'vat and his cultists. This final insult was almost more than she could handle.

Benny Hathaway was more clinical in his description.

"I had wondered why they apparently only overloaded the engines and caused an explosion. Surely they knew the blast proof would protect the ship. It now appears they were counting on their explosive devices to have ruptured the blast proof as the engines overloaded. Some shoddy engineering work on their part saved everyone on board."

"Neither Um'vat nor his fellow conspirators had the training or education to construct these devices," said Tar'lol. "They had help. This wasn't some last act of defiance. This was planned and orchestrated treachery."

It was hard for any of them to truly understand, Peter MacGregor realized. For her, these events were fresh, the wounds recent. But these actions had, in fact, happened thousands of years ago, the conspirators were long dead.

He said none of this, of course.

Catching the eye of Col. Andrew Todd, he could tell the other man was thinking the same thing. Obviously, Peter wasn't sure what the mission attached to the Seventh Ark would encounter, but he knew that if they did find descendants of Um'vat out there, Col. Todd would need to be whispering to his host reminders about the length of time that had elapsed.

The explosives were removed, analyzed, catalogued, and made inert in short order. When the wreckage was finally removed, the *Shackleton* – having been modified with unwieldy clamping docks along its keel – was fitted into the recesses of the much larger vessel.

From the perspective of the larger ship's gravity-drive assembly, the *Shackleton* was now simply part of the Seventh Ark. In very real ways, the *Shackleton* would become the brain of the vessel. The superior computers on the smaller ship would take over the propulsion and navigation systems, which Hathaway and his team had found to be an easier task than originally thought. For convenience, the engineers had wired the *Shackleton*'s controls to be accessible from the Seventh Ark's command level.

Engineering, he said several times, was a truly universal language. Peter MacGregor quietly suspected that sentiment would be tested in the years to come.

The available stasis boxes for use by command-level personnel meant the mission could include only twenty four people. The selection process had been tedious, but Peter was proud of the team that had been assembled – even if slightly sad he was not including himself in their number. He was please to find, on self-examination, he was more excited about the arrival of the *Henson*, and the realization he was closer to seeing his father cured.

Ambassador Smith-Davies and Col. Todd would lead the twenty-four member delegation, though Charlotte would be the final operational authority. Engineer Hathaway would serve as technical advisor, with the *Henson*'s Adriana O'Neil, *Shackleton*'s Paul Bratton and three junior engineers keeping the vessels operating.

Dr. Regan and three nurses would provide medical the chief medical officer. Over the initial concerns of his father, Jeff Prasadh would serve as the communications officer.

The resident astronomer, Thomas Newcome, would advise on navigational issues and serve as the scientific leader of the team that included ten other scientists. Their fields ranging from exobiology to geology. And, finally, the son of Thomas and Charlotte's son, Grayson Newcome.

"You're sure you want to do this?" Peter asked the young man, not exactly wanting to dissuade him.

"You mean, leave my final year of high school, skip tests, college admissions, and instead go explore space?" the young man asked, sounding a bit too much like himself.

"I see your point, but I was thinking of friends and experiences back home."

"I figure I'll be able to make friends out there."

The young man's optimism was infectious, and Peter hoped it would remain so. Tar'lol planned to follow the thirteen-millennia-old mission protocols and awaken her compliment of Pra'oo engineers and command-level staff after the first jump. That is when she would explain what had happened, and introduce their new crewmates.

Transferring people and cargo between the *Henson* and the *Shackleton* proved to be a logistical dance. While the *Shackleton* was now officially going to be crewed by just twenty-four people, there was very little space unoccupied by spare equipment and materials. An empty stasis room on the Seventh Ark, a space the size of a gymnasium, became the storehouse for perishable items.

With more than three weeks to spare, the Seventh Ark and *Shackleton* were ready to leave. At this point, the astroid hurtling toward them was visible to the ship's onboard equipment. The predicted path of the rock's orbit, which had necessitated the flurry of activity, had been dead-on accurate. A strike would be devastating. It was not actually fair to call it a rock or even an astroid. It was closer to being a planetoid, slightly smaller than Pluto's moon Charon.

The crew playfully decided to nickname it "Um'vat." This was a designation Tar'lol heartily enjoyed.

"It is large, dumb, and will be similarly unsuccessful."

CHAPTER 83

Command Level, The Ark of Kaziok, Kuiper Belt.

Hours before leaving, Charlotte Smith-Davies officially transferred command of the *Henson* to Linda Bletchley. For his part, Peter had decided the *Shackleton* would be the first and last of the Second Generation Engine ships he would command. He relegated himself to engineer second class and went to work helping prep the *Henson*'s for its return to Earth. He could have simply sat back as one of the company's owners, but that wasn't in his DNA.

Charlotte reflected on the quality of parenting he and his sisters had received from Ian and Jessica MacGregor that each of them were so driven to productive work. Charlotte glanced across the Seventh Ark's command level to where her husband and son were quietly talking; their nervousness had translated into catching up on each others' lives. Charlotte was pleased her son had such role models.

Only a few of her mission crew were manning stations on the command level. Several were in the engineering room, and the rest were down in the *Shackleton*. This first slip of the Seventh Ark into the gravity stream would take them five light years from Earth, or – in what Albert Einstein would decry as a complete violation of the laws of the universe – approximately one year of travel. Not one year from her perspective, but one actual year from that of an observer on Earth. The theoretical physicists would be arguing for a long time over how this was possible, once they were told.

She suspected that, should the medical treatments be successful, when Ian MacGregor awoke he'd love knowing the cursed speed limit had been broken.

The crew would spend two weeks monitoring the systems and making observations, then everyone would be nestled into stasis boxes for the trip. They would be awakened only when the ship dropped out of the stream.

Over the last several hours, the *Henson* had maneuvered into a position outside the gravitational interaction area of the Seventh Ark, the ship headed by the House of Kaziok but now temporarily crewed by humans. On one of the large monitors Hathaway's team had installed, the *Henson*'s bridge now appeared.

"Captain Kaziok Tar'lol, on behalf of the men and women of the Quantum Advantage, and of all Earth's children, we wish you well in this journey to locate your people," said Peter MacGregor. "To Ambassador Smith-Davies and Col. Todd, serving with you as been a privilege. It is my prayer that our orbits cross again."

Tar'lol thanked MacGregor for his kind words and generous aid, and then turned to Smith-Davies.

Charlotte smiled. "Peter, Captain Bletchley, and all my friends on the *Henson*, each of us are excited about this voyage into the unknown. When Jason Roberts took the *Henson* on its maiden flight, he quoted its namesake, Matthew Henson. In thinking of the many difficulties that brought us here, together, and now forward, I thought I would remind us of Ernest Shackleton's words, 'Difficulties are just things to overcome.' Let us continue overcoming difficulties together, no matter how far apart we may be."

A ripple of applause spread across the command level of both the *Henson* and the Ark.

Col. Andrew Todd smiled. "I also wanted to quote Mr. Shackleton," he said. "Before his trip to the South Pole, he wrote, 'Men Wanted: For hazardous journey. Small wages, bitter cold, long months of complete darkness, constant danger, safe return doubtful. Honour and recognition in case of success.' They had no idea what that honor and recognition would look like, and neither do we, but they were up for the adventure. So, like them, I think it's time we got started."

Captain Tar'lol looked at these new additions to her crew, then at the monitor to Peter MacGregor. A slight smile mixed with bemusement appeared on her face. "You people use a lot of words. Nice words, but we will be leaving now."

She glanced at Andrew Todd and nodded before turning to Engineer Hathaway. "If you please, Benny, initiate the drive sequence."

EPILOGUE

The sunrise was beautiful. It was going to be a perfect Arrival Day celebration.

Perfect, except that Tresden Kaln did not want to give the speech. He hated giving speeches, and he was certain everyone hated hearing him give speeches. But he had a job to do, and so he had set an early alarm. He wanted to re-read what was to be the final version of his speech before practicing it in front of his household staff. They would lie and tell him it was wonderful.

He set his tea down and picked up the leafs of paper, then dropped them back to the table. Maybe everyone would let him skip the speech?

Not a chance.

Giving the speech was not an option. It did not matter he was the newest member of the council. The Arrival Day speech was given in a particular order around the council places. Whoever was serving in the role of councilor for that particular House, would give the Arrival Day speech. It is how things were done. Tresden took another sip of his tea, steeled himself, and picked up the papers again.

It did not matter that this was the two-thousandth anniversary of the Arrival. He would give the speech because it was the turn of the House of Kaln, in the order of rotation established two thousand years ago. And he was now the Councilor of the House of Kaln.

Whether he liked it or not. And at this moment, *not*.

"This was the world that had been promised to us by the Great Master." There would be some who disliked the religious tone from the start. Fine. They could give the speech. Tresden was not a particularly religious man himself, but this was Arrival Day. He continued reading:

When our Pra'oo *ancestors set off from Dareq, the world of our birth, they were following the prophecy of the Great Master. That old world,* dar'Eq *as they called it, was dying but the Great Master assured our ancestors that a new world waited for them. By the reckoning of the old calendar, nearly thirteen thousand years ago, everyone left. They knew the ancestral world would live without us, and would thrive under the new stewards. During the thousands of years of sleep as measured on Dareq, the mighty preservers of our people kept a valiant watch. They endured the cold, deep void between the stars. They explored countless hundreds of star systems. Many of those had planets, but they were not suitable for life.*

Some were too hot, many were too cold, all of them were too barren.

There were even some in that historic generation who began to lose hope. They feared the Great Master had been wrong, that this voyage would be the doom of our people. They set those doubts and fears aside. They pressed forward. They persevered. They were seeking a newer world.

But then, word came that a world had been glimpsed. Blue and brown. It was lifeless, yes, but it held the hospitable building blocks for our life. The Great Master had said our people would find a planet with an orbital period the same as the old world. The Great Master said the days and nights, the variations in temperature, would be perfect for our people and livestock, the beasts of the field, and even the creatures of the sea. And on this world, on Eqhar, the promises took their fullest form.

When the first ship, the ship captained by my own ancestor, the great Kaln Tre'sen – *or Tresen Kaln, in our modern speech – when it set down on this new home, he and his crew released the seeds and animals in their order. Faster than anyone imagined possible, the land flourished and even the seas began teeming with life. On this day, two thousand years ago exactly, he then awakened a joyful people. Joyful, for they had Arrived. They had travelled for nearly eleven thousand years to find this home.*

Today, we must ask ourselves if we the Praoh are living as people who have arrived. Does our work do honor to our Pra'oo ancestors, the Great Master, and, yes, those who will come after us? Just as they stepped boldly into the darkness thirteen thousand years ago to find this world, let us each re-commit ourselves to making this day, and every day, one of bold action. Let every day be a Day of Arrival!

Tresden Kaln placed the papers down and rubbed his forehead. He felt more like vomiting than celebrating.

He was the fifty-sixth Councilor of the House of Kaln. It was his obligation as the second born child to now serve on the Council of the Ten Houses, just as it had been his mother's before him – and would be his young son's after him. He briefly wondered if the Council would allow his toddling two-year-old to give the speech today? *The child couldn't do worse.*

Tresden's mother was supposed to give the speech, but she had unexpectedly died thirty-one days earlier. After the official twenty-eight days of mourning, he had been installed as councilor from the House of Kaln. The Laws of Praoh required that the second-born child of the House's councilor assume the office, as long as the heir had achieved the age of twenty-five years on or before the twenty-seventh day after the death of the predecessor. Otherwise, a temporary councilor would be appointed in year-long terms until such time as the heir reached the required age.

He had come of age on the twenty-sixth day after his mother's death. If only he could have been born, say, two days later then he had, someone else would be giving this speech.

This was foolish thinking, he reprimanded himself. He was now the councilor of the House of Kaln; he must act like it.

His brothers and sister were obligated to manage the affairs of the House business without him. While the Council met for only a few days every cycle, the work – as he had seen in his mother's life – seemed to never end.

Tresden knew his first council session, which was to began just after the Arrival Day speech while everyone else was celebrating, was going to be horrible. The agenda arrived by messenger last night before dinner, and had mostly ruined his appetite.

Under the Rule of Arrival, no one was allowed to return to the ancestral world. It was the first rule of boarding and the first rule of disembarkation. Everyone had born under that rule; it was a basic law of their society. Even the path back through the stars was a carefully guarded secret held by less than a dozen people at any given time. Eventually, if he lived long enough to be the First or Second elder of the Council of the Ten Houses, he would learn those details.

The Great Master told them their race would die if they remained. It was a tenent of the Praoh faith that a return would bring death to those who made the voyage and end all life on the ancestral world.

That was the belief, anyway.

Now, some thirteen thousand years since departure, and exactly two thousand years after arrival, there were those who wanted to not exactly go back, but to send robotic probes. They wanted to use the ancient technologies to skip through space and see what had become of that world and all that had been left behind.

They were curious.

As his father loved to say, curiosity was a deadly indulgence. That was a sentiment shared by many of the Praoh people.

If Tresden was honest with himself, he appreciated their interest in the ancestral world. Of course, maps from the Age of Travel still existed as important reminders of their race's birthplace. But, still, like everyone, he wondered at times how it would look today. Was it a wild place? Had the Opub risen as promised?

As a boy, he loved the speculative fiction of Grolot Mult, in which their people had not left the ancestral world. Mult's stories were aimed at entertaining youthful readers, even as they carried a scandalous message for adults. Mult believed fervently in the cause of Opub here on Eqhar. It would have been unthinkable in the Age of Travel and even on through to Mult's own time to *actually* consider the Opub as much more than clever animals. Yet, in the safety of Mult's fiction, they had become intelligent beings who could think and love – even if not yet truly equal to the Praoh.

Because of Mult's inspiration, the House of Kaln had freed its own Opub to the planet's subcontinent three generations earlier. They were allowed to live in freedom, without control – benevolent or otherwise – from any Praoh masters. Seven of the other Houses had done likewise, and with each passing year, pressures on the two holdouts grew. Soon, perhaps in Tresden's own life, the cruel institution of Opub servitude would finally be abolished and those poor creatures set free.

That, also, had been prophesied by the Great Master – though it was one most everyone chose to ignore, even the most religious.

Every single child was raised knowing that everything prophesied for the people had come to pass. One had to close one's eyes not to see it. Their life on this world was evidence in and of itself, after all.

Kaln Tre'sen's ship still stood at the center of the capital city. The last three of the arks to arrive still circled overhead. They served as a reminder of the blessing that they had been given. There was no need to look backward.

According to the agenda for the Council's meeting, a group of researchers wanted to use the ancient exploration pods remaining on one of the legacy ships overhead to build their probe.

Just one, they promised. *Maybe two.*

Tresden knew, of course, the council would vote no. Even with his own (sinful?) curiosity, he would vote no and do so proudly. This was the First Rule of Arrival. It was central to their civic faith. Doing otherwise would violate the essence of what it mean to be a Praoh living on Eqhar.

But the process of getting to that vote would be tedious. Debate would be had. Everyone would posture. Tresden wondered, again, why his own birthday couldn't have been delayed by several days.

He hadn't heard his wife, Leana, take a seat beside him. As he absently stretched out his arms, he became aware of her presence. "I'm sorry if I woke you."

She shook her head, picking up the pages of his speech. "I am surprised you do not mention the two ships that were lost in the voyage, and the two that chose a different path?"

He nodded his head. "I thought about it, but my goal was to be short, and forward looking. With an emphasis on short."

"You will do wonderful, Councilor Tresden Kaln," she said, putting her hand on his. "I enjoy your use of the old pronunciations of names. You remember how my father insisted that the priest at our marriage ceremony use *Pra'oo* rather than Praoh?"

"Yes! I thought the poor old priest was going to die from the stress of your father glaring at him throughout the ceremony, making sure he used the old words correctly." They laughed at the memory. "I suspect besides you, your father might be the only one who appreciates it. Everyone just wants to get on with the celebrations and not be reminded of what came before."

Leana was about to respond, but a loud knock at their front door disturbed the morning quiet.

"Who could that be?" asked Tresden as he stood, heading to the front of their home. He got to the door just ahead of his head butler, who was himself rubbing sleep from his eyes.

"No worries, Graat, I have it." Tresden pulled open the door... and found no one there. Instead, a simple, flat package was laying at the doorstep. "Urgent" was scrawled across the top. Nothing indicated who left it.

Tresden picked it up gently, craning his neck but finding no one up or down the lane. He shut the door and came back inside. Graat and Leana looked on with unabashed curiosity as he unsealed the envelope. Several sheets of heavy photographic paper spilled onto the table.

A note rested on top of them: "Do not be deceived. Not everyone left. The Seventh Ark, the Ark of Kaziok, was not lost. It stayed and built an extravagant civilization."

Trseden's brow furrowed; he'd heard that libelous tale since childhood.

His eyes darted over the color photographs; his wife began moving them around the table so they would all be visible.

They seemed to have been taken from orbit over the ancestral world. Perhaps they were clever forgeries, but something told him they were... real.

Like everyone, he could recognize the land masses of the ancestral world from history classes almost as easily as those of this world. He saw what could only be city lights on the night side of the planet. A civilization was thriving there, *if* these pictures were real. No picture was closer than low orbit, but even still he could tell the cities were grand – far surpassing anything even here on Eqhar. Again, assuming this was not just a clever hoax.

He looked back at the note. The last line read, "We must reclaim what is ours. We must return."

THE END

ACKNOWLEDGEMENT

I would never have become a first-time novelist without the encouragement of my amazing wife and our three kids. When I mentioned I had started (yet another) outline for a story, they uniformly urged me onward. Without them, I never would have inflicted this on an unsuspecting world.

Special thanks to my copy editor, Rae Liput, who patiently pointed out missing words, problems with subject-verb agreement, and even a pesky issue of two characters with unintentionally confusing names. I often took her recommendations. Any errors you find are mine, and not hers!

ABOUT THE AUTHOR

Michael Quinn Sullivan

'Sullivan' is the 93rd most common name in the United States, with 'Michael Sullivan' making up 2.3 percent of them.

This one lives in Texas, where he grew up devouring the works of Asimov, Heinlein, Clarke, and Nivon. While a writer by profession, "Finding the Void" is his first work of fiction – though some detractors might disagree.

By day, he is the publisher of the Texas Scorecard.

www.ingramcontent.com/pod-product-compliance
Lightning Source LLC
Chambersburg PA
CBHW030500260626
47157CB00015B/2365